Sons of Ellyrion

ELDAIN SAW CAELIR stab the Everqueen, yet still could not believe what his own eyes were telling him. He'd known his brother's purpose in coming to Avelorn, but to see it enacted was worse than he could ever have imagined. Though it was over in an instant, Eldain saw everything, from the tiniest detail to the full panorama of the murderous deed. Alone of all those in the garlanded arbour, it seemed that he must bear witness to the full horror of events as they unfolded.

Was this his punishment for being the treacherous architect of this assassination, to see every detail and feel every nuance of the bloody deed?

He saw the black sheath of Caelir's dagger crumble away, blown by perfume-scented winds like cinders from a dead fire. The blade itself, dulled by old blood and reeking of ancient murders, crossed the all too short distance between Caelir's fist and the Everqueen's chest. Yet though he had come to Avelorn on a mission of murder, Caelir's face was not the face of an assassin, but that of a horrified witness.

A WARHAMMER NOVEL

SONS OF ELLYRION

GRAHAM McNEILL

BLACK LIBRARY

To everyone who kept demanding I finish this story.
Thanks for waiting for me...

A BLACK LIBRARY PUBLICATION

First published in Great Britain in 2011 by
The Black Library,
Games Workshop Ltd.,
Willow Road, Nottingham,
NG7 2WS, UK.

10 9 8 7 6 5 4 3 2 1

Cover illustration by Marek Okon.
Map by Nuala Kinrade and Karl Kopinski

A CIP record for this book is available from the British Library.

UK ISBN: 978 1 84970 067 2
US ISBN: 978 1 84970 068 9

See the Black Library on the internet at
www.blacklibrary.com

Find out more about Games Workshop
and the world of Warhammer at
www.games-workshop.com

Printed and bound in the UK by CPI Mackays, Chatham ME5 8TD

THIS IS A DARK age, a bloody age, an age of daemons and of sorcery. It is an age of battle and death, and of the world's ending. Amidst all of the fire, flame and fury it is a time, too, of mighty heroes, of bold deeds and great courage.

AN ANCIENT AND proud race, the high elves hail from Ulthuan, a mystical island of rolling plains, rugged mountains and glittering cities. Ruled over by the noble Phoenix King, Finubar, and the Everqueen, Alarielle, Ulthuan is a land steeped in magic, renowned for its mages and fraught with blighted history. Great seafarers, artisans and warriors, the high elves protect their ancestral homeland from enemies near and far. None more so than from their wicked kin, the dark elves, against whom they are locked in a bitter war that has lasted for centuries.

THESE ARE BLEAK times. Across the length and breadth of the Old World, from the heartlands of the human Empire and the knightly palaces of Bretonnia to ice-bound Kislev in the far north, come rumblings of war. In the towering Worlds Edge Mountains, the orc tribes are gathering for another assault. Bandits and renegades harry the wild southern lands of the Border Princes. There are rumours of rat-things, the skaven, emerging from the sewers and swamps across the land. And from the northern wildernesses there is the ever-present threat of Chaos, of daemons and beastmen corrupted by the foul powers of the Dark Gods. As the time of battle draws ever nearer, Ulthuan, and all of the civilised lands, need heroes like never before.

Nagaroth

Blighted Isle

Shrine of Khaine

Chrace

Phoenix Gate

Shadowlands

Anlec

Dragon Gate

Unicorn Gate

The Sunken Lands

Griffon Gate

Ellyrion

Eagle Gate

Gaen Vale

Sea of Dusk

Tor Elyr

Tor Anroc

The Sunken City

The Inner Sea

Shrine of Asuryan

Tiranoc

The Dragon Spire

Vaul's Anvil

150 Miles

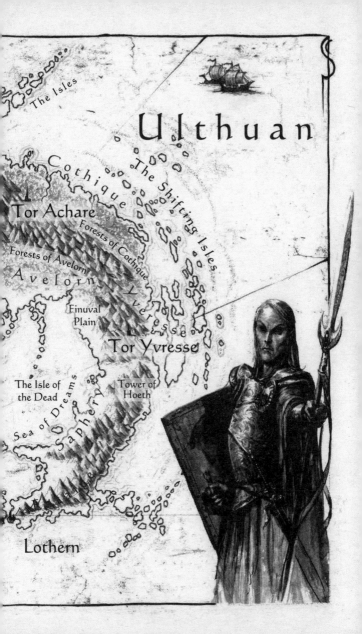

Ulthuan

The Isles

Cothique

The Shifting Isles

Tor Achare

Forests of Cothique

Forests of Avelorn

Avelorn

Yvresse

Finuval
Plain

Tor Yvresse

The Isle of
the Dead

Tower of
Hoeth

Saphery

Sea of Dreams

Lothern

BOOK ONE
HEROES

CHAPTER ONE

TEARS OF ISHA

ULTHUAN WAS WEEPING.

Waterfalls and wailing rivers carried its tears to the sea. The clouds gathered in solemn thunderheads and the wind howled its sorrow through the air, which hung torpid and heavy over even its most carefree inhabitants. Not since the days of the Sundering, when brother had slain brother and a race favoured by the gods turned on one another, had the realm of the elves known such grief.

The skies above the mist-shrouded island faded to black, the sun unwilling to bear witness to such horror. Only the shimmering emerald orb of the Chaos moon dared show its face on such a night, but the clouds over Ulthuan hid the torment of its inhabitants from such a leering gaze.

Ulthuan's brightest and most beauteous star had been torn from the heavens, and that grief was for her people alone.

The masked statues upon the Shrine of Asuryan wept blood from their hidden eyes, and the waters around Tor Elyr broke and seethed with anger, shattering crystal bridges that had stood for thousands of years. Roaring waves heaved the surface of the Inner Sea, capsizing the few silver-hulled ships that plied its waters and dragging sorrowful mariners down to their doom.

The lands of the Inner Kingdoms, golden realms of eternal summer, knew at last the touch of winter as cold winds blew from the north and ignoble rains battered the balmy plains. Magical sprites, capricious things of glittering mischief, transformed in an instant, their mischief turned to spite, playfulness to malice. The forests of Chrace echoed with the sound of enraged beasts, and lone hunters abroad in the shadowed depths sought the sanctuary of caves or tall trees.

Towering breakers battered the rocky coastline of Cothique as the ocean surged with fury, desperate to spill over the land. Within the Gaen Vale, the mountain of the crone maiden rumbled as though ancient geological faults tore open, and black smoke clawed from its summit. From Sapherian villas and the coastal mansions of Yvresse, to the rocky, cliff-top towers of Tiranoc and palaces of such beauty that they may only be told of in song, the land of the elves knew pain and sorrow.

The great statues of the Everqueen and the Phoenix King that stood sentinel over the mighty port of Lothern trembled upon their mighty footings. The light of a thousand torches illuminated Lothern, but the marbled Everqueen remained shrouded in the deepest shadows, and all who looked upon the regal features of the Phoenix King saw the stern and unflinching countenance crack, like the carven track of a single tear.

Ulthuan's warriors, mages, poets and peacemakers alike wept with their magical home. That shared woe passed from the elves to the land, and from the land to the air. And as Ulthuan mourned, it spread on the winds of magic throughout the world until even distant kin in ports as far away as Tor Elithis breathed in the sorrow of the Everqueen's fate.

The distant asrai of Athel Loren grieved with their long lost brothers and sisters, the slumbering Orion and fey queen Ariel dipping the branches of their forest home in shared anguish. Though the paths of the asur and asrai had taken very different turns through the ages of the world, their shared heritage was still a bright thread of connection between them.

Even the crude and unsophisticated race of man felt something amiss in the world. Children – who alone of the race of men retain their sense of wonder – woke from troubled dreams with a scream on their lips, and those forced to pass the long watches of the night in wakefulness felt the touch of the grave draw ever closer. Dramatists and dreamers felt an aspect of beauty pass from the world, while those whose lives had been touched by the asur in some way felt an unreasoning grief they could not explain when the sun's rays once again illuminated a world that seemed just a little less bright than before.

If the dwarfs of the mountain holds felt anything of these events, none could say, for elf and dwarf had long since lost any love for the other.

Only the fallen elves of Naggaroth revelled in this time of suffering. As drops of blood fell to the loamy earth of Avelorn, cold laughter echoed from the crooked towers of the druchii's accursed cities of dark iron and blood-stained stone.

Leading his army of invasion against the gates of Lothern, the Witch King himself, greatest and most hated son of Ulthuan, bellowed with laughter astride his midnight-skinned drake perched atop the Glittering Lighthouse. The ocean boomed and crashed far below him, but his mirth drowned the noise of the furious water.

In her gaudy pavilion of debaucheries before the embattled Eagle Gate, Morathi the Hag Sorceress whipped her devotees into bloody paroxysms of opiate-fuelled madness before bathing in a cauldron of their hot blood.

The myriad voices of the world spoke with a million voices in a million ears, subtly different every time, but all singing the same lament.

Alarielle, the Everqueen of Avelorn, was dead.

ELDAIN SAW CAELIR stab the Everqueen, yet still could not believe what his own eyes were telling him. He'd known his brother's purpose in coming to Avelorn, but to see it enacted was worse than he could ever have imagined. Though it was over in an instant, Eldain saw everything, from the tiniest detail to the full panorama of the murderous deed. Alone of all those in the garlanded arbour, it seemed that he must bear witness to the full horror of events as they unfolded.

Was this his punishment for being the treacherous architect of this assassination, to see every detail and feel every nuance of the bloody deed?

He saw the black sheath of Caelir's dagger crumble away, blown by perfume-scented winds like cinders from a dead fire. The blade itself, dulled by old blood and reeking of ancient murders, crossed the all too short distance between Caelir's fist and the Everqueen's chest. Yet though he had come to Avelorn on a mission of murder, Caelir's face was not the face of an assassin, but that of a horrified witness.

Eldain willed the magic of the Everqueen to turn aside the blow, hoping that some innate power possessed by the chosen of Isha to undo harm or malicious intent before it could be wreaked would save her. No such magic intervened, and the black wedge of ensorcelled iron plunged into her breast. Blood welled from the wound, each droplet that stained her gown of silk and starlight shockingly bright in the darkness that fell like the last night at the end of the world.

The Everqueen did not cry out or scream or give voice to the pain of her wounding. A single tear spilled down her cheek as her body fell like the most graceful tree in the most magical forest hewn by the axe of an unthinking dwarf. Though no living race was quicker and more agile than the asur, not one amongst those assembled before the Everqueen's gilded pavilion moved so much as a muscle to save her.

Acrobats, poets, warriors, singers, musicians and tale-tellers had gathered in this leafy bower of Avelorn to witness the Everqueen walking among her people, to bask in her divine radiance and feel the joy of her breath play across the sculpted lines of their perfect features. The land had welcomed her arrival, fresh blooms springing up in her footsteps, and the leafy canopy parting with every grateful sigh of the wind to allow the sunlight to caress the Everqueen's radiant skin. Those blooms now withered and died, and the treetops closed over this scene of murder with an ashamed rustle of branches. The patter of rain fell from a cloudless sky.

The Maiden Guard, resplendent in their ivory robes, bronze breastplates and long spears, could do nothing as their mistress fell. Not since the days before Finuval Plain had they lapsed in their duty of protection, and each warrior woman felt as though Caelir's blade had pierced her own heart.

Eldain saw those closest to Caelir, a soft-bodied poet and a wiry woman with the body of a dancer. The male fell to his knees, his hands clasped theatrically over his cheeks as he howled with loss. The woman's fists were clenched, the corded muscles in her arms and legs bunched in readiness to fight.

No matter where his gaze fell, Eldain's eyes were always drawn back to the Everqueen as she fell with languid grace to the soft grass. She struck the ground with a sigh of silk and a gasp of pain. Her eyes met those of Eldain, and he felt the awful weight of his betrayal in that tawny-gold gaze. She saw past the mask he presented to the world, and into the secret heart of him. In that unbreakable moment of connection, Alarielle did the one thing he could never do for himself.

She forgave him.

Her head rolled to the side and golden tresses woven from sunlight and joy fell across her face, mercifully covering her alabaster features. The moment of connection ended and Eldain's splendid isolation from the flow of the world's time was at an end.

He slid from the back of his horse as an inchoate roar of aggression sounded from a hundred throats. Though the grief was too raw and too powerful for mere words, the sentiment was clear.

Blood must answer for blood.

* * *

CAELIR'S HAND BURNED from holding the dagger, his palm scarred with the imprint of its hateful grip and his soul rebelling at the memory of the thousand assassinations and uncounted lives it had ended on the sacrificial altar. He watched the Everqueen fall away from him, as though she tumbled into the deepest chasm from which there could be no escape. Her gaze did not condemn him, such eyes could hold only love, and he looked away, unable to bear the shame of her forgiveness.

Instead he looked across the twilight glade and saw an elf whose countenance was the mirror of his own. Softer and without the harsh lines of Caelir's angular cheekbones, he finally recognised his older brother, Eldain. Rhianna stood beside him, and his heart broke anew to see the matching pledge rings upon their hands. Next to them, a warrior woman in the garb of a Sword Master had her blade drawn, but Rhianna's restraining hand was on her shoulder.

Caelir knew everything now. Washed up on Ulthuan's shores without his memory, he had been a weapon primed by the Witch King and his hellish mother, and aimed at their most powerful enemies. Teclis of the White Tower had already been laid low, and now the Everqueen had fallen victim to Caelir's unwitting treacheries. Yet even as he saw his part in these attacks, he knew that none of this would have been possible but for Eldain's betrayal in Naggaroth.

'You left me to die, brother,' he said, his voice softer than a whisper, but flying like blazing arrows to Eldain's heart.

His life was forfeit. There could be no return from a deed of such unadulterated evil, and Caelir awaited the pain of a hundred arrows piercing his flesh and silver lances plunging into his body to split his worthless heart in two. Briefly he cursed the Fates that he would die without first taking his revenge, but the fading light of the Everqueen spoke of the futility of such notions. Vengeance only begat vengeance and thus was the cycle of hatred perpetuated.

Yet even as he awaited death, a voice in his head whispered his name. The sound was a zephyr of wind across the Ellyrion plains, the rumble of hoof beats from the Great Herd, and the boom of thunder from the Annulii. Soft, yet with a power stronger than the roots of the earth itself, it told him one thing, and Caelir could not disobey.

Flee, it said. *Flee and forgive…*

RHIANNA SAW CAELIR'S blow as it landed, the magic within her leaping to her fingertips as soon as she felt the weight of the hateful dagger's evil. As the Everqueen fell away from Caelir, she wanted to unleash that magic in a torrent of fire. Hotter than Vaul's forge and brighter than Asuryan's fire, it would unmake Caelir in a heartbeat.

No sooner had that intent surfaced in her mind than it was quashed.

This was the boy she had loved and had planned to wed.

Caelir was the reckless scoundrel who had taken her on wild rides across the plains of Ellyrion upon the backs of the most incredible steeds of Ulthuan. He had taken her into the Annulii, higher than anyone else would have dared, and shown her the majesty of the untamed magic that boiled within the thunder-haunted peaks. His roguish charms had won her away from Eldain, but his loss in the Land of Chill had ended their dream of a life together before it had begun.

She could not bring herself to undo the memory of that young boy. She had loved him once, and saw the same innocence behind his tortured face she had seen that day in the mountains when she had first lost her heart to him.

Those around her showed no such restraint and she saw their horror turn to anger in a heartbeat. Bows were bent and silver-bladed lances brought to shoulders, ready to spill the blood of this traitor. Caelir stumbled away from his black deed, turning to Eldain and running towards him as though the whip of a Tiranoc charioteer was at his back. As fast as Caelir was, there was no way he could possibly reach his brother before the arrows of the Everqueen's protectors cut him down.

The dark-haired leader of the Maiden Guard that had brought them to the Everqueen's bower had her horse-hair bowstring taut, an arrow fletched with feathers from a white raven aimed at Caelir's heart.

Save him and you will save me…

The words lanced into Rhianna's mind, the mantra she had kept close to her heart ever since her journey into the cave of the oracle. Though they seemed contradictory, she knew better than to doubt the words of the high priestess of the Gaen Vale.

A score of Maiden Guard bows creaked and loosed in the same instant, and each shaft arced through the air with accuracy no other race could match.

This time the magic flew from Rhianna's hands without restraint and she poured it into the towering oak beside her. Shimmering light spilled from its cracked bark, and the flurry of arrows arcing towards Caelir veered from their course like iron drawn by a navigator's lodestone to hammer the ancient wood.

Splinters of bark made her duck as a second volley was similarly torn from its natural course. Cries of anger and frustration echoed from the forested glade as the Maiden Guard cast aside their bows and took up their lances. They bounded through the crowds of panicking elves, intent on slaying the killer in their midst.

'Caelir, wait!' yelled Eldain, but his brother was in no mood to listen. He vaulted onto the back of Eldain's steed with the grace of one to whom being on horseback was as natural as breathing. Caelir settled onto the back of Irenya, the reins leaping into his hands as he turned the beast's rearing into a curving turn.

With a wild yell, Caelir leaned low over the horse's neck and it surged to a run in the time it took to take a breath. The Maiden Guard were superlative warriors, but their martial skill could not defeat the horsemanship of an Ellyrion rider. Their lances struck only empty air as Caelir twisted his mount left and right, and no arrow, no matter how skilfully loosed could find its target thanks to Rhianna's magic.

Caelir galloped into the depths of the forest, the trees closing around him as though accomplices in his escape. Groups of bronze-armoured warrior women set off after Caelir, but Rhianna knew they would not capture him. An Ellyrion horseman would only be caught if he wished to be caught. Only the forest could prevent Caelir's escape, and Rhianna had a suspicion that the ancient sentience that dwelled in the soil, air, water and wood of Avelorn had prescience beyond even the asur, and would thwart every attempt at pursuit.

Rhianna felt the magic drain from her and dropped to her knees as a keening wail of abject loss split the night with a depth of fury no mortal could know and sorrow beyond the reach of even the most broken hearted. Yvraine was at her side in a heartbeat as groups of warriors and poets gathered around the fallen Everqueen.

'What did you do?' asked the Sword Master in disbelief.

'What I had to,' said Rhianna, staring at the fallen Everqueen.

Alarielle's hair spilled around her head like a pillow of spun gold. A single droplet of blood marred the illusion that she was simply resting, and tears welled in Rhianna's eyes.

She looked up as a shadow halted before her.

Through tear-blurred vision, Rhianna saw the leader of the Maiden Guard, her dark hair wild and unbound beneath her bronze helm. Cold fury glittered in her amber eyes, and a terrible grief was held in check only by centuries of training. Her lance was aimed at Rhianna's heart, and the urge to drive it home was evident in every taut sinew and bunched muscle.

'You will come with me,' hissed the Maiden.

Ten warriors of the Maiden Guard led Eldain, Rhianna and Yvraine into a deeper part of the forest, one where what little light remained to the day was filtered through a damp mist of drizzle. Though the ride from their landing at the River Arduil had been frantic, Eldain had not been blind to the soaring magical nature of the forest, yet here its beauty was as flat and dull as any forest of the Old World. The trees here looked dead and withered, devoid of magic and light.

Eldain felt the potent anger of the Maiden Guard, the hostility that came off them in waves, but also the fear that they would be held accountable for this disaster.

'Are we prisoners?' whispered Rhianna.

Eldain shrugged, unsure of their status in Avelorn. 'I don't know, maybe.'

'But we came with a warning,' said Yvraine, chafing at the loss of her greatsword. The Maiden Guard had divested them of weapons, and to take away a Sword Master's blade was like taking a limb. 'We tried to stop this.'

'But you did *not* stop it,' said the Handmaiden with midnight tresses. She removed her helm, setting it down on a moss-covered rock carved with spiralling vines. He face was beautiful, but with its angular lines and narrowed eyes, her beauty took on a twilit aspect that chilled Eldain's blood. 'You aided the Everqueen's attacker in his escape.'

'And he's only getting farther away,' pointed out Yvraine. 'You are wasting time.'

'Your deeds are known to me, Yvraine Hawkblade,' said the Handmaiden, 'so I will not take you to task for your youthful impudence. I am Lirazel, Chief Handmaiden of Everqueen Alarielle, and I do not like others telling me my business.'

'Every moment we tarry here, Caelir slips beyond our grasp,' pressed Yvraine.

Lirazel said, 'For now he is beyond my reach,' and Eldain saw how much it hurt to say those words.

Rhianna saw it too and said, 'Then let us go. We know Caelir. We have been following him since the attack on the White Tower. I have to save him.'

'Save him?' demanded Lirazel, stepping close to Rhianna with a white-knuckled grip on her silver lance. 'After what he did? Who are you, and why would you say such a thing?'

'I am Rhianna Silverfawn, child of Saphery and daughter of Mitherion Silverfawn' said Rhianna. 'And I can say this because I once loved Caelir. We were to be wed in a gentler time I can scarce recall.'

Lirazel's eyes flicked from the pledge ring on Rhianna's hand to the matching one upon Eldain's. Her eyes narrowed as she took in the contours of his features.

'You are kin to Caelir,' she said.

'I am his brother, Eldain of House Éadaoin,' said Eldain, feeling the Handmaiden's gaze strip him bare. Lirazel had failed to protect the Everqueen from one assassin's blade, and she wasn't about to take the chance that murder ran in the family.

'You are one of the horsemasters?'

'Indeed,' agreed Eldain. 'My family has trained with the herds for a thousand years, and none know the way of the horse as we do.'

Lirazel nodded, and said, 'Do you also desire to save Caelir?'

'I do not wish him dead,' replied Eldain, hoping she believed him. In truth, Eldain wasn't sure what he desired. To see Caelir dead would allow him to live the life he had only recently won back, but the chance for redemption that had come with the reawakening of his brother's true self would die with him. The Everqueen might have forgiven him, but hers was not the forgiveness he craved.

'Tell me how you came to be in Avelorn,' said Lirazel. 'Leave nothing out.'

Eldain told how Yvraine had escorted them to the Tower of Hoeth at the behest of Rhianna's father, of how they had arrived in the midst of a terrible battle between the Sword Masters and nightmarish creations of raw magic unleashed by a trap laid in Caelir's memories by Morathi.

Rhianna took up the tale as they sailed across the Inner Sea to the Gaen Vale and travelled the hidden paths on the isle of the Mother Goddess. Her voice fell to little more than a whisper as she spoke of what happened at the island's heart, her soft tones heard only by Yvraine and Lirazel. Eldain made no attempt to hear what passed between the oracle and Rhianna, for it was clearly not meant for the male of the species.

'Save him and you save me,' said Rhianna as she concluded her tale of events on the Gaen Vale. 'I do not understand what it means, but it is all I have.'

From the island of the Mother Goddess they sailed for Avelorn and there the tale ended as Yvraine described their ride through the forest to reach the Everqueen before Caelir. When their tale reached its conclusion, Eldain saw Lirazel's suspicion ease a fraction, and let out a pent-up breath.

Lirazel planted her spear in the earth and ran her hands through her hair. Her skin was tanned from a life spent in the forest, yet her pallor was deathly, as though her wellbeing was contingent on some external factor.

Eldain realised there was one question no one had yet asked.

'What of the Everqueen?' he asked. 'Did Caelir… I mean… is she…?'

'No,' snapped Lirazel. 'And do not say the words. Her mortal flesh hangs in the balance, and the connection to the power within her remains intact only by the slenderest of threads.'

'She's alive,' breathed Rhianna.

'For now,' agreed Lirazel. 'All Ulthuan would feel it were it not so.'

'How can we help?' asked Yvraine, as one of the Maiden Guard appeared at her side bearing her sheathed greatsword. The Sword Master looped the belt around her shoulders, the soft shagreen scabbard slipping exactly into place. 'I am bound to House Éadaoin and Silverfawn by the Oath of the Sword Masters. Where they go, I go.'

'There is little that can be done,' admitted Lirazel. 'Though perhaps the soft wretches that brought Caelir within the borders of Avelorn can shed some light on how they managed to avoid the snares and delusions that should have enraptured any evildoers.'

Eldain looked over his shoulder as he heard a commotion at the edge of the trees, and saw several Handmaidens usher a group of gaudily dressed elves into the clearing. He recognised two as the poet and dancer who had been next to Caelir as he plunged the dagger...

No, don't think it!

'Please!' begged the poet, 'this is all a terrible misunderstanding. We had no inkling that Caelir was a killer. You have to believe us!'

'Shut up, Narentir,' hissed the dancer, with a venom that surprised Eldain. 'You might not have known he was a killer, but I did.'

'Sweet Lilani,' said the poet. 'You have a most delectable mouth, but please, for the love of Loec, keep it shut or you will see us all slain! And lover of new sensations though I am, the embrace of Morai-Heg is not one I am keen to experience.'

'I don't think that is up to me,' said the dancer as Lirazel plucked her spear from the earth.

'Actually it is,' said the Handmaiden.

* * *

IN THE SPACES between life and death, magic and reality, Alarielle floated in an ocean of pain. Her lifeblood was all but spent, drawn out by the dark magic bound to the blade of cold iron, and her spirit was adrift in a place where she was alone.

No, not alone. Alone would have been a blessing.

She heard the howls of the banshees in the distance, far away, but closing on her with all the dreadful hunger for which they were rightly feared. The hounds of Morai-Heg, their keening wail was a portent of death, and Alarielle wondered if this was to be her time to pass from the embrace of the Everqueen.

Her body lay on a bed of leaves somewhere impossibly distant, held fast to her spirit by the slenderest of silver cords wrapped around her wrist. What floated in this abyssal darkness was not the crude matter of flesh, but her ageless, immortal essence of magic. One could not exist without the other, and as one sickened so the other faded.

Alarielle felt the banshees gathering, like ocean predators with the scent of blood in the water. Their wailing laments echoed in the void, but their cries were not for her. All around the island of Ulthuan, elves were dying. War had come to her fair isle, the druchii once again bringing hate and blood to the land they had forsaken all those centuries ago.

That age was a time of legend to Alarielle, but little more a blink of an eye to the power that dwelled within her. Chosen since before her birth to take up the mantle of Everqueen, she had studied and trained for decades before rising to become one of Ulthuan's twin rulers. She remembered the day of her coronation, the terror and awesome sense of multiple threads of fate converging upon her.

Though complex rituals of magical preparation had readied her for the moment of surrender, nothing could have prepared her for the surging torrent of power that coursed through her. The crown upon her brow was a living connection to every queen who had ruled in Avelorn, their memories were her memories, and she struggled to hold on to all that was Alarielle.

What the asur called the Everqueen rose up within her, claiming her for its own ancient purpose. The lives, loves, hopes, dreams and nightmares of all who had held the title before her filled her mind with ancient knowledge. Her mother and grandmother rose up to greet her, easing her into the embrace of the Everqueen and welcoming her to their numberless sisterhood. The line of motherhood stretched back to time immemorial, and Alarielle felt the strength of her lineage steel her to retain her own identity in the face of the vast, elemental power of the Everqueen.

That power was a distant memory, lost to her now as though carved away by a butcher's blade. She could feel it somewhere in the darkness: directionless and unfocussed without a mortal host. It was angry, though such a small word did no justice to the roiling fury that sought her in the darkness. Alarielle felt a great weariness closing in on her, and the magical cords binding her spirit and flesh loosened, unwinding from her wrist like a silken glove, and she felt herself drifting away from the earthly realms. The swirling black shapes of the banshees closed in, their faces hidden, but with gleaming fangs bared and sharpened claws uncurling from gnarled fists.

Hold fast, my daughter, your time in the realm of mortals is not yet over…

It was not one voice, but many, and she knew them all. Hundreds of voices layered into one spoke to her, and each was right to call her daughter. The banshees wailed, this time in anger as this most succulent of morsels was drawn away from them.

Alarielle gripped the silver cords tighter.

'I cannot hold on,' she whispered to the voices within her.

You can. You must. Ulthuan yet needs you…

The voices spoke with one purpose, but a hundred voices, each one subtly different and seeming to come from a multitude of places within her skull. So many voices, so many lives, she could only retain her sense of self thanks to the decades of preparation and her own mastery of the winds of magic. A lesser being would have been driven to madness the instant the crown had been placed upon their brow.

Alarielle held to the voices, letting them guide her back towards her destiny. She followed their gentle urgings, feeling her strength grow the closer she came to the colossal power that lay at the heart of Ulthuan. Leave the Phoenix King his comforting fiction of a shared rule, the power of the Everqueen dwarfed that of any male sovereign.

In her was embodied the true power of creation, what *king* could match such a gift?

At last she felt the power that made her whole, the power she had been wedded to since her birth and which had been waiting for her since before even that.

The banshees retreated, realising there would be no prize beyond the hundreds of souls being sent to them daily from the blood being spilled on Ulthuan's ancient soil. Alarielle felt the pain and suffering of her children, and surrendered herself to the gathering power of the Everqueen.

Her body was wounded unto death, but the frailties of a mortal vessel were insignificant in the face of the Everqueen's ability to heal and renew. She knew there would be pain, and braced herself for a return to the world of flesh.

With a cry of agony, Alarielle opened her eyes.

And the Everqueen looked out.

CHAPTER TWO

WAR CALLS

THE BLUE-FLETCHED ARROW leapt from Alathenar's bow, arcing through the cold air to punch through the cheek-plate of a druchii helm. The warrior fell from the ramparts of the Eagle Gate, and Alathenar nocked another arrow to his bow. His fingers were raw and callused, his limbs weary beyond imagining. Once again he loosed, and once again a druchii warrior was pitched from the ramparts.

Beside him, the Shadow Warrior, Alanrias, loosed shafts with a speed and precision that put his own rate of fire to shame. Each black-shafted arrow thudded home in the belly or neck of an enemy fighter, hits that would take them out of the fight, but leave them writhing in agony for days.

Alanrias paused only to take a drink from a ceramic wine jug placed behind the toothed parapet.

'Thirsty work, killing druchii,' he said, as though they

were shooting at targets instead of fighting for their lives.

Alathenar wasted no words on the Shadow Warrior, seeing in him a reflection of the druchii army that battered itself bloody against the mighty fortress that guarded this route through the Annulii to Ellyrion. He reached for another shaft, but his hands closed on empty air. His quiver was spent.

'Here,' said Alanrias, tossing him a full quiver of black leather.

'My thanks,' said Alathenar, drawing an arrow from the quiver. It was lighter than he was used to, fashioned from some withered tree of Nagarythe, and the iron tip was barbed to make it next to impossible to remove. Its length was spiked with tiny thorns that would cause ghastly torment to any victim as they writhed in pain.

Alathenar said nothing, but nocked the arrow to his bow. The string was woven with strands of hair from his beloved Arenia, and her love gave his arrows an extra ten yards at least. The string slipped, as though rebelling at so vile a barb, but Alathenar whispered words of soothing magic and the bow was appeased.

He scanned the walls of the Eagle Gate, looking for a target worthy of his bow.

There were plenty to choose from.

The walls of the fortress stretched across the mountain pass, its white and blue stonework marred by weeks of war and magical attack. An unbroken line of elven warriors, wondrously arrayed in tunics of cream and gold, blue and silver, held the wall against thousands of dark-armoured druchii and human fighters in burnished plates of iron and baked leather. The defenders of the Eagle Gate were magnificent and proud, yet there was a brittle edge of desperation to their fighting.

An assassin's blade had ended the life of the Eagle Gate's commander, Cerion Goldwing, and the heart of the defenders had died with their beloved leader. Alathenar glanced towards the Aquila Spire, and a splinter of ice wormed its way into his heart. The warriors of the Eagle Gate were fighting to protect their homeland against the bitterest of foes, yet Cerion's successor had yet to wield a blade alongside them.

A flitting shadow darted overhead, and Alathenar cursed his inattention. Screeching, bat-like creatures with a repellent female aspect swooped overhead, darting down to tear at the defenders with ebony dewclaws. He sent a shaft into the breast of one of the flying creatures, sending it tumbling down to the floor of the pass, where druchii beastmasters goaded even more terrible creatures into battle.

Chained draconic things with a multitude of roaring heads sprayed the wall with caustic fire and bellowed in pain at their master's tridents. Beside them, mindless abominations with elastic limbs and forms so abhorrent they resembled no creature known to the Loremasters of Hoeth, clawed and howled as they smote the reinforced gateway. The air crackled and fizzed with unleashed magic as elven mages countered the sorceries of the druchii, and protective runes worked into the parapet blazed with powerful light.

Druchii warriors clambered up black ladders, only to be met with asur steel, and the carnage was terrible to behold. Precious elven blood made the ramparts slick, and the healers were stretched far beyond their ability to cope with the number of wounded being carried to them by stretcher bearers.

Alathenar saw Eloien Redcloak fighting at the centre

of the wall, where once a mighty carven eagle head had stared into the west. His sword was a blur of silver, his cloak a darting wing of blood as he wove a path of destruction through those druchii who gained the walls. The warrior of Ellyrion was the master of war from horseback, but was just as lethal on foot.

A towering brute in crudely strapped plates of iron daubed in lurid blue rose up behind Redcloak, and Alathenar sent a borrowed arrow through the gap between his neck torque and helmet. The enemy warrior dropped and Eloien raised his sword in salute, knowing full well who had loosed the fatal shaft. Alathenar soon found other targets, a druchii climbing the face of the Aquila Spire, another poised to deliver the death-blow to a fallen asur warrior, a screeching monster that swooped down on a wounded archer. Each time his arrow slashed home with deadly accuracy, though none were killing strikes.

'Is it my imagination, or are these arrows spiteful?' he shouted to Alanrias.

The Shadow Warrior grinned. 'I crafted them from the trees upon which the blood of the druchii fell after Alith Anar nailed seven hundred of them to the walls of Griffon Pass. If there is spite within them, it is of their own making.'

'They say your people are touched by the Witch King,' said Alathenar, slotting another arrow to his bowstring. 'I can well believe it.'

'Do not presume to judge me, warrior of Eataine,' snarled the Shadow Warrior. 'Wait until your land and home is destroyed by the druchii and see how much mercy fills your heart for their worthless lives!'

Alathenar recoiled from the warrior's anger.

'I will kill them, and I will return to them the pain my people have known tenfold.'

'*Your* people?' hissed Alathenar. 'We are one people. We are the asur.'

'Think you so?' said Alanrias nodding in the direction of the tallest tower still standing upon the Eagle Gate. 'You would count him amongst us?'

Alathenar knew exactly to whom the Shadow Warrior was referring. Within the impregnable walls of the Aquila Spire, Glorien Truecrown, the commander of the Eagle Gate was ensconced with his dusty books and ancient treatises on war. While the defenders fought and died upon the walls of the Eagle Gate, Glorien fretted over the words of long dead scholars instead of leading his warriors with the courage and nobility expected of an elven prince.

'The commander of a fortress is its heart,' said Alanrias. 'And no living thing can fight without its heart. You know this to be true, archer.'

'I know those words could see you executed,' said Alathenar.

'The warriors of this fortress look to you to lead them, not Truecrown,' replied Alanrias. 'I know what must be done to win this day, and I see from your eyes that you know it too.'

Alathenar bit back a furious retort. He wanted to chastise the Shadow Warrior for his sedition, to reprimand him for his lack of loyalty, but he could not find the words. The realisation tasted of ashes in his mouth, and he felt the splinter of ice harden his heart.

For he knew Alanrias was right.

* * *

WITH EVERY MILE he rode, Caelir expected death. With every mile that passed without it, he wondered why. He had slain the Everqueen. The fact of that deed was evident in the grey sky, the weeping rain and the sagging branches of every tree. The life had bled out of the forest, the magic that had sustained it for an eternity now ended in one treacherous dagger thrust.

His clothes were plastered to his body in the rain, an impractical mix of silks and satin that looked like they belonged to some courtly nobleman, not a horseman of Ellyrion. The rush of memory was still raw and rough edged, his abused mind struggling to cope with the return of a life unremembered. He thought his skull might burst with the torrent of images, sensations and vivid recall that flooded his senses. He could remember the succulent taste of roast stag, hear a forgotten sound of crystal bells and feel the lost warmth of a mother's embrace.

Caelir fought to hold onto the present, blinking tears and raindrops away as he rode madly through the depths of Avelorn Forest. Blurred shapes passed him, oaks, ash, and willow. He heard chittering voices, capering sprites and the ancient creak and groan of creatures older than the elves as they moved unseen in the darkness. To ride like this was madness; a hidden burrow or a concealed root could trip his horse and break its leg. This beast was no Ellyrian mount, but one of Saphery, its coat lambent and silky with magical residue. The black steed he had ridden to Avelorn…

Lotharin!

Yes, Lotharin, that was Eldain's mount. His brother had scoffed at the naysayers who said that a black horse would bring its rider ill-fortune. He remembered the

vision he had experienced in Anurion the Green's overgrown villa on the coast of Yvresse, that of a dappled
grey stallion galloping through the surf.

Aedaris...

On the heels of that memory came the pain of knowing that his beloved Aedaris was dead, her flanks pierced
by druchii bolts in the dockyards of Clar Karond. He
recognised the mount that bore him now, a powerful
mare by the name of Irenya, who galloped with sure and
steady grace through the haunted forest. Once she had
borne a retainer of his father's villa, but that warrior had
died...

More memories intruded, Rhianna, Kyrielle, Lilani
and all that had happened since his return to Ulthuan.
Caelir wept to know that he had been used as an instru-
ment of murder, but the guilt he felt was tempered by
the knowledge that there were few alive who could have
withstood the tortures and unclean magic that had been
worked upon his flesh and spirit.

'You should have killed me, Eldain,' he wept. 'Better
dead than left to the druchii.'

His horse flicked its ears in annoyance at the name of
the dark kin from across the ocean, and Caelir rubbed
its neck as it ran. Trees and lightless arbours flashed past
him, and Caelir could not fathom why the forest had
not killed him.

He sensed its hostility in every looming tree, every
grasping branch that whipped him as he passed. Yet
for all their bitter spite, they did not stop him, did not
unhorse him and seemed to close up behind him as
though reluctantly aiding him. The steed rode paths of
the forest unknown to even the Maiden Guard, travers-
ing the secret ways known only to the trees and denizens

of Avelorn who had made their home here before the coming of the elves.

Caelir had no idea where the paths of the forest were leading him, or where his horse was taking him. In truth, he didn't care. There was nothing left to him now, no refuge, no friends and no loved ones to take him in or offer him succour. Caelir was alone in the world and every place of goodness and decency would surely reject him. In such times where could anyone go?

The first Caelir was aware of how far he had ridden was when he heard the sound of rushing water, and smelled the scent of the Inner Sea. His head came up and he saw the forest thin ahead of him; thick, ancient-bodied trees giving way to younger, more vigorous saplings hungry to break the borders forced upon them by elfkind. Though still many miles before him, the escarpment of the Annulii reared up in a towering white cliff that soared beyond the clouds. The majestic peaks of the distant mountains were shawled with tumbling streams of raw magic drawn to Ulthuan by the long lost mages of Caledor Dragontamer.

He rode from the trees, seeing a wide river before him and knowing it as the Arduil, the watercourse that marked the boundary between Avelorn and Ellyrion. A small ship rode high in the water, a mid-sized sloop with runes etched into its prow that named it *Dragonkin*.

Its crew were already aboard, and the ship was ready to make sail, but its captain made no move to take her out, as though waiting for something or someone to return. Caelir rode to the edge of the river, and the captain of the ship came over to the gunwale. His skin was ruddy from a life spent upon the waters, and his keen eye took in Caelir's unusual garb with a curious glance, which surprised Caelir. This was Avelorn, and this sea-farer must have borne stranger travellers than he to the Everqueen's realm.

'My lord,' said the captain. 'I dreamed I would see you again. Yet I dreamed you older, not younger.'

Caelir knew in that instant how Eldain had come to Avelorn, and shook his head.

'You mistake me for another, friend captain,' said Caelir, turning his horse away. 'When you see my brother again, ask him if it was all worthwhile.'

'You are not Lord Éadaoin?'

'No, nor will I ever be,' said Caelir, riding away towards a point where Irenya could cross the river. Caelir glanced over his shoulder. The crew of the boat were watching him, and he gave the captain a wave. No such gesture was returned, and Caelir guided his mount down the muddy slopes of the bank and into the river. The riverbed was barely a yard and a half below the surface, a depth that would have been impassable to any ships but those of the asur.

The water was cold, icy from its journey down the flanks of the Annulii, yet Caelir welcomed its frozen touch. He rode into the centre of the river and stopped, feeling the water churn with the agitation of nymphs beneath the surface. They called to him with tiny splashes and gurgles, capering around his horse's legs with fearful burbles.

'I have no tears left to spare,' he said, and they sped off upriver with hurt splashes.

Caelir paused a moment before resuming his crossing, bathing in the cold magical energies of Ulthuan's waters. He tipped his head back and spread his arms, letting the touch of the river wash him clean of the dark enchantments surrounding him. He closed his eyes and let loose an almighty shout, a primal scream of loss, anger and catharsis.

All that had been done to him poured out in his cries, and he yelled till he was hoarse.

When it was done, he tapped his heels to the horse's flanks and rode towards the far shore. Like Avelorn, low clouds smothered Ellyrion's beauty, the enduring summers that warmed its wide, trackless steppes and unbroken wilds banished in the face of the grief that engulfed the land of Ulthuan.

Even shrouded in sorrow, Ellyrion was a tonic for the spirit. A wind blew across its face, carrying the scent of the wild herds, the open plains and the long grass that waved in gentle breezes that caressed the skin like a lover.

Caelir rode from the cold waters and onto the soil of Ellyrion, feeling the land welcome him as a prodigal son. In the shadows of the mountains lay Ellyr-Charoi, the marble-walled villa where he had grown to manhood and learned the ways of the horse lords from his father. This was where he belonged, in a wild, untamed land where elf and steed roamed free and answerable to no one.

Ellyrion was a golden kingdom, and no sorrow could dim its radiance for long.

The clouds parted somewhere far to the south, and a single brilliant beam of sunlight broke through to shine on a distant city of crystal castles, silver bridges and fabulous, soaring towers of gold and silver.

It was the most beautiful thing Caelir had ever seen.

'I am home,' he said.

* * *

IN ALL HIS long life, Prince Tyrion of Ulthuan had never known weakness like this. Though he had been wounded before, by those few foes skilled enough to penetrate his defences, the pain that was now his constant companion cut deeper than any sword thrust or axe blow.

This was a wound of the spirit.

He clung tightly to Malhandir's reins as a wave of pain washed over him, and only his superlative mastery of his own body kept him in the saddle. His aquiline features, so noble and yet so harsh, were now drained of colour and his eyes held the emptiness of a corpse long lain within its tomb.

The dusty plain before the mountain castle was thick with druchii dead, their plum-coloured cloaks stained with ignoble blood. Though this had been little more than a skirmish, a prelude to the slaughter to come, it felt good to kill again, and shed the blood of those who dared invade his homeland and strike down his loved ones.

Such terrible lust to kill was not born within Tyrion, but far to the north upon the Blighted Isle, where the ancient blade of Aenarion reared proud from its blood-soaked altar and called to the cursed descendants of that legendary hero. The pleasure Tyrion took in slaughter was the Sword of Khaine's gift to him, driving his blade home and giving him the strength he needed to slay his enemies.

In times of peace its song was a curse, in times of war a boon.

Tyrion hated that its keening wail of murder made him feel so alive, yet what other power could keep his grief and pain at bay?

Every instinct screamed at him to abandon Lothern

and ride with dragonspeed to the forest realm of his beloved Alarielle. He was the Everqueen's champion and he was far from her side at her hour of greatest need. She lay on the cusp of death, yet he could do nothing for her. So fleet was Malhandir that Tyrion could be in Avelorn by nightfall, yet his promise to Alarielle bound him to the defence of Lothern with chains of duty stronger than the finest ithilmar.

He had promised her that he would heed his brother's counsel, and Teclis had bade him fight alongside the Phoenix King's warriors in their desperate battle against the druchii invaders. King Finubar and his White Lions fought with the warriors of Eataine on the ramparts of the Emerald Gate, and he had entrusted Tyrion with securing the castles on the rocky shoulders of the mighty portal that blocked entrance to the Straits of Lothern.

'Keep my flanks secure, Tyrion,' Finubar had urged him as they parted in the shadow of the great statues that towered over the wondrous port. 'If the druchii take but one of the castles then the Emerald Gate must be yielded. I would not see it so, my friend.'

'Nor I, my king,' Tyrion had promised. 'I will hold it as long as I can.'

The memory faded and Tyrion slumped over Malhandir's neck as his strength ebbed, like the tide around the bloody, bone-choked shores of the Blighted Isle. His vision blurred and he pictured the plain of bones and the smouldering black sword of his ancestor. Even over so great a distance the Sword of Khaine called to him with promises of the power to win victories undreamed.

Tyrion shook his head, eyes closed and teeth gritted together to resist its call, for damnation and ruination would fall upon any who drew the cursed blade.

Belarien rode alongside him, his sword wet with enemy blood. They had fought as brothers since the last great invasion of the druchii, and spilled blood together on the blasted plain of Finuval. They had sailed the great oceans of the world and seen its wonders side by side. Only Teclis, it was said, was closer to Tyrion than Belarien.

'My lord,' cried Belarien as Tyrion swayed in the saddle. 'Are you wounded?'

'By this rabble?' hissed Tyrion, ramming Sunfang back in its red-gold scabbard. 'Not unless I have lost every skill I once possessed.'

The battle Tyrion and Belarien's Silver Helms had fought before the gate of the castle had been brief and bloody. The druchii had been poorly led, overconfident and scattered by their ill-disciplined charge. Easy pickings for the finest heavy cavalry in the world.

His ancient blade had drawn deep from the well of druchii blood, and reaped many souls to send to Morai-Heg. Yet no sooner had they crushed this first attack beneath the glittering hooves of their steeds than Tyrion had felt the dagger thrust as though it had plunged into his own heart.

'Lead us within the walls,' hissed Tyrion. 'Now!'

Belarien waved to the Silver Helms' clarion and a shrill note was blown from an icy trumpet that rallied the triumphant riders to their prince. Steeds of dappled grey formed up around Tyrion, their flanks gleaming with their own inner light. Tyrion spun his horse, taking up position at their head as the Silver Helms moved off. No commands, no vulgar blows from a whip or raking violence of spurs had been needed, for these steeds understood their masters' will as though rider and mount shared one mind.

Tyrion gripped tight to Malhandir. The steed felt its rider's pain and bore him with all swiftness to the safety of the castle. The gate shut behind them, and a volley of arrows hissed from the gleaming ramparts as the druchii gathered for another attack. Tyrion had seen the opportunity to ride out against the last attack, but the enemy would not be so incautious again.

A squire took Malhandir's bridle, and Tyrion nodded his thanks. He slid from the saddle, and hissed with pain as the impact of his landing jarred the phantom wound in his heart. He placed his hand upon his chest. Though the golden scales of Aenarion's armour remained unbroken, Tyrion felt the cold touch of death drawing ever closer to his heart.

'My lord?' said Belarien, dismounting next to him and handing his steed's reins off to another squire. 'The pain is getting worse.'

Tyrion took a deep breath, marshalling his strength.

'No,' he said at last. 'It is the same.'

'I was not asking a question.'

'I know,' said Tyrion, accepting a goblet of water from a warrior in the livery of the Eataine citizen levy. Belarien removed his helmet, a gleaming silver artefact adorned with a host of battle honours, ribbons and eagle feathers. His thin face was etched with concern for his prince, his pale grey eyes glittering with flecks of amber. He too accepted a goblet, and drained it in one long swallow.

'Are we not friends enough that you can speak to me truthfully?' asked Belarien. 'I saw you almost fall from your saddle.'

'Malhandir would never allow it,' stated Tyrion.

'Maybe not,' agreed the High Helm of Tyrion's riders. 'But I saw what I saw.'

Tyrion saw Belarien would not be dissuaded from his questions, and sighed.

'You are my dearest friend,' said Tyrion. 'But some burdens are mine to bear alone.'

'Only because you choose to make it so,' pressed Belarien, taking Tyrion's arm. 'Remember you have friends with wide shoulders.'

Tyrion smiled and said, 'I know. Asuryan and Isha have blessed me with my companions in war and peace, but weakness is for mortals, not those upon whom the survival of their race depends.'

Belarien saw the truth of Tyrion's pain. 'You still feel the Everqueen's wound.'

'I do,' admitted Tyrion. 'It is like a slow-moving dagger pushing towards my heart. Only with Teclis do I share a closer bond, but his near death at the hands of the traitor Caelir was a swiftly forgotten ailment compared to this weakness. Until Alarielle heals I will share a measure of her pain as she once bore a measure of mine when the forests of Avelorn burned and the assassins closed in.'

'Then is there nothing I can do?'

'I fear not. Every battle host draws its will to fight from its leader, and I must be as strong and powerful as ever to the warriors around me. More so, now that I need them stand fast in the face of an unwinnable fight.'

'You do not believe we can hold this castle?'

On the ramparts, archers loosed volley after volley at the druchii beyond the walls. Here and there, a scream punctured the clear sky as a bolt of black iron from an enemy crossbow felled one of the defenders.

'You and I will not ride like that again, Belarien,' said

Tyrion. 'The druchii leader was a glory seeker, but the next assault will be commanded by a more cautious warrior.'

'And we will hurl his rabble back too,' promised Belarien.

'Your ardour does you credit, my friend, but this castle was not built to resist anything other than skirmish troops or a probing force. No one foresaw the need for it to be stronger. It will fall eventually, that is certain.'

Belarien replaced his helm and fixed Tyrion with a determined gaze. 'Then we will make them pay for its walls in blood.'

Tyrion drew Sunfang from its sheath, and the Silver Helm mirrored his movement in one fluid unveiling of glittering silver steel.

'That we shall,' promised Tyrion, his proud voice carrying to every warrior within the castle. 'I promised the Phoenix King that I would hold this place, and no scrap of Ulthuan will be yielded without an ocean of druchii blood spilled in its name.'

He raised Sunfang high, the weak light catching the radiant blaze of its shimmering blade. For one shining moment, the grief and hideous twilight of the Everqueen's pain was banished in a burst of brilliant sunlight. The cold fire in Tyrion's chest was no less diminished, but pain was fleeting, legends would last forever.

'For the Everqueen and Ulthuan!' yelled Tyrion, leading the Silver Helms towards the ramparts. That the castle would fall was inevitable, but Tyrion would make its doom so bloody for the druchii that this battle would live in their memories for all eternity.

On the Blighted Isle, the Sword of Khaine simmered with anticipation in its dripping, reeking altar.

CHAPTER THREE

VOICES FROM ANCIENT DAYS

BIRDSONG HAD RETURNED to Avelorn, though Eldain hardly noticed. He wandered the shadowed groves and garlanded arbours of the forest, letting its twisting paths guide his steps rather than any conscious thought of a destination. Sunlight and joy had drained from the enchanted forest, but it had not been extinguished.

The Everqueen had survived Caelir's blow, though none yet knew what damage had been done to her. Eldain knew well how the weapons of the druchii could cause such hurt as to leave the body intact but destroy the life within. His own father had fallen to such a weapon, his wasting flesh lingering long after his spirit had withered and died.

Eldain had not thought of his father in some time, and the guilt of that was another cold nail hammered into the hard muscle of his heart.

How much could any soul endure before it became too heavy a burden to bear?

Plants and trees bent their backs away from him and the path turned him around, this way and that, as he roamed at random through the leafy depths. He had no idea where he was, and that was dangerous in a place like Avelorn. No one, not even the Everqueen or her Maiden Guard, knew the full extent of what lay at the forest's heart. To stray with such lack of care in a place of magic was reckless beyond words.

Eldain looked up from the path, hearing voices raised in song. Not a lament, this was a song of love triumphant and the joyous union of souls. Notes struck from a lyre of glorious timbre drifted through the trees and where they fell, the leaves shone a vivid green, and grass once withered bloomed anew. It was music to lift the heart and refresh the soul. Anger touched Eldain. What right did anyone have to sing such songs in times of woe? The more he listened, the more the music and joyous lyrics seemed to mock him, as though chosen with deliberate irony.

His fists bunched at his sides, and he set off in the direction of the players, seeing drifting forms in gossamer-thin robes of silk through the foliage. Riotous colours fluttered in the spaces between the trees and bushes. Eldain saw elves of both sexes, none wearing the white of mourning as they danced and swayed to the wondrous tunes of the musicians.

A figure stepped from behind a tree before he could intrude on the recital, a female elf of striking appearance. Clad in a twisting weave of auburn silk and crimson damask, her body was lithe and hard with wiry cords of muscle. Her hair fell about her shoulders in golden tresses, and Eldain recognised the dancer that had stood beside Caelir and who been brought before the Maiden Guard.

'Whatever you are about to do, think again,' she said, her voice hard and pitiless.

'They mock my pain,' hissed Eldain.

'No, they celebrate the Everqueen's survival,' said the dancer. 'There's a difference.'

Eldain nodded in understanding, ashamed he had allowed music and laughter to enrage him so. He gripped the branch of a tree, feeling thorns prick his skin and the leaves shake in irritation at his touch.

'You and the forest are not friends?' asked the elf maid, seeing a drop of blood on his arm.

'I have no friends,' said Eldain. 'Least of all in Avelorn.'

'I am Lilani,' said the dancer with a seductive purr. 'I could be your friend.'

'You don't know me.'

'I knew your brother,' said Lilani. 'You look a lot like him. Sadder, though.'

'I saw you beside Caelir when the Everqueen…' began Eldain. 'How did you know him?'

'We met crossing the Finuval Plain,' she said, linking her arm with his and leading him towards the musicians and dancers within the grove. 'He and I were lovers for a time.'

Eldain was taken aback at her frank admission, but knew he shouldn't have been. Avelorn was a realm where the normal rules of conduct and etiquette were proudly flouted. What would have shocked the polite society of Lothern or Tor Elyr was a daily occurrence within the Everqueen's realm.

'I didn't know that,' he said, hating how prudish his words sounded.

'Why would you?' she said.

Eldain shrugged, trying to think of something to say

that wouldn't make him sound like more of a dullard than he already felt. Lilani led him into a wide clearing, across which had been spread a riotously garish spread of blankets. Elves lay sprawled throughout the clearing, drinking dreamwine from crystal goblets that sparkled like ice in the evening twilight.

A goblet appeared in his hand, though Eldain could not recall anyone passing near enough to have given it to him. Within the goblet, the dreamwine swirled like a miniature whirlpool of glittering quartz and mist. He hesitated to taste it, remembering when he had drunk a similar vintage with Rhianna before leaving for Naggaroth.

'You've drunk dreamwine before, haven't you?' said a fluid voice before him.

Eldain looked up into the eyes of the elf poet the Maiden Guard had spoken to in the wake of Caelir's attack.

'I have,' agreed Eldain, turning his wrist and upending the goblet. 'And it didn't agree with me then either.'

'What a dreadful shame,' said the poet as the dreamwine floated away like a whispered secret. 'And a terrible waste. Good dreamwine is hard to come by, especially now. Still, I am sure the wind will enjoy it, though what the wind dreams of only fools and eagles know.'

'You are Narentir?' said Eldain.

'How wonderful to be recognised,' said the poet, clapping his hands in delight. 'You have read my work?'

'No,' said Eldain. 'I saw the Maiden Guard drag you before them.'

'Ah, yes, an unfortunate business,' said Narentir, turning away from him and threading his way through the lounging elves. Lilani followed him, taking Eldain with her, and he found himself powerless to resist. Her beauty was intoxicating, her touch magical and exhilarating.

Narentir stopped beside a brightly painted wagon and lifted out a gleaming breastplate and a sword encased in a scabbard of sapphires and rubies.

'Your brother, for I see by the proud jaw, aquiline nose and brooding eyes that you are related to our erstwhile companion, has caused us quite a considerable amount of trouble. Merely for the crime of knowing him, the members of our happy troupe were subjected to many hours of objectionable questioning by the Everqueen's protectors, though, given her current condition, I use that description laughingly.'

Eldain took his arm from Lilani and nodded. 'I am Caelir's brother, yes.'

'Well of course you are, dear boy,' said Narentir, casting his gaze up and down. 'Though I fear young Caelir alone inherited the family talent for song and rhyme.'

'He performed for you?'

'For some more than others,' grinned Narentir, with a sly look at Lilani. The elf maid did not blush or show any sign of embarrassment at the poet's lascivious comment. Eldain ignored Narentir's unabashed tone and looked around the gathering of elves.

'How long did you travel with Caelir?' asked Eldain, as a pair of musicians again began to play their instruments. This time, the music was melancholy, bittersweet and full of regret. Eldain felt his anger at these performers abate, for what had they done except take Caelir in as a travelling companion?

With a start, Eldain realised that the clearing had begun to fill without his noticing. Dozens of elves had silently slipped through the gloaming, appearing in the gaps between the trees in greater and greater numbers until hundreds had gathered around the colourful stage of blankets.

'He came upon us at the northern extent of Finuval Plain,' said Narentir, apparently oblivious to the swelling numbers of observers. 'A curious fellow, and no mistake, but I saw the soul of a rake and a rogue in him, a fellow traveller on a whimsical road that leads everywhere and comes from nowhere.'

Narentir sighed. 'How I was mistaken, for though Caelir was all those things and more, a darkness was hidden within him and I, in my innocence, failed to see it. Woe unto the poet that he should always seek the best in others.'

A single note of music chimed, and Narentir smiled with theatrical zeal.

'But, alas, I must take a turn as a poor player before my audience, for in times such as these, what is left to us but tales of valour to rekindle hope and stir the hearts of those who will defend us?'

Eldain turned to Lilani, the poet's overblown manner beginning to irritate him. 'Do you know what he's talking about?'

She nodded and said, 'Come. Sit with me awhile and you will see.'

NARENTIR TOOK CENTRE stage on the blankets, clad in his gleaming breastplate and with his gilded scabbard belted at his side. He wore a cloak of brilliant blue, which billowed around him, though not a breath of wind stirred the leaves and grass of the clearing. A winged helm sat upon his head, such as might be worn by an elven prince of a forgotten age. The ensemble should have been ridiculous, for Narentir was clearly no warrior, but Eldain found himself picturing the poet as a great hero, a leader from distant times who none now remembered, save in song.

'Let me tell you of a time long passed, when gods walked the earth and mighty heroes were as common as gemstones upon the fingers of an Eataine princess. Let me tell you of the doom of the Ulthane and the glorious time of their rebirth. Let me tell you of ultimate evil unleashed, and the bright heroes of legend who stood against it!'

Despite himself, Eldain felt himself caught up in Narentir's words. Flitting will-o'-the-wisps bobbed through the clearing, casting a diffuse glow over the gathered elves. Eldain saw every face enraptured by the poet's presence, the cadence and rhythmic flow of his delivery perfectly capturing the spirit of the age.

Narentir prowled the stage of rugs, his arms spread wide and his head thrown back as he told the epic of Aenarion, when the land of Ulthuan had burned with the touch of daemons from beyond the great gateway. Hearts thrilled to the tales of battles fought in the shadow of impending destruction, and though all knew the outcome – for the legend of the Defender was taught to every child upon their mother's knee – tears were spilled and breath caught at each twist in the tale.

At last Narentir came to the tale of Caledor Dragontamer, Aenarion's greatest and most trusted friend and architect of the final victory against the daemons. Eldain felt Lilani press herself to him in fear as Narentir told of how the great Chaos powers laid siege to the Isle of the Dead to prevent Caledor from completing his great ritual to deny the daemons their source of power.

Eldain found himself able to picture the limitless hordes of daemons battling to overcome Aenarion's brave defenders. As Narentir leapt and spun, slashing the air with graceful sweeps of his sword, Eldain saw the epic confrontation between the mighty daemon lords and the Phoenix King. He flinched with every depiction of that incredible battle, and when the poet was done, Eldain wept as he heard of how Caledor and his fellow mages had drained the world of volatile magic, leaving the daemonic host powerless and dying, like fish stranded by the tide. The price of that success was beyond imagining, for Caledor and his fellow mages were now trapped forever in a vortex of powerful magic upon the Isle of the Dead. They now existed in a place beyond time and beyond the reach of mortals.

Eldain shivered at the mention of that accursed island. He remembered the shifting mists and bitter taste of old magic as the *Dragonkin* had sailed close to its unnatural boundaries. The sea around the Isle of the Dead was gloomy and bleak with timeless melancholy, and Eldain swallowed a sudden bilious nausea at the thought of that doomed island out of time.

He blinked, listening as Narentir recounted the last flight of the mortally wounded Indraugnir, greatest of dragons, who carried the dying Aenarion to the Blighted Isle. A respectful hush fell across the audience, and heads bowed at the memory of the fallen Phoenix King. He and Caledor had been the greatest of the asur. Their selfless deeds ensured the world would live on, though none beyond the shores of Ulthuan would ever know of their incredible sacrifice.

Yet as the tale wound to its well known conclusion, Eldain saw that Narentir was not finished. His tale had more to reveal, and like all good tales, it grew in the telling.

'Greatest master of magic though he was, not even Caledor could tame such forces as were unleashed by the first masters of the world,' sang Narentir. 'Though his great ritual drew the storms of magic to Ulthuan that they might be drained from the world, not all enchantments can be so neatly caged.'

Narentir prowled the stage, his sword now sheathed and his hands grasping the air as though struggling to contain some unseen power that flitted just beyond his grasp.

'Cracks there were in the world, for the devastation wrought in the great cataclysm that brought Chaos to the world was like nothing seen before or since. Wild magic seeps into the world through those cracks, like water through a crumbling weir. In enchanted groves, spellbound forests, mist-wreathed marshes or mystical caves, that magic lights the world around it, gives it life and fills the hearts of all those who look upon them with joy, though they know not what beguiles them. But not all such cracks are places of wonderment, some are gateways to the terrible powers that almost destroyed the world, and such places must be guarded by those with hearts as pure and strong as the first dawn.

'Such warriors were the Ulthane! Heroes cast in the image of Aenarion and Caledor combined, yet none here know their names, for they desired not fame nor riches nor glory, for they served a higher purpose. The gods had chosen them, granting them power beyond the ken of mortal and asur alike, for they stood watch on the one place Caledor's spell could not seal, a bloody isle unknown to maps or seafarers, yet which lived in the hearts of men as a dark tale of shipwrecks and lost souls.'

Narentir paused before Eldain. The poet's eyes shone with the vibrancy of his tale, as though a portion of that dark time passed from that age to this. Even the shimmering forest lights had dimmed, and the elves gathered around Narentir held their breath as they waited for him to continue. The poet knew his craft, letting the anticipation of his next words build before pressing on with his tale.

'The gods of Chaos are cunning, and, worst of all, patient. They knew that no creature of this world could fully tame the tides of magic, and they waited for their chance to strike. The Dark Powers sent their minions to that island, and laid siege to it as once they had besieged Ulthuan. With the light of Aenarion gone from the world, they knew of no enemy that could stand before their numberless hordes. Yet for all their cunning, they knew not of the Ulthane, for each among them had shed their former lives and vanished from the pages of history, becoming nameless warriors in the service of order. The Dark Gods could not see them, could not know them, and could not defeat them.

'Upon the shores of that black island, a battle to save the world was waged. A host of daemons fell from the skies, and an army of leviathans rose from the deepest ocean trenches. The very rock rebelled at their touch and writhed in new and terrible forms. And upon that once-fair isle, the blood ran in rivers, turning the waters red for leagues in all directions, yet not once did the Ulthane falter! Their swords were thunder-forged lightning, their shields ice-wrought mirrors. A hundred daemons fell with every blow, and beneath the Ulthane's red-lit eyes, no creature born of Chaos could stand but be withered and cast back to its diabolical abode.'

Eldain could dimly remember hearing legends of the Ulthane when he had been a child, but the memories were hazy and indistinct, like a fleeting dream that escapes recall upon waking. Though Narentir told his tale with vigour and charm, its details were already fading from his mind, as though the memory of the Ulthane dared not linger in the memories of those who heard of them for fear the Dark Gods of the north might learn of their existence.

'And like Aenarion before them, the Ulthane hurled back the foe, fighting a hundred battles in as many days. Though the foe attacked without mercy, neither did the Ulthane stop to lament their fallen brothers nor pause to take sustenance. Their swords smote mightily, and little by little, the attacks of the monstrous horde lessened until, at last, the Dark Powers abandoned their assault.

'The battle was won, but at a fearful cost. Barely a handful of the Ulthane remained, and all knew that there could be no return to the lives they had known. Another attack would come, from the daemons or some other foe intent on seizing the incredible power that lay at the heart of the island. The Ulthane gathered at the twisted heart of the island and swore mighty and unbreakable oaths to stand guard upon its shores forever more.

'Though ages of the world came and went, the Ulthane stood sentinel over the island, summoning up an enchanted mist to keep the island from the thoughts of lesser races and never once relaxing their penetrating gaze. And should a time come where the world needs their blades again, the Ulthane will return, thunder-forged swords and shields of mirrored ice out-thrust to whatever enemy dares to wreak harm upon the world they have sworn to defend. And such times are upon us now, dear friends. The shadow of the Witch King lies long upon the lands of Ulthuan as he and his damnable mother strike at the heart of our fair isle. In this time of woe, shall not the greatest heroes of the age rise to our salvation? Shall not every heart be filled with martial pride and towering fury to drive these invaders away? Though darkness claws at the horizon with iron nails, we must not forsake hope. Though our enemies gather like wolves around a wounded stag, we will not despair, for even the sly wolf knows the stag can fight back. Hold to hope, my friends, for Ulthuan has never yet fallen, and nor shall she fall now!'

Thunderous applause erupted from every elf in the clearing and from thousands more unseen in the forest's depths. Eldain joined in, bruising his palms with the vigour of his clapping. He surged to his feet, convinced the towering forms of the Ulthane were about to march from the trees with their thunder-forged swords held high.

Lilani uncoiled from the ground, vaulting into the air and landing on an overhanging branch. She loosed a wild shout of joy, an exultant cry that was taken up by all the gathered elves until it seemed the entire forest was yelling with one voice.

Only when three bronze-armoured Maiden Guard entered the clearing did the thunderous noise begin to diminish. All heads turned to the grim-eyed warrior maidens as they marched past the exhausted Narentir. Eldain watched them also, knowing in a heartbeat that they had come for him.

Lirazel came at their head, her silver-bladed lance held

at her side as she fixed him with a steely-eyed gaze that left no doubt as to what would happen if he tried to resist. Eldain had no intention of resisting, for he knew where they would be taking him.

Lilani dropped to the leafy floor of the clearing beside him and clutched his arm tightly. She leaned in close and whispered urgently in his ear.

'Remember Narentir's words. Do not forsake hope. Never give in to despair.'

With those words she sprang away, vanishing from sight amid the gradually dispersing crowd of elves. With the taleteller done, their whims and fancies carried them away like leaves in an autumn wind.

Lirazel halted before Eldain, and her eyes held the promise of winter in their amber depths. Something awesome shimmered beneath her skin, a fragment of a presence incalculably ancient and merciless. The elemental power of Avelorn lurked within this warrior of the Maiden Guard, and Eldain felt his heart hammering in his chest at its nearness.

'I know why you are here,' he whispered. 'You will have no need of lances or bows.'

'Then let us begone from these minstrels and troubadours,' said Lirazel in a voice that echoed with the weight of ages and an unbroken line of life that stretched back to the birth of Ulthuan itself.

'For we are the Everqueen,' said Lirazel. 'And we would know the truth of you, Eldain Éadaoin.'

DAWN WAS CREEPING into the eastern horizon, bringing an end to the welcome respite from the fighting brought by darkness. Beyond the walls of the Eagle Gate, the fires of the enemy burned with queerly shimmering flames, lighting the white stone of the Annulii with writhing shadows. Menethis almost tripped on the steps leading to the Aquila Spire, exhaustion making him as clumsy as an orc.

He couldn't remember the last time he had slept in a bed.

Injured warriors brought food and water to those who defended the ramparts, and healers worked their way along the wall, using what little magic remained to them to seal sword cuts and mend broken bones. Their powers gave strength to weary limbs, but such boons came at a cost, and every one of the fortress's healers stumbled like a dreamwalker, their own reserves of energy drained by the effort of tending to so many. Though he knew little of magic, Menethis knew the healers were at the limits of their endurance.

'Much like the rest of the garrison,' he whispered, before chiding himself for the disloyal thought that came hard on its heels. He straightened his tunic and did his best to smooth down his hair. They may be under siege, but Glorien tolerated no laxness of behaviour or appearance.

He reached the top of the stairs and knocked on the reinforced door. The wood was scorched where a bolt of rogue magic had burned it. From inside the tower, Menethis heard a clatter of metal, and wondered what new foolishness Glorien was attempting.

'My lord,' he said. 'It is Menethis. May I enter?'

'Menethis! Thank Isha, yes, come in, I need you!'

Menethis pushed open the door and entered the cramped tower. Intended as a perch for the commander to watch an unfolding battle before drawing his plans, it had become Glorien's refuge from the horrors below.

Stacks of books were strewn on the wide table, unrolled scrolls lay in limp piles, and balls of crumpled parchments rolled across the floor as Menethis opened the door.

Glorien Truecrown stood before a full length mirror, its edges wound in silver wire like interleaved vines. He wore his wyvern skin boots and a mail shirt, over which was a finely cut tunic of softest cream. Glorien once claimed he had hunted the wyvern himself, and Menethis had made admiring sounds, though he knew the lie for what it was.

A breastplate of ithilmar hung from Glorien's chest, its straps loose and flapping as the commander of the Eagle Gate spun around, trying in vain to buckle himself into his armour.

'It's so frustrating,' said Glorien, as Menethis entered.

'My lord?'

'This armour. Whoever designed it must have been a blind idiot. It's impossible to put on, Menethis. Is that not the most foolish thing you've ever heard? Armour that can't be worn!'

'A noble of Ulthuan should have his squires to armour him, my lord,' said Menethis. 'He would not be expected to gird himself for war alone.'

'Of course,' said Glorien, with a relieved sigh. 'Squires. Of course. I completely forgot about squires. It's this warrior's life; it drives all thoughts of civilised behaviour from your head. I required your help, so why were you not here? Remiss of you not to attend upon me, when I needed you.'

Menethis bit back a harsh retort and said, 'I was on the walls, my lord. The druchii and their barbarous allies sorely press us.'

'Fighting, yes,' said Glorien. 'And that is why I need you. If I am to fight, then I must be armoured in the proper fashion. A prince of Ulthuan must shine like the sun when he goes to war.'

Menethis forgot his anger in a heartbeat, and he took a step towards Glorien.

'You fight with us now?'

'Of course,' said Glorien. 'Whatever gave you the impression I wouldn't?'

Menethis looked at the scattered books and scrolls, the words of ancient warriors and scholars on the arts of war. For as long as the enemy had been before the walls of the Eagle Gate, Glorien had buried his head in the pages of his beloved books, seeking solace and inspiration from their inked wisdom. Until now, Menethis had thought it panic that had kept Glorien locked within the tower, but had it been prudence after all? Had Glorien found what he sought in the words of these long dead warriors?

'Nothing, my lord,' said Menethis. 'It lifts my heart to know you fight with us. Your warriors will fight like Aenarion reborn with you at their head.'

'No doubt,' said Glorien. 'Now help me into this damned armour.'

Menethis lifted the carven breastplate, a wondrously sculpted artefact with more than a hint of the enchanter's art woven into its metal. It was light, and Menethis felt the magic tingling at his fingertips as he strapped it to Glorien's body. As he added each piece of armour, Glorien at last began to resemble the noble elven warrior he needed to be.

Menethis glanced down at the scattered books.

'If I might enquire, my lord,' he said. 'Which author

finally convinced you it was time to don armour and draw your sword?'

'None of them,' said Glorien with a dismissive glance towards the books that had held him prisoner within the tower. 'Last night as I slept amid these treatises on war, the truth was revealed to me in a great dream.'

Menethis had heard of the gods sending dreams to their chosen champions, but Glorien hardly seemed a likely candidate to be such a warrior. But then, the ways of the gods were mysterious, and who could say what made them chose one individual over another?

'You believe it was a true vision, my lord?'

'I do, Menethis, for I dreamed of a Phoenix King of old.'

That was certainly auspicious, for dreams of ancient kings were often heralds of great deeds. It was said that Finubar had dreamed of Caradryel the night before his coronation in the Flames of Asuryan.

'Which of the Phoenix Kings did you dream about?' asked Menethis, lifting a gleaming pauldron of silver and gold from the armour rack in the corner of the tower.

'I dreamed of Tethlis.'

'Tethlis?' said Menethis, his hand hovering over the buckle. 'The Slayer?'

'Indeed,' answered Glorien. 'In my dream I found myself upon the mist-wreathed shores of a black island, the rocks and sand awash with blood and bones. It was quite the most frightful place I have ever seen.'

'The Blighted Isle!' gasped Menethis, making a protective ward symbol over his heart.

Glorien nodded. 'I should have been deathly afraid, but I was at peace. I felt no fear as I saw a figure farther up the shore. And when he beckoned me, I felt compelled to obey.'

'And you believe this was Tethlis?'

'I know it was,' said Glorien. 'He was exactly as I remember him from the Phoenix Gallery in Lothern. I walked towards the king, and the mist parted. I saw corpses all around me, thousands of them, maybe more, but still I was not afraid. In some places the dead host lay a hundred deep. Blood streamed from their ruined bodies and into the sea, and I knew that the bloody lance in Tethlis's hand had seen every one of these warriors slain.'

'A dream of Tethlis is one of ill-omen, my lord,' breathed Menethis. 'None know for sure how he met his end on that dread island. Found dead at the foot of the Altar of Khaine, some say his own warriors cut him down, lest the Sword of Khaine twist his soul into that of a bloody-handed tyrant who would lead Ulthuan to its doom.'

Glorien shook his head. 'I have heard those tales, but I do not believe them. No elf of the asur would turn his weapon on his betters.'

'Tethlis's rages were well known, and I have heard stranger things than a leader cut down by his own warriors. Tell me, my lord, did Tethlis speak to you in this dream?'

Glorien's mouth opened, and he cocked his head to one side, as though struggling to remember an elusive fact. He started to speak, but could not find the right words. At length, he said, 'I heard no words, but the Phoenix King bade me draw my sword, for the enemy was upon us. The mist gathered around us, and within it I saw ghostly apparitions, shadowy warriors closing in on us with bared blades. Though I could not remember unsheathing it, my sword was in my hand. The Phoenix King and I were back to back as the foe let loose a terrible yell and charged towards us.'

'What were they? Druchii?' asked Menethis.

'I do not know,' said Glorien. 'I could not see them clearly. But we fought them, Tethlis and I, killing them with cut and thrust, lunge and riposte. We fought for an age, and when the foe was done, Tethlis turned to me, and his gaze bored into me with eyes of fire. His command was clear, and I knew the time had come for me to wet my sword in druchii blood in the waking world. I have studied my books long enough, Menethis, and there is little I do not know on the theory of war, but it is time to stand with the warriors of the Eagle Gate and let them see me fight alongside them.'

Glorien saw the look in Menethis's eye before he could mask his surprise and said, 'I admit I was... wary of standing in the battle line with weapon in hand, but the druchii's axes will fall on my neck whether I remain in this tower or on the walls.'

Menethis looked upon Glorien with new eyes, seeing the proudly straight back, the strength in his bearing that had always been there, but which fear had masked. Clad in his battle armour of gold and silver, and with a shimmering helm of ithilmar upon his head, he was the image of the heroes of song and verse. The transformation was nothing short of miraculous, and Menethis wondered that he had not seen the young prince's potential before now.

'Your warriors will be joyous at your presence, my lord,' said Menethis, and meant it.

Glorien smiled, and Menethis felt his heart swell with pride. He had despaired of this moment ever coming, fearing that the death of Cerion Goldwing had doomed the Eagle Gate.

But with this dream, true vision or not, perhaps they had a chance.

'Dawn is almost upon us, Menethis,' said Glorien, 'and it is time for me to take my place on the Eagle Gate as a warrior.'

'A new dawn,' said Menethis. 'A time for fresh beginnings.'

Menethis opened the door to the Aquila Spire, and Glorien stepped onto the top step. The first rays of sunlight caught the gold of his armour, glittering like the fires of the phoenix, and Menethis felt the exhaustion that hung around his neck like a tombstone fall away from him.

Glorien marched down the steps, and the faces of the asur turned towards him, recognising that something had changed, but not knowing what. Menethis saw hopeful looks passed from warrior to warrior, following each glance as the news of Glorien's arrival flew around the fortress.

This was hope reborn. This was the fire of victory lit in every heart.

But Menethis's step faltered as he saw the brooding countenance of a hooded warrior crouched in the gloom of the parapet. Alone among the garrison, this warrior's face remained impassive, and Menethis quailed at the unflinchingly hostile stare of this dark-cloaked archer.

Though he could not see the warrior's face, there was no doubt as to his identity.

Alanrias, the Shadow Warrior of Nagarythe.

Menethis thought of Glorien's dream of Tethlis and his newfound hope turned to fear.

Chapter Four

Bitter Truths

Eldain had wandered aimlessly through the forest, but the Maiden Guard took a more direct path towards the Everqueen. They marched with grim purpose, and Eldain knew that whatever awaited him at the end of this journey would change his destiny forever. The gloom that had hung over the forest was now lifted, and fresh sunlight shone through the tops of tall trees that lifted their branches towards the sun once more.

New growths budded on the ends of limbs of wood, and the grass beyond the invisible paths shone with new-found lustre. Lirazel had said nothing to him after her demand that he accompany her to the Everqueen, and Eldain had not attempted to engage her in conversation.

The crowds that had gathered to listen to Narentir's tales vanished into the forest, yet he could feel them nearby, as though they watched with accusing eyes from the shadows. The forest was alive again, but it was not the life of Avelorn as it had been; it was rampant, vital and unchecked.

Wild magic seeped into the roots of Avelorn, and it was responding to that touch with unfettered growth.

New blooms choked older plants, aggressive saplings fought for light and the earth churned with competing life. As unrestrained as Avelorn had seemed before, now it reminded Eldain of the tales he had heard of the wild wood of Athel Loren. The growth of the asrai's domain was kept in check by powerful waystones, but whatever power had held the full power of Avelorn in check was now absent.

Eldain heard the creak and groan of new wood, the breath of forest creatures as they stalked the undergrowth like hunters. The entire forest had turned hostile.

No, not hostile exactly, but the power that had once turned the thoughts of the creatures of Avelorn to joy and carefree abandon had become violent and predatory. Even the Maiden Guard walked warily, their bows bent and spear points aimed outwards. Not even the protectors of the Everqueen could travel these paths without caution, it seemed.

Eventually Lirazel halted before a woven archway of green wood, the sap running along newly formed shoots like glistening amber. The smell of growth and fecund life was almost overpowering, and the scent of life resurgent was a powerful taste in the back of Eldain's throat.

'You must enter,' said Lirazel.

'You are not coming in?' asked Eldain.

'We need no protection of blades,' replied Lirazel, though the voice was not her own. 'The only life at risk is your own. Enter and follow the path.'

He followed Lirazel's instruction, and stepped through the archway into a verdant grove of dazzling light. The brilliance blinded him, and his every step was taken without the knowledge of where it might lead. He walked until a powerful sensation that he had reached his destination swept over him.

The veil of light withdrew from his senses, and Eldain blinked in the sudden rush of colour. Everywhere he looked, new blooms sought to outdo one another with the brilliance of their hue. Shimmering roses of glittering ebony wove around tree trunks garlanded with flowers that Eldain had never seen before. Plants of vivid purple, gold, white and azure grew wherever they could, and the sheer mass of growth was like the grandest arboretum ever devised.

In the centre of it all sat the Everqueen.

Not Alarielle.

The Everqueen.

Eldain appreciated the difference without even realising there had been one until now.

Clad in a shimmering robe of ice and rainbows, she sat upon a throne of roots and grass that split the ground beneath her and pulsed with the magic that sustained it. Light surrounded the Queen of Avelorn, radiance that sheened the grove in warmth and breathed vitality into everything it touched.

She was simultaneously clad in her robes of light and magic, and naked. Her ivory flesh was sculpted and perfect; no trace of the wound Caelir had done her visible through the mist of glamours that surrounded her. She was just as Eldain remembered her, but so much more.

Her golden hair framed a face of such aching beauty that Eldain wanted to drop to his knees and declare his love for her. At that moment he would have cast aside everything he held dear just to be allowed to devote his life to her. With an effort of will he lifted his gaze to the Everqueen's face, her cold and lethal face.

Though everything around her exploded with life, her eyes held only the promise of death.

Outwardly, the Everqueen was exactly as she had been before, but a force more powerful than any known to the asur beat within her breast. Eldain understood immediately that this was old magic, perhaps the oldest in the world. The first heartbeat of creation empowered her, the birth cry at the beginning of the universe sighed from her lungs, and the power to create everything that was or could be shone in the light that bathed her.

Rhianna was here too, similarly enraptured by the Everqueen's brilliance, and it was all Eldain could do to acknowledge her. She spared him the briefest glance before returning her fervent gaze to the force at the centre of the grove.

The Everqueen shifted in her living throne of roots, raising her hand and beckoning Eldain closer. He could no more disobey that gesture than he could stop his own heart from beating.

'Eldain Éadaoin, called the Fleetmane,' said the Everqueen. Her voice was the sound of new life, and Eldain felt the years melt from him at the sound of his name on her lips.

'My Lady,' said Eldain. 'How would you have me serve you?'

She smiled, but it was the smile of a cat with a helpless mouse in its claws.

'I would see your truth unveiled,' she said. 'I would see you undone and your secrets revealed before those you love.'

Eldain fell to his knees, and shooting buds of new wood erupted from the ground, writhing like fast-growing vines to wrap around his wrists and pull his arms wide. The Everqueen's throne groaned as the roots twisted and bore her towards Eldain. She reached out and cupped his chin with her glistening fingertips. Eldain's skin thrilled at her touch, even as he realised she could destroy him utterly.

Her eyes locked with his, and Eldain felt the primordial energies that danced within the frail mortal frame of the woman before him. She poured into him, and he cried out at the touch of such enormous power. It burned him, and his entire body felt afire with its surging, ancient force. It hollowed him out, scouring his body for every memory, thought and deed that made up his long life. In a heartbeat she knew him entirely, understood what he loved, hated and desired. In that one moment of connection, she knew him better than he knew himself.

'You left your brother to die,' said the Everqueen, looking up at Rhianna. 'For her. You told yourself it was for love, but nothing so noble turned you away from him. Jealousy, spite and hurt pride drove you. You deluded yourself that good could come from evil, but all that springs from evil is tainted by it.'

With the comforting shield of his denial stripped from him, the full force of Eldain's guilt rose up in a choking wave of horror. He saw Caelir's outstretched hand, the silver pledge ring glinting in the cold, bleached light of Naggaroth. Eldain relived that moment a thousand times in the space of a heartbeat, experiencing the shame of his betrayal over and over again.

He had told himself that the love that bloomed anew between he and Rhianna made his betrayal a small thing. Time and unconscious self-preservation had built walls around the memory of Caelir's abandonment, but the power of the Everqueen smashed them asunder and forced him to confront what he had done.

In that moment, he had hated Caelir, hated that he was more liked, more carefree, more beloved and naturally luckier. Caelir took everything that was once Eldain's, and he did it with such ease that no deed of Eldain's could ever compete. The world fell into Caelir's lap without effort, and in that glinting instant, Eldain let a lifetime's worth of bitterness spill out in one terrible mistake.

A moment of weakness, that was all it had taken to betray his life, his love and his own flesh and blood. Eldain wished he could take it back, undo the damage his actions had set in motion, but it was too late for regrets. Too late by far.

'I could have saved him,' said Eldain. 'Lotharin was strong enough to carry us both clear. Caelir ran to me. He called for me to save him, but I ignored him. Worse, I told him I was leaving him to die. I *wanted* him to know why he was going to die. Oh, Isha forgive me!'

'You left him...?' gasped Rhianna, experiencing the full weight of Eldain's betrayal as it filled her mind with the memory of that black night. 'You returned from Naggaroth and lied to me? I loved Caelir and you left him to die!'

'I loved him too,' said Eldain, but Rhianna wasn't listening. Her hands seethed with magical fire, incandescent in the presence of the Everqueen's power. Tears of grief and horror spilled down Rhianna's cheeks as the certainties of her life crumbled around her. Eldain felt the build up of killing magic, and awaited his just punishment. Rhianna would kill him, and it would be a death well deserved.

Before the fire could erupt from Rhianna's hands, the Everqueen snapped her fingers and the roots entwining Eldain's limbs withdrew into the ground like retreating snakes. Unseen hands jerked him to his feet and sheathed him in protective energies as Rhianna's magic blazed. Blue flames washed over Eldain, licking hungrily at his body. But like a Phoenix King of old, not a single hair upon his head was so much as singed by the fire.

The roaring of incredible magic burned the air around him, the air fizzing and cracking with its violence, but none of it touched him. The fire retreated, and Rhianna fell to the ground, sobbing with aching loss and sickness. Her eyes blazed hatred at him, and Eldain welcomed it.

The Everqueen rose from her throne, and Eldain said, 'Why did you save me? Let me die, please. I deserve everything Rhianna's hatred can do and more.'

'Think you that I am so limited in view as mortals?' said the Everqueen. 'There is purpose that might yet be served by my mercy.'

'There is nothing left for me,' begged Eldain. 'I beg of you, let me die.'

The Everqueen shook her head, and her spun gold tresses were like corn before the scythe. Eldain felt himself lifted from the ground by invisible winds, his body suspended before the awesome force that claimed the Everqueen's body.

'No, Eldain Éadaoin, called the Fleetmane,' said the Everqueen, and Eldain thought he heard the faintest echo of the mortal vessel that contained her power. 'You will live with the guilt, the shame and the torment all your remaining days. Now go, little elf, fly away before my forgiveness is spent.'

With a flick of her wrist, the magical winds holding

Eldain aloft gusted with hurricane force, and he was hurled from the grove like a dust mote in a thunderstorm. Trees and branches and leaves whirled past him in a blur as he spun through the forest.

Cast forever from Avelorn like a banished spirit.

COLD WINDS BLEW over the Eagle Gate, carrying the smoky tang of sensual oils and gaudy incenses. Alathenar could taste the seductive promise of fleshy delights they offered in every breath, like the scent lamps in a Lothern pleasure court. The smell made him hungry and angry, for he knew it was a lie. Nothing that blew on the wind from the druchii camp could be trusted; it was an art as black as the land that birthed it.

Morathi had yet to rejoin the battle, her debaucheries within the silken pavilion leaving her no time to fight alongside her mortal allies. Any other army would have balked to have an ally take so little part in the fighting, but these northern barbarians had such a hunger for battle and bleeding that they cared little for the inequalities of blood shed to carry the fortress.

Their battle cries were vulgar obscenities as they climbed barbed ropes that sliced their palms or raced up scaling ladders of heated iron. Alathenar had emptied six quivers of arrows, and once again had taken a fresh quiver from Alanrias. The Shadow Warrior seemed always to have arrows to spare, and Alathenar hated that he relished using such spiteful shafts on the foe.

He knelt beside the splintered remains of the left wing of the eagle that had once proudly kept watch over the pass, loosing arrow after arrow into the mass of tribesmen. They were big men, brutish giants with bloated bodies of muscle and fur and iron. Iron axes and wide-bladed broadswords smashed through elven armour, and their frothing madness gave them strength enough to withstand injuries that would have slain any normal mortal twice over.

The walls were thick with fur-cloaked warriors, grappling and slashing to gain a desperate foothold on the ramparts. They bit and clawed without grace or skill, relying on strength, narcotic roots and ferocity to keep them alive long enough to win. Eloien Redcloak fought from the ramparts high on the eastern flank of the fortress, protecting the few bolt throwers left to them.

Redcloak cut down enemy warriors with darting sweeps of his curved sabre. It was a weapon designed for use on horseback, but it was a perfect weapon for slitting throats, slashing tendons and opening bellies as he danced past clumsy mortals as though borne on a fine Ellyrian steed.

In the centre of the wall stood Glorien Truecrown.

Surrounded by a dozen asur warriors, his lack of skill as a warrior was hopelessly exposed. He despatched dying humans, stabbed and flailed with his sword at foes that had been disarmed by his protectors. Alathenar saw that Glorien thought he was fighting like Tyrion himself. He yelled and whooped in delight, and the warriors assigned to protect him by Menethis had to fight twice as hard as any other. The garrison's morale had shone at the sight of Glorien on the walls, but that had soured as his lack of ability became plain.

'Truly it is like Aethis reborn,' said Alanrias, looking over Alathenar's shoulder at Glorien's wild attacks.

Alathenar started. He hadn't heard the Shadow Warrior approach. He wanted to contradict Alanrias, but the comparison was an apt one. Aethis had been Phoenix

King over a thousand years ago, a poet and dreamer who had scorned the arts of war in favour of decadent plays, indulgent artwork and grand public performances.

'I'm not sure I like the comparison,' said Alathenar.

'What do you mean?'

'Aethis was slain by a trusted friend. A poisoned dagger to the heart, if I remember my history.'

'You do,' said Alanrias, loosing a shaft over Alathenar's head. It took a tribesman low in the groin, and the man fell from the wall with a squeal of pain.

'Ha! No sons to bear your name into the future!' shouted Alanrias.

Alathenar couldn't read the Shadow Warrior, and never knew if the words he spoke were intended to be laden with hidden meaning. Was his naming of Aethis simply to deride Glorien's skill or was it a further nail in the young prince's coffin?

Alathenar watched as Glorien's protectors saved him from a baying mob of tribesmen. Two fine warriors were cut down in the process, lives that might not have been lost were their efforts bent to their own battles instead of another's. Even on the walls, Glorien was costing them dearly.

A heavy metal clang shook dust and rock splinters from the parapet behind them. Alathenar spun to see a smoking ladder of hissing iron bounce from the stone. A flailing hook swung up over the battered parapet and he rolled aside as it bit where he had knelt a moment before. Callused hands appeared in the embrasure, and a muscular warrior clad in soft ermine and baked leather strips vaulted onto the rampart. He bore a short, stabbing sword in his free hand, and a long length of chain in the other.

Alanrias put an arrow in his belly, but the warrior didn't even blink. Two more fur and leather-wrapped tribesmen clambered up the ladder and onto the rampart. Alathenar dropped his bow, and his sword was in his hand a second later. Before the warriors could drop to the walls, Alathenar's sword lanced into a belly and emptied its entrails. The man shrieked as he died, but before Alathenar could turn to face the second human, a hobnailed boot slammed into the side of his head.

He dropped and rolled as stinging light flared before his eyes. He kept moving, bringing his sword up to block a killing sweep. Crude, steppe-beaten iron slammed into gleaming steel from a craftsman's forge, and Alathenar grunted at the brute strength of the blow. He went with it, letting himself roll backwards to his feet as his attacker came at him again. The human was a fang-toothed warrior with hideous brands burned into his cheeks, and his eyes blazed with drug-induced fury. Behind the tribesman, more enemy warriors had gained the ramparts, and Alanrias fought three of them as he tried to keep them from taking this part of the walls.

'We need more warriors!' shouted Alanrias.

'There are no more!' returned Alathenar. The fang-toothed warrior came at him again, but Alathenar was ready for him this time. As the tribesman swung his axe, Alathenar spun in low and rammed his sword, two-handed, into his belly. He used his forward momentum to drive the blade up into the man's heart, twisting the blade and sliding it clear in one motion.

The tribesman grunted in pain, and dropped to his knees as his lifeblood poured out. Alathenar was disgusted to see a look of exquisite pleasure twist the man's features as he died. Another six enemy warriors had gained the wall, and Alathenar saw it was hopeless to try and plug this breach. Alanrias bled from several wounds, and was backing steadily away from the wall. The northern barbarians could scent victory and their baying cries rose in volume.

A clear elven voice cut through their raucous bellows, like a beam of sunlight through a thundercloud.

'Get down,' it said.

Alanrias and Alathenar obeyed without hesitation as a hissing cloud of starwood bolts scythed the air above them. A dozen, then a dozen more flashed past in a blur of pale wood and glinting leaf-bladed barbs. The volley of bolts swept the walls clean of barbarian warriors, and Alathenar looked up to see Eloien Redcloak on the far side of the fortress with an Eagle's Claw bolt thrower turned towards their struggle.

He started to wave his thanks, but stopped as he saw a look of horror on his friend's face.

Alathenar rolled to his feet as a monstrously muscular warrior clad in a patchwork of contoured plates held fast to his tanned flesh by a mass of leather coils dropped to the rampart. His armour glistened like flayed meat, branded with the rune of the Dark Prince, and his body reeked of a hundred scented oils. The warrior smiled, and Alathenar was struck by the hammer-blow of his fierce beauty. This was not the mask of a killer; this was the face of a lover, a poet and a dreamer.

Then Alathenar saw his eyes, cruel and hateful, filled from a well of hate and indulgence, seeing through the mask of beauty a moment before the glamoured warrior would have killed him. A curved and barbed sword with too many blades cut the air with a scream, and Alathenar hurled himself to the side. A hooked barb cut into his chest, slicing through his mail shirt and tearing the skin beneath. Blood flowed down his body, and Alathenar fell onto his haunches, desperately scrambling backwards to escape this madman's blows.

'I am Issyk Kul!' roared the warrior. 'And this wall is mine to do with as I please!'

Half a dozen elven warriors rushed to secure the wall so recently cleared of enemy fighters, but the ferocious enemy champion cut them down in as many blows. His sword flew faster than any of the elven warriors could match. Its blade was surely woven with dark enchantments, for none in the mortal realm were swifter than the asur. Alanrias was struck, hurled down into the courtyard by a savage blow. Alathenar watched him fall, but could not see whether he yet lived.

Issyk Kul towered over Alathenar, and he heard his name shouted from behind him.

'Time to die, frail thing,' growled Issyk Kul, his voice the rasping growl of a jungle cat.

Alathenar heard a powerful *thwack* of starwood and coiled rope, and spat his defiance at the worshipper of the Dark Gods.

'For you,' he said as the single, mighty bolt of an Eagle's Claw flew straight and true.

Kul's sword swept up and the enormous bolt was smashed from the air with a single blow.

The champion grinned and looked up at the Eagle's Claw that even now was being made ready to fire once more. Kul sprang onto the broken stumps of the battlements and aimed his sword at Alathenar.

'The gods bid me spare you for a reason,' he said with a gleeful laugh.

Another bolt from the Eagle's Claw punched the air, but Kul had already slid back down the ladder, leaving Alathenar breathless on a rampart filled with the dead. He slowly picked himself up, resting on the blood-slick parapet as the enemy host withdrew once again.

Alathenar heard a wild yell of triumph, and turned to see Glorien Truecrown thrust his sword towards the sky, as though this reprieve was a victory he had won single-handed.

Anger filled Alathenar, and he looked back into the courtyard as Alanrias climbed painfully from the ground, his bow arm cradled close to his chest. Alathenar's eyes locked with those of the Shadow Warrior.

He saw the question, and slowly, Alathenar nodded.

And their pact of murder was sealed.

THE GROVE WAS silent, the winds that had billowed its branches and shaken the leaves from the trees now stilled. Rhianna watched Eldain snatched from sight, and hot tears spilled down her cheeks. She wept for Caelir, for herself and the world that had suddenly changed in the time it took to draw breath. Rhianna knew betrayal was in the blood of mortals, but to know that one of the asur could turn on another was like a dagger of ice to the heart. She clenched her fists, as anger began to overtake horror, and coruscating sparks of fire rippled around her arms. Reflected power from the Everqueen shone in her eyes, and it pulled Rhianna to her feet.

She had thought the grove silent, but now saw that wasn't true. Birds had returned to the trees and slender-limbed deer nuzzled at bushes at its edges. Doves mingled with ravens, peacocks and kingfishers. Hawks settled on the tallest branches, attended by white-plumed falcons and red-breasted warblers.

Shapes creaked within the heartwood of the trees, suggestions of faces and limbs formed by the groan of roots and branches. Darting lights spun through the foliage, and giggling laughter echoed on the last breath of drifting zephyrs. They floated through the grove in hopeful loops, gathering above the Everqueen and bathing her in their dream-like radiance. Rhianna shielded her eyes as that brightness was taken into the Everqueen's body, filling her with such brilliance that it seemed a second sun had come to Avelorn.

The light spread through the forest, suffusing every living thing it touched, travelling on the wind, the earth and the water until its power was spent. Whatever the light of the Everqueen touched would never be the same, and a part of their spirit was forever filled with joy and wonder.

The effect on Rhianna was instantaneous, and she felt her anger ebbing away. The wrathful magic that suffused her limbs dimmed until, finally, it was gone. She took a deep breath and wiped her eyes free from tears as the light of the Everqueen began to fade. Rhianna bowed her head as the Everqueen came towards her, gliding over the soft grasses of the grove and leaving only new life in her wake.

A slender hand, with soft fingers and delicate nails lifted her chin.

Rhianna looked into warm hazel eyes that knew no hate, no bitterness or spite.

'You are Alarielle,' said Rhianna.

'For now,' agreed the Queen of Avelorn. 'The Everqueen slumbers, regaining her strength, even as I do. Alarielle speaks to you now, but while our flesh heals, my power will wane and the Everqueen's will wax like the turning of the seasons. But the light of the forest shines once more, and the balance between us will be restored soon.'

Rhianna looked into the Everqueen's eyes

'Why did you let him live?' asked Rhianna.

Alarielle smiled. 'I would never have harmed Eldain, for all the asur are my children. I could no more strike him down than I would strike you down.'

'It looked like you were going to kill him.'

'The power of the Everqueen might have killed Eldain, but it spared him for some purpose I do not understand.'

Rhianna turned away from Alarielle. 'I wish she had killed him. He deserves to die. I hate him for what he did. To Caelir. To me... to Ulthuan. Why did he do it? You saw inside him, I know you did. Why did he leave his brother to die?'

The light of Alarielle followed her, and Rhianna felt a gossamer-thin touch upon her shoulder. Its warmth flowed into her, but she resisted it, hanging onto her anger in the face of the soothing balm of forgiveness.

'He did it for love,' said Alarielle. 'At least he once believed that was why.'

'For love?' hissed Rhianna, spinning to face Alarielle. 'What kind of love brings about such pain and suffering?'

'Mortal love,' said Alarielle. 'For it is bound by the confines of a life, and is therefore fleeting. Swords have been bloodied throughout the history of the world in the name of love, Rhianna. Love of a land, a colourful flag, an ideal. A beloved wife...'

'Eldain's betrayal had nothing to do with love,' said Rhianna, as fresh tears spilled out. 'I will hate him forever for what he did.'

The light of the grove dimmed at her words, and Alarielle's eyes shone with the light that had passed into the forest. Rhianna felt its healing properties, magic that could heal a heart broken into a thousand pieces.

'There is no hurt in the world that cannot be undone by the power that lives in me,' said Alarielle, 'but you have to let it in. The heart that does not want to heal cannot be remade.'

'Maybe some hearts should not be remade.'

'And be left only with hate to fill them? No, hate is a poison that will turn the purest soul to the blackest deeds. It is a seed that can only flower in bitter soil. Do not feed it, and it will wither away. Do not water it with your tears and it will never grow again.'

Rhianna sobbed and sank to her knees. 'How? I do not know how.'

'You will learn,' promised Alarielle. 'You must if you are to fulfil your destiny, for what you hold in your heart will shape Ulthuan for all time. For all our sakes, do not let it be hate.'

'I don't understand,' said Rhianna.

'No, but you will.'

Alarielle closed her eyes, and Rhianna saw a tremor pass through her. When next the queen looked upon her, a measure of the Everqueen had become part of her again.

'But the time for talking is over,' said the Everqueen. 'The hate of which I speak has flowered in the hearts of those who stand against the druchii in the west. All too soon it may bear bitter fruit, and we must be ready to fight.'

'You will go to war?' said Rhianna.

The Everqueen nodded, and the light inside her

swelled until it seemed as though her body could no longer contain it. The warmth in her eyes became a furnace, and Rhianna thrilled to the passion of the Everqueen's emotion.

'I will summon the army of the forest,' said the Everqueen with a sound like thunder in a clear sky. 'The treemen of the deep woods, the dryads of the bracken, the great eagles, the faun, the sprites and the fair folk. All the kith and kin of magic shall heed my call. The Maiden Guard, the singers, the poets, the dancers, the warriors, the playwrights and the acrobats, all shall delight at gathering beneath my banner of ice and song. The raven shall carry my words to Chrace, the dove to Cothique. All shall heed my summons!'

Rhianna felt the elemental power of the forest pass to every creature that filled the grove. Every bird that could fly took to the air to carry the Everqueen's command. Each beast of the forest that could run took to its heels to gather its kind.

The Everqueen turned her blazing gaze upon Rhianna, and she saw the fierce exultation in those ancient eyes at the thought of gathering her magical army.

'Avelorn marches to war!' cried the Everqueen.

CHAPTER FIVE
LOST SOULS

ELDAIN AWOKE FROM troubled sleep by the lapping banks of a river. He felt refreshed and unhurt. He had expected neither after the Everqueen had stripped him of his armour of self-denial. Eldain had thought the light of the Everqueen would burn him to cinders in punishment for his terrible crime. He could not think of a single reason why she might spare him. A memory of fire lingered in his mind, a vast portal and a silent sentinel, but he could make no sense of it.

He pushed himself to his feet, looking around to gain a sense of where he was. Across the river was an impenetrable wall of trees, their leaves shimmering with their own inner light, a luminosity that could have but one source. Though the river was shallow here, Eldain knew it would be suicide for him to re-enter the woods of Avelorn. He had been cast from beneath its magical boughs, and to return there would be the death of him.

To the west, the Annulii scraped the clouds from the sky and gathered them like cotton haloes around their magical summits. He turned to the south, already feeling his heart lighten at the thought of what he would see.

Ellyrion.

Land of his birth, it opened out before him like a mother's embrace. Its golden fields and wild steppe spreading as far as the eye could see. The sight of so wild, so untamed, so free a land made Eldain weep. He had no right to be here. No right to see so fantastical a land and certainly no right to receive its welcome. He had betrayed one of its sons, and as he had been banished from Avelorn, so too should he be banished from every kingdom of Ulthuan.

Yet, as much as he knew he deserved to feel no sense of welcome or homecoming, its presence was as potent as any he had known. This land had been birthed in an age beyond Eldain's imagination, and would endure long after he was dust in the wind. It had no need to pass judgement upon anything as petty as the affairs of the mortal creatures that crawled upon its body like ants on a fallen tree.

Ellyrion was his home, and it welcomed him as its son.

His joy was short-lived as he thought of his likely future. Beyond Ellyrion he would receive no welcome. He would be shunned as a pariah, hated for what he had done, and a bleak mood settled upon him as he thought of how far he had fallen since the heady days before the raid to Clar Karond. He was alone, and would be alone forever.

Forever was a long time for one of the asur.

Would he be able to bear the weight of the centuries alone? Could he stand to face the long years locked behind the walls of Ellyr-Charoi, withering and diminishing with every passing century? The Everqueen had spared him, but death would have been preferable to such a grey end to a life. To lessen with the years, growing dim and haunting the ruins of his villa until it too collapsed into forgotten rubble at the foot of the mountains.

His would be a life measured by despairing centuries and spent in eternal regret.

That was to be his fate, and Eldain accepted it.

It was a long walk to Ellyr-Charoi, but no sooner had he taken his first step south, than a familiar scent came to him as the wind shifted. Eldain knew that scent better than anything, hearing the welcome sound of hoof beats on good earth. He turned to the long grass of the west in time to see a black horse galloping towards him with fierce joy in every step.

'Lotharin!' he cried, running towards the midnight steed.

The last he had seen of his faithful mount had been when Caelir had ridden him from the Tower of Hoeth. He had assumed the horse now roamed within the borders of Avelorn, but no steed of Ellyrion could be kept long from its homeland. Eldain had known Lotharin since his birth, both elf and horse growing to adulthood with a bond closer than any mortal rider could ever hope to understand.

'I have missed you, old friend,' said Eldain. The horse nuzzled him, and Eldain rubbed its neck. Lotharin's coat was freshly brushed and shone with fresh vitality.

'Time in Avelorn has done you good.'

The horse tossed its mane, and Eldain saw that no matter what he had done, Lotharin would always be with him. Nothing could break the bond between an Ellyrion horseman and his steed, and Eldain thanked Asuryan that he had been lucky enough to be born in such a wild, passionate land.

He vaulted onto the horse's back, needing no saddle, bridle or reins.

Though he rode to his eternal doom, Eldain welcomed this last ride upon so fine a mount as Lotharin.

'Come, Lotharin,' said Eldain. 'Homewards. To Ellyr-Charoi.'

THE SUN FELT good on his skin, and Tyrion turned his face towards it, hoping its golden rays would send him a measure of his beloved Everqueen's warmth. Druchii blood coated the golden scales of his armour, and his azure cloak was stiff with the stuff. Sunfang lay unsheathed across his lap, though not a drop stained its gleaming blade. The caged fire within its heart burned any impure blood away.

Days had passed since his arrival at the castle, and, as he had predicted, the druchii had indeed attacked with greater skill and cunning after their first, abortive, assault. He had been proved right, though he took no pleasure in that. The Naggarothi were descendants of the asur. Of course they would be skilled.

More of the dark-cloaked warriors were even now assembling beyond bowshot, together with heavy bolt throwers and monsters that roared and bellowed behind hastily thrown up walls of boulders. Soon there would be a force thrown at the castle that not even he could fight against.

Already Tyrion had given Finubar more time than could be expected. The Phoenix King had sent word that the Sea Guard and Lothern citizen levy was taking position on the Emerald Gate, but every minute Tyrion could give him was vital. It was a heavy burden Finubar had placed upon him, but such was the way of kings, to ask great things of those that served them.

'Resting when there are druchii still to slay?' said Belarien, returning from the crumbling keep with two platters of bread, cheese and fruit. He sat down beside Tyrion, and set the food down on his lap.

'I am trying to, but you are making it difficult,' answered Tyrion.

'We shall sleep when we are dead, eh?'

Tyrion tried to smile. He had said those same words before the battle at Finuval. Rescued from a mighty daemon prince of Chaos by Teclis, he had gone on to fight the Witch King's greatest assassin in single combat though his spirit had almost been lost in the abyss. Then, those words had been defiant, now they sounded hollow. Belarien saw the emptiness in Tyrion's eyes and was immediately contrite.

'Apologies, my lord. I spoke without thought.'

'No need,' said Tyrion. 'I should watch what I say in future if I cannot stand my own words quoted back at me. And you are right. I will sleep when this is done.'

'How is the pain?'

'Happily lessened,' said Tyrion. 'Alarielle yet lives, and grows stronger. I can hear the birds of Ulthuan sing again. She will recover, and each day I feel her pain less and less.'

'Then why the grim mood?'

'We face an enemy who will soon gather enough force to overwhelm us. Is that not reason to be grim?'

'You've faced worse odds than this and prevailed,' said

Belarien. 'I know, I was there for all of them and I still bear the scars.'

Tyrion said nothing. How could he tell Belarien of the dark siren song of the Widowmaker? Every time he closed his eyes, he saw the black, blood-veined altar and the smoking blade buried in its heart. The bones of the dead and the yet to be slain rattled around it, unquiet in their death and looking to him to give their deaths meaning. Every blow he struck against the druchii was a pale shadow of the destruction he could wreak with the Sword of Khaine in his hand. With its power he could end the threat of the Witch King forever, take the war across the sea and destroy their blighted homelands in one bloody sweep.

He let out a breath, knowing these were the Widowmaker's thoughts, not his own.

They were not lies, these thoughts. Lies would be easier to dismiss. The sword *would* give him all the power it promised, but it was power that could never be given back. Aenarion had learned that lesson too late, dooming his lineage to forever be bound to that black blade of murder and bloodshed.

Belarien knew the stories of Aenarion as well as any in Ulthuan, but he could never really understand the terrible attraction the Sword of Khaine had for Tyrion.

'My lord?' said Belarien.

Tyrion was saved from answering by the glorious note of a hunting horn. Cheers went up from the garrison, as a group of warriors marched into the castle through the Autumn Gate in the western wall. Tyrion rose to his feet as he saw the shimmering sea-serpent banner that went before these axe-wielding killers, each one clad in tunics of sumptuous cream and embroidered with golden thread and fire-winged birds. Their helms were bronze, and about their necks were mantles of brilliant white fur, taken from the bodies of the deadly lions that hunted the mountains of Chrace.

LED BY A giant with a pelt cloak so voluminous that it seemed impossible it could have come from a single beast, the White Lions escorted a singular warrior clad in scarlet dragonscale armour and a shimmering cloak of mist and shadow.

'The Phoenix King,' said Belarien.

'None other,' agreed Tyrion, pushing himself to his feet and sheathing Sunfang. As highly regarded as he was, not even Tyrion would dare stand before the Phoenix King with a bared blade. Korhil, the towering master of Finubar's bodyguard, would never allow it, and the mighty, double-bladed axe slung at his shoulder was a potent deterrent against such foolishness.

Tyrion went to meet Finubar, the Seafarer as he was known, and bowed as the White Lions parted smoothly to allow their king to meet his greatest champion.

'My king, you honour us,' said Tyrion.

'My friend, how many times do I need tell you that you should not bow to me?'

'A king must always be bowed to, or else none shall know him as a king.'

'Prince Tyrion quotes Caledor the Second,' said the broad-shouldered White Lion at Finubar's side. 'Even as he shows respect, he mocks.'

The words were said without anger, and Tyrion smiled. 'Ah, yes, I always forget that you Chracians actually know how to read and write, let alone study history.'

'Careful, Tyrion,' warned Finubar with a smile.

'Korhil's blood is still afire after he slew the champion of a druchii witch cult yesterday.'

'He is welcome to test that lumbering tree-cutter against Sunfang any time he wishes.'

'Tree-cutter?' growled Korhil. 'Chayal would find your neck before you could pull that shiny toothpick from its sheath.'

Tyrion smiled and said, 'It is good to see you, Korhil.'

The White Lion bellowed with laughter and swept Tyrion into a crushing embrace. Rightly it was said that Korhil was the strongest elf of Ulthuan, and Tyrion felt his ribs creak in the powerful embrace.

'Enough,' said Finubar. 'As much as I always enjoy your games, there is little time for them now.'

Korhil released Tyrion and stepped back behind his king. Tyrion drew in a breath and stood tall before his friend and his king. Finubar was handsome and had the look of one whose eyes were always seeking the next horizon. His blond hair was almost as pale as the cloaks of his White Lions, and the green of his eyes matched the thousands of gems set within the gate that led to the Straits of Lothern.

'How goes the fighting here, Tyrion?' asked Finubar. 'The castle on the far side of the Emerald Gate yet resists. Thanks to a few scattered survivors of the battle before the gate, no force of any significance has managed to land on the southern coast. It is here the druchii will bend their every effort.'

'Then they fare better than we do, my lord,' said Tyrion. 'Every day the druchii bring up more warriors across that damned bridge of boats. Tell Aislin to send those scattered survivors to destroy the bridge and we may hold this castle.'

Finubar sighed. 'You know Aislin, my friend. Not even the counsel of a king will sway his thoughts. He and Kithre Seablaze rally whatever ships will answer their call from the Inner Sea, thinking to sail out and win this war in the water before the Emerald Gate.'

'Then he is a fool,' snapped Tyrion.

'Choose your words with more care, Tyrion, Aislin is still a prince of Ulthuan, and Seablaze is his protégé,' warned Finubar. 'And we will need their ships if the Emerald Gate is ever yielded.'

'Which it must be if this castle falls,' said Korhil.

As if to prove the point, the hatefully discordant blare of a druchii war horn echoed from the mountainside. Its echoes faded, only to be replaced by the cold-hearted chants of advancing warriors and the bellows of blood-hungry monsters.

Tyrion smiled grimly at Korhil. 'Time to put that axe of yours to good use,' he said.

Korhil glanced at Finubar, who nodded.

'Could you use us on the walls, Prince Tyrion?' asked the Phoenix King.

'Always, my lord,' said Tyrion.

THE ATTACK WAS led by the beastmasters. Two iron-scaled abominations, each with a writhing mass of serpentine necks and snapping, biting heads, stalked ahead of a host of marching warriors in lacquered armour of crimson. The monsters' bodies were dark and rippling with iridescent scales, their eyes glossy and reflective. Teeth like swords of yellowed horn dripped blood and venomous saliva.

Driving the pair of monstrous beasts forwards with cruelly barbed goads, the beastmasters loosed ululating cries from strange horns and yelled jagged words that could only be commands.

'Khaine's blood,' hissed Finubar, drawing his starmetal sword. 'Hydras!'

Tyrion could not take his eyes from the king's weapon, its blade curved in the manner of southland warriors, and golden like the last arc of sunset. The blade had been a gift from one of the coastal potentates of Ind, a land of exotic spices and strange ritual. Finubar had saved the life of the king's daughter, and had received this wondrous blade in return. No smith trained in the Anvil of Vaul could unlock the mysteries of its creation, but the power of the magic worked into its blade was beyond question.

'Some heavy meat for Chayal to cleave,' grunted Korhil, unfazed by the sight of so terrible a pack of monsters. His White Lions hefted their heavy axes, resting them on their shoulders with nonchalant ease.

Tyrion took a calming breath as the dark presence of the Sword of Khaine eased into his thoughts. With that blade in his grip, these beasts would be carved into bloody chunks in moments. He forced thoughts of murder from his mind and sought the peace Teclis had taught him, the state of mind that allowed him to fight unencumbered by doubt, free from anger and able to find the space to kill with complete precision.

'I am the master of my soul,' he whispered under his breath. 'Aenarion's curse is not my curse. I wield my blade in the service of my kind and my home. No thought of selfish gain, no lust to rule, no urge to slay shall guide my arm. I am Tyrion, and I am the master of my soul.'

He felt Korhil's gaze, but ignored him, feeling his heart

slow and his senses sharpen to the point where he could pick out the individual faces of every single druchii warrior in the advancing army.

'They are so like us,' he said.

'They are nothing like us,' said Korhil, and Tyrion blinked, not realising he had spoken aloud. He did not allow Korhil's gruff voice to distract him from achieving oneness with his sword. Its grip grew hot in his hand, and he smiled as though welcoming a long lost friend.

'Eagle's Claws!'

At Tyrion's command, the castle's bolt throwers spoke with one voice, and three long shafts streaked towards the hydras. One plunged into the flank of the most eager hydra, yet even the power of such a weapon could only drive the point a hand span through the creature's scaled flesh. Another skidded clear and the third was snatched from the air by a darting, draconic head and bitten in two.

'They'll not be stopped by bolts,' said Korhil.

'No,' agreed Tyrion.

More bolts leapt from the war machines, swiftly followed by a volley of goose-feathered shafts from the archers leaning over the parapet. Volley after volley billowed up into the sky as archers in the courtyard loosed over their comrades' heads. These fell among the druchii warriors, but most thudded home in heavy wooden shields or bounced away from burnished helms. A hundred, two hundred, three. Enough arrows to fell these invaders thrice over hammered down, but barely a handful died. Answering flurries of repeater crossbow bolts clattered against the walls. Iron-tipped bolts shattered on the hard stone, but screams of pain told Tyrion that many were finding their mark.

Tyrion lifted a sapphire blue amulet from around his neck and kissed the smooth stone. Encased within the blue gem were woven strands of golden hair, preserved like flies in amber, and he felt it respond to his touch.

'Be with me, queen of my heart,' he said. 'Watch over me this day.'

Arrows hammered the druchii line, and more were falling as the enemy cast down their shields and heavily armoured warriors ran towards the walls bearing scaling ladders. The first hydra was limping badly, two heavy bolts jutting from the rippling swathes of muscle around its neck. The second beast was being driven at the gateway, and its heads coiled back over its shoulder.

Tyrion knew what would come next.

'Get down!' he yelled.

The many heads of the hydra shot forward with their mouths gaping wide. Ashen smoke and fire belched from the guts of the monster in a torrent of volcanic destruction. Like a frothing wave of evil red light, the fiery breath of the hydra broke against the walls of the castle. Sulphurous flames billowed over the ramparts and asur warriors screamed as their tunics caught light. Flames rippled along the wall as the first beast exhaled its volatile breath of fire and fumes.

Asur warriors dropped from the walls, blazing from head to foot as the monster's fiery breath consumed them. Tyrion coughed and spat as black smoke roiled around the parapet, instantly turning day into night. Sunfang shone brightly, a beacon in the darkness, and he vaulted to his feet as he heard the smack of wood on stone.

'To arms! The enemy is upon us!'

A druchii helmet appeared in the embrasure, and

Tyrion removed it with a brutal thrust of his blade. The headless body dropped from the ladder, as another druchii warrior clambered up to take its place. He died screaming, and Tyrion leapt into the gap between the merlons, bringing Sunfang's blade down in a two-handed sweep.

The ladder split asunder, spilling armoured warriors into the seething haze of fire and smoke that boiled at the wall's footings. Tyrion watched the druchii die, trying to maintain his equilibrium in the face of so much death. He turned from the destruction he had wrought as yet more ladders thudded into the length of the wall. Druchii leapt over the parapet and formed fighting wedges to allow the warriors behind them to gain the walls.

Swords and axes clashed as the ancient enemies spilled bitter blood. Beside him, Belarien slew druchii with cold, economical thrusts and slashes. Without the skill of Tyrion, his friend killed the druchii with the classic sword strokes of one schooled by the best. There was no flamboyance to his killing, simply the efficient blows of a killer.

Finubar fought with his golden sword, slaying the druchii as quickly as they climbed the walls. The Phoenix King was a fine swordsman, but his talents were those of peace, not war, and the White Lions were called upon to protect their liege lord on more than one occasion.

The White Lions fought like the grim hunters they were, each hacking blow measured and merciless. Their axes clove through druchii armour with ease, and they bellowed coarse Chracian insults at their slain enemies. Korhil's axe wove a silver web of destruction around him, the twin blades crashing through armoured plates, breaking bones and slicing flesh with horrifying ease.

Even as he slew enemy warriors, Tyrion couldn't help but be impressed. Korhil was a giant, broad shouldered and more powerful than any elf Tyrion had known, and he wielded his axe with a speed that belied his massive form. A duel between them would be a dance of blades to savour.

A druchii blade scraped over Tyrion's chest, and he spun around, driving his elbow into his attacker's face. A bronze cheek-guard crumpled and the warrior staggered. Sunfang plunged through a crimson breastplate and the warrior screamed as the weapon flared with power, burning him alive from the inside.

Tyrion kicked the charred corpse free of the blade and danced down the length of the wall, finding the spaces between the fighting to stab, cut, slash and chop as he went. He flowed into the gaps, always with enough time and space to take the killing blow. Belarien followed him, but could barely keep up with his incredible skill and speed.

The castle wall shook and the fighting stopped for the briefest second as a trio of monstrous heads on sinuous necks appeared over the battlements. One darted forward and an elven warrior was snatched up in its jaws. He screamed briefly before the teeth bit through his armour. Fire spewed from the jaws of the other heads, and an entire section of the wall was suddenly empty as Tyrion's warriors burned in the searing fire.

'With me!' shouted Tyrion, charging along the ramparts towards the beast as its forelegs, each the thickness of a tree, grasped the stone of the parapet. A dozen elven warriors followed him, readying long-bladed lances to fight this giant creature of nightmare. It hauled its bulk up and onto the walls, screeching as its masters jabbed its hide with their barbed goads. The rampart crumbled beneath its weight, cracked masonry falling to the base of the wall.

Tyrion sprang onto a piece of crumbing stone and leapt towards the nearest head.

Sunfang flared with dazzling brightness as Tyrion brought the magnificent blade around and clove through the beast's neck. The head flew clear of the stump of neck, and the monster roared in pain. Tyrion landed lightly and rolled, slashing his sword across the beast's chest. Blood frothed from the wound, and the rampart split as the beast's claws tore at the walls.

Elven lances plunged into the hydra's body and drew spurts of stinking blood, yet even as the blades plunged home, wounds already inflicted stopped bleeding and the scaled hide reknit. Tyrion swayed aside as a head snapped down, bringing Sunfang down like an executioner's blade. Another head was severed, and Tyrion knew that this wound would never heal. No living thing could withstand so incredible a blade.

'Tyrion!' cried a voice amid the monster's screaming roars of pain, and he spun around as the second hydra hauled its enormous body onto the walls. Flames rippled around its body, hazing the air with the hellish heat of a forge of the damned. Finubar and Korhil appeared in the swirling morass of smoke, as a heaving breath of fire and heat erupted from the hydra's reeking jaws. Tyrion threw his arm up before him as the battlements were engulfed.

The flames roared and heaved like an ocean of fire, and Tyrion wept at the sound of elven screams as his warriors died around him. Their bodies burned like warlords of the northmen on their pyres, consumed by the monster's infernal breath. But the armour of Aenarion had been forged in the depths of Vaul's Anvil, quenched in the blood of the mightiest dragons of ancient times and shaped with hammers touched by the smith god himself. No magical by-blow's fire could defeat its protection, and Tyrion stood like an invulnerable god before its hellish breath.

Tyrion saw Finubar and Korhil further along the wall, sheltering in the lee of the sagging parapet and swathed in the Phoenix King's dragonscale cloak. Korhil rolled away from the king and beat out smouldering embers in his cloak before swinging his axe to bear once more. The hydra's heads swayed above them, hissing; jelly-like ropes of saliva drooling from its smoking jaws.

Finubar ducked a snapping bite and thrust his blade into the hydra's mouth. He uttered a word of power and molten light filled the hydra's skull, streaming from its eyes in golden fire before the head exploded in a welter of boiling blood and bone. Korhil swung Chayal in a mighty, two-handed sweep, cutting another head from the hydra's body with one blow.

Tyrion turned back to the beast he had first fought, its one remaining head coiled away from him as it dragged more of its bloated body onto the wall. Cracks split the rampart, and Tyrion felt the wall shift beneath him as its foundations crumbled. A mighty foreleg smashed down, but Tyrion had seen it coming and dived beneath the blow. Nimble as a cat, he sprang to his feet and thrust Sunfang up into the beast's belly, wrenching the sword to open a wide tear. Dark fluids gushed from the wound, drenching Tyrion in stinking, Chaos-touched blood that ran from his armour as water from a fowl's back.

The beast's body shuddered, yet its head remained beyond his reach. It spat a mouthful of corrosive bile at him, but Tyrion swatted it aside with his blazing sword. As the creature reared up to slash its front legs at him once more Tyrion aimed his sword at its head and felt the powerful surge of magical energy pulsing in his blood.

'In Asuryan's name!' shouted Tyrion, and a blazing spear of white light erupted from the sword blade. The hydra screeched in agony as the furnace heat burned the flesh from its skull and boiled the brain in its head. The blackened stump flopped lifeless to the wall, and its body slid from the rampart as its life was extinguished.

Without waiting to watch it fall, Tyrion turned in time to see Korhil and Finubar despatch the second hydra. The White Lion's axe was drenched with the hydra's blood and the Phoenix King's cloak smoked from the heat of the battle. Korhil bellowed a Chracian victory oath, as Finubar shouted for fresh warriors to defend this portion of the castle.

The wall was a blackened ruin, stripped of merlons and embrasures by the attack of the hydras. If the druchii came at this portion of the castle again, there would be no protection for the defenders as they awaited the enemy scaling ladders. Tyrion saw Belarien driving the enemy from those sections of the wall the hydras had not demolished, and breathed a sigh of relief to know that his friend had survived this attack.

The druchii fell back from the battle, limping, bloodied and broken. They had thrown their all into this assault, but they would be back with warriors fresh and eager to swarm over the walls of the castle. Arrows punched through the backs of the fleeing druchii, but they were few and far between.

A crossbow bolt smacked into a stump of rampart, reminding Tyrion that even in victory there was danger. He darted over to Finubar and Korhil, as more elven archers took up position on the wall. Both warriors were spattered with blood, but how much of it was their own, Tyrion could not tell.

'Not so terrible now, are they?' beamed Finubar, between breaths.

'No, but there will be more of them, my king,' said Tyrion. 'And this castle is ruined.'

Finubar squared his shoulders, immediately catching Tyrion's implication. 'I will not yield, Tyrion. We fight on. We must.'

'We will not,' stated Tyrion, as the calm spaces in which he had fought faded away.

'You defy your king?' demanded Finubar.

Anger, hot and urgent and bloody filled Tyrion. 'I will not throw my warriors' lives away in a battle I cannot win.'

Before Finubar could speak again, Korhil said, 'The prince speaks the truth, my king. The walls offer no protection, the gate is burned and there are few enough left alive to fight for it.'

The Phoenix King said nothing for long moments before letting out a sorrowful breath. He nodded reluctantly as he took in the cost of repulsing this latest attack. Scores of elven warriors were dead, and many more were horribly burned. At best, a hundred warriors remained to defend the walls.

'I know,' said Finubar. 'Yet if this castle is lost, then so too is the Emerald Gate. I do not relish my legacy to be the first Phoenix King who allowed the druchii within the Straits of Lothern.'

'You have no choice,' said Tyrion, feeling the pulse of an ancient and malevolent heartbeat keeping time with his own. 'War seldom allows us the luxury of doing as we might wish. We must do whatever it takes to survive.'

'We must do more than survive, Tyrion,' said Finubar. 'We must triumph.'

The captain of the White Lions stepped between the two warriors, pulling at the fur of his cloak as he put a hand on Tyrion's shoulder. 'I think I understand what Prince Tyrion is proposing, my king. It's like when I hunted Charandis. I drew that great lion farther and farther away from the mountains for days on end until his strength was weakened and I could choke the damned life from him. So you see, my lord, we're giving them the gate, and drawing them into the Straits of Lothern. It's a killing ground. We draw the druchii in, and hit them from all sides. Even as they come at the Sapphire Gate, every fortress along the length of the straits will be hammering them with bolts and arrows and magic. And if Aislin and Seablaze want to sail out to fight the druchii, they've got the perfect opportunity to earn some glory. Trust me, it will be a slaughter.'

Korhil turned to Tyrion and fixed him with his cold gaze. 'Isn't that right?'

'Yes,' said Tyrion with relish. 'That's right. A slaughter.'

Chapter Six

Embers

No song of the elves was older than dragonsong. The red-lit caves beneath the Dragonspine Mountains echoed with the ringing chants of fire mages as they sang of ancient days, when dragons soaring over the highest peaks were as common a sight as doves in Avelorn. Hot steam and a magma glow suffused the glistening rocks of the caves, and braziers burned with aromatic oils said to be pleasing to the senses of dragons.

Ghostly figures moved through the cavern, exhausted mages whose voices were hoarse with singing the songs forgotten by all save the line of dragonriders. Hidden by the acrid smoke, vast forms of scale and claw and wing lay coiled around the hottest vents, their mighty chests rising and falling with the slow rhythms of their ancient hearts.

The dragons of Caledor slumbered on, and none could reach them.

The old songs of valour could not rouse them from their dreams, and the clarion call to wake fell upon deaf ears. As the mountains had cooled, so too had the ardour of the dragons to shake themselves from their centuries of sleep. Only the younger dragons awoke now, and even that was becoming rarer and rarer.

Prince Imrik sat cross-legged before a great split in the rock, through which hissed a curtain of sulphurous smoke and the heartbeat of creatures older than any now living could remember. His white hair hung in wet ropes around his thin face, and droplets of sweat ran down his cheeks like tears. He had sung every song of elfkind, even the secret ones taught to him by his master so long ago.

Nothing was working, and though the naysayers of Lothern woefully claimed the fire of the dragons had gone out, Imrik refused to believe that, not when so many still lived in these mountains. A species as noble and ancient did not just slip away as their hearts cooled.

He knew things these naysayers did not.

Once, as they had flown through storms raging around the Blighted Isle, Minaithnir had told him that the dragons of Ulthuan would all die together in the last battle against the Dark Gods. It had been an uncharacteristic pronouncement, one perhaps brought on by the proximity of the Widowmaker, and the dragon had made Imrik promise never to repeat his careless words.

Imrik had told no one of Minaithnir's grim prophecy, but he held to its promise of a reawakening as he gathered his strength for another song. His brazier had burned low, and he threw another handful of heartleaf into the flames. The plant burned white gold, and its light had been used in ancient times to guide dragons to their riders in times of war. As the flames took hold and the aromatic leaves filled the air with the pungent tang of sulphur and blood, Imrik felt the presence of another elf.

He looked up, seeing a fire mage in billowing robes of crimson making his way across the cavern floor towards him. His steps were uneven, like those of a drunk, and Imrik knew Lamellan had not slept in weeks.

'My friend,' said Imrik, 'What news? Have any of your brothers had their songs answered?'

Lamellan shook his head. 'No, my lord,' he said, his voice little more than a whisper. 'The great drakes do not heed our calls. One of the younger sun dragons almost rose from its slumber, but slipped back into sleep before we could renew the song of awakening.'

'We must keep at it, Lamellan,' pressed Imrik, rising smoothly to his feet. He had long ago discarded his armour as too clumsy and restricting to fully perform the dragonsongs, and was clad only in a long white robe tied at the waist with a golden belt. His features were sunken and pale, for dragonsong drew upon a warrior's heart and soul for its power.

'The dragons do not heed us,' said Lamellan. 'My brother mages are beyond the limits of their endurance, and there is little more we can do. The dragons sleep on, and they will wake or sleep in their own time.'

Imrik sighed, letting the frustration of the last few weeks pour from him.

'I refuse to accept that,' he said. 'The dragons will come! If we die, they die, and the dragons of Caledor will not be slain in their sleep by druchii invaders. I will not allow that, do you understand me?'

'I do, my lord, but I do not know what else we can do,'

said Lamellan. 'We have sung all the songs we know, and they do not reach the dragons. Only the songs known by the dragons themselves will rouse them now, and none among the asur know them.'

Imrik paced the cavern floor, the red light of countless braziers and the shimmering reflections of dragonscale casting stark reflections over his noble countenance.

'That is not strictly true, my friend,' he said at last.

'What do you mean, my lord?'

'I know them,' said Imrik. 'And you are right; the dragons will not wake with the old songs of the asur, so we need to sing the songs of the dragons themselves.'

'How can you know these songs?' asked Lamellan. 'Teach us how to sing them and we will fill these caverns with our voices. With such songs, even the most ancient dragons of Ulthuan will wake!'

'I cannot teach you these songs,' said Imrik. 'Minaithnir taught them to me, but had me swear that I would never sing them in the presence of any save dragonkind.'

'Why?'

'The songs of the dragons are powerful, and not meant for the minds of mortals, even ones as long lived as the asur, for it is said these songs are powerful enough to reach the minds of even the oldest star dragons. But they hold the true names of all the dragons of Ulthuan, and such secret knowledge should never be used lightly.'

'Tell us!' demanded Lamellan, the glittering light of fire magic crackling in the hazel of his eyes. 'Ulthuan is lost without the dragons.'

Imrik placed a hand on the fire mage's shoulder and shook his head, speaking with all the calm he could muster. 'In all the years you have known me, have I ever broken an oath to a friend?'

Lamellan sagged. 'No, my lord. Never.'

'And never shall I,' said Imrik with a weary smile. 'Now gather your brothers and return to the surface. Seal the caverns behind you, and let none enter on pain of death. Ulthuan will have need of the fire mages, with or without the dragons.'

'And you will sing the songs of the dragons alone?' asked Lamellan.

'I will.'

'Then you will die. If such songs are as powerful as you say, then there will be nothing left of you by their ending.'

Imrik drew himself up to his full height, and his skin shimmered with vitality; the earlier fatigue that had threatened to overwhelm him vanished. Just the thought of singing the songs of the dragons filled him with energy, as though the song itself ached to be sung.

'Have faith in me, old friend,' said Imrik. 'I will rouse the dragons, and I will lead you all in battle as we fall from the skies upon the druchii!'

Lamellan bowed and shook Imrik's outstretched hand.

'We will burn them from Ulthuan together,' said Lamellan.

'Count on it,' replied Imrik.

POWERFUL AROMAS OF flesh on the fire and incense created from rendered bones filled the silken pavilion, together with the reek of human sweat. Morathi luxuriated in the delicious scents filling her senses, letting each one linger on the tongue before savouring the next. The air had a sluggish, greasy texture in the aftermath of powerful sorcery, and she could still feel the phantom caresses of her daemon lover.

Sated bodies lay strewn around her, marbled flesh quivering and beaded with sweat and oil. Coiling wisps of smoke streamed from candles and the flames from hanging censers danced on the walls. Her flesh was newly restored; iron-hard and unblemished after the blood of a dozen captives had been drained to make it so.

She ran her fingers across her flat stomach and down her thighs, relishing the cold smoothness of her skin. Rolling onto her side, she found a ewer of spiced wine that had somehow avoided being spilled during the carnal revelry, and poured it into a goblet of ice she formed in her other hand. Fingers from beneath a wolfskin rug pawed her, but she ignored them, sliding into an upright position and taking a long draught of the wine.

It was bitter, the creature she had summoned to pleasure her having soured it, but she drank it down nonetheless. Morathi knew enough of creatures from beyond to know that it was never wise to decline their gifts, intended or otherwise. The wine tasted of blood, but that was of no consequence to her. She had tasted far worse in her thousands of years of life.

Many of her lovers tonight would not live to the dawn, their throats and bellies opened in the frenzy of coupling that had brought forth the daemon. Such was the price of approaching the flame too closely. Slaves, captives or willing participants, it made no difference to Morathi, each was a pleasure to be taken by force or by seduction.

A chill wind blew through the pavilion, snuffing out several of the candles, and she felt a wistful pang for her homeland across the sea. Immediately she corrected herself. *This* was her home, and had been for many years before she and Malekith had been cast from their rightful place as rulers of Ulthuan. The thought angered her, and she wondered if it was being back on this island that made her moods so unpredictable.

Morathi pulled a thin robe from the floor, and wrapped it around her youthful body. Lustrous dark hair spilled around her shoulders, thick and glossy and black as night. She had the body of a maiden, but the eyes of a crone. Suffering the likes of which mortals could not imagine had paraded before those eyes, and no matter how much blood she spilled to preserve her youth, nothing could wash away the weight of ages in her gaze.

She poured more wine into the crackling goblet of ice and moved to the entrance of her pavilion. Lithe elves in armour of banded leather that barely covered their flesh lounged upon velvet blankets, seemingly in repose, but poised and ready to react to danger in the blink of an eye. Servants of the witch cults, they looked up languidly before returning their gaze to the fortress wall in the east.

The Eagle Gate still barred the way to the summer-lands beyond. The white of its walls was stained with blood and fire, and the eagle carved into its ramparts was barely recognisable. Its towers were ruined, and only what the defenders built up during the night served as battlements now. Torchlight and the soft hue of magical light shimmered beyond the walls, like a frozen moment of time just before the dawn. Moonlight glittered from spear points and helmets.

Wards beaten into the stone of the fortress prevented her from casting her spirit gaze beyond its walls, but she knew well enough what it protected. Lands of eternally golden summer, fecund soil and pure waters like the clearest crystal. In days past she had ridden those lands without a care, confident in the path her future would take, but those days were gone, and only bitterness remained in her heart. What Morathi could not have she would destroy.

Or if not her, then another…

Morathi remembered the last time she had seen Caledor, and the threat he had made. She wondered if he even remembered it. The magic of the vortex had all but driven him mad, and Caledor would sooner destroy this land than allow her or Malekith to claim it.

She wondered if the asur knew that.

Once she could not have allowed her thoughts to stray to Caledor and the magical vortex at the heart of Ulthuan, for fear that he would become aware of her presence. But many centuries had passed since their last meeting, and her knowledge of the arcane arts had grown immeasurably – enough that she could weave spells to hide her from the archmages' sight. Morathi was not deluded enough to believe that she was the equal of Caledor Dragontamer, but she had one advantage over the trapped mage lord.

She wasn't utterly insane.

Morathi smiled as she wondered if that were true.

Her sinuous guards uncoiled from their supine positions, long-bladed daggers appearing in each hand as a towering figure in armour like flayed skin appeared at the edge of the torchlight. Handsome to the point of ridiculousness, his body was as fine a specimen of mortal flesh as could be imagined.

'Is it safe to approach?' he enquired with a wry grin. 'Or must I again send you my best warriors to die under your knives?'

'Approach, Issyk Kul,' said Morathi. 'I am, for the moment, sated.'

The warrior emerged fully into the light, and Morathi

took a moment to appreciate the sheer dynamism of his body. So raw in its muscularity and power, so blunt in its threat. So different from the slender bodies of Naggaroth.

'How goes the fighting?' she asked.

'You would know if you fought instead of rutted,' said Kul, 'though there's pleasure to be taken in both. Perhaps we should swap roles.'

Anger flared momentarily, but she quelled it, knowing the warrior of the Dark Prince was simply goading her. He relished her anger, and she was in no hurry to indulge him. Not yet.

'Why should I fight when you and your tribesmen take such pleasure in it?' she said.

'There's truth in that,' agreed Kul. 'The blood flows freely, and the asur fight well. It is a battle of blood, of pain and of exquisite wounds. The kiss of an ithilmar blade stings like no other.'

'In any case, my battle is fought in subtler ways,' said Morathi.

'I like subtle,' said Kul, and Morathi laughed.

'So I see,' she said.

Kul drew his many-bladed weapon from the sheath across his shoulder, and Morathi's witch cultists were at her side in a heartbeat. Kul grinned, exposing his tapered fangs.

'Tell your witches to beware,' he said. 'I do not wish you dead until I have taken my fill of your flesh.'

'When the war is won, you will have your prize,' said Morathi, letting her robe fall open to reveal a slice of her toned thigh. Kul's gaze lingered on her body, following its contours from her hips to her breasts to her face. His grin was one of pure lust, and it never failed to amaze

Morathi how much importance mortals placed on physicality. Copulation was the least of the ways in which a
soul could be pleasured, the easiest, the most direct and
the most human.

Issyk Kul would never satisfy his base, animal needs
with her.

He would be dead before then.

'Your son still lays siege to Lothern?' said Kul, picking
up a discarded cup and holding it out to her as though
she was some kind of servant girl. She bit back her anger
and poured the soured wine into his cup.

Kul drank it down in one gulp. 'Pungent,' he said.

She dropped the ewer, letting its contents ooze out
onto the rock of the pass.

'Malekith enjoys success at Lothern,' she said. 'The
Emerald Gate is his, as are the shoulder castles on the
cliffs. Every day fresh warriors cross the bridge from the
Glittering Lighthouse to the mainland. It is only a matter
of time until Lothern is ours.'

'From what I hear, getting to the next gate will be a
fight of great magnitude.'

'It will be bloody,' admitted Morathi.

'Mayhap we will be in Lothern before your son,' sug-
gested Kul playfully.

'Not if this fortress continues to stand.'

'It will fall soon,' promised Kul. 'It is a certainty. And
it will be soon.'

'What makes you say that?'

'There is one among the elves who is touched by the
Dark Gods.'

'An asur?'

'Aye. An archer, I think.'

'They are all archers, Kul,' pointed out Morathi.

Kul shrugged. 'You elves all look the same to me,' he said. 'Pale skin, strange eyes and pointed ears. I could have killed him, but I saw the touch upon him as clear as midnight. His soul is at war, and all it will take is a small push to make him ours.'

'How small a push?' asked Morathi.

'One you could easily provide,' said Kul.

ALATHENAR TOOK A seat on the carved bench at the foot of the walls, and let out a relieved breath. He rested his bow against the wall and placed the plate of bread and cheese beside him. He was too tired to eat, but knew it was the only chance he was likely to get to satisfy his hunger. His muscles ached abominably and the sword cut on his hip had reopened. Blood stained his leggings, and he had loaned his needle and thread to one of the healers whose magic was exhausted. He tried to remain still, knowing that the wound would seal eventually, and grateful for this chance to rest. The walk from the mess hall had all but drained him, and he knew that he could not survive much longer without rest. He leaned his head back against the wall and closed his eyes, but sleep would not come. Too many images of hacked open bodies and friends screaming in pain paraded before him to allow him to sleep.

He wondered if he would ever sleep again.

The defenders of the Eagle Gate were in a sorry state. Barely eight hundred of them remained alive, and only two-thirds of those were fit to fight. Rumours kept circulating that reinforcements were being gathered, but they had yet to see any sign of them. Stories of far off battles filled the fortress; bleak tales of war being waged at Lothern, human fleets ravaging the coasts of Cothique and

Yvresse, and assassins striking at the leaders of the asur.

No one knew what to believe anymore.

Warriors gathered in small groups, talking in low voices, and he wondered if they gave voice to the same thoughts as slithered around his skull. Healers moved from group to group, using what little magic remained to them, and victual bearers brought water to parched throats.

'We are battered, but resolute,' he said. 'But for how much longer?'

'Not much longer if Glorien keeps wasting lives,' said Alanrias, walking over from the direction of the mess hall. The warrior of Nagarythe carried something beneath his cloak, but Alathenar could not tell what it was. Eloien Redcloak came with the Shadow Warrior, and though the he still bore his scarlet cloak, it was torn and burned in so many places that it seemed foolish to retain it. His features, already hardened from a life in the saddle, had been hardened further by his time at the Eagle Gate.

'I was about to eat,' said Alathenar, ignoring the Shadow Warrior's obvious barb.

'A delightful feast indeed,' agreed Eloien, taking a slice of bread from Alathenar's plate. He bit into the bread and grimaced before spitting it out. The Ellyrian wiped his lips with the back of his hand.

'You don't like the bread?' asked Alathenar.

'It is stale.'

'Stale? Elven bread does not go stale.'

'Then you had better tell the bakers,' said Eloien. 'Either this bread has been in the stores since the time of Bel Shanaar or the sorceries of the druchii have found new ways to make us miserable.'

Alathenar took a mouthful of bread and was forced to agree with Eloien. Elven bread could last for years without going hard and tasteless, but this was like stone or the bread the dwarfs were said to favour.

'It seems you are right,' he said taking the half-chewed lump from his mouth.

'Enough prattle about bread,' hissed Alanrias. 'I saw you on the wall, we made a compact. I saw it in your eyes. Let us be about our business.'

Alathenar sighed and looked toward the Aquila Spire. Soft light emanated from the windows, where Glorien Truecrown rested in comfort.

'Yes,' he said. 'We did, but that does not mean I take pleasure in what we must do.'

'I don't care whether you take pleasure in it or not,' hissed Alanrias. 'Only that you do it.'

'Be at peace, brother,' soothed Eloien. 'Alathenar knows what must be done. It does him credit that he takes no joy in its necessity.'

The Shadow Warrior sat back and shook his head. 'We are on the brink of ruin and you dance around the issue like children. On the walls tomorrow. That is when it must be done.'

Anger flared in Alathenar's heart and he rounded on the Shadow Warrior. 'If you are so ready to spill Glorien's blood, then why not do it yourself?'

'You are the best archer in the garrison,' said Eloien. 'You are the only one who is certain not to miss.'

'You think you can move me to murder with flattery?' hissed Alathenar.

'If need be,' said Alanrias. 'You saw how many died protecting him today. How many will die tomorrow? How much longer can we bear his incompetence?

Until the fortress falls and we are all dead?'

Alathenar started to reply, but before he could form the words to respond to Alanrias, he tasted a bitter metallic flavour in his mouth and a bilious wave of resentment washed over him. He wanted to tell Alanrias that he would not kill one of his own kind – murder was beneath him – but all those noble sentiments were swamped by images of the dead and maimed.

He did not like Alanrias, but could not deny the truth of his words. Glorien's foolishness had cost them all dear, had seen brave elves die and brought them to the edge of defeat. His half-hearted attempt to win back their favour by taking to the walls was an insult to the warriors who had died in his name.

This was the true face of Glorien Truecrown, a petty martinet, a strutting popinjay who saw war as a means of advancement. To have fought on the walls of the Eagle Gate would be just the posting to secure influence and prestige for his family. No matter that it would be bought with the lives of warriors who had spilled their precious elven blood under his command. Behind this tide of anger, part of Alathenar rebelled at what the dark voices were telling him, but the greater part of him embraced it.

Alathenar's expression turned to stone and he said, 'I cannot do the deed with one of my arrows. Nor even yours, Alanrias. We cannot be implicated.'

'We have thought of that,' said Alanrias.

The Shadow Warrior moved aside his cloak to reveal what he had brought to their plotting. It gleamed in the moonlight, the stock fashioned in polished ebony and the wound strings woven from a coarse horsehair. Alathenar reached out to touch it, but his fingers stopped short of the iron bolt resting in the groove of the weapon. It was a weapon of brutal yet elegant design.

A druchii hand crossbow.

Alathenar's fingers slipped around the weapon's handle. It felt natural, as though the weapon had been crafted just for him.

'Tomorrow then,' he said.

MORATHI LET THE drained body fall from her grip, the blood dripping from her fingertips as the last of the spell faded away. It had been a tiny thing, requiring only the blood of a single sacrifice, for the daemons of hate were simple to conjure, and needed little encouragement to venture into the realms of the living.

Brought forth beneath the light of the Chaos moon, and loosed on the winds of magic, it had been a matter of moments for the daemonic spirits to ease their way through the cracked and broken defences of the fortress. Wards that had kept her sorcery at bay for weeks were now virtually exhausted, simplicity itself for creatures of Chaos to overcome.

She felt the surge of hatred within the fortress, and laughed.

Warriors who had been brothers moments ago now traded hurtful words, and tiny grievances now swelled to monstrous insults. It would be short lived and swiftly forgotten, but potent while it lasted.

'Is it done?' asked Kul, licking his lips with anticipation.

'It is,' confirmed Morathi. 'Though how a single moment of hatred will serve our cause is beyond me. By morning the asur will not remember their sudden anger.'

'Do not be too sure,' said Kul. 'A moment of weakness matched to an instant of hate, and the course of a life can be changed forever. My divine master is patient, and swift to snare any soul that lowers its defences, even for a second.'

'And you think this brief hatred is enough?'

'Once the dark prince has a claim on a heart, there is no escape,' hissed Kul. 'You of all people should know that. Your bloody-handed god is jealous of his followers, but Shornaal cares not from where the souls come. Only that they be ripe for corruption.'

Kul laughed and strode away from Morathi.

'Tomorrow,' he said. 'This ends tomorrow.'

CHAPTER SEVEN

BLACK SWANS

ELLYRION OPENED UP to him, its rolling fields endless and its skies huge. The land before him was a thin strip of golden corn, the heavens an unending bowl of blue skies and streamers of silver clouds. Eldain's ride across the land of his birth was a revelation, like he was seeing it with new eyes. Eldain had believed he and Lotharin had ridden every path of Ellyrion, but his senses were alive with the pleasure of discovery.

Every hill and forest seemed new and freshly risen, each dawn as though it had been wrought just for him. Eldain had no idea why his homeland should welcome him as it did, for the kingdoms of Ulthuan kept no secrets from one another. What the land knew in Avelorn, it knew in Ellyrion and Saphery and all the other realms of the asur.

Eldain had taken an indirect route to Ellyr-Charoi, keeping clear of the main settlements and pathways.

He slept by streams gurgling towards the Inner Sea, and ate plants that grew on their banks, rising each morning more refreshed than before. He had lost track of the days, but knew he could not be far from his home. His clothes were travel-stained and had begun to smell, but Eldain didn't mind. This ride was what it meant to be an Ellyrian, free from the constraints of society and its rules.

Here and there, he would see herds of wild horses grazing or drinking at a pool of crystal water. Most of these herds ignored him, but others would gallop over and ride alongside for a time, conversing with Lotharin in a series of whinnies and snorts. It felt good to be with the herds of Ellyrion, and brought back a particularly fine memory from his youth.

'You remember it too, don't you?' he said, as Lotharin tossed his mane and stamped the ground. His mount broke into a run at his words, and he laughed as the joy of that day returned with the potency only a memory of the asur could render.

He had ridden out with Caelir when they had been no more than twelve summers old, taking their still-wild steeds out into the plains to gallop alongside the Great Herd. Once every few decades, the countless wild herds of Ellyrion would gather somewhere on the plains, drawn by some nameless imperative to run together in a thousands-strong stampede of fierce exultation.

Every son of Ellyrion longed to ride with the Great Herd, to mingle with the powerful beasts as they joined together in one thunderous ride to glory. Only the best riders dared join with the herd, for these steeds were wild and cared nothing for the safety of the mortals in their midst. Many an experienced rider had been crushed to death beneath the thundering hooves of the Great Herd.

Eldain and Caelir took their horses out by the light of the moon and rode north from their home to the burned copse where Laerial Sureblade had slain Gauma, the eleven-headed hydra.

Here they followed the tracks of the lowland steeds, and joined the smaller herds as they crossed a confluence of rivers that foamed white as though desperate to be part of the ride. Eldain remembered seeing hundreds of horses all around them, the numbers growing with every passing moment as the white herds of the south were joined by the dun and dappled beasts of the mountains. The greys of the north and the piebald mounts of the plains galloped in, proud and haughty, to be met by the silver herdleaders of the forests.

Here and there, a black steed galloped in splendid isolation, honoured and shunned in equal measure by its equine brothers. Soon the plains were filled with thousands of wild horses in a mighty herd that stretched from horizon to horizon, and the blood surged in Eldain's veins to be riding with such a host.

Beside him Caelir whooped and yelled, standing tall in Aedaris's stirrups and waving an arm over his head like a madman.

'Sit down!' Eldain had yelled. 'You'll be thrown and killed!'

Caelir shook his head and vaulted onto his horse's back, his limbs flowing like water as he bent and swayed to compensate for the wild ride. Dust billowed in thick clouds as the Great Herd galloped for all it was worth. The earth shook and the pounding beat of unshod hooves on the hard-packed earth was like the storms that boomed and rolled over the Annulii when the Chaos moon waxed full.

Eldain saw groups of Ellyrian horsemen riding through the herds, listening to their laughter and hearing their passionate cries. A herd of dun mares jostled him and he hauled the reins to the right, but pulled into the path of a group of pale stallions with the light of madness in their eyes. Lotharin was struck from both sides, and Eldain fought to stay on his back. Like Eldain and Caelir, their steeds were youthful and much smaller than these powerful beasts.

He felt the panic in his mount, and struggled to disentangle himself from the stallions. The horses had their head, and he was enclosed from all sides. Lotharin was tiring fast and to slow in such a desperate gallop would be suicide.

'Eldain!' shouted Caelir, and he looked over to see his brother sat astride Aedaris once more. 'Ride to me!'

Eldain pulled Lotharin through the barging, heaving mass of horses towards his brother, but Lotharin's strength was fading fast. Sweat stung Eldain's eyes and his muscles burned from the effort of keeping upright. Caelir was less than five yards to his right, but a bucking mass of wild horseflesh occupied the space between them.

'Jump!' shouted Caelir. 'Lotharin can break free if he does not need to worry about you!'

Loath as Eldain was to abandon his horse in the midst of this pandemonium, he knew Caelir was right. An Ellyrian steed would die to protect its rider, but that loyalty would see them both killed here.

Eldain kicked his boots free of the stirrups and leaned over his mount's neck.

'Run free, my friend, and I will see you after the ride is done,' he said.

Lotharin threw back his head and whinnied his assent. Eldain sprang onto Lotharin's back, the black horse a lone spot of darkness amongst the pale grey stallions. Caelir fought to hold Aedaris steady at the edge of the heaving mass, holding his hand out to Eldain.

'Jump, brother!' Caelir yelled.

Eldain swayed on Lotharin's back, gauging the right moment to leap. One misstep and he would fall through the press of horses and be crushed beneath their hammering strides. The horses were turning now, leaning into a sharp left turn. It was now or never.

Eldain jumped, hurling himself from Lotharin's back and into the air. He came down on the bouncing shoulder blades of a white stallion and sprang onwards, twisting to come down behind Caelir. His brother gripped him as he slid back, and they rode clear from the crescendo of galloping horses.

Caelir rode until they were cantering on the fringes of the Great Herd, content to watch the majestic sweep of the mass of horses as they let loose their untamed hearts and shared the joy of a wild ride with their brothers and sisters. Eldain slid from Aedaris's back at the foot of a jutting scarp of rock, knowing that Caelir wasn't yet done with the Great Herd.

'Go,' he said. 'Ride with the herd; I know you want to.'

'Without you, Eldain?' laughed Caelir, though Eldain could see the fierce desire in him to ride back into the herd. 'Where would the fun be in that?'

'Don't be foolish, how often does the Great Herd gather? Go!'

Caelir loosed a wild yell and Aedaris reared up before charging headlong into the swirling mass of dust and thundering horses. Eldain watched him go, proud to have so fearless a brother and, he could now admit, a touch jealous that he would not get to spend the day amid the frantic, pulse-pounding energy of the Great Herd.

As night fell, and the Great Herd began to break up into myriad smaller groups, Caelir rode Aedaris to the rock where Eldain had watched the ebb and flow of the mad stampede. Sweat-stained and exhausted, Caelir was nevertheless exultant, his cheeks ruddy with excitement and joy. His mount's flanks were lathered with sweat, but he too was overjoyed to have been part of something so ferocious. Lotharin followed his brother's horse, similarly drained, but equally joyous.

Together they had ridden back to Ellyr-Charoi, and Eldain spent the entire journey hearing of the magnificent sights at the eye of the herd, the swirling mass of horses and the madness of the jostling, barging, crashing herds. Eldain revelled in his younger brother's tales, laughing and yelling with each telling of Caelir's reckless stunts. Dawn was lighting the eastern horizon by the time they passed through the gates and allowed the equerries to take their horses from them.

Though that ride had been many years ago, Eldain still remembered it like it was yesterday. That all too brief moment of sheer, unbridled joy as he rode with the Great Herd was like nothing he had ever experienced before or since. It was a golden memory, and he silently thanked the land for its boon. Lotharin gave a long whinny of pleasure, and they rode on in companionable silence. The horses of the wild herd that had accompanied him for many miles now turned and galloped for the mountains. Eldain waved them on their way.

'Farewell and firm earth,' he said, as the last horse

vanished over an undulant hill fringed with pine. At the foot of the hill, a jutting rock carved by childish hands into the shape of a rearing horse poked from an overgrown tangle of thornspines, and Eldain smiled as he recalled carving it for Rhianna, the first summer she had come to visit from Saphery.

Time had weathered the poor carving, and obscuring plant life had grown up around it, making it look like an ambush predator was dragging the horse down. Eldain shivered at the image that conjured, and tried not to think of it as an omen.

He was close now, that carving had been made when they were little more than children and not permitted to venture far from the villa. Eldain cut south until he found a hill trail that led south, a hidden pathway that none save an Ellyrian would know. Eldain saw it had been travelled recently, the hooves of a horse not native to Ellyrion having come this way. For an hour he followed the trail, winding through the high gullies and forest lanes until he emerged onto a rolling hillside of lush green grass.

Below him lay a glittering villa set within a stand of orange-leaved trees that nestled between two waterfalls.

Ellyr-Charoi.

Home.

LIGHT WAS FADING from the sky by the time Eldain reached the villa, and the evening sun reflected from the many gemstones set within its walls. Azure capped towers surrounded a central courtyard, and the tinted glass of their many windows shone with a rainbow of colours. Autumnal leaves drifted on the winds around the villa, and withered vines climbed to the tiled copings of its walls.

Eldain took a deep breath and tried to feel something other than foreboding at the sight of his home. Ellyr-Charoi grew from the earth, wrought with great cunning by its builders to merge seamlessly with the landscape and become part of its surroundings. As was the fashion of Ellyrian dwellings, it was elegant and understated, without the riot of gaudy decorations common to Ulthuan's more cosmopolitan cities.

He rode slowly down the path until he reached the overgrown track over a gently arched bridge. So many memories jostled for attention. Sitting on the bridge with Rhianna and throwing in flower petals. Racing Caelir to the bridge on their new steeds. Cheering as his father rode to join a warrior host setting out for Naggaroth.

Weeping as the white-clad mourners brought his mortally wounded father home.

The gates were open, and the wind blew through like a moan of grief, whistling through cracked panes of glass on the tallest towers and filling the air with dancing leaves of gold and rust. No one challenged him as he rode into the courtyard, where once warriors had stood sentinel on the walls with bows bent and arrows nocked. Those faithful retainers were long gone, and Eldain felt the villa's abandonment settle on him like an accusing glare.

He slid from his horse's back and turned slowly, taking in the neglected villa's disrepair. Where once an autumnal air had held sway, now winter was in the ascendancy. The fountain at the heart of the Summer Courtyard was empty of water, and only dead leaves filled the pool. A marble-tiled cloister bounded the courtyard, and Eldain made his way towards the elegantly curved stairs that led from the courtyard to his chambers at the top of the

Hippocrene Tower. He climbed the first step, and paused as he heard the brittle sound of fallen leaves crumbling beneath a riding boot.

Knowing what he would see, Eldain turned around.

Caelir stood by Lotharin, clad as Eldain remembered him from Avelorn. Like him, he was travel-worn and tired, but unlike Eldain, Caelir was armed. He carried a slim-bladed sword with a blue sheen to its edge. Eldain recognised it as their father's sword, the weapon he had borne to Naggaroth on the eve of his death.

'Caelir,' said Eldain. 'I hoped you would be here.'

His brother took a step towards him, and ran a hand down Lotharin's lathered flanks.

'A true horseman would see to his mount before anything else,' said Caelir. 'But then we both know you are no son of Ellyrion, don't we brother?'

BY MIDMORNING THE armies of Morathi and her mortal allies had launched two major attacks upon the Eagle Gate. Both attacks had been repulsed, though the defenders had suffered heavy losses, for the Hag Sorceress had held nothing back from these assaults. Flitting she-bats swooped from the skies, bellowing hydras unleashed breaths of fire, and rock-shielded bolt throwers hurled enormous, barbed shafts at the fragmenting walls.

Morathi herself took to the air, unleashing black sorceries from the back of her midnight pegasus, and every magicker in the fortress bent their efforts to keep her at bay. Her spiteful laughter rang over the battlements, driving her warriors to ever greater heights of suicidal courage.

It sat ill with Menethis to think of the druchii as

possessing so noble an attribute as courage, but there was no other word for it. The blood in their veins came from the same wellspring as did his, and for all their other hateful qualities, courage was, unfortunately, not a virtue they lacked. Yet it was not the equal of asur courage, he knew, for its origins lay not in duty, honour or notions of self-sacrifice, but in fear.

The mortal followers of the dark prince attacked with reckless disregard for their own lives, many of them seeming to welcome the stabbing blades of the elves. The towering warrior in the flayed-flesh armour bellowed his challenges from the top of each ladder he climbed, killing any who came near him with chopping blows of his many-bladed sword.

Three times he had gained the rampart, and three times he had been hurled from the walls, only to rise from the ruin of broken ladder and splintered bodies to seek a new way up. The deformed monsters dragged towards the fortress in chains battered its crumbling walls, and the musk of their excretions drifted over the battlements in nauseating waves.

Yet for all the ferocity of these attacks, Menethis sensed a growing sense of something else behind the dark helms of the attackers. He wanted to believe it was desperation, for the walls of the Eagle Gate had held far longer than he would have thought possible. Designed to be impregnable, the garrison had been steadily run down over the years until only a token force remained. The warriors fighting and dying here were now paying for that foolishness with their lives.

Perhaps our enemies know they are on borrowed time, he thought, thinking of the sealed scroll that had arrived in the hands of a rider from Tor Elyr moments before the second attack had hit the walls. Glorien had read it first, then handed it to Menethis. With every word he read, a growing sense of euphoria filled him.

'We have done it,' Glorien had said, his eyes alight with the prospect of victory. 'This will be over in days. All we have to do is hold a little longer.'

Arandir Swiftwing, the lord of Tor Elyr, was mustering an army and his foremost general, Galadrien Stormweaver, was marching to their relief. Every able-bodied warrior had been summoned to Lothern, but as more and more of the citizen levy had answered their lord's summons, another army took shape on the martial fields around Tor Elyr.

A portion of that army would reach the Eagle Gate in two days.

Perhaps that was why the three great eagles had flown from the fortress, sensing that their aid was no longer required. Some had seen it as a bad omen when the three mighty birds had flown over the northern peaks of the mountains, but the news of their relief made sense of their departure.

There had been no time to disseminate the wondrous news of Stormweaver's imminent arrival, for the enemy were attacking once more. Menethis watched the armoured host of enemy warriors marching towards the walls as a host of white-shafted arrows slashed towards them. Stocks of arrows were low, and Glorien had decreed that only the best archers be given an extra quiver. The Eagle's Claws were out of bolts and their crews stood on the walls with their fellow warriors, spears glittering in the high sun.

Menethis drew back the string of his bow, picking out a druchii warrior without a helm at the forefront of a group of ladder-bearers. The warrior's face was pale, and a glistening topknot of black hair hung down to the nape of his neck. His armour was bloodstained and carved with jagged runes. Between breaths, Menethis let fly, watching the arrow arc downwards before plunging home in the druchii's neck. The warrior fell, clutching at his throat as blood squirted from the wound.

The enemy broke on the walls with a thunderous crash of iron and wood. Ladders were thrown up and looping grapnels sailed over the makeshift battlements. Menethis leaned out over the crumbling rampart and loosed arrow after arrow into the mass of surging warriors below. Each shaft found its mark, punching through the top of a helmet or slicing home in a gap between armoured plates.

Menethis did not waste his arrows on the mortals; only druchii warranted his attention. Within moments, his quiver was emptied and he drew his sword as the enemy climbed their ladders. Hundreds of screaming warriors were coming to gain a foothold on the walls, in a mass of stabbing blades, hewing axes and streaking iron bolts.

'Steady now,' said Menethis, hearing iron-shod boots on metal rungs.

A druchii appeared at the top of the ladder. An asur spear stabbed out but was blocked, and the warrior hauled himself through the embrasure. Menethis plunged his sword into the warrior's chest. Twisting the blade, he kicked the druchii from the wall and chopped down into the head of the enemy behind him.

'The ladder!' yelled Menethis, seeing that the iron hooks at its end had not bitten into the stonework of the parapet. 'Help me!'

He gripped the top of the ladder and heaved with all his strength. Three more elves ran to help him, but the first dropped as an iron bolt hammered into his throat. The two elves took position either side of Menethis and leaned into the task. Another druchii reared up and stabbed his blade into the warrior beside Menethis. He gave a strangled cry and dropped to his knees, but with the last of his strength he gripped his killer's blade tightly, trapping it within his flesh.

The ladder squealed with a grating scrape of iron on stone, but Menethis felt it pitch past its centre of gravity. Powerless to prevent the ladder from falling, the druchii released his sword and leapt onto the walls with a dagger aimed at Menethis's heart. A black-shafted arrow sliced out of nowhere and thudded home into the druchii's armpit. Arterial blood flooded out and the warrior fell as the ladder was cast down. Screaming druchii tumbled to the base of the wall, and Menethis sought out his rescuer.

He gave a begrudged nod of thanks as he saw it had been the Shadow Warrior, Alanrias, who had loosed the arrow. The cloaked warrior sketched a casual salute and bent his bow once more, picking off druchii warriors who were in danger of forming a fighting wedge on the ramparts. All along the length of the wall, a tidal wave of druchii and barbarians were pushing hard. The ramparts were slick with blood, and though the asur line was bending, it was holding.

In the centre of the wall, Glorien stood in the midst of the garrison's best warriors. His sword was bloody and his armour would never be the same again, but he was fighting hard. Even Menethis had to admit that Glorien's skills with a blade left much to be desired, but war forced a warrior to be a swift learner. Though there was not an elf in this fortress Glorien could best in a clash of blades, there were the makings of a fine warrior coming to the fore.

Perhaps Glorien's dream vision was just that; a dream, not some nightmare premonition of doom. Menethis had kept a wary eye on Alanrias throughout the fighting, but the Shadow Warrior had done nothing untoward, calmly and methodically killing druchii with lethally accurate arrows.

Menethis crouched behind the crumbling rampart and removed his helm, pulling his hair back and securing it in a long ponytail. He reached up to wipe a film of sweat from his brow and blinked as he saw something out of place. A stillness, amid the frenetic scrum of battle raging along the length of the wall.

A lone warrior crouched in the shadows at the base of the Aquila Spire with a druchii crossbow resting on a broken stub of rock. His eyes were cold and merciless, the eyes of a murderer. Menethis opened his mouth to shout that a druchii assassin had scaled the walls unde-tected, when he saw that this assassin wore a cloak of pale blue, muted in the shadows, but unmistakably of asur design.

'Here they come again!' shouted a voice, and Menethis heard the clang of iron ladders and the biting of grapnel hooks into stone. He ignored them, and ran along the wall, ducking and weaving a path through desperate combats.

'No!' he shouted, knowing where the iron bolt of the crossbow was aimed.

The assassin loosed and Menethis screamed a denial as the bolt slashed through the air and hammered through the temple of Glorien's helmet. The commander of the Eagle Gate was punched from his feet, falling against the parapet as blood poured down his stricken face.

His protectors tried to catch Glorien, but the shock of the impact stunned them to the point where not even their superlative reflexes were swift enough. Glorien toppled forwards, his body falling from the walls to land in the midst of the enemy.

A terrifying howl of triumph erupted from below, for there could be no doubt which of the asur had fallen. Glorien's armour clearly marked him as the commander of the Eagle Gate, and Menethis ran to the edge of the wall in time to see Glorien's body torn to pieces by the frenzied savages who served the barbarian warlord.

A palpable wave of grief and horror swept over the defenders of the Eagle Gate, a physical sensation of loss and despair. Few had any love for Glorien Truecrown, but seeing their commander slain so suddenly tore the heart from everyone who saw it. Even the healers and the wounded beyond the walls felt the pain of Glorien's death.

Wracked with grief, the defence faltered.

Just for a moment, just for the briefest instant, but it was enough.

Scores of ladders thudded against the fortress as Menethis and the defenders wept for their lost master. Enemy warriors hurled themselves over the ramparts, and this time, there would be no stopping them.

Menethis turned towards the Aquila Spire, the need for vengeance fanning a terrible fury in his heart. He saw the druchii weapon thrown from the wall as the assassin who had wielded it stepped from the shadows, confident that no one had seen his perfidy.

Menethis gasped as he saw who had loosed the treacherous bolt.

'Alathenar!' he screamed.

ELDAIN HAD DREADED this moment, but now that it was here, he felt strangely relieved. Ever since that fleeting moment when he had allowed hateful feelings of jealousy to overcome a lifetime of brotherly love, he had known he would have to answer for his crime. The blade in Caelir's hands would exact the price he would have to pay.

'Do you want to kill me?' he asked.

'Can you think of a single reason I shouldn't?'

'No,' said Eldain, stepping down into the Summer Courtyard. 'I deserve your hatred.'

The wind sighed through the gates, blowing the leaves from the inlaid marble flagstones into miniature whirlwinds. The last embers of sunlight shone from the colourful windows of the villa's towers and the evening-hued blade in Caelir's hands.

'Tell me why, Eldain,' demanded Caelir, and Eldain wanted to weep at the wrenching sorrow he heard in his brother's voice. 'Tell me why you left me to die. I need to know.'

Eldain shook his head. 'It will not make any difference.'

'It will make a difference to me, Eldain!' roared Caelir. 'I rode day and night from Avelorn, trying to comprehend why my own flesh and blood would betray me to the druchii, but I could think of no reason, no reason at all. So make me understand, brother. Tell me what great insult did I do to you that made you hate me so much?'

'Hate you, brother? No, never that. I loved you.'

'You loved me? You must have a strange definition of the word.'

Eldain circled the fountain, and Caelir mirrored his movements, keeping the waterless centrepiece between them.

'Perhaps you are right,' said Eldain. 'I no longer know. I loved you and was jealous of you in equal measure. Nothing I did could ever match what you would accomplish. Anything of worth I could achieve, you would outdo. Wherever I shone, you shone brighter.'

'I only sought to be like you, brother,' cried Caelir. 'You were my inspiration!'

Eldain shook his head. 'When our father died, who took care of our estates? Who kept our family name alive and dealt with the necessities of life? I did. Not you. I was the one who took care of us when father died, you ran like a spoiled child. Hunting, carousing and riding with the herds was the life you led, being the heroic warrior I had not the time to be.'

'And for that you betrayed me?'

'You stole everything of beauty that should have been mine!'

'What are you talking about?'

'You took Rhianna from me!' cried Eldain, turning and walking towards the tall building at the edge of the Summer Courtyard. He pushed open the ash doors of the Equerry's Hall, and a gust of leaves followed him inside. Within was dimly lit and smelled of neglect, though it had been only weeks since he had last set foot in this grand hall. Hunting trophies and faded portraits of former lords of the noble Éadaoin family hung from the walls, and a long oval table filled the centre of the echoing space.

Eldain sank into the high-backed chair at the end of the table as Caelir stood silhouetted in its wide doorway by the last light of day. The sword in his hand sparkled in the gloaming. Caelir shut the doors behind him and stepped inside, letting his eyes adjust to the thin light coming through the vents in the roof. In ages past, the lords of the Éadaoin would gather here to feast and sing songs of the wild hunt, but those songs were sung and no more would they lift the rafters with their wild notes.

Caelir sat at the opposite end of the table from Eldain, and laid the sword before him.

'I did take Rhianna from you,' he said at last. 'I knew it was wrong, but I did it anyway. It was that ride into the Annulii. We were attacked by the druchii and I fought them all. We should have ridden away, but I *wanted* to fight them. I wanted her to see how strong and brave I was. Foolish, I know, but back then I was a little in love with death I think.'

'She was never the same after that day,' said Eldain. 'I accused her of being infatuated with you because of your reckless bravery. I spoke harshly to her, and she did not deserve my anger. I had too long ignored her happiness, and all but forced you together.'

'I did not mean to fall in love with her, but…'

'But you did,' said Eldain. 'She is a woman impossible *not* to fall in love with.'

'And you married her,' said Caelir. 'I saw the pledge rings. You came back from Naggaroth and told her I was dead. You betrayed me and took up your life where you had left off now that the inconvenience of Caelir was removed.'

'That is true,' admitted Eldain. 'But I think that it was not hatred of you, but love of Rhianna that was my undoing.'

'Again, your definition of love is a mockery of the word.'

'Perhaps, but love is a powerful emotion, one that blinds us to many things. Love is also the gateway to other, darker, emotions: jealousy, paranoia, possessiveness and lust. I told myself I loved her, and anything that brought us together could not be altogether evil. I was wrong, I know that now. And though it can make no difference to how this must end, I ask your understanding if not your forgiveness.'

Caelir rose to his feet, his face reddening as through Eldain had slapped him. 'You speak of forgiveness? Of understanding? You left me to the druchii and told the woman I loved that I was dead. You cannot know the things the dark kin did to me, how they made me do… terrible things and cause untold harm to my own kind.'

'I know what they made you do, I understand–'

'You understand nothing!' screamed Caelir. 'Hundreds of people are dead because of me, because of what you did. Don't you understand? Kyrielle, Teclis, the Everqueen… Our enemies used me as a weapon!'

Caelir vaulted onto the table and charged along its length, scattering dusty plates and cutlery. He hurled himself at Eldain and the two brothers crashed to the floor in a tangle of flailing limbs. The sword lay forgotten on the table, as Caelir straddled Eldain's chest and wrapped his hands around his neck.

Eldain struggled in his brother's grip, holding onto Caelir's wrists and fighting to take a breath. The light of madness was in Caelir's eyes, yet behind it was an ocean of sorrow and pain and guilt. That guilt was rightfully Eldain's, that sorrow his legacy, and he knew he had more than earned Caelir's vengeance. This death was a small thing, the last gift he could give his brother in lieu of any means to make amends.

Caelir's grip tightened, and Eldain's throat buckled under the pressure. He could take no breath, and he released Caelir's wrists, letting the grey at the edges of his vision deepen to black until he could see no more.

At last, Eldain knew peace.

CHAPTER EIGHT

AMENDS

No sooner had the bolt left the druchii crossbow than Alathenar knew he had made a terrible mistake. He watched it cut the air, hoping for a freak gust of wind or a chance movement that would see it plunge home in an enemy's chest. He closed his eyes as the bolt punched through Glorien's helm, and sent a whispered prayer to Asuryan that he might, one day, be forgiven for this murder.

'What have I done…?' he said as Glorien fell from the wall.

Alathenar hurled the druchii weapon away as though it were a poisonous serpent, and took up his bow as he swiftly stepped from the shadows. He pulled his cloak tight, feeling his soul already growing heavy with the enormity of his deed. He had slain a fellow elf, one of the asur. No less a warrior than his commanding officer. He was no better than the dark-armoured warriors who threw themselves at the walls with bloody war cries.

He heard his name shouted, and saw Menethis running along the battlements. He knew immediately that Menethis had seen him loose the fateful bolt, and part of him was glad. He didn't think he could bear the weight of such a dark secret.

The defenders of the Eagle Gate were paralysed by Glorien's sudden death, as horrified by his ending as they had been by Cerion Goldwing's. Sword arms were stilled and bowstrings went slack as they watched their fallen leader's body savagely torn apart by the enemy. No matter that he had been derided for many weeks, he was a noble of Ulthuan and had finally begun to live up to that title. Only now, when it was too late to undo the deed, did Alathenar understand what Glorien might have become.

The druchii swarmed the walls, and Alathenar saw the barbarian warlord in his crimson armour scramble onto the ramparts. His sword swept out and three elves were torn apart in a spray of blood. He bellowed his triumph, keeping the defenders at bay with wide arcs of his monstrous blade. Dozens of leather and fur-clad warriors in crudely strapped armour gained the walls behind him, massing for a push outwards along the length of the rampart. Elsewhere, heavily armoured druchii with long, executioner's blades forced a path onto the wall, and more of their plate-armoured brethren came with them.

The wall was lost, any fool could see that.

Menethis slammed into him and bore him to the ground. Alathenar's sword slipped from its scabbard, and he sprang to his feet as Menethis came at him again.

'You murderer!' yelled Menethis, slashing wildly with his blade. 'I will kill you.'

Alathenar leapt away from each attack. Grief and anger

had made Menethis clumsy, and he sobbed even as he fought.

'Wait!' cried Alathenar, backing away.

Glorien's lieutenant paid his words no heed and launched himself at Alathenar again. He had no choice but to block the blows with the stave of his bow, feeling every bite of the sword's edge, and mourning every splinter broken from the weapon.

'Menethis!' he shouted. 'The wall is lost, but the garrison might yet be saved!'

Another blow slashed towards his head. He ducked and spun inside Menethis's guard, hammering an elbow into his temple. Menethis was knocked from his feet and Alathenar stepped in to snatch up his fallen sword.

He knelt beside Menethis and rested the tip of the blade on his throat.

'You will kill me too?' snapped Menethis. 'How long have you been a servant of the druchii? You are a worthless traitor, and I spit on you.'

'I am no servant of the druchii,' he said. 'Suffice to say I allowed the bitterness of others to poison my thoughts and upset the moral compass of my heart. But I make no excuses; I have no defence for what I have done.'

'Because there *is* no defence! You murdered Glorien just as he was becoming the warrior he needed to be.'

'I fear you are right, but we have no time for debate or regrets.'

Menethis glanced away from the blade at his throat to the fighting on the walls. The elven line had not yet broken, but it was a matter of moments only.

'You and your plotters have condemned us all to death,' said Menethis. 'You know that?'

'No,' said Alathenar. 'For you will lead what is left of

the garrison to Ellyrion. There are horses aplenty in the landward stables, enough to carry the bulk of our warriors to safety.'

'The druchii will break through and cut us down before we have a single horse saddled.'

'Not if I hold them back,' said Alathenar.

Menethis laughed, a bitter, lost sound that cut Alathenar deeply.

'You are a fool as well as a traitor,' he said.

'You'll get no argument from me on that account,' said Alathenar, standing and lifting the sword from Menethis's neck. 'But regardless of your opinion of me, you must go now if any lives are to be saved.'

He reversed the sword and held it hilt-first before him.

Menethis took the weapon, and Alathenar could see the urge to plunge the blade into his throat in his eyes. The hurt anger diminished and Menethis sheathed the weapon. He took a deep breath and turned to the steps leading down to the esplanade behind the doomed wall.

He glared back at Alathenar. 'All Ulthuan will know what you did here,' he promised.

Alathenar nodded. 'So be it. If I am to die hated, then that is all I deserve.'

Menethis gripped his sword and said, 'Your honour is lost and will never be regained, Alathenar. Your death here will not even the scales of Asuryan.'

Alathenar took up his damaged bow and said, 'When I stand before him in judgement, I will be sure to remind him of that.'

ELDAIN OPENED HIS eyes and found himself looking at the tapered ceiling of the Hippocrene Tower. His throat ached abominably and it was painful to draw a breath.

He turned his head, seeing that he was lying on his bed, still fully clothed, and was the chamber's sole occupant.

What had happened to him?

His last memory was of Caelir throttling him and the black mist of death reaching up to drag him down. Eldain reached up and ran his fingertips along his neck, feeling the skin there swollen and bruised.

Eldain sat up, feeling every ache in his body magnified. Holding his throat he took a painful breath and swung his legs onto the floor. Everything here was just as he had left it when he and Rhianna had followed Yvraine to Saphery. It seemed like a lifetime ago that he had been called to attend upon the young Sword Master, and Eldain was reminded of how swiftly a life could change its course

He rose from the bed and stood at his walnut desk. Sheaves of curling scrolls lay strewn across its surface, along with a quill stone and inkpot. Bookshelves surrounded him, each one filled with the works of great scholars, poets, dramatists and historians.

Eldain had read every book in his library, yet their worth seemed transitory and meaningless in the face of how the world now turned. Would the druchii keep any of these books? Would they build a new library in the ruins of Lothern? Would any of the works composed over the thousands of years since asur and druchii had gone their separate ways survive this invasion?

He realised such questions were irrelevant, and moved to one of the eight windows set into the compass points of the tower's walls. Eldain leaned on the western window's stone frame and looked up at the enormous peaks of the Annulii. Their peaks were wreathed in magical storm clouds, roiling thunderheads of magical energy that spat lightning bolts of raw power into the earth.

Contained within those peaks were the titanic energies bound by Caledor Dragontamer in the time of Aenarion, and it never failed to humble Eldain that a mage of Ulthuan had mustered such power.

Eldain turned from the panoramic vista and his thoughts moved to more immediate concerns. That he still lived was a surprise and a mystery.

Why had Caelir not killed him?

He more than deserved death, and his last sight had been of Caelir's grief-wracked face as he choked the life from him. There had been no mercy in those eyes, so why had his brother carried him upstairs to his chambers? Part of him wanted to remain in this tower, isolated and without the need to venture into a world that despised him.

Eldain recognised that for the cowardice it was, and opened the door.

He descended the steps that led to the Summer Courtyard, finding it deserted and echoing with the ghosts of long-passed glories. Leaves gusted around the silent fountain, and he scattered them with his boot as he walked a circuit of the courtyard. Once, this had been a place of joy, where laughter and song had breathed life and colour into the world. Ellyrians were a proud people, haughty and free-spirited, with a love of life that the people of other kingdoms saw as quick-tempered.

Yet as quick as an Ellyrian was to anger, he was just as quick to forgive.

Eldain heard the sound of horses, and knew where Caelir would be.

He swept his fingers through his platinum-blond hair and made his way towards the rear of the villa where the stables were situated. In any other kingdom, stables were simply functional structures, designed to house mounts and nothing more. Horses were equals in Ellyrian households, and a noble of this land lavished as much care and attention on the building of his stables as he did on his own quarters.

Ellyr-Charoi's stables were crafted from polished marble and roofed with clay tiles of stark blue, each stone rendered with intricate carvings and gold leaf representations of heroic steeds from family history. The starwood doors were open, and Eldain heard his brother talking to the horses in a low, soothing tones.

Though elf and horse did not converse as such, there existed a bond that allowed each to sense the needs of the other. When steed and rider were together, there was no division between them, their thoughts were one and they moved and fought with perfect synchronicity. No other cavalry force in the world could boast so intuitive a connection, and rightly were the riders of Ellyrion known as the horse lords.

Eldain rounded the chamfered columns of the door, and the warm welcome he always felt in Ellyr-Charoi's stables enfolded him. A central passageway ran the length of the building, with twenty stalls to either side, though it had been many years since each one had been filled. Lotharin and Irenya were ensconced in neighbouring stalls, and Caelir fed them handfuls of good Ellyrian grain. A grain-fed horse would have stronger bones, more powerful muscles and could easily outrun a grass-fed horse.

Caelir looked up as Eldain entered.

What could he possibly say to his brother?

'Hello, Eldain,' said Caelir. 'I think we need to talk, don't you?'

'Will that talk end the way of our last?'

Caelir shook his head. 'No, brother. Not unless you desire vengeance.'

'Vengeance? No, there is no malice left in me.'

'Nor in me,' agreed Caelir.

'Why?' said Eldain, wary of opening so raw a wound, but needing to understand why he still lived.

'Why what?'

'Why did you not kill me?' asked Eldain.

'Because you are my brother,' said Caelir.

ALATHENAR RAN TO the edge of the wall, loosing shaft after shaft into the surging host of enemy warriors. Blue-cloaked elves streamed from the walls, obeying the trumpeted order to retreat even as isolated groups stood firm to deny the enemy the slaughter of pursuit. Alathenar ducked a sweeping axe blow and sent a shaft through the eye of a screaming tribesman at point blank range. Another sliced open the throat of a druchii bearing a heavy, two-handed blade, and another punched through the heart of a warrior reloading his ebony crossbow.

The hordes of the enemy strained at the few defenders remaining on the wall, yet they could not break through such determined resistance. Bound by shared guilt at Glorien's death, these were the warriors who had wished for his death, or had imagined his fall and now knew the true cost of such disloyal thoughts. Without any orders needing to be given, every warrior of the Eagle Gate knew in a heartbeat whether he should remain until the bitter end or escape the slaughter to come.

Alathenar fought like Alith Anar himself, weaving a path through the enemy warriors like a ghost. Across the rampart, he saw Eloien Redcloak, cutting enemy warriors down with graceful sweeps of his cavalry sabre. Like

Alathenar, the terrible nature of what they had done was etched on his hard features, and the Ellyrian wept as he killed.

Alanrias crouched on a jutting perch of stone, sending the last of his barbed arrows into the sweating, grunting mass of enemy warriors. The savage humans could smell victory. It was just within their reach, but these last, few elves were denying them the full splendour of slaughter. Alathenar had not known whether the Shadow Warrior would remain to face the consequences of their conspiracy, but should have known better. For all his dour and bitter pronouncements, he was still one of the asur.

His quiver emptied, Alathenar broke his bow across his knee and swiftly unwound the string from the notches at either end. Woven with tresses from his beloved Arenia, he was not about to have it fall into the hands of the druchii. He wrapped the bowstring around the fingers of his right fist and swept up a fallen sword.

He looked down into the courtyard, seeing Menethis hurriedly organising the evacuation of the fortress. Hundreds of elven warriors saddled horses and prepared to ride eastward. Many of the escapees were from Ellyrion and were already riding for their homeland. The majority of what was left of the garrison would escape, but Menethis needed more time to get everyone clear.

A hellish bellow of rage echoed from the sides of the pass, and Alathenar saw Issyk Kul slay the last of the defenders holding his barbarous warriors back. A tide of unclean and perverse humans surged onto the walls, bellowing with triumph as they swept left and right along the ramparts.

'Redcloak! The stairs!' he yelled, running towards the head of the western steps. One warrior could hold the steps for a short time only, but perhaps that would be enough. Eloien Redcloak took up position at the head of the eastern steps, while Alanrias kept up a relentless stream of killing arrows. The Shadow Warrior let fly with no thought for spite in his barbed arrows. Each shaft tore out a throat, plunged through an eye socket or into a heart.

Three warriors against an army.

There could be no redemption for any of them, but at least they would die in the service of Ulthuan.

A screaming tribesman came at Alathenar, and he ducked beneath the slashing blade of a heavy broadsword. His blade lanced out, opening the man's belly and hurling him to the courtyard below. A warrior with an arm covered in weeping sores that looked like eyes leapt at him, and Alathenar hammered his sword across his neck, all but severing his head.

A hurled spear tore a gash in his hip, and Alathenar staggered as blood washed down his leg. The wound in his side reopened and he knew he had moments at best to kill as many of these dogs as he could. Three more tribesmen died by his blade, and he risked a glance over to the eastern stairs to see Redcloak bleeding from a score of wounds. His right arm hung uselessly at his side, but he fought equally well with his left.

A druchii warrior with a full-faced helm of bronze came at Alathenar with a long, hook-bladed spear. He could see the druchii grinning beneath his helm and anger flared at the relish he saw in his enemy's face.

'Come and die, dark one!' he shouted.

The druchii ignored him and thrust with his spear; Alathenar batted it aside and lunged forward. No sooner had he moved, than he realised he had been lured into the attack. The druchii stepped back and swept his spear to the side, the haft slamming into Alathenar's torso and pitching him over the edge of the steps.

Alathenar felt himself falling, and reached out to grip the spear with his free hand. The druchii warrior gave a cry of surprise as Alathenar dragged him from the top of the steps, and the two of them fell from the wall.

Alathenar slammed into the cobbled esplanade, screaming in pain as the bones of his legs shattered with the force of the impact. The druchii landed next to him, his skull smashed to splinters and blood pooling around his caved-in helm. Alathenar rolled onto his side, crying out in pain as the broken bones of his legs ground together. Enemy warriors streamed down the steps into the fortress, and Alathenar wept to see one of Caledor's great fortresses fall.

Through tear-blurred vision, he saw Eloien Redcloak cut down by the warlord of the tribal host. The champion's horrific sword opened the Ellyrian from collarbone to pelvis, and sent his ruptured body tumbling to the courtyard. An ivory figure astride a winged black horse dropped through the sky to land at the centre of the wall. Morathi's laughter rang from the sides of the pass, and Alathenar had never hated anyone with greater passion.

A flickering stream of black light erupted from her outstretched hand, and Alathenar watched in horror as the deadly fire engulfed Alanrias. His cloak ignited and the archer vanished in a pillar of searing flame that burned hotter and darker than any natural flame could possibly burn. The black fire quickly dissipated, leaving only a smeared ashen outline on the wall where the Shadow Warrior had once stood.

Alathenar tried to sit up, but the pain from his broken

bones was too great. He closed his eyes and brought his hand to his mouth. He kissed the bowstring wrapped around his fingers, picturing the beautiful elf-maid who had so delicately cut strands of her hair for him.

'Forgive me, Arenia,' he whispered.

He kept the image of her perfect beauty in his mind as a talisman against the pain, wishing he could have done things differently, that he had not loosed that fatal bolt.

A shadow fell upon him and he cried out as the vision of Arenia vanished. Alathenar opened his eyes and saw the towering form of Issyk Kul looming over him. The warlord's bulk blotted out the sun, and Alathenar saw the dark halo of the Dark Gods' favour rippling around his cruelly beautiful features.

'I knew the gods had me spare you for a reason,' said Kul.

Alathenar tried to spit a defiant answer, but his mouth was full of blood.

Issyk Kul knelt beside Alathenar, and pressed a broken sword into his bloodied palm.

'No warrior should die without a blade in his hand,' said Kul. 'It is one of the few things the worshipers of the Blood God and I agree upon.'

'Kill me,' gurgled Alathenar.

Issyk Kul smiled, exposing sharpened teeth and a glistening tongue.

'All in good time,' he said. 'All in good time.'

ELDAIN AND CAELIR spent the next hour in silence, brushing their steeds and carefully grooming them as though they were soon to participate in one of the grand ridings of Tor Elyr. The use of the farrier and stableman's tools was second nature to them, and Eldain found the work cathartic and restful. There was a rhythm and peace in caring for horses that could be found in no other labour. Lotharin and Irenya stood proudly as the two brothers brushed their coats, wound iron cords through their tails and cleared their hooves of stones and earth.

At last they stood back from their mounts, satisfied their work was done. Both brothers had worked up a powerful thirst and appetite, and though Eldain's throat was still bruised from Caelir's earlier assault, he was pleasantly out of breath by the time the two steeds were fully groomed.

'I will fetch food and drink from the kitchens,' said Caelir. 'Clean up and I will see you in the Equerry's Hall.'

Eldain nodded and watched as Caelir left the stables through a side door. Both horses watched him go also, and Eldain stroked their necks. Lotharin's hide gleamed like shimmering oil, while Irenya's dun flanks were like polished mahogany.

'I do not deserve such loyalty,' he said, knowing it was true, but grateful beyond words to know that he was not yet beyond redemption. The horses nuzzled him, and he indulged them momentarily before heading outside. Midmorning sunlight filled the Summer Courtyard, and though he and Caelir were alone, the villa felt more like a home than it had in years.

Eldain made his way to a dry trough built into the eastern wall of the villa. Diverted water from the streams on either side of Ellyr-Charoi should be flowing through these troughs, but only dead leaves filled them now. Eldain bent to scoop leaves from the carved horse's mouth that channelled water out of the trough and back to the stream, then did the same at the other end. No sooner had he scooped out the first handful than water splashed over his hands in a gloriously refreshing spray.

Icy water from the Annulii gurgled into the trough, swiftly filling it and flowing along its length.

He washed his hands and splashed water onto his face, relishing the shock of its coldness. The water tingled with the residue of magic, but what else could he expect when its source was high in a range of mountains suffused with the most elemental energies of the world?

Eldain washed in the glittering water, and by the time he was finished, his skin shone as though rejuvenated. He ran his hands through his hair, aware now of how unkempt he appeared. Riding alone with the wild herds, it was acceptable to look like a rustic, but Eldain was still a noble of Ulthuan, and Ellyr-Charoi was not the open plain.

Refreshed, Eldain climbed the steps of the Hippocrene Tower and stripped out of the clothes he had worn for days. His wardrobe still had a wide sartorial selection, and he chose a tunic of pale cream, over which he slipped a gold edged shirt with silver embroidery at the collar. Next, he selected leggings of soft buckskin and high riding boots of tan leather with a wide heel. Finally, he snapped a black belt around his waist, and fastened it with a golden buckle worked in the form of interlocking horse heads.

With his ensemble complete, Eldain took a silver comb and ran it through his long hair until he was satisfied he had worked out the burrs and knots of the last few weeks travelling. He plaited several iron cords into his hair, and pulled it back into a loose ponytail before securing it at his temples with a circlet of polished ithilmar inset with a liquid sapphire.

Eldain looked in the mirror to check his appearance, and gave himself a curt nod; satisfied he was the equal of his position in attire. A thin smile touched the corner of his lips, as he realised that this was the first time in many a month he had been able to look in the mirror without despising the reflection.

He left his chambers and made his way back down to the Summer Courtyard.

Eldain smiled as he saw that his labours in removing the leaves from the villa's walls had brought water back to more than just the trough. The fountain in the centre of the courtyard now frothed and burbled, the pool slowly filling with cold mountain water. Leaves floated on the surface, and the wind gusted those lying within the courtyard out through the open gates.

'Ellyr-Charoi returns to life,' he said, tilting his head back and allowing the sun to warm his skin. The smell of toasting bread drew his attention to the open doors of the Equerry's Hall. It had been days since Eldain had eaten anything other than berries and leaves, and only now did he realise how famished he was.

He crossed the courtyard and entered the hall. The smell of sweet tisane and toasted bread made his mouth water. The inside of the Equerry's Hall was bright and airy, its shuttered windows now thrown open and the dust of neglect being swept away by a warm wind that blew from the high rafters with soft sighs. Platters of toasted bread and cheese, together with copper ewers sat on the table, and Eldain saw his father's sword lay where his brother had placed it the previous evening.

Caelir stood before a tall portrait depicting a noble elf atop a pure white steed as he slew a foul, mutated beast of the Annulii. Like Eldain, he too had cleaned and washed himself. He wore earthy riding clothes of fine quality, with dark boots and a short cloak of sky blue. A leather circlet wound with bronze cord secured his hair and Eldain smiled to see his brother dressed as an Ellyrian once more.

'I didn't know I looked so heroic,' said Caelir, gesturing towards the picture with what remained of a slice of bread. 'This is me, isn't it?'

'Yes,' said Eldain. 'I had the picture commissioned for Rhianna upon my return from Naggaroth.'

'Ah,' said Caelir. 'It is a memorial.'

'It was,' agreed Eldain, helping himself to a slice of toasted bread. 'Now it is just a portrait, I suppose.'

'It is a good likeness,' said Caelir. 'Who painted it?'

'An artist of Lothern by the name of Uthien Sablehand.'

'He is talented.'

'He ought to be for the money I paid him.'

Caelir turned away from the portrait, and Eldain was struck by how his brother had aged. Though only a few years separated their births, Caelir had always possessed youthful good looks that made that gap appear much larger. Though his features still bore a roguishly handsome cast, his eyes were those of a veteran.

'Nobles of Ulthuan in all their finery,' said Caelir, taking in Eldain's fresh appearance.

'It felt right,' said Eldain.

'It should, brother,' agreed Caelir. 'We are home. Can you feel it welcoming us?'

'I can,' agreed Eldain. 'It is a good feeling and has been too long in coming.'

Caelir finished his bread and poured a goblet of warm tisane. 'Whatever happened to Valeina?' he asked. 'I saw no sign of her in the kitchens or the maids' quarters. Did you dismiss her?'

'No,' said Eldain, accepting the goblet as Caelir poured another for himself. 'When Rhianna and I left for Saphery, she was still here. Perhaps she rejoined her family in Tor Elyr when word came of the attack on the Eagle Gate.'

Caelir nodded and said, 'More than likely.'

Eldain sipped the tisane. It was sweet, but the aftertaste stung the tongue with its sharpness. Eldain recognised the blend of flavours, and was instantly transported back to when he and Caelir were little more than callow youths.

'Mother's recipe,' he said.

'Yes, it seemed appropriate,' said Caelir. 'She was always the one who brought us together after we quarrelled. Father would be content to let us squabble and bicker, but mother could never bear it when we fought.'

Eldain smiled at Caelir's reasoning, and took a seat at the table. He placed the goblet before him and let the familiar smell of wild lemon and honey fill his senses.

'So what do we do now, Caelir?' he asked.

'We talk, brother,' said Caelir, taking the seat next to Eldain.

'What is there left to say that your hands on my neck did not already say?'

Caelir sipped his tisane before answering. 'Tell me all that has happened since your return from Naggaroth.'

'Why?'

'Because I wish to know.'

Eldain began haltingly, telling Caelir of how he had taken care of Rhianna upon his return from the Land of Chill, eventually taking her as his wife. Caelir's jaw tightened at this retelling, but he said nothing as Eldain went on to tell of Ellyr-Charoi's gradual decline and the arrival of Yvraine Hawkblade, the Sword Master from the Tower of Hoeth. He told of their journey across Ulthuan to Saphery, the voyage to the Gaen Vale and finally their arrival in Avelorn.

In return, Caelir told him of his return to Ulthuan, washed ashore on the coastline of Yvresse, and the beautiful girl who had found him on the beach. Caelir's eyes misted over as he told of how Kyrielle Greenkin had nursed him back to health, and Eldain remembered meeting her grieving father on the blasted summit of Bel-Korhadis's tower. Caelir spoke of his journey across the Finuval Plain and his meeting with Narentir's troupe as they made their way to the forest of the Everqueen.

Here again, their stories became intertwined as they relived the moment the dark power hidden within Caelir unleashed its darkest sorcery yet. Both brothers had been cast from the forest and ridden to the one place in Ulthuan where they knew they would find sanctuary.

Ellyr-Charoi.

Worn thin by their respective tales, Eldain and Caelir sat back, their tisanes cold and the bread forgotten. Silence fell, but it was not uncomfortable. At last, Caelir sat forward.

'I wanted to kill you, brother. And I nearly did,' he said. 'But when your eyes closed, all I could think of was a voice I heard in Avelorn.'

'What did you hear?' asked Eldain.

'I think it was the Everqueen,' said Caelir. 'I stood before her with the dagger in my hand and I heard a voice like the most beautiful sunrise of Ellyrion.'

Caelir paused, as though reliving that wondrous voice.

'What did she say?' asked Eldain.

'She told me to flee. And to forgive.'

'Do you think she was talking about me?'

'There is no one else who needs my forgiveness,' pointed out Caelir.

Eldain thought of the last time he had stood in the

presence of the Queen of Avelorn. He remembered the killing light in her eyes, the ancient power that had passed from mother to daughter down the ages since the world was young. There had been little forgiveness in those eyes, yet she had not killed him. The mortal goodness of Alarielle tempered the merciless power of the Everqueen, and *that* had spared Eldain's life.

Now it had spared it again.

'You have a good soul, Caelir,' said Eldain. 'Better, I think, than most. I deserve your hatred, and to let me live speaks greatly of your heart.'

'My soul is not so pure, Eldain, you know that,' said Caelir. 'And I do not hate you. I did, but I believe that is what the Everqueen meant when she told me I had to forgive. Hatred is the root of all evil, brother. It turns good hearts bad, and sows the seeds for all that is ignoble in this world. I will not carry hate in my heart. Not any more.'

'Not even for the druchii?'

Caelir shook his head. 'Not even the druchii. Once they were like us, and perhaps they can be again.'

'The druchii will never let their hatred of us dim,' said Eldain.

'Most likely not,' said Caelir, 'but I will not hate them. Not any more.'

'The Everqueen touched you deeper than you know, brother.'

Caelir laughed, a sound Eldain had never thought to hear again. His younger brother leaned forward and said, 'You may be right, Eldain. She has power beyond anything you or I will ever understand. Something inside me has changed for the better.'

Caelir took Eldain's hand, and Eldain felt closer to his brother now than he ever had before. The connection was powerful, and Caelir's words touched him deeply.

'I was foolish, vain and selfish and cared not a whit for the wants and needs of others,' said Caelir. 'We both had a duty to Ellyr-Charoi and Ulthuan after father died, but I ignored mine. You shouldered my burden, and one soul is not meant to carry the weight of two.'

'Then are we at peace, brother?' asked Eldain.

Caelir said nothing for a few moments, looking over at his portrait.

'Not yet,' he said, 'but I believe we will be. There is still one matter to discuss.'

Eldain knew what this would be without Caelir having to voice it.

'Rhianna,' he said.

'Rhianna,' agreed Caelir. 'She is your wife.'

'Not for long, I would think,' pointed out Eldain. 'She hates me now.'

'For a while she will, but Rhianna is a better person than you or I will ever be. Hate will find no place to lodge within her.'

Eldain dearly hoped so, but knew that even if Caelir was right, he could not remain wedded to Rhianna. He had won her heart through lies, and no relationship could survive being built upon such rotten foundations. He wondered if she would become Caelir's wife, and was surprised to find the thought brought no jealousy or pain.

'So what do we do now?' asked Eldain.

'We ride for Tor Elyr,' said Caelir. 'And we make amends for the damage we have done.'

'Why Tor Elyr?'

'We are sons of Ellyrion, and our land is at war,' said Caelir. 'Where else would we go?'

CHAPTER NINE

WAR CALLS

ELDAIN WALKED LOTHARIN through the gates of Ellyr-Charoi, enjoying the scent of wild flowers borne on the warm summer breeze from the plains. Caelir pulled the gates of their home closed, and Eldain wondered if he would ever return here. Lotharin tossed his mane, stamping at the ground, and Eldain rubbed his neck.

'Patience, great heart,' he said. 'The plains of Ellyrion will be yours to run soon enough.'

'He is impatient,' said Caelir. 'I don't blame him.'

'No, I suppose not. It has been too long since I let him have his head on the steppe.'

Caelir checked Irenya one last time, rubbing her flank with his palm before vaulting into the saddle. For so short a ride to Tor Elyr, a saddle was not necessary, but if they were to ride to war, then it would be madness to fight without one.

'You are a fine steed, of that I have no doubt,' said

Caelir, 'but I miss my Aedaris. He was wide-chested and powerful, with long strides and a heart as big as the ocean. You would have liked him.'

Irenya snorted, and Eldain grinned. 'Spoken like a true steed of Ellyrion,' he said.

Caelir had a fine double-curved bow of yew and star-wood looped over his shoulder, and a host of quivers strapped to Irenya's flanks. A long, curved-bladed sword hung at his hip, for Caelir had insisted that Eldain bear their father's sword.

That blade now hung at Eldain's side, and the weight of duty and responsibility it represented was formidable. He had failed in his duty as a noble of Ulthuan, but he would not fail again. The black handle was wound with thin silver wire, and a polished onyx gleamed at the pommel. He held tight to the sword, its legacy of dutiful service tethering him to this land and his responsibilities more surely than any sworn oath.

Along with his father's sword, Eldain too was armed with a bow, and though other Ellyrians might consider him a competent archer only, that still put him head and shoulders above most others of Ulthuan. He mounted up, and settled himself onto Lotharin's back. This was where he felt most at ease, feeling the land below him through the motion of a fine steed that knew his moods, his skills and his heart better than any other.

They rode down the pathway towards the bridge, enjoying the gentle sway of their mounts and the clear air between them. As they crested the bridge, Eldain felt closer to his brother than he had his entire life.

'It feels good to be riding from Ellyr-Charoi with you, Eldain,' said Caelir. 'Even if it must be to war.'

Eldain nodded and rubbed Lotharin's neck as a shiver

of prescience made him look back over his shoulder.

'I fear war is riding to us,' he said.

Caelir shielded his eyes from the sunlight reflecting on the glittering peaks of the western mountains and the sparkle of magic at their summits. He followed Eldain's gaze towards the cleft in the peaks where the Eagle Gate spanned the pass through the mountains. Thin trails of smoke marred the pale blue of the sky, but it was to the cloud of dust that his eyes were drawn.

'Riders,' said Caelir. 'How many do you think?'

'Maybe three or four hundred,' replied Eldain. 'They are not druchii.'

'No,' agreed Caelir. 'But whoever they are, they are riding at speed.'

'From the Eagle Gate, do you think?'

'They must be,' said Caelir. 'And there can be only one reason why so many horsemen would ride swiftly from Eagle Pass.'

Eldain nodded grimly, and they urged their mounts to greater speed as the pathway wound its way up the hillside towards the road to Tor Elyr. The road they followed was visible only as pale lines in the landscape; nothing so crude or mannish as stone formed the roads of Ulthuan. After an hour, the land levelled out, and Eldain saw the vast sweep of the landscape at a meeting of four roads that converged from the corners of Ellyrion. A tall waystone carved with interlocking circles and images of rearing horses rose from the confluence of the roads like an obsidian fang, and the air around it shimmered with agitation.

'The stone is troubled,' noted Caelir.

'Likely with good reason,' said Eldain, riding Lotharin in a tight circle around it.

To the east, the glittering spires of Tor Elyr were visible as a shimmer of gold and silver against the brilliant blue of the bay in which it sat. A mist from the waters rolled out over the fields and outposts before the city, while to the south, a pall of dark cloud hung low over the landscape. Dancing lights shimmered on the northern horizon, like the glow that smeared the sky when the magic contained within the Annulii surged with vitality.

The western road was known as the Aerie's Path, and Eldain halted Lotharin at its edge as he awaited the arrival of the riders from the pass. It would not be long, for he had set their pace in order to reach the waystone just before them.

Sure enough, the vanguard of the riders from Eagle Pass emerged from a forest of mountain firs. They saw Eldain and Caelir and spurred their mounts onwards.

'Khaine's blood,' swore Caelir as the mounted warriors approached. 'They have ridden their mounts into the ground!'

Eldain felt his brother's anger and recognised it in himself. To treat a horse with such disrespect was inexcusable.

He bit back on his own anger. 'Be calm,' he said. 'Your emotions are being amplified by the waystone's magic.'

'But those horses–'

'Are not ours,' finished Eldain. 'And you do not know from what these warriors ride.'

Caelir said nothing, but urged Irenya away from the waystone, letting his emotions become less volatile. The first warrior rode towards Eldain and raised a hand in greeting.

'Are you from Arandir Swiftwing?' he demanded.

'I am not,' said Eldain. 'I am Eldain Éadaoin, lord of Ellyr-Charoi. This is my brother, Caelir.'

'You have not come from Tor Elyr?'

'No. It is to Tor Elyr that we ride. Have you come from the Eagle Gate?'

The rider nodded. 'We have,' he said breathlessly. 'Or what is left of it. The fortress is taken, and the druchii are marching on the Inner Kingdoms.'

Though Eldain had known that could be the only reason these warriors would ride with such recklessness, it was still a shock to hear that one of Caledor's great mountain fastnesses had fallen to the druchii.

'Are you the commanding officer?' he asked.

'I am now,' said the rider. 'Menethis of Lothern. Adjutant to Glorien Truecrown, who was slain by a traitor in our own ranks, a vile serpent known as Alathenar.'

'Slain by one of your own?' hissed Caelir, riding in from the shadow of the waystone.

'If you can believe such a thing,' said Menethis. 'Barely three hundred of us remain.'

'Why did you ask if we were from Arandir Swiftwing?' asked Eldain. 'You were expecting reinforcements from the lord of Tor Elyr?'

'So said the last missive we received,' agreed Menethis. 'His general, Galadrien Stormweaver, was marching to our relief.'

'We have seen nothing of any relief force,' said Eldain. 'But we have only just ridden from our villa.'

'Then join us in heading east,' implored Menethis. 'For the west is lost.'

Caelir leaned in towards Eldain. 'Most of the warriors of Ellyrion will have gone to Lothern. If Lord Swiftwing has raised an army, it will be the citizen levy only.'

'And what of it?' asked Eldain.

'They will be footsoldiers,' said Caelir. 'If we are to have an advantage in Ellyrion, they must fight on horseback.'

'There will not be enough horses left in Tor Elyr to mount enough of them to make a difference,' pointed out Eldain.

'I know, but there are more than enough on the Ellyrian steppes,' said Caelir. 'Eldain, we have to gather the Great Herd.'

'I know of this Great Herd,' said Menethis, 'but I was led to believe that no one can say for sure when it will gather, and we do not have time to wait. The druchii will be at the gates of Tor Elyr within days.'

'That is indeed true, Menethis,' said Eldain, though his heart beat faster in his chest at the idea of gathering the Great Herd. 'But this is our land and I know the steeds of Ellyrion will heed our call.'

Menethis saw the determination in their faces and said, 'Then I beg you, gather as many as you can and ride to Tor Elyr. I will see you there, and pray to Isha and Asuryan that the stories of your people are true.'

Caelir tugged at Irenya's reins and rode off to the northwest with a wild yell, and Eldain could not resist a flourish of showmanship as Lotharin reared up and pawed the air with his forelegs.

'Farewell, Menethis of Lothern!' he cried, turning his horse to ride after Caelir. 'In two days I will see you in Tor Elyr. And we will have all the herds of Ellyrion at our backs!'

THE UPPER REACHES of the Tower of Hoeth were being rebuilt. Priests of Vaul shaped stone from the Annulii, and the mages in service to Hothar the Fey lifted them into the air on magical currents. At the top of the tower they were set with such precision that none but a master mason could spot the joints between them.

Already the walls destroyed in the aftermath of Caelir's unwitting attack had been raised, and shipwrights from Cothique were singing songs to shape the heartwood beams of the roof. Teclis turned his scarred face to the circle of sky above him, letting the flavoursome tang of woodsap carried on magical currents fill his senses.

He stood with the support of his moon-topped staff, his body not yet healed from the damage done to it in the recent attack. A gift from the Everqueen, the staff was a conduit to the healing magic of Ulthuan, but Teclis had found himself relying on restorative potions brewed by the light of the moons more and more often. Healer-mages had done their best to alleviate the pain, but their power was wholly inadequate to restore him to health.

That Teclis lived at all was little short of a miracle, for the terrible energies unleashed had been at the limits of control, and only magic beyond the reach of any save the mages of old could completely undo the damage. Many others would never get the chance to heal: mages, Sword Masters and Kyrielle Greenkin, daughter of Anurion the Green. The darkness hidden within Caelir by the Hag Sorceress had consumed her utterly, using her innocence as fuel for its destruction.

'How like Morathi to twist purity into a weapon,' he whispered, as a measure of guilt for Kyrielle's death settled upon him. Her father remained at the Tower of Hoeth, channelling all his energies into aiding the priests of Vaul in their war-magic, accelerating the growth of arrow shafts that were as straight as sunlight to be fitted with enchanted arrowheads that could pierce even the thickest armour. Anurion grew spear shafts that would seek out an enemy's flesh in forests around the tower, and shaped bowstaves of golden heartwood for the citizen militias of Saphery.

Teclis could understand such industry, knowing it was always better to avenge a loss with positive action instead of wallowing in grief. Anurion would not rest until the druchii were cast from Ulthuan, but the true measure of his character would come when the war was over. Teclis knew that vengeance was a poor motive for action, but in times such as these, it was more common than any other.

Once more he cursed his obsessive need to know everything, to understand the workings of the universe and all its complexities. Morathi had known he would not be able to resist plumbing the depths of Caelir's mind and unlocking the barriers within.

But just as Morathi knew Teclis, so too did he know her.

The Witch King would be content simply to destroy the asur, but so mundane a thing as annihilation would not satisfy Morathi. No, her ambitions went beyond simple conquest into the realms of madness.

She wanted more, and Teclis had an idea what that might be.

He drew on the power of his staff and sent his magesight over the landscape of Saphery, swooping low over the ravaged landscape around the tower. He rose into the sky, passing through the clouds and pulling away from the world below. Teclis found peace here, a refuge from the pain of his weakened flesh, and a measure of calm that could only be achieved without the pull of flesh to intrude.

Much of his recovery had been spent in such fugue states, his consciousness divorced from his body and roaming the land on the currents of magic that flowed around Ulthuan. He had seen the bolt that killed Glorien Truecrown, and watched as his twin pulled the elven forces back from the shoulder fortresses at the Emerald Gate.

Druchii ships now roamed the mouth of the Straits of Lothern, but they did not yet dare to push on the Sapphire Gate. The floating mountain that housed an army of druchii lurked somewhere off the southern coast of Ulthuan, but even Teclis could not penetrate the cloaking shadows that concealed it.

An enemy army now bore down on the defenders of Ellyrion, and it was only a matter of time until the warriors at Lothern were under full attack. Teclis let the currents of magic carry him into the north, hoping to learn more of the Everqueen's plans. A wall of mist and magic shimmered at the borders of Avelorn and not even he would risk attempting to scry beyond its boundaries.

Teclis opened his eyes and let the full weight of his body return as his spirit-self settled back in his bones. Never had Ulthuan needed him more, and he was weaker than at any other time in his life.

'Why must we always face such times at our worst?' he whispered.

'Because war never comes when your enemy knows you are strong,' said the voice of Loremaster Belannaer. Teclis smiled to hear his old master.

'Always the teacher, my friend,' said Teclis.

'You may have surpassed me in ability, but you will never surpass me in age and hoary wisdom.'

Teclis turned and gave a short bow, acknowledging

the venerable Loremaster's words. Swathed in a glittering robe that shimmered with captured starlight, Belannaer wore his long white hair unbound by circlet or helm, and his long face was old even among a race that lived on the edge of immortality. Belannaer had worked his enchantments when Bel-Hathor ruled the asur, and only Teclis had a greater understanding of the workings of magic.

Two other mages stood with Belannaer, Anurion the Green and Mitherion Silverfawn – father of Rhianna Silverfawn. Both were drawn and tired looking after many weeks of imbuing weapons and armour with war-magic. Four Sword Masters accompanied them, for no mage of Saphery walked unescorted now. Their presence helped Teclis settle back into his flesh, for they were elves firmly rooted in the physical world.

'My friends,' said Teclis. 'It is good to see you.'

'And you, Teclis,' said Mitherion Silverfawn. 'You are looking better every day.'

'And you are a rogue, Master Silverfawn,' said Teclis, moving to sit on the padded litter that had been his sickbed since the attack. 'I am weary and heartsick, but I appreciate the sentiment. How does your work proceed?'

'It progresses, Warden,' said Mitherion. 'I have studied the celestial movements closely, and, well, the signs are not good.'

'Elaborate, please.'

Mitherion retrieved a series of scrolls from the Sword Master behind him and unrolled the largest on a table already piled haphazardly with heavy books, hourglasses, moonstones and empty glass vials. Teclis limped over and studied the astronomical chart, its midnight blue surface covered in arcing silver orbits, geometric patterns and intersecting lines. Teclis knew enough to know that he was looking at a map of the heavens, but so cluttered was it with Mitherion's notes, observations and postulations that it was next to impossible to read.

'Damn you, Mitherion,' said Anurion, scanning the map. 'This is unreadable.'

'There's a system, Anurion,' said Mitherion. 'You just need to know the system. It's really quite simple.'

'Then how is it that only you know it?' demanded Anurion, his tolerance for Mitherion's eccentricities wearing thin.

'Because no one else has the patience to learn it,' snapped Mitherion. 'Now, if I may continue?'

Teclis nodded and Mitherion traced a slender finger over a curving line that arced across the page to intersect with a number of other lines, some geometric, some arrow-straight and others curved.

'The stars move strangely, Warden,' said Mitherion. 'The Chaos moon passes close to our world and introduces many variables of incalculable complexity into any equation. Which means any conclusion drawn from such equations must be viewed with a degree of uncertainty.'

'In other words, nothing you say can be trusted to be accurate?' said Anurion.

'Not as such,' said Mitherion, ignoring Anurion's hostility. 'I can read the patterns of the stars and offer insight into aspects of the world. But any prediction, no matter how apparently certain it might be, is always subject to the vagaries of chance.'

'What have you learned?' asked Teclis, forestalling another comment from Anurion.

'The stars are not right,' said Mitherion.

'Not right?' asked Belannaer. 'What does that mean?'

Mitherion tapped the map and said, 'In every path of the future I have followed, the stars move out of alignment with the routes they currently trace across the sky.'

'What could cause that?' asked Anurion.

'Only one thing I can think of,' said Mitherion.

'Well don't keep us in suspense,' demanded Anurion. 'What?'

'The only way we would be seeing an effect like this would be if our world were no longer following the same course it is now,' said Mitherion. 'You must understand that even a tiny shift in this world's path would be catastrophic. Depending on whether we are carried closer or farther from the sun, our world could be doomed to an eternal ice age or every living thing might be burned from its surface.'

'What could cause the world to shift like that?' asked Belannaer.

'A vast outpouring of magic,' said Teclis.

'That is what I thought at first,' agreed Mitherion, 'but there is no magicker on this world capable of wielding such power. Not even the lizard lords in their jungle temples can cast magic that powerful. It must be something else.'

'I believe I know what is powerful enough to throw our world out of its proper place in the heavens,' said Teclis, bowing his head and sighing deeply. 'I had hoped I might be wrong, but I believe your calculations have confirmed my worst fear, Master Silverfawn.'

Belannaer moved to stand beside Teclis and put a hand on his shoulder.

'She would not dare, Teclis,' said the ancient Loremaster. 'Caledor would know of it and he will not allow his great work to be undone.'

'Perhaps so,' agreed Teclis. 'But five millennia have passed since those days. Who can say what remains of Caledor and his convocation? Morathi is cunning beyond measure, and she has had a long time to find a way to hide her presence from his mage-sight. We can afford to take nothing for granted.'

'Isha preserve us,' hissed Anurion as he grasped the horrific scale of the threat to Ulthuan and the world.

Teclis looked up and the weakness that had plagued him earlier returned with greater potency. He sagged against the table, and but for the hand of Belannaer and Mitherion, he would have fallen to the floor. They carried him to his litter and laid him upon it.

He tried to muster a smile to allay their fears, but saw they were unconvinced.

'In the days to come, the armies of the asur will have need of our powers,' he said. 'I cannot take to the field of battle, so you must lead my mages and Sword Masters to war. I regret that I must ask even you, Belannaer, to take up the blade of Bel-Korhadris one last time.'

'It will be my honour to fight for Ulthuan, Teclis,' said Belannaer. 'I always knew there would be one last challenge ahead of me before I might find my peace.'

'Lead the mages of fire and water to Lothern,' said Teclis. 'Counsel Tyrion and Finubar, for they are warriors and are ruled by the heart. They will have need of your wisdom in the dark days to come, Tyrion especially…'

Teclis turned to Anurion and Mitherion. 'My friends, you must take the mages of sky and earth to Ellyrion. Morathi herself leads a host of dark warriors from the mountains, and she must be stopped before the walls of Tor Elyr, whatever the cost may be.'

A shadow passed over Teclis's features, and his gaze

fell upon the celestial map belonging to Mitherion Silverfawn. 'And I fear it will be a bitter cost to bear.'

THEY CHASED THE sun as it edged across the vastness of the sky, angling their course towards the rivers that flowed from the Annulii to the Inner Sea. The herds roamed freely over the wide steppes of Ellyrion, but Eldain knew they would not stray too far from water. He rode Lotharin hard, letting the horse have its head as it stretched its muscles in a flat out run. Caelir galloped beside him, letting Irenya understand a measure of Lotharin's strength.

She was an Ellyrian steed, haughty and proud, but she quickly grasped that she was not the equal of Lotharin. It felt good to ride the steppe, letting his mount choose their path, for he was bound to this land in ways Eldain would never understand, and knew where the leaders of the herds were likely to be found.

They rode past scattered villages, all now empty of elves, and isolated woods of larch and evergreens. The landscape felt empty, and the soft light of eternal summer spread an indolent blanket over the horizon. Heat haze rippled from the undulant hills of the middle distance and the gauzy cornfields of their surroundings.

Eldain could see no horses, and his heart sank at the prospect of finding none of the herds. He had proudly boasted that they would bring the Great Herd to Tor Elyr, but Ellyrion was silent, even the capering sprites and darting creatures of magic that haunted the hidden places of magic and mystery keeping far from sight.

He halted Lotharin at the top of a rounded hill, letting his mount catch his breath as Caelir and Irenya drew alongside.

'Where are the herds?' asked Caelir.

'They feel the coming of the druchii and are keeping to their secret watering holes,' said Eldain. 'They know the dark kin will try to break them and force them to serve our enemies.'

'So how do we find them?'

Eldain considered the question. Even a warrior of Ellyrion could search the plains for a lifetime and never find the hidden ranges of the herds. Such places were known only to horsekind, and the first elves to settle in Ellyrion had always respected their privacy. It would be impossible to find the herds unless they wished to be found.

'We have to bring the herds out onto the plains,' said Eldain.

'And how do we do that, brother?'

Eldain looked out over the majestic sweep of Ellyrion, drinking in the wondrous vista before him like a tonic. His eyes lost their focus as his soul was drawn into the magnificence of this bounteous kingdom, feeling the heartbeat of its unchanging season as a slow warmth in his blood. The golden land stretched as far as the eye could see, a verdant paradise of bountiful fields, rolling plains and endless acres upon which to ride. Thick forests of evergreens shawled the foothills of the mountains to provide the herds with shade, rivers of fresh water fed their watering holes and the vast expanse of flat earth was their playground.

No finer land for horses existed in the world, as though the gods had crafted this land for the herds and not the asur.

'Brother?' said Caelir.

'The steeds of Ellyrion know this land better than the asur,' said Eldain, his voice soft and dreamlike. 'It is through the land we will reach the herds.'

'What do you mean?'

'I mean we must ride!' shouted Eldain, standing tall in his saddle and galloping down the hillside. 'Ride like the horse lords of old!'

Lotharin surged downhill, his long legs bunching and stretching as he thundered across the plains. Grassland and forest, hill and stream flashed past as he galloped faster and harder than ever before. Eldain hung on tight, letting the horse remember its heritage as a proud steed of Ellyrion.

Caelir and Irenya followed him, the mare galloping for all she was worth, and feeling the power of the land surging through her as she strove to keep up with Eldain and Lotharin. Eldain held tight to Lotharin's mane, feeling the magic of Ulthuan in every pounding hoof beat and every sway and stretch of the horse's back. This was what it meant to be an Ellyrian, to ride like the gods across the face of the world and feel the land respond.

Eldain risked a glance over at Caelir, and laughed as he saw his brother holding on for dear life, terrified and exhilarated in equal measure. No words needed to pass between them, for both understood that this was the ride of their lives. Even were they to die in the next few moments, neither would have any regrets.

Never had Eldain ridden so fast, not even when escaping the shipyards of Clar Karond. His hair whipped his face and his eyes watered in the wind as he leaned low over Lotharin's neck. He whooped and yelled with a mixture of fear and excitement, knowing that at such speed, the slightest mistake would see him hurled from the saddle. An Ellyrian steed would never normally allow its rider to fall, but even Lotharin would not be able to save him were he to lose focus for even a second.

Ellyrion whipped past in a blur. Eldain had no idea where they were; fields, forest, rivers and hills flashing by in a golden-green blur. Lotharin eased into a sweeping curve, and Irenya came alongside, her eyes wide and ears pressed flat against her skull. Ellyrion responded to their wild ride, and the earth beneath the horses released its magic in a shimmer of starfire that billowed from the ground like mist. Eldain felt the power of his homeland in every breath, like taking in a lungful of cold air on a frosty morning.

It filled him with light, and he saw the pulsing lines of magical energy running through the world, a rainbow hued storm that roared across the face of the landscape. These iridescent colours disturbed not a blade of grass or so much as a single leaf, yet they flowed through every living thing, leaving behind a measure of their essence. Eldain gathered that power within him, shaping it into a wordless cry of supplication.

He loosed that power not with words, but through the might of his steed, letting it carry his message to the Ellyrion herds through the thunder of its hooves upon the earth. Lotharin ran faster than he ever would again, blowing hard as he leapt a wide streambed. Irenya could not match his leap, and Caelir turned her towards a shingled ford as Eldain and Lotharin rode ever onwards. The river of colour faded from sight, and he let out a cry of loss as his mortal eyes lost the sight of his homeland's magic.

Yet as the blinding light of magic faded from his sight, he saw that he no longer rode alone. Dozens of horses surrounded him, duns, blacks, greys, whites, dappled and bay, piebald and silver. Herds from all across Ellyrion galloped over the plains beside him, and more were coming with every passing moment. They emerged from forest shadows, from hidden gullies and sheltered dips in the land. They answered the call of one of the sons of Ellyrion, and they came in their entirety.

Eldain watched with tears in his eyes as the Great Herd formed around him. The silver horseleaders ran with Lotharin, unspoken communication passing between them. Caelir and Irenya were behind him, galloping in the midst of a host of white-gold horses. Caelir waved at him, and Eldain's heart surged with joy to see so many had answered his call. Billowing clouds of dust hid the true numbers of the herd, but the beating war drum of their hooves and the snorting bellows of myriad herds told Eldain that more than enough had come.

At last, Lotharin could run no more, and Eldain gently eased the horse into a wide turn that bled off his speed. Lotharin's flanks heaved and bellowed, and Eldain knew his steed had run himself to the edge of destruction. Even a horse as mighty as Lotharin had his limits, and they had reached them.

The Great Herd followed his lead, slowing until Eldain and Caelir sat in the midst of a thousands-strong herd of proud steeds. His brother rode alongside him, both he and Irenya blown and exhausted. Yet the thrill of the wild ride across the face of Ellyrion had left its mark on them both. The mare's eyes shone with delight, and Caelir's face was that of an excited child.

'Brother,' gasped Caelir. 'Not even Tyrion and Malhandir could have ridden like that.'

Eldain reached out and gripped his brother's shoulder.

'The ride of our lives, eh, Caelir?' he said.

'No one has gathered a herd like this in ten lifetimes,' swore Caelir. 'Even the first Ellyrians never knew such joy.'

'We called and they came,' said Eldain. 'And now we ride for Tor Elyr.

Chapter Ten

The Glittering Host

Considered by many of the asur to be the most beautiful city in Ulthuan, Tor Elyr nestled on the shores of the Sea of Dusk within a placid bay of mirror-smooth water. Glittering castles of silver rose from forested islands of smooth marble, each like sheer pinnacles of ice crafted by a master sculptor. Tapered domes of azure and gold capped these towers, and finials bearing pennants of emerald and ruby snapped in the wind blowing off the sea.

A web of crystal bridges linked the hundreds of island castles, grown from the living rock by spellsingers of old, and a handful of crimson-sailed ships plied the waters beneath them. Tendrils of mist coiled around the base of each island, and faint songs of lament echoed from the peaked castles as the mothers and wives of Tor Elyr sang to the gods to watch over those who rode to war.

High atop a carven balcony, the lord of Tor Elyr,

Arandir Swiftwing, listened to the songs of his city and pondered on the vagaries of time. The asur were a long-lived race, yet their survival might yet come down to a matter of days. In the end, didn't everything depend on timing? A warrior might deflect an enemy's blow, and a heartbeat later could be struck down by another or dodge aside at the last moment.

Or a poison-tipped crossbow bolt might slay a beloved steed so swiftly that she could not prevent herself from rolling over her rider and crushing him beneath her weight...

As always when he thought of Sarothiel, Lord Swiftwing's hand strayed to his twisted and misshapen hip. Slain beneath him in a skirmish with druchii raiders seeking to plunder the northern herds of Ellyrion, his steed had rolled on top of him and smashed his pelvis. The healers had been unable to reknit the bone, and his muscles had reformed wrongly around the ossified mass.

Thirty years later, he still walked with a painful limp, and his days of riding out with his warriors were over.

He hated the Fates of Morai-Heg that she had cursed him so. A lord of Ellyrion who could not ride. It would be funny if it were not so painful to think about.

Lord Swiftwing pushed aside these bitter memories, and stared into the west. The storm-wreathed Annulii dominated the horizon, and though the mages advised it best not to stare too long into the clouds of magic, he could not tear his eyes from the seething cauldron of power that thundered between their peaks.

Morathi's army was marching on his city from those mountains.

Impossible as it was to believe, the Eagle Gate had fallen, and the three hundred survivors of that disaster

painted a bleak picture of the power and size of that
host. Lord Swiftwing could defend Ellyrion against Morathi's army with more warriors, but the Phoenix King
had all but emptied Tor Elyr for the battle at Lothern.

He had baulked at the idea of sending the majority
of his warriors to Lothern, but Finubar had assured him
that none of the gateway fortresses could be taken. Tor
Elyr was quite safe, Finubar had said, and Lord Swiftwing
felt his lip curl in a sneer at the thought of the Phoenix
King's empty promises.

'That's what you get when you choose a king who
thinks only of lands far from home,' he whispered, as
the light moved from afternoon to the gloaming. He dis-
liked this time of day, for it was a shadowy cloak that
concealed assassins or spies, and returned to the candle-
lit warmth of his chambers.

As befitted a noble of Ellyrion, his quarters were clean
and sparsely decorated, with only a few trophies taken in
his time as a Reaver Knight hanging on the walls. Numerous bookshelves sagged under the weight of treatises on
mounted warfare, with one such essay penned by no less
a figure than Aenarion himself. Admittedly, his tactical
writings dealt with fighting from the back of a dragon,
but the fact that the Defender's hand had touched that
scroll was reason enough to treasure it. These days, warriors of Ulthuan were fortunate if they had even *seen* a
dragon, let alone fought from the back of one.

He paused by a table heaped with hastily scrawled des-
patches and idly flicked through them, carefully reading
those that caught his eye, and discarding those that did
not. Much of what he read was concerned with the current muster of citizen soldiers. With the majority of his
city's warriors now fighting at Lothern, Lord Swiftwing

had been forced to spread the net of his levy far wider than at any other time in Ellyrion's history. He had mustered an army and sent its most experienced warriors with his best general into the west to relieve the beleaguered defenders of the Eagle Gate.

But what a difference a few days could make.

Barely had the relief force departed Tor Elyr than word had come that the fortress was lost. Galadrien Stormweaver had returned the previous evening, and Lord Swiftwing had watched the general's dejected riders climb the crystal bridge to Castle Ellyrus, the gateway to Tor Elyr. A warrior named Menethis of Lothern had brought three hundred warriors who had escaped the slaughter at the Eagle Gate to Tor Elyr this morning. It was a paltry force, but any additions to Lord Swiftwing's army were welcome, especially as they were veterans.

And Asuryan knew, he needed veterans!

Nearly eight thousand citizen soldiers were now under arms in Tor Elyr, yet Lord Swiftwing knew that number concealed the fact that many of these would normally be considered too young or too old to fight in the battle line. With nowhere near enough horses in his stables, most of these soldiers would need to fight on foot, which was anathema to warriors of Ellyrion.

A door opened, and a gust of wind blew out a handful of candles. Irritated, Lord Swiftwing glowered at the venerable elf that entered his chambers with a wooden tray bearing a steaming goblet of honeyed wine and several bottles of warmed oils.

'Casadesus, you are as clumsy as an ogre,' snapped Lord Swiftwing.

'My apologies, my lord,' said Casadesus. 'I shall

endeavour to ease the winds around your tower before I enter next time.'

Casadesus had served Lord Swiftwing for the entirety of his adult life, since before the ascension of Finubar to the Phoenix Throne. He had borne Lord Swiftwing's banner when the Ellyrians rode to war, they had watched friends pass away and, as was the way of things, they had grown old together. Lord Swiftwing's wife was long dead, his daughter apprenticed to a mage at the Tower of Hoeth and his sons abroad somewhere in the Old World. Casadesus was the only family he had left, and no one got under Lord Swiftwing's skin like family.

'Whatever happened to the notion of bondsmen showing respect?' he grumbled.

'I suspect the same thing that happened to nobles having nobility.'

Lord Swiftwing grunted and said, 'You should have gone to Saphery. Or Yvresse. It's not safe in Ellyrion anymore.'

Casadesus shook his head. 'I am where I need to be, my lord.'

'I released you from your service to me a century ago, there is no need for you to stay.'

'I remain here for the same reason you do, my lord,' said Casadesus, placing the tray on the table and handing Swiftwing the goblet.

'And what reason is that?'

'Duty, my lord. You have yours and I have mine. Now, drink the wine and sit down.'

Lord Swiftwing knew better than to argue, and took a long draught of the warmed wine. It was sweet and cloying, just the way he liked it, and the medicinal powders sprinkled through it gave it a grainy texture. Immediately, he felt its soothing balm and lowered himself onto the specially carved chair that allowed him to sit with the least amount of discomfort.

Casadesus sat on a stool opposite and lifted Lord Swiftwing's leg to rest upon his knees. He grunted in pain, but knew better than to complain. Slowly and with deft finger strokes, Casadesus worked the warmed oils into the knotted muscle tissue of his leg. Alchemists and healing mages had produced a poultice that eased the pain of his wound, though it could never undo the damage. Every night, Casadesus would massage his ruined leg, and every morning he would be able to walk without pain until the effect of the poultice wore off.

'I hear Stormweaver is back,' said Casadesus, working his thumbs deep into the muscle of Lord Swiftwing's thigh.

'That he is,' agreed Lord Swiftwing.

'Then it is true? The Eagle Gate has fallen?'

'You already know the answer, so why ask the question?'

'I was taught to only trust first hand information, not rumour or hearsay.'

'Yes, the Eagle Gate has fallen, and yes, Stormweaver has returned,' snapped Lord Swiftwing. 'Anything else?'

'I wondered if you had received any responses to the messages you sent to King Finubar and the Warden of Tor Yvresse,' said Casadesus without looking up.

Lord Swiftwing sighed. 'No, there have been no responses, and nor do I expect any. Finubar has stripped my city of warriors and is not about to send them back when his own city is threatened. As to Eltharion, he broods in his miserable city of shadows and pretends the rest of the world does not exist. His land is free of invaders, yet he sends no warriors to me or to Finubar!'

Casadesus paused in his massage. 'Tor Yvresse is a city of ghosts, my lord. There are fewer warriors in Lord Eltharion's city than in Tor Elyr. If our situations were reversed and he sent *us* a request for aid, would you send him any troops?'

'With so few warriors left to defend my city? No, I would not,' said Lord Swiftwing with a wry smile. 'There you go using logic again. Did I not tell you that it is unwise to point out the flaws in a noble's reasoning?'

'You did, but I chose to view that as advice rather than an order.'

Before Lord Swiftwing could respond, a single note from an elven war horn blew from one of the northern islands. Both men looked up as other horns joined it, the glorious trumpeting growing in power until a chorus of triumphant music was blowing from every tower of Tor Elyr.

Casadesus helped Lord Swiftwing to his feet, and together they made their way out onto the balcony over-looking the city and the endless plains beyond. The pain in his leg was forgotten as Lord Swiftwing gripped the stone balustrade and his heart leapt with excitement at the sight before him.

'I don't believe it…' gasped Casadesus.

Lord Swiftwing wept tears of joy, knowing he would never see so fine a sight in all the days left to him. The wide open plains before the city were awash with horses, thousands of wild animals galloping towards the gate in a thundering herd of many colours. At their head rode two warriors, one mounted on a midnight-black steed, the other upon a dun mare.

'The Great Herd,' said Lord Swiftwing.

'How is this possible?' asked Casadesus.

'I do not know, but Asuryan has smiled on us this day.'

Though hot steam filled the air of the cavern, Prince Imrik felt a chill deep in his bones. Clad only in a loincloth, his muscular body was now thin and gaunt, like the starved prisoners he had rescued from a druchii slave ship so many years ago. He sat cross-legged, with his arms hanging at his side and his breath coming in long, soft breaths.

He had lost track of how long he had been here, for nothing ever changed in the cave of dragons. Their great, slumbering hearts beat ever on with gelid slowness, never varying their cadence or tempo. Sleep had stolen upon him in the times between songs, and his dreams had been filled with the faces of lost loved ones and never-won glories. Each time he would wake and curse the weakness that had seen him sleep. Then he would sing, filling the air with the wondrous sound of dragonsong.

Minaithnir had taught him these songs many decades ago, placing the words that were not words and the music that was not music directly into his mind. Until now, he had never heard the songs sung aloud, and he wept as he finally gave them voice. Their soft beauty was quite at odds with the creatures that created them, and Imrik dearly wished his race had known of these songs in ages past.

His eyes closed as he felt the dragonsong draw on his strength for sustenance, for such magical sounds could not be sustained simply by a mortal's voice. His breathing slowed as the song flowed from him and Imrik felt as though his mind was sinking into a forgotten trench at the bottom of the ocean where monstrous beasts made their lairs.

The darkness was complete, yet this was as close as he had come to reaching the vast, unfathomable consciousnesses of the dragons. In this deep, dark, unreachable place, their minds roamed free, too vast and too far beyond mortal comprehension to be confined within their skulls. In this place of emptiness, the dragons dreamed of distant stars and the myriad worlds that circled them.

The dragonsong surrounded Imrik, and he felt the steady heartbeat of something infinitely more colossal than he could ever imagine pounding in the darkness. If the heartbeat of the dragons was infinitesimally slow, this was yet slower. He had no idea to what he was listening, but no sooner had he wondered at its origin than the answer was given to him.

This was the heartbeat of the world, and Imrik at last recognised the truth of the dragons.

They were linked with the world in ways too complex to fully understand, but Imrik knew enough of dragons to know that as the world cooled, so too did their hearts. The dragons were as much a part of the world as were its rivers and forests, its mountains and deserts. As one rose, the other rose; as one declined, so too did the other.

Imrik felt the colossal presences of the dragons as their minds finally registered his intrusion into their shared dreamspace. As a man might regard a fleabite, so Imrik was to the dragons; an irritant; something so trivial and minor that he was virtually beneath their notice.

Yet they *had* noticed him.

Though he knew his body did not exist in this darkness, he sang the dragonsong with ever more passion, allowing the wordless music free rein within his flesh.

Take of me what you must, but hear me dragonkin! I am Imrik, and Ulthuan needs you!

Other minds, still immense, but smaller than the glittering, star-filled presences of the most ancient dragons, darted around him. They looked at him as a curiosity, a diversion to be toyed with and enjoyed for a brief spell while they slept away the ages. It was the tiniest connection, but it was more than he had managed in all the days he had been singing.

A yellow eye, slitted like a cat's, opened in the darkness before him. Enormous beyond words, it filled the void, a sensory organ as vast as a landscape. It regarded Imrik curiously, before deciding he was unworthy of attention. The mind's eye closed and Imrik was once again plunged into sightless oblivion. He screamed his frustration into the void as his hold on the dragonsong faltered.

No sooner had its ritual rhythms been disrupted than his connection to this dream world was ended. His spirit was hurled back to the world above, and Imrik opened his eyes with a great intake of breath and a cry of frustration bursting from his throat.

He had been so close!

Feeling as weak as a newborn foal, Imrik calmed his frayed nerves and slowed the rapid tattoo of his heart. His hands were shaking and his throat was raw with the effort of shaping songs that no mortal was ever meant to sing.

'You heard me!' he wept. 'Why do you not wake?'

He knew the answer, and his heart sank with the knowledge that he could never reach the minds of the dragons. The world was dying, and the magic of Ulthuan faded with every passing moment the druchii stood upon its soil.

The heat of the cavern enfolded him, yet Imrik felt only the cold of the grave.

Though he knew it would eventually kill him, Imrik began the dragonsong once more.

THE CASTLE AT the heart of Tor Elyr had been built by the first horsemasters of Ellyrion, and was the ancestral dwelling place of the city's master. Such was its age that no difference could be seen in the stone of its walls and the rock upon which it was built. As though its alabaster walls had grown from the island, the castle soared gracefully from the water like a linked series of stalagmites carved in glistening marble and polished quartz. Its many towers were studded with windows and roofed in gold, but it was in the chamber at the castle's heart where Lord Swiftwing gathered his most trusted warriors for councils of war.

Known as the Reaver Hall, its walls were fashioned from cream marble threaded with gold veins, and its icy rafters were hung with ancient and colourful banners depicting galloping horses, proud manes and crossed lances. Many of these were from the time of Caledor the Conqueror, and one was even said to have been borne alongside Caradryel as he ordered the last retreat from the Old World.

It never failed to move Lord Swiftwing whenever he came here, for it was a potent reminder of the long and faithful service of Ellyrion to the Phoenix Throne. His own banner bore the image of a rearing silver horse upon a crimson field. That banner still had pride of place above his starwood throne, which sat at the head of a

long oval table that filled the bulk of the chamber, but
never more would Casadesus bear it into battle.

He smiled as his earlier reflections on the nature of
time returned to him.

A lifeline had been thrown to the warriors of Tor Elyr
this day.

And not just one.

Less than an hour after Lord Éadaoin and his brother
had brought the Great Herd to Ellyrion, a silver-hulled
vessel had emerged from the mists at the mouth of the
bay and docked with the great castle at the centre of Tor
Elyr. None of the sentries had spotted the vessel, but
upon seeing the silvery moon emblazoned upon the vessel's sail, Lord Swiftwing understood how such a vessel
could have escaped detection.

The ship had sailed from Saphery, and many of its pas-
sengers were mages of that enchanted kingdom. In the
space of a single day, Tor Elyr had been blessed by the
arrival of enough horses to mount whole companies of
the citizen levy, and a convocation of mages powerful
enough to lay waste to any enemy that dared attack the
city.

Galadrien Stormweaver stood at the head of the table
with his most experienced Reaver Knights close to him,
as the commanders of horse he had appointed took their
seats. As nobles and bringers of the Great Herd, Lord
Swiftwing had graciously allowed the brothers Éadaoin
to attend this meeting.

As the masters of the Sapherian mages entered the
hall, Lord Swiftwing immediately knew that had been
a mistake.

The mage known as Anurion the Green blanched at
the sight of Caelir Éadaoin, and Lord Swiftwing felt the

powerful build up of magic. Clad in an emerald robe tied at the waist with a belt of woven ferns, Anurion's eyes flashed with hostility and his hand snatched at the silver pendant around his neck.

'You!' he cried, and everyone in the hall staggered under the force of his words. Killing fire leapt to life around Anurion's hands, and the lethal taste of war-magic filled the air in the Reaver Hall with an actinic flavour like the aftermath of an Annulii lightning storm.

Lord Swiftwing's knights reached for their swords, but he stopped them with a gesture, knowing it would be suicidal to intervene when such powerful magic was involved. The other warriors in the hall rose from their seats in alarm, but took their lead from Lord Swiftwing and did not intervene.

The elf next to Anurion, a tall, distinguished mage in a cobalt blue robe, named Mitherion Silverfawn, put a hand on Anurion's shoulder, but it was angrily shrugged off.

Caelir Éadaoin stood, and Lord Swiftwing saw the terrible guilt etched on his face. The boy's brother stood, but Caelir shook his head and he sat back down.

'Anurion,' said Silverfawn. 'Control yourself.'

'He killed my daughter,' said Anurion, tears of sorrow spilling down his face.

'No,' said Mitherion. 'Not him. He was an innocent victim of the Hag Sorceress.'

'It was him,' wept Anurion. 'I saw Kyrielle die, Mitherion. I saw my daughter die.'

Caelir moved around the table, taking measured steps towards Anurion the Green, and Lord Swiftwing held his breath. The tension was almost unbearable, for the proximity of such bellicose magic surged through every warrior's veins like the first moments of battle.

'Master Anurion,' said Caelir, bowing to the powerful mage. 'You have every reason to hate me, and I would not blame you if you were to kill me. Isha knows I took your daughter from you after she was kind enough to welcome me into your home. You gave me shelter and tried to help me. I repaid you with betrayal, and for that I am truly sorry.'

Anurion took a step towards Caelir, and the deadly fire wreathing his hands shone from the marble walls of the Reaver Hall. Lord Swiftwing saw Galadrien Stormweaver ease his sword from its sheath and shook his head firmly. The sword emerged no further from the sheath, but neither was it replaced.

'She was the light of my life,' said Anurion. 'Of all the wonders in my life, none was brighter and more beautiful than her. And you ended her…'

Caelir nodded and said, 'I understand, and I share your pain. Not a day has passed since that moment I do not think of Kyrielle and the light I took from you and Ulthuan. I am truly sorry for what happened, but I swear I knew nothing of the darkness within me.'

'The boy speaks the truth, Anurion,' said Mitherion. 'You heard Teclis say the same thing.'

'When she died I swore I would destroy you,' said Anurion, placing his hand on Caelir's chest. 'I dreamed of killing you every day.'

'If that is what you wish, then I will not stop you,' said Caelir.

As though in response, the wooden floor buckled and warped as new buds sprouted from the living wood and swelled upwards with surging growth. Pulsing tendrils of sapwood writhed like kraken tentacles as they wrapped themselves around Caelir's legs. Upwards they climbed, enveloping his torso and upper body, and Lord Swiftwing knew that they could crush Caelir Éadaoin to death in an instant.

'I loved her so much,' said Anurion, as the sweet-smelling branches tightened on Caelir's body. 'You took everything she had and everything she was going to do. Ulthuan is the poorer for her absence.'

Caelir nodded and said, 'I loved her too, and could never have knowingly hurt her. But do with me as you will, Master Anurion. You deserve your vengeance.'

Anurion's fist clenched and Lord Swiftwing felt sure he would do as Caelir Éadaoin bid. Slowly his fingers uncurled, and he lowered his hand. The roots holding Caelir released their grip, the incredible growth reversing as suddenly as it had begun until no trace remained that they had existed at all.

'Kyrielle would never forgive me,' he said as the last of the magic faded. 'I know it was the crone of Naggaroth who killed my daughter, but it is painful for me to look upon your face, Caelir Éadaoin.'

'I understand,' said Caelir.

Mitherion Silverfawn eased Caelir away from the grieving mage, and led him back to where his brother sat. The mage spoke quietly to the Éadaoin brothers, and Lord Swiftwing saw there was clearly some connection between them as they embraced with the sadness of grieving relatives instead of friends.

Anurion the Green took a seat at the table and folded his arms. Lord Swiftwing let out a relieved breath and waved everyone in the hall back to their seats. He blinked the last remnants of Anurion's magic from his eyes and pushed himself to his feet. He winced in expectation of pain, but none came, and he smiled at such an unexpected boon.

'Now that we are all friends again, I suggest we turn our attention to the coming war with the druchii,' said Lord Swiftwing. 'Unless there are any more dramatic reunions to be had.'

THE HORSEMAN ELDAIN and Caelir had met on the Aerie's Path began the council of war, telling of Morathi's host and the fall of the Eagle Gate. Eldain listened in disbelief as Menethis told of how the men in thrall to the Dark Gods had hurled themselves at the wall, letting themselves be cut down by the defenders while the druchii watched. Whether it was a lingering after-effect of Anurion's magic or simply the power of Menethis's retelling, but Eldain found himself caught up in the emotion of his tale. He soared as the fortress repulsed wave after wave of attackers, and despaired as he heard again of the treachery of the vile Alathenar that saw Glorien Truecrown slain.

Lord Swiftwing's general, an angular-featured warrior known as Galadrien Stormweaver demanded specifics on the enemy from Menethis: numbers, dispositions, weaponry, order of battle, discipline and a host of other morsels of information. Eldain took an instant dislike to Stormweaver. His manner of questioning left Eldain in no doubt that he viewed Menethis as a coward for not dying at the Eagle Gate, as though the senseless loss of elven life in so futile a gesture would have been better than their survival.

Menethis answered Stormweaver's increasingly belligerent questions in calm, measured tones that spoke of a warrior in love with the logistics of war.

In a pause between questions, Eldain leaned over the table and said, 'How many warriors do you have at Tor Elyr, General Stormweaver?'

The warrior looked over, his irritation at being interrupted plain.

'A little over eight thousand, Lord Éadaoin,' said Stormweaver, and Eldain did not miss the emphasis the warrior put on his title.

'And how many of them have seen battle?'

'Perhaps a third.'

'A third? Then it seems to me that you would do well to be less antagonistic to the warrior who commands three hundred veterans. Spreading his warriors throughout your force will help steady those that are yet to be blooded.'

Stormweaver glared at Eldain. 'You think to teach me how to wage war? I am a general in the army of Tor Elyr!'

'And I have led warriors into the heart of Naggaroth,' said Eldain. 'Have you?'

Stormweaver did not answer, and it was Lord Swiftwing who spoke next.

'Lord Éadaoin,' he said, 'I am grateful to you and your brother for bringing us the Great Herd, but had I known how volatile a presence you would prove to be, I might have thought twice before allowing you to join this council of war.'

'I apologise, my lord,' said Eldain.

'Now you, Stormweaver,' said Lord Swiftwing.

The general nodded and gave a curt bow of the head. 'I apologise, Lord Éadaoin.'

'Now is there anyone else who needs to vent before we return to the business of defending these lands? No? Good. Now, Casadesus, the map if you please.'

The robed elf who had stood silently at Lord Swift-wing's shoulder stepped forward and unrolled a long map of Ellyrion. It was a work of beauty, each river, hill, forest and village picked out with the care of an artist who knew his work would endure for centuries to come.

Eldain smiled as he saw Ellyr-Charoi rendered in loving detail, captured perfectly by someone who had clearly visited the lands around the villa. He felt a pang of homesickness at the sight of his villa as Lord Swift-wing addressed the gathered warriors and mages.

'Our enemy has the initiative for now, and that offends me,' said the lord of Tor Elyr. 'As an Ellyrian and a Reaver Knight, I understand how vital it is to keep the enemy off balance. Under normal circumstances, we would have harried the druchii all the way from Eagle Pass, but these are not normal circumstances. Stormweaver, what do your scouts tell you about the enemy's movement? How soon will they get here?'

'Tomorrow. Dusk at the earliest,' said Stormweaver.

'Then we still have time,' said Lord Swiftwing, turning to Menethis of Lothern. 'I want you to take your riders and give the druchii a bloody nose. Jab and cut them, but keep out of their reach. Stall their advance and let them know that we will give them a fight they will not soon forget.'

'My lord,' began Menethis. 'My warriors are exhausted. They need rest and–'

'Nonsense,' said Lord Swiftwing. 'They need a victory. Their spirits are stained with the loss of the Eagle Gate, and you need to wash it away in druchii blood. Restore their honour, Menethis, and they will fight all the harder when battle is joined on the fields of Tor Elyr.'

'It will be done, my lord,' Menethis assured him, and

Eldain saw the great warrior Lord Swiftwing had once been as he turned his attention to the mages across the table.

'Master Silverfawn, tell me what you bring to this fight, and I warn you I have no time to indulge in any lengthy digressions. I know how you mages love the sound of your own voices, so be swift and clear in your answer.'

Mitherion Silverfawn rose and nodded to the assembled gathering.

'Loremaster Teclis sent us to you with a company of Sword Masters and forty mages,' said Mitherion. 'Mages whose specialisations are in the realms of air and earth.'

'What does that mean?' demanded Galadrien Stormweaver.

'It means that we can summon mists to conceal our attacks and confound their crossbowmen,' snapped Anurion the Green. 'It means we can bring forth walls of spikethorns to entangle their warriors as we make their flesh irresistible to every arrowhead on the battlefield. It means we can help defend this city. What more do you wish to know?'

'We can also counter the sorceries of Morathi,' cut in Mitherion smoothly. 'The Hag Sorceress possesses a mastery of the dark arts beyond any other living being. Without our help she will freeze the blood in your veins, conjure your worst fears and make them real or drag your soul screaming into the Chaos Hells.'

'Must you work together to do this, or can you spread yourselves throughout the army?' asked Lord Swiftwing.

'It will be best if we spread our presence, with each mage accompanied by his Sword Masters,' said Anurion. 'The mages of Saphery fight not with blade or spear, but the flames of Asuryan. Wherever we fight, we will rain that fire down on the druchii.'

Lord Swiftwing nodded and turned to Eldain and said, 'You say you led an expedition to Naggaroth, Lord Éadaoin?'

'I did,' confirmed Eldain without looking at Caelir. 'My brother and I led a raiding force to Clar Karond and burned the druchii shipyards to the ground. We toppled one of their floating castles and then… then we made our escape.'

'Then you will lead a detachment of my Reavers,' said Lord Swiftwing. 'I will give you command of a hundred of my bravest knights. When the druchii arrive before my city, I want you tearing at their flanks. Make them fear to take so much as a single step forward.'

'My lord, you can count on me,' said Eldain.

'And you, Caelir Éadaoin?' asked Lord Swiftwing. 'Will you fight in Tor Elyr's army?'

Caelir rose to his feet and placed a hand on his heart. 'It will be my honour.'

BOOK TWO
SACRIFICES

CHAPTER ELEVEN

BATTLELINES

THE SEA IN the Straits of Lothern was troubled, churned to white foam at the base of the cliffs that formed its sheer sides. Captain Finlain of *Finubar's Pride* gripped the gunwale of his ship and craned his neck to look up at the escarpments either side of his vessel. The tops were lost to him, hidden by low clouds that were emptying their cargo of rain over the fleet that bobbed and jostled in the swells that made for a treacherous sea.

Finlain stared at the wreck of an elven warship near the mouth of the straits, its sunken remains hauled to the surface atop a rocky outcrop pushed up from the depths. He wondered which ship it was, and what, if any, omen could be read in why it had chosen this day to rise to the surface. The ship's prow was garlanded with seaweed, and the name carved into the hull was impossible to read, but Finlain felt a profound desire to learn its identity for fear that his own vessel might share its fate.

Twenty ships were all that remained of the once-proud asur fleet that had sailed out to meet the druchii in battle before the Emerald Gate. Spread across the straits, they formed a thin silver line of warships with the *Mist Maiden* at its centre. A navy blue sail emblazoned with a stooping hawk was furled to the mast of Lord Aislin's golden, eagle-prowed flagship, and its many banks of rowers had their oars pulled in hard to the hull.

Many of Aislin's fleet still bore the scars of battle, and *Finubar's Pride* was no different. Her silver prow was burned black in patches, and her armoured hull was splintered where scores of crossbow bolts had struck.

Finlain still had nightmares of that battle, recalling the terrible sight of Malekith himself dropping from the thunderous skies on the back of his black dragon to rip the masts from foundering vessels. Finlain took a measure of comfort in knowing that the Witch King would not dare fly his dragon within the straits. High above the warships of the asur, tier upon tier of fortifications cunningly wrought into the rock of the cliffs ran the length of the straits, making it a death trap of Eagle's Claws and archers.

Nor were these defences the only danger an attacker must face.

Sandbars rose and fell throughout the channel in unpredictable ways, tides might change in a heartbeat or winds that had been gentle could suddenly rise to become dangerously unpredictable squalls and dash a ship against the cliffs. All of which made navigation hazardous for even experienced captains. Finlain had sailed these waters for decades, but knew better than to take their good graces for granted. Many an arrogant captain had found out the hard way that the waters of Ulthuan were capricious and punished those who sailed without the proper respect for the sea.

Dark clouds massed at the mouth of the straits, and a curtain of rain obscured the ocean beyond. When the Emerald Gate had been flanked, the druchii had fired the castles to either side, draping the corpses of those they had slain from the mighty sea gate. Despite the best efforts of Lothern's mages to protect the mechanisms controlling the gate, the sorcery of the Witch King had undone their enchantments, and the gate had swung open as dawn climbed over the Annulii.

Within the hour, Lord Aislin had mustered his surviving vessels and sailed out from the Sapphire Gate to meet the invaders. Twenty ships was not enough to defend these waters, and everyone aboard knew it. Today would see elven blood stain the sea red, and Finlain just hoped that none of it would belong to his vessel's crew.

'Not much of a fleet,' said Meruval, echoing Finlain's unspoken thoughts while shielding his eyes from the rain. 'At least *Finubar's Pride* is still sailing. That's got to count for something.'

'We may not have the numbers,' replied Finlain, 'but we have ships and crew worth ten times any druchii galley.'

'True enough,' agreed Meruval, gripping the top edge of a kite-shield slotted home in the gunwale as a vicious wave broke against the hull. Water spilled onto the deck and the spray of salt water soaked into their cloaks.

'Bad seas,' noted Meruval. 'I miss Daelis. Isha's tears, I never thought I'd say such a thing, but he knew his way around a whimsical seabed.'

Finlain smiled. Daelis had been their mage-navigator, and though he had been hard to like, he had always steered them true in dangerous waters. A druchii cross-bow bolt had taken his life off the coast of Tiranoc, and *Finubar's Pride* had lost a valuable member of its crew.

'Yes, he was a prickly character, but we could use him now.'

'The water is in a foul mood,' said Meruval. 'Not the kind of sea anyone should be sailing. One of the crew told me he dreamed of the Conqueror last night. He drowned at sea, you know.'

'I know, Meruval,' said Finlain. 'It was a bad end for a great king; but neither dreams, portents nor omens will stop us from venturing out today. Lord Aislin has decreed it, and I doubt even the Phoenix King could stop him.'

Meruval leaned in close to Finlain. 'You know it is madness to sail when the sea is acting up like this. Lord Aislin might not care, but I can see you agree with me. I've served with you long enough to know your thoughts, captain.'

Finlain shook his head. 'For the sake of morale aboard ship, I am going to pretend you did not speak such seditious words, Meruval. Lord Aislin has commanded that we sail, and that is the end of the matter. The druchii are massing their ships at the mouth of the straits, and it behoves us to show them that we will not yield these waters without a fight.'

Meruval glanced over at the *Mist Maiden*, and Finlain saw that threats of disciplinary action were not going to dissuade him from speaking his mind. Under normal circumstances, Finlain valued Meruval's plain speaking, but not today.

'I understand that, captain, but look above you!' said Meruval. 'Castles, ramparts, Eagle's Claws beyond number. Archers and spearmen, mages and warriors. These waters will not be taken without a fight, but to sail into harm's way when there are such defences in place seems like recklessness, not bravery. Aislin felt the Phoenix King's wrath at the defeat before the Emerald Gate, and now he seeks to regain his honour in this desperate gamble.'

'I could dismiss you for this,' said Finlain.

'But you won't because you know I'm right.'

'No, it is because if we are to keep *Finubar's Pride* afloat, I need you at the helm,' said Finlain. 'Now be silent and listen, for your rank aboard this vessel depends upon it.'

Before Meruval could reply, Finlain took a deep breath and walked along the deck of *Finubar's Pride*. The vessel's forecastle had been repaired after the battle with the black ark, and a pair of fearsome bolt throwers had been mounted on a rotating platform at her prow.

He vaulted nimbly onto the edge of the hull, balancing on the rows of shields and gripping the sweeping bow of the nearest Eagle's Claw as he drew his sword with his free hand. The crew of his vessel gathered on the deck, each one sensing their captain's need to speak.

'Warriors of *Finubar's Pride*, listen well to me,' he cried. Lightning arced in the gloom, and Finlain pointed to the rain and darkness filling the mouth of the straits. 'The druchii are out there, ready to sail into this channel, and all that stands between them and Lothern is us.'

Thunder rolled overhead as the sea did its best to unseat Finlain from his perch. The vessel rolled to starboard, but Finlain leaned with the motion of his ship.

'Many of you are wondering why we sail out to fight the druchii at all when there are such strong defences worked into the cliffs. Why risk our lives in battle when we can fight our enemies from afar? You all know me, for I have captained *Finubar's Pride* for many years, and I know warfare as well as any and better than most. So I tell you this; if we yield the straits without a fight, we hand the initiative to the enemy. They will believe that we have no will to fight, and their warriors will be heartened by so easy a victory. When the time comes, which it will, to give battle on the Sapphire Gate, the druchii will fight all the harder, believing that we are already defeated.

'*That* is why we must give battle here! We will tell our enemies that no part of Ulthuan will be surrendered without a fight. They must learn that every yard they advance will exact a fearsome toll in blood. Yes, this will be dangerous, and yes we may see our ships sunk, but not to sail out is the most dangerous thing of all. We are *Finubar's Pride*, and does anyone fight harder than us?'

His crew yelled at the stormfront advancing through the straits, and Finlain dropped from the row of shields with their cheers ringing in his ears. The cheering was taken up by the crew of *Hammer of Vaul*, the vessel sailing alongside *Finubar's Pride*, and spread along the line of elven warships until the entire fleet was shouting its defiance.

The cheering died moments later as a lightning-shawled mountain emerged from the cloaking shadows wreathing the Emerald Gate. A rearing crag of black rock, its impossible bulk smashed the edges of the towering gate and sent its towers and ramparts tumbling downwards. Thousands of tons of rock crashed into the sea, throwing columns of water hundreds of feet into the air and sending a surging wave towards the fleet of elven warships.

Rock ground on rock as the black ark forced it way into the channel, the sound like continents colliding or a never-ending avalanche as the glittering marble of the straits was crushed to powder. Fire from infernal furnaces within the mountainous abomination burned at its spiked summit, and lit the inner faces of the straits with hellish orange light.

Though he had seen this sundered peak once before, Finlain still felt his heart clamped in the grip of icy terror. How could any fleet fight something so unimaginably vast? Like a gnarled plug of cooling magma forcing its way down the neck of a dying volcano, the black ark ground its way, inch by inch, into the straits of Lothern.

And surging from its base came a hundred raven-hulled warships.

THE SUN HAD passed its zenith as the druchii army marched into sight of Tor Elyr. It came in a cloud of dust, with the sky darkening and the land growing silent before it. The scent of freshly spilled blood was carried on the cold winds surrounding the dark host, as though a cocoon of winter shielded the warriors from the balmy climate of Ellyrion.

Ahead of the druchii came Menethis of Lothern and his Reavers. They rode hard for Korhandir's Leap, the crystal bridge to the southwest of Tor Elyr said to have been built in the first days of Ellyrion, with scattered groups of dark-cloaked riders in pursuit. Eldain's practised eye told him the druchii would not catch Menethis before he crossed the river. No sooner had Lord Swiftwing's council of war broken up than Menethis had taken his warriors west, and Eldain was pleased to see that most had returned from their reaving.

But others had not, and all of Ulthuan would grieve their loss.

The pursuing druchii gave up the chase as they came within bowshot of the River Elyras, and Eldain watched Menethis lead his Reavers over the glittering bridge with a heavy weight in his heart.

It had been Eldain's betrayal that had brought the druchii to Ellyrion, and he would bear a measure of guilt for every life that was lost in its defence. He tried to keep that thought from distracting him from his role in the coming battle, but as he looked around at the faces of elves surely too young or too old to fight, he could not help but picture them as headless corpses or rotting feasts for the carrion birds that followed any druchii host.

Menethis rode up the slope towards Eldain, his horse breathless and lathered with sweat. The warrior's face was lined with joyous exhaustion, his ivory cloak was bloodstained, and the riders who followed him were alight with exultation.

'Lord Éadaoin!' cried Menethis. 'We return triumphant!'

'You return alive,' said Eldain. 'That is what is most important to a Reaver.'

'All night we harried them,' said Menethis. 'We slew their sentries, scattered their horses and fired their tents. Perhaps three or four hundred dead, many more injured.'

'Good work, Menethis, we will make an Ellyrian out of you yet,' said Eldain. 'Now ride to the centre. General Stormweaver will have orders for you and your warriors.'

'Indeed,' said Menethis, turning his horse with a flourish and leading his riders towards the grassy flatlands that spread before the backdrop of Tor Elyr. As Eldain watched Menethis ride off, his gaze was drawn along the glittering battle line of Lord Swiftwing's army.

Arrayed in serried ranks of shimmering spear points, azure cloaks, polished helms and gleaming breastplates, the army of Tor Elyr occupied the slopes overlooking the southern banks of the river. The army had assembled as dawn's first light bathed the land in its honey gold warmth, marching from the city under Galadrien Stormweaver's direction.

This close to the sea, the river was wide and deep, yet its waters flowed languidly and without urgency. Blocks of spearmen and lines of archers held the field, with a mass of heavy horse at their centre. Beneath a banner of crimson, Stormweaver led the Silver Helms of Tor Elyr from the back of a mighty steed the colour of a winter's sky. As though carved from silver, the horsemen stood silent and unmoving, perfectly disciplined and courageous beyond mortal reckoning.

On each flank of the army, a thousand Reaver Knights strung their bows or sharpened the already keen edges of their spears. Thanks to the gathering of the Great Herd, most of Ellyrion's citizen levy was now mounted, and Eldain hoped it would be enough to tip the balance in their favour.

Scores of Eagle's Claw bolt throwers had been set up on the high ground behind the archers, and several weapons had been assembled further south upon small hillocks overlooking Korhandir's Leap and in the north on the slopes of a hill crowned by a circle of waystones. No druchii warriors would be able to cross the river without suffering beneath a relentless hail of powerfully driven arrows.

Eldain lifted a hand as he saw Caelir riding across the plain towards the left flank of Lord Swiftwing's army. His brother waved back, elated to be defending his homeland at the head of a hundred Reaver Knights.

Caelir was a war leader now, a noble of Ellyrion riding out in defence of his homeland, and Eldain felt pride that was almost paternal in its strength. Only now did he understand that the jealousy he had felt towards Caelir had been completely unnecessary. They had never been in competition, but the wild spirit of Ellyrion had driven them both to foolish acts of betrayal. They were part of a race of near immortals on the brink of extinction, and yet they could still fall prey to damaging emotions just as easily as the mortals of the Old World they looked down upon. More so, in many cases, for the pulls of the heart endured by mortals were but pale shadows of those that drove the asur. That the wounds between Eldain and Caelir were healing was his only consolation as the druchii emerged from the penumbra of shadow that swathed them like a shroud.

Rank upon rank of warriors in dark cloaks and oil-sheened armour the colour of obsidian filled the centre of the plain with the tramp of their marching feet. Blood-red cloaks billowed in the icy winds that followed them, and their black-hafted spears were tipped with bronze. Heavily armoured warriors atop snarling, snapping reptilian steeds rode in the southern wing of the army, and beastmasters goaded roaring beasts with many writhing heads towards the river.

Hideously malformed creatures of raw flesh, wailing, fang-filled mouths and unnaturally jointed limbs hauled their corrupted bulk alongside these beasts. Sweating mortals held them on chains, hard-muscled men of the north clad in furs, brazen iron and horned helms.

Though allied, Eldain saw there was clear division in how the enemy host would give battle. The druchii would attack to the south of Tor Elyr over Korhandir's Leap, while the tribal barbarians would force a crossing in the north. It seemed a foolish plan, for there was no bridge in the north, and the savage warriors of the Dark Gods would be forced to wade through the river while enduring endless volleys of arrows from the citizen levy's archers.

The bloodshed would be terrible, but from the scarred, wild and hungry look of these warriors, Eldain suspected they would welcome the pain. Certainly the mighty warrior atop a fleshy steed with a silver saddle stitched to its naked hide could barely contain his eagerness to ride into the water. A dark halo that looked like naked flames seemed to coil across the warlord's skin, and Eldain wondered if he was even aware of it.

A chill took hold of Eldain's heart as the plain across the river filled with regimented ranks of druchii and howling mobs of axe-wielding savages. He had hoped the battle before the walls of Eagle Gate might have bled this host of its power, but the army of Lord Swiftwing was still outnumbered by at least four to one.

A lone rider emerged from the ranks of the enemy army, and a fierce, ululating scream of worship and devotion was torn from every druchii throat.

She was ivory-skinned and clad in leather armour that revealed more flesh that it protected. A twisted crown of dark iron and bone encircled her brow, and she bore a dread weapon that dripped blood and made Eldain clutch his chest as though it might tear his heart from his body even from so far away. Eldain knew exactly who she was; her name was a byword for unnatural perversions, ancient hatred and endless spite.

'Morathi,' he hissed, spitting the name like poison sucked from a wound. She was the architect of Caelir's transformation from loyal son of Ellyrion into a weapon aimed at the heart of Ulthuan's best and brightest. She had tortured his brother and driven him beyond sanity with her excruciations and seductions.

Eldain gripped his sword hilt tightly, hoping that the chaos of battle would see him face to face with his brother's tormentor. As though sensing his hatred and savouring it, the Hag Sorceress turned her mount in his direction. Morathi's steed was blacker than the heart of the most merciless tyrant, its eyes a simmering furnace red, and a pair of nightmarish wings were folded in at its flanks.

Morathi raised her pale arms above her head with a crack of displaced air. The sky split with thunder and a wind straight from the Land of Chill swept across the river and into the army of the asur. Not a heart failed to miss a beat, not a sword arm did not tremble, and not one amongst the defenders of Tor Elyr failed to hear the banshee wail of Morai-Heg.

Yet not one warrior took a backwards step.

A host of discordant war-horns sounded from the enemy host, and with a clash of swords and shields, Morathi's army marched on Tor Elyr.

THE ORDER CAME from Lord Aislin's ship, and the asur fleet surged towards the shadow-cloaked vessels at the base of the black ark. It was a wondrously foolish charge, but the nineteen captains of the Sea Lord obeyed instantly, sailing south in the direction of the open sea. Kithre Seablaze led the western half of the fleet, Lord Aislin the east, and it was the Sea Lord's lieutenant that struck first.

Racing ahead of the rest of the ships, Seablaze ran his ships at speed towards the druchii raven ships as a mist arose from the surface of the water. No natural sea mist was this, but one conjured from the foamy wave-tops that swirled around the druchii ships like a winter's fog. It clung to their dark hulls, gathered in their sails and confounded the warriors on the prow-mounted dart throwers.

Seablaze sailed into the mist, and no sooner had his ships reached its edge than the mist sank back into the sea. Cries of alarm echoed from the decks of the raven ships as their crews saw the sleek vessels of the asur bearing down upon them. Eagle's Claws loosed withering hails of bolts into the packed ranks gathered on the decks, and fearful was the carnage. Another volley flashed, hurling scores of arrows through the druchii Corsairs. One final volley of darts was loosed before Seablaze gave the order to turn about.

Even as his ships pirouetted on the ocean, additional Eagle's Claws mounted on the quarterdeck loosed their shafts. While the enemy crews reeled from the slaughter wreaked on their decks, the Eagle's Claws let fly with heavy ithilmar-tipped bolts designed to punch through the hull of a ship. Aimed below the waterline, three druchii vessels were holed and began wallowing in the swells as their lower decks began filling with seawater.

Black bolts from the prows of the enemy ships flashed through the air, but loosed too swiftly they were poorly aimed. Yet with so many unleashed, some found their targets, and blood was spilled across the decks of the elven ships.

As Seablaze raced back to the asur fleet, a rain of arrows and bolts fell from the castles and ramparts carved into the cliffs of the straits. Hundreds slashed down onto the raven ships, punching through armour, cutting ropes and slicing sails. The heavier bolts smashed through decks to slay dozens of slave rowers or even punch through the bottom timbers of the hull.

In answer, swarms of iron crossbow bolts flew from the black ark, and the battle below was fought beneath a sky darkened with deadly projectiles. Monstrous balls of flaming pitch were hurled from the summit of the black ark, arcing through the air with languid ease to slam into the pristine walls of the defensive castles. Fires blazed across the cliff side defences and thick columns of black smoke curled skyward.

Finlain sent *Finubar's Pride* racing towards the unnamed ship wrecked upon the new island, aiming his prow for the narrow gap between it and the eastern scarp of the straits. *Hammer of Vaul* came with him, and he waved to its captain as they sailed on this gloriously mad course. Despite what he had said to his men, Finlain knew this was a desperately risky gambit. No matter how skilled a sailor, the odds of winning a victory against such numbers was practically zero, but this fight was not about victory, it was about making a statement.

In the centre of the fleet, Lord Aislin's ship rode the crest of the waves, a host of glistening, bottle-green wyrms breaking the water either side of his prow. The creatures of the far ocean had come at Aislin's command, predators of the deep with the strength and ferocity to sink even the largest ships. The Sea Lord's blue sail caught the last rays of light in the straits, and it shone like the skies at the centre of the Sea of Dusk.

More mists oozed from the sea, coiling over the gunwale as it cloaked the asur ships from the sight of the enemy. Finlain held to his course, knowing that he could afford no mistakes in his heading or else be dashed upon the rocks.

'Steady as she goes, Meruval!' he yelled, his voice deadened by the mists.

'Aye, captain,' returned his helmsman, as *Finubar's Pride* cut the waters of the straits.

'Eagle's Claws ready?'

'Ready, aye, captain,' came the shouted reply.

The wind caught the sails and *Finubar's Pride* leapt forward, keeping her prow low to the water as she cut the waves like a knife. A druchii bolt flashed overhead, grazing the mainmast, and spinning off into the mist.

'They know we're here,' said Finlain.

The rocky island of tumbled blocks and dripping seaweed emerged from the mist. Finlain saw a fallen statue of Isha lying on its side, with seawater dripping from her granite eyes like tears. Behind the statue the sagging hull of the wreck hid his ship from the druchii, and Finlain glanced over his shoulder to see that *Hammer of Vaul* was still with him. Up ahead, rising like the sheer face of a mountainside, the black ark smouldered like the sea volcanoes that rose without warning in the southern oceans. A wall of water went before the black ark like a surge tide, bearing all manner of detritus from the bottom of the ocean in its oily foam.

Light glimmered evilly from the many towers and garrets built haphazardly on the scorched flanks of the black ark, and the dull hammer of iron on iron echoed from within. Hideous screams and bloody chants to Khaine accompanied the metallic cacophony, and Finlain knew he took a terrible risk in coming this close to such an abominable creation.

Across the straits, druchii sorcery battled with asur magecraft as the mists conjured by the sea-mages of Lord Aislin were dissipated by roiling clouds of fire. Blazing ships foundered in the channel, and burning elves hurled themselves from the decks of their doomed vessels rather than be consumed by the flames.

The druchii's advantage in numbers was now paying off, as Kithre Seablaze found himself trapped against the walls of the straits. Swifter raven ships pushed north into the straits as more heavily-laden galleys engaged Seablaze's vessels. In such close confines, the deadly rams affixed to the hulls of the raven ships were next to useless, but the druchii had other means of taking the elven ships.

Corvus boarding ramps with heavy iron spikes in the shape of barbed beaks slammed down on the decks of the elven ships, shattering gunwales and embedding themselves firmly in the timbers of the deck. Corsairs in scaled cloaks charged onto the elven vessels, and the slaughter was prodigious as these merciless killers butchered the crews of the eagle ships. With nowhere to run, two elven ships were run aground, their hulls broken to splinters and their crews dashed upon the rocks by the powerful waves.

Lord Aislin's ships cut a wedge through the centre of the druchii line, Eagle's Claws sweeping the crew from the decks of raven ships with volley after volley of arrows. His sea-mages dragged two raven ships beneath the waves in a crushing, whirling vortex of water, while another was left becalmed as its crew were bewitched by the glamours of oceanid song that rose from the haunted deeps.

Fire fell from above in blazing lumps of pitch as the castles on the cliffs burned, and flames caught the sails of the close-packed druchii ships. Those that could not fight the fires were sunk by their fellows, and the sea filled with screaming Corsairs who fought to reach a spar of broken timber before the weight of their armour dragged them to their deaths.

Captain Finlain watched the battle raging across the width of the straits, and felt his heartbeat quicken. They had sunk their own number of druchii vessels at least, and many more were aflame or sinking. Yet for all that, the asur fleet now numbered only seven vessels. Even as he watched, Finlain saw Kithre Seablaze's vessel ride up onto a fang of rock at the base of the western cliff. The hull of his vessel broke apart like matchwood, and its crew spilled like seeds into the dark waters.

'Meruval!' shouted Finlain. 'On my word!'

The seas bucked and heaved at the base of the black ark, and Finlain saw its lower ramparts and donjons through the mist and sea spray. Shouting druchii warriors pointed at them as they emerged from the mist, but before they could do more than shout a warning, scores of arrows flensed the lower walls of the black ark.

'Come about!' cried Finlain. 'Now, Meruval, now!'

Finubar's Pride heeled hard to starboard, the ship leaning down into the water and exposing its silver underside to the black ark as it spun around to make a perfect course change of ninety degrees. *Hammer of Vaul* followed her round, and the two vessels surged forward into the flanks of the druchii fleet, borne aloft on the thundering bow wave driven before the sea-borne mountain. Finlain gripped the ropes tied to the mast to keep his feet as *Finubar's Pride* rode the waves faster than she had ever done before.

Crossbow bolts smacked into the deck, and Finlain looked over his shoulder to see druchii crossbowmen racing to the ramparts of the black ark.

'Keep our backside clear!' ordered Finlain, and his best archers took up position on the quarterdeck. Arrow after arrow flew from their bows, any druchii who dared show their face punched from his feet by the volley. Finlain turned and ran to where Meruval wrestled with the tiller, his face contorted with the effort of holding their course. The prow of *Finubar's Pride* was aimed towards the sea, and the power of the wave they rode was like nothing Meruval had sailed before.

Finlain threw himself at the tiller, adding his own strength as they guided their vessel into the druchii fleet.

A raven ship trading arrows with the *Mist Maiden* was the first to feel their wrath.

Finubar's Pride slammed into the druchii ship, her reinforced prow smashing through the raven ship as though it were a child's toy and not a ship of war. The vessel broke in two and the screams of its crew were short lived as the oncoming wave swallowed them.

Two more ships were smashed to pieces in this way before Finlain was forced to give the order to turn *Finubar's Pride* to the north. His archers loosed until they had no more shafts in their quivers, and his Eagle's Claws exhausted their supply of heavy bolts a moment later.

The surface of the ocean was awash with broken timber, burning ships and drowning sailors. Castles burned high on the cliffs, and savage lightning crackled from the sorcerers' towers of the black ark. A towering column of fire erupted beside *Finubar's Pride*, and Finlain watched in horror as *Hammer of Vaul* was struck dead centre by one of the giant balls of flaming pitch. Immediately, the vessel was ablaze from bow to stern, and Finlain knew there was no saving her.

'Captain!' cried Meruval. 'Help me.'

Finlain shook off his sorrow at the loss of his fellow captain's ship, and bent his efforts to helping Meruval control their wild course. Iron bolts thudded into the quarterdeck and mast now that the druchii in the black ark could target them without fear of reprisals.

'Time to get out of here,' advised Meruval.

'Agreed,' said Finlain, and they hauled the tiller around until they were aimed to the north and the gleaming blue glare of the Sapphire Gate. Using the power of the wave surging ahead of the black ark, the vessel shot away from the vast mountain, passing the rocky island of the wreck. Viewed from this angle, Finlain could see the faint outline of the runic carvings worked into this side of the newly revealed prow.

Morelion.

Finlain felt a stab of hope at the sight of the name, for it was that of the firstborn twin of Aenarion and Astari-elle. In the ancient war against the Chaos powers, the daemons of the Dark Gods had fallen on Avelorn in a tide of bloody claws and slaughter. The Everqueen had been slain and Morelion and Yvraine thought lost to the daemons, but an ancient forest spirit of Avelorn had kept Aenarion's children safe and eventually returned them to their people.

Though the asur fleet was scattered and sunk, Finlain did not despair, for as Morelion had survived impossible odds to fight again, so too would *Finubar's Pride*.

'Blood of Khaine!' hissed Meruval, making Finlain flinch with the invocation.

'Watch your tongue,' said Finlain. 'I'll not have the murder god's name spoken aloud on my ship.'

'Apologies, captain,' said Meruval. 'But look!'

Finlain followed Meruval's outstretched hand, and was almost moved to give voice to the bloody-handed one's name himself.

Her navy blue sail ablaze, the *Mist Maiden* sailed into the heart of the druchii fleet with two raven ships locked alongside her, their corvus boarding bridges wedged tightly in her decks. The sea around the ships churned with blood as sea wyrms tore at hideous monsters loosed from the bowels of the black ark, and purple lightning set the water ablaze with magical fire. Elven warriors fought in the leaping shadows of the flames, and Finlain saw the magnificent form of Lord Aislin as he swept the curved blade of his ithilmar sword through the Corsairs attempting to capture his vessel.

For a brief moment, Finlain dared hope that the Sea Lord might yet break free of the druchii vessels. But as the water churned with strange lights and a groaning roar of something beneath the ocean, that hope was cruelly dashed.

Something vast and scaled broke the surface beneath *Mist Maiden*, and her keel broke like a dead sapling as she was lifted out of the water. Like a kraken of the deep, the monster had eyes the size of chariot wheels and row upon row of ivory teeth in an obsidian gash of a mouth. Its fangs closed on the *Mist Maiden*'s hull and the ship exploded in a welter of smashed timber and elven bodies.

The creature fell back into the water with a thunderous boom of crashing waves, and Finlain blinked away tears of anger and sorrow. He turned from the Sea Lord's death and let the fierce winds and pounding waves carry *Finubar's Pride* towards the postern of the glittering sea gate ahead.

'The straits are lost,' said Meruval accusingly, as though unable to believe the words.

Finlain nodded, too grief-stricken to answer.

Only the Sapphire Gate now stood between the druchii and Lothern.

Chapter Twelve

First Blood

CAELIR DREW IN the reins of his horse at the foot of the domed hill to the north of Tor Elyr. Its summit was crowned by a ring of white stones, each taller than two elves, and cut with sigils of ancient power. In days long since passed, it was said that the mages of Ulthuan could travel to other dominions with a single step through such portals, but none now lived who were powerful enough to walk between worlds.

His Reaver Knights were eager for action, hungry to take the fight to the druchii, and Caelir liked that aggressive spirit. A Reaver Knight needed a reckless streak, yet one tempered with iron control. It was a contradiction of wildness and discipline that only a very few could understand or master. Above his warriors, a line of Eagle's Claw bolt throwers were being loaded with arrows, and Caelir waved to the warriors that crewed them.

Across the river, the enemy host milled and stamped, beating axes and swords against iron-bossed shields. It was grim theatrics, designed to intimidate, and against another army of mortals it might have worked, but directed at the asur, it was failing miserably. The braying of horns echoed over the river, and Caelir felt his pulse quicken as the enemy moved towards the river.

Though they were but mortals, the warriors across the river were powerful and wolf-lean, bred tough by a life spent on the verge of extinction. Living in the harsh tundra of the north meant that only the strongest, most ruthless survived, and only by a man's strength and power could he be measured against his foes. Clad in beaten plates of iron, wolf and bear pelts, these northern savages had a primal ferocity that could not be under-estimated. Though crude, a club to the head would kill you as surely as the finest blade. They howled a guttural refrain, a deafening war-chant that was discordant, melo-dious, ear-splitting and hideous all at once. It spoke of delirium, the loss of control and the pleasure that could be had from surrendering all restraint.

Caelir shifted uncomfortably in his saddle, feeling the clashing sounds touching some deep part of his soul. He recognised the urge to allow desire to overrule control, and hated that he shared even this scrap of connection with the enemy. The northern warriors did not advance; content simply to bang their swords and shields, lift their bloody banners high, and hurl vile taunts across the wide river.

Instead, the beasts charged.

Terrible perversions of nature, these hybrid abomina-tions were taller and more powerfully built than all but the mightiest tribesmen. Their bodies were covered in rank, matted fur and most carried heavy clubs or crude axes. No two were identical, but each bore the unmistakable trait of some forest beast, be it mastiff, bull, fox, bear or wolf. They walked on two legs in imitation of the noble creatures of the world, but nothing could disguise the horror of their condition. Caelir almost felt sorry for them.

The beasts plunged into the river, howling and braying as its purity burned their Chaos-tainted flesh. Where a mortal warrior would be dragged to the bottom of the river, the beasts swam with powerful strokes, and hundreds of shaggy-haired monsters drew near the gently sloping banks of the river. Archers positioned on the northern flank of the army let fly with a volley of arrows, and the river ran with blood as they slashed down into the warped flesh of the beasts.

Another volley hit home, and another, but the beasts' hides were thick and their flesh leather-tough. Some sank beneath the river, but many more pressed on through the waters to the far bank. Raucous cheers from the tribesmen drove them on, and Caelir saw that arrows alone would not stop the beasts from reaching the riverbank.

'With me!' shouted Caelir, hauling on the reins and urging Irenya to a gallop.

His knights followed instantly, riding north in a curving loop to come upon the beasts at an oblique angle. Caelir stood tall in the saddle, and craned his neck to see that numerous other Reaver bands had followed his example. Perhaps five hundred riders thundered across the plain as blocks of spearmen advanced to fill the gap they had just left.

The first of the monsters had reached the shoreline and were dragging their hulking bodies onto dry land.

They shook their fur free of water and bellowed their challenges as more arrows thudded home. Caelir saw a towering monster with the head of a horned bull and a breastplate of beaten iron strapped to its body snap a pair of arrows from its stomach and roar its hate at those whose bodies were unblemished.

The Eagle's Claws on the hill unleashed flickering volleys of arrows, and several beasts fell, pierced by a host of shafts. Scores of monsters had gained the riverbank, as Caelir raised his left fist and chopped it down to his hip.

As one, the Reaver Knights wheeled their horses, changing direction in an instant and riding towards the monsters. Caelir hauled back on his bowstring and loosed at the bull-headed monster. His arrow plunged into its side, but it seemed not to feel the impact. Arrows flashed past him as his fellow knights let fly, but only a handful of the beasts fell. Many hundreds of the terrifying monsters had assembled on the banks of the river, and were advancing towards the glittering elven lines with a bestial, loping gait.

'Fly, Irenya!' shouted Caelir. 'Ride like never before!'

Though Aedaris had been the faster horse, Irenya was still a proud steed of Ellyrion, and she rode as if all the daemons of Chaos were on her tail. The ground thundered beneath her, and Caelir loosed three more shafts before exerting pressure with his left boot and swinging his mount around.

Less than a hundred yards separated the beasts and the asur battle line, and Caelir led his Reavers into that gap. He twisted in the saddle, drawing and loosing arrow after arrow with swift economy of movement. His arrows plunged into eye sockets and open mouths, the only vulnerable areas of soft flesh on the beasts' bodies.

'Turn about!' yelled Caelir, as Irenya pirouetted and reversed her course.

The gap between the elves and beasts was shrinking rapidly, and Caelir hoped he hadn't left it too late to ride out. He looped his bow around his shoulder and flicked his spear free of the leather thong holding it to his saddle.

A wolf-headed beast leapt for him, and he rammed the spear into its throat. The beast howled and fell beneath Irenya's hooves. Shimmering speartips slashed and stabbed in a terrifying scrum of bodies. Howls and grunts filled the air as the beasts fought to drag the Reavers down, but such was the speed and agility of their steeds that not a single knight was slain. Blood sprayed and his arm ached with the effort of driving his spear into iron-hard flesh. This close to the enemy, Irenya was a weapon too, her hooves caving in skulls and chests with every stride.

Then they were clear, and Caelir whooped with the sheer bliss of riding free. His weapon and armour were drenched in bestial blood, but he was alive. They had ridden into the jaws of death and spat in the eye of Morai-Heg before riding out. His heart beat a racing tattoo within his chest, but no sooner had he brought Irenya to a canter than the charging beasts struck the elven line like a hammer-blow.

Spears shivered and snapped with the impact, and a braying, honking, roaring mass of furred flesh slammed into the silver line of lowered spears. The elven line bent back, but held. Warriors in the ranks beyond the fighting rank thrust their spears forward, driving the razor-sharp points into the unclean flesh of the beasts.

Great axes and monstrous clubs slammed into the elven warriors, hurling broken bodies through the air or pounding them into the earth. Screams carried over the clang of weapons and armour, and Caelir fought the urge to ride into the fray. With their spears lowered, the Reaver Knights would wreak fearsome harm, but getting bogged down in such a brutal fight was not where they excelled.

Instead, Caelir wheeled his horse back to the river as yet more bestial creatures forded the waters. Behind them came mortal warriors from the Old World, chanting, jeering and screaming tribesmen in leather breastplates and bronze helms. They carried fleshy banners daubed with obscenities and blasphemous runes dedicated to gods whose names should never be spoken.

Riding at the head of these brutal warriors was a towering warlord, his armour a mix of leather, bronze and iron, his helm beaten to resemble a raven with swept-back wings at the sides. Caelir felt the power and threat of this champion, knowing that this was surely the master of the mortal horde. The warrior sat astride a mountainous horse, its raw-meat bulk and saw-toothed snout marking it as an abomination of Chaos.

This warrior of the Dark Gods bore a sword with many blades, a weapon that glittered with cruel light and infinite malice. Caelir had tried to keep the memories of his many torments in the depths of Naggaroth buried in the deepest, darkest recesses of his memory, but the sight of this warrior unlocked the blackest of those horrors.

He sobbed as he remembered the many violations wreaked upon his flesh, the pain and the loathsome pleasures designed to break him down to his component parts in order to rebuild him in a manner pleasing to the Hag Sorceress. He remembered this warrior's face leering down at him, a vision of perverse beauty that repulsed and beguiled in equal measure.

'Issyk Kul,' whispered Caelir, his anger and hate rising to the surface in a bilious tide.

Between them, Kul and Morathi had tainted everything of worth in his soul, and Caelir would never forgive them for that. As the warriors of the Dark Gods approached the riverbank, Caelir waved his spear in the air and loosed an aching cry of grief and pain.

Irenya reared up, startled by his sudden outburst, and his Reaver Knights milled around in confusion. Caelir spun his spear and scanned the battle raging between the elven line and the beasts. More of the beasts were pouring into the fight, punching ragged holes in the elven host, which were swiftly filled with warriors from the rearmost ranks. Blue-fletched shafts dropped amongst the beasts from archers behind the spears, plunging into shoulders and skulls.

A cold wind, icy and filled with the actinic tang of magic flowed across the river, and Caelir saw the surface of the water grow sluggish and gelid. Frosted patterns crazed across the river as rippled ice began to form. Ellyrion was a land that never knew the touch of winter, yet the northern stretch of the river was freezing solid.

A carnyx formed from the bones and skull of some long-dead leviathan echoed over the frozen waters, and Issyk Kul led his warriors onto the ice.

'Reavers, with me!' shouted Caelir, riding for the river.

POETS TOLD THAT the goddess Ladrielle had woven Korhandir's Leap from starlight and moonbeams when the gods first shaped Ulthuan for the asur. Given to the horse lords in ancient times in gratitude for their aid during the coming of the daemons, it was a trysting place for the young of Tor Elyr, and the young bucks of the city would leap into the river from its crystal arches to impress their chosen fillies.

Now it was a killing ground.

Druchii warriors bearing kite-shaped shields emblazoned with the heraldry of their dark houses charged asur warriors positioned at the midpoint of the bridge on the crest of its grandest arch. Wide enough for only twenty warriors to stand abreast, it was a perfect choke point to stymie the druchii advance. Silver-tipped spears splintered shields and drew chill blood, as cold-forged iron hacked through mail shirts in return. Warriors heaved against one another, grunting and stabbing and cutting.

This was battle at its most primal, strength against strength, blood upon blood until one force could stand no more of the slaughter. It was the kind of war fought by savages, not the elegant, sophisticated warriors of the asur. Yet all too often, war chooses its own form, regardless of who fights it, and warriors either adapt or die.

Eldain rode Lotharin along the banks of the river, loosing shafts across the water to slay druchii warriors crouched on the opposite bank who unleashed iron-tipped crossbow bolts into the flanks of the warriors defending the bridge. His Reavers traded barbs with dark-cloaked druchii kin with ebony weapons pulled in tight to their shoulders, like the uncouth black powder weapons of the dwarfs. Loosing several bolts from top-mounted magazines with every squeeze of the firing bar, they were lethal at close quarters, but lost power swiftly at range.

Eldain's bow suffered no such loss in power and most of his shafts sent a druchii warrior tumbling into the river. The battle on the bridge was the key to the southern flank of the elven army. Hold the bridge and the druchii could not bring their superior numbers to bear. Lose the bridge and their flank would be turned.

Along the line of battle, the elven host sent arching flocks of arrows over the river, and Eldain relished the thought of the suffering the enemy would be enduring. Flickering bolts of pellucid white flames zipped across the river, answered by crackling arcs of purple lightning and cold streams of icy air as the mages sent from the White Tower did battle with the magickers of the Hag Sorceress.

Freezing fog obscured the land to the north of the battle line, and Eldain saw only the faintest outline of the hill of waystones. He could see nothing of Caelir's Reaver Knights, and whispered a short prayer to Asuryan to look kindly on his younger brother. Eldain cast his gaze over the river, watching the enemy host jostle for position as yet more blocks of infantry moved up to the river, spear-armed warriors, heavily armoured warriors with executioners' blades, screeching hydras and rank upon rank of crossbowmen crouched at the edge of the river.

Movement far to the south caught his eye, and Eldain saw numerous groups of black-cloaked horsemen apparently riding away from the battle. They were pushing their mounts hard, and though their direction made no sense, Eldain guessed their destination; a gently curved portion of the river that foamed white where buried rocks broke the surface. Eldain immediately saw the danger and turned to his lieutenant, a rider named

Alysia. Her hair was crimson and gold, held in place by a silver pin shaped like a butterfly.

'The river, can it be forded there?' he demanded, pointing to the river's curve.

'When the rains are mild,' she said. 'But it is too deep for even one such as Korhil to cross.'

'But not so deep that it would trouble a lightly-laden cavalryman,' snapped Eldain, dragging Lotharin's reins around and urging him southwards. 'Ride! All of you, with me!'

Eldain's Reavers swirled around him as he rode south along the riverbank, forming a wedge of horsemen with him at its tip. The druchii riders, seeing their manoeuvre was discovered, threw off any pretence at subtlety, the disparate groups coming together and galloping for the river.

Laurena Starchaser's Reaver band joined Eldain's knights, and he waved to their flame-haired leader. He had met Starchaser the night before, her long limbs, auburn hair and strikingly angular features reminding him of a hunting bird. With both bands joined together, nearly two hundred warriors now rode to intercept the flanking riders.

The enemy had the lead on them, and reached the ford first, splashing into the river and striking for the far bank. The water reached up to their horses' necks as they crossed the ford, walking slowly but surely through the river. Eldain cursed that neither Lord Swiftwing nor Galadrien Stormweaver had thought to mention this ford. Forty riders had made the crossing already, and hundreds more were already halfway across.

Eldain nocked an arrow to his bow and let fly. The shaft pitched a druchii from his saddle, and a host of arrows flashed past Eldain to engulf the cloaked riders. Only a handful fell, for these riders were almost as nimble as his Reavers. Like the enemy warriors by the riverbank, these riders were armed with the deadly repeater crossbows, and swarms of deadly bolts were fired in return.

Eldain heard screams as his knights were struck, and loosed another shaft. His target swayed aside at the last moment, raising his crossbow and firing a pair of bolts in return. Eldain leaned low over Lotharin's neck as one bolt flew past his ear and the other ricocheted from the ithilmar boss on his mount's bridle. More of the dark-cloaked riders had gained the riverbank, enough to pose a threat, but not enough to outnumber them.

Eldain slung his bow and raised both his arms, before spreading them out to the side. Both groups of Reavers split apart, Eldain's heading straight for the druchii, Starchaser's swinging around in a sweeping curve to come at them from the flank. Arrows and crossbow bolts sliced the air, and Eldain ducked and swayed in the saddle to avoid being struck.

The druchii charged out from the river, but Eldain's larger band of warriors met them spear to spear. Warriors and horses screamed as the two hosts met in a clash of blades and flesh. The black horses of the enemy were vicious beasts, biting and butting heads with their Ellyrian cousins, but such steeds were not without their own fire. While the warriors in the saddle fought with spear and sword, the horses kicked their back legs and pawed the air with shod hooves to crush ribcages and pitch riders from their mounts.

Eldain thrust his spear into a druchii's belly, twisting the blade and pulling it clear before the suction of flesh could trap it. He slammed the haft into a screaming warrior's face; then reversed the weapon to open the throat of a crossbowman as he reloaded. His spear spun, stabbed, blocked and thrust, drawing blood, breaking bones and parrying slashing blows of swords. The noise of battle was incredible: grunting, snorting horses, shrieked calls of the murder god's name, and the shrill clash of blades and armour.

Lotharin bucked as a crossbow bolt sliced across his rump, cutting a long furrow, but not lodging. His back legs snapped out, cracking into the thigh of a druchii circling around him. The warrior howled as his femur was crushed, and he dropped the sword he had been about to plunge into Eldain's back.

'My thanks, old friend,' said Eldain, as Lotharin snorted in a way that perfectly captured an admonishment to watch his back.

Warriors swirled around each other in a chaotic, heaving mass of desperate combat. There was little shape to the battle, simply horses and warriors weaving an intricate, formless dance around one another as they fought for a killing position. The Reavers were having the best of the fight, and many more of the black horses were without riders than the brown and silver horses of Ellyrion.

More of the dark-cloaked riders were crossing the river, but not in so great a number that gave Eldain the fear that they would be overwhelmed. His spear snapped as a druchii sword slashed down and took a chunk out of the haft. The lower half of the spear spun away, but Eldain grabbed what was left of the speartip and plunged the blade into the swordsman's heart. The broken weapon was wrenched from his hand, and he drew his sword as Starchaser's Reavers slammed into the battle.

Eldain's knights and the druchii had struck together,

but Starchaser hammered into the druchii with all the power of an Ellyrian charge. Her warriors attacked with spears lowered like lances, and the druchii were skewered like meat on a spit. Picking out one horseman to strike in the midst of such a frenetic battle was a feat beyond any but the most skilled riders.

Child's play to an Ellyrian Reaver Knight.

Nearly a hundred of the druchii riders were killed in the first moments of the charge, and Eldain rode into the stunned survivors as they reeled from this sudden reversal. He killed three warriors in as many blows, and laughed with the primal ferocity of this fight as the druchii fell back in disarray towards the river. He rode after a fleeing warrior, and lanced his sword into his back. The druchii fell from the saddle, and Eldain saw the riders in mid-crossing pause as they realised the battle on the riverbank had been lost. They milled in confusion until a barking command was shouted and a hunting horn blew.

Eldain lifted his gaze to the far bank and his heart chilled as he saw the group of bolt throwers dragged there. The crews slammed home heavy magazines of bolts on the firing mechanism and worked the windlass in readiness to fire.

'Back!' shouted Eldain. 'Get back from the banks!'

The Reavers obeyed instantly, but even that was too slow, as the bolt throwers spoke with a whickering voice that filled the air with hundreds of black-fletched arrows. Elves and horses went down in the withering hail, dozens pierced by four or more shafts. Eldain turned Lotharin away, making him a smaller target. An arrow sliced over the skin of his neck and another struck him between the shoulder blades. The impact was painful, but his armour held firm and the arrow dropped free without piercing his skin.

Arrow-pierced horses flailed on the ground, screaming in pain and kicking their legs as the barbed tips of the arrows tore their flesh. Reaver Knights lay where they had fallen, many shot through the head and neck. Eldain and Lotharin galloped away from the riverbank as the bolt throwers' crew worked to unleash another volley.

Eldain saw Starchaser, her shoulder and hip streaming blood.

'We must yield the bank,' she cried.

'No,' said Eldain, riding alongside her and turning his horse. 'Enough of us remain to hold them here. We wait until the druchii gain the bank and then charge in again. They won't shoot while their own warriors are in the way. We can do this!'

'I do not doubt it, but if we do not pull back we will be cut off from the rest of the army! Look yonder to Korhandir's Leap!'

Eldain twisted in the saddle and saw the druchii warriors on the bridge fall back as bulky reptilian quadrupeds of dark scale and wide, fang-filled jaws lumbered onto Korhandir's Leap. Eldain knew of these creatures, called Cold Ones by their masters, but had never seen one in the flesh. Monstrously powerful, and ridden by tall warriors in plate of black and gold, their eyes were dull and listless, and frothed saliva drooled from between teeth like daggers. The druchii upon their backs carried long lances and their helms were fringed with flaring blade-wings.

'The warriors on the bridge will not be able to resist such a charge,' said Starchaser, and Eldain knew she was right. 'If we stay here, we will be trapped. Druchii to the left and right and the sea at our backs. Not a place any Ellyrian should find themselves.'

The idea of yielding the riverbank galled Eldain, but the idea of being trapped offended his Reaver Knight sensibilities even more.

He nodded and turned Lotharin back to Korhandir's Leap.

'Then we form a new line at the bridge,' he said.

THE SOUNDS OF battle drifted over the centre of the elven line, the sounds tinny and distant, though blood was being shed and lives were being lost no more than a few hundred yards from where Menethis stood. A thick fog had gathered over the river to the north, obscuring the fighting until only the tips of the waystones atop the rounded hill could be seen.

Beyond Korhandir's Leap, a sprawling clash of horses raged, though Menethis could not tell who was in the ascendancy. He supposed the Ellyrians could, but even after his ride with them to harry the druchii vanguard, Menethis was still a foot soldier at heart. He preferred the ground beneath his feet as he fought; a longbow or sword as his weapons of choice.

Menethis stood in the front rank of the citizen levy of spear gathered by Lord Swiftwing, for the rank of sentinel had been bestowed upon him for his service at Eagle Gate. The two-hundred strong host was largely made up of warriors who had already lived a life of war and had hoped never to see another battle. Others had yet to see the ugly face of war, and it was these warriors Menethis was heartbroken to see arrayed in armour and bearing long-hafted spears. These were the young of Ulthuan, the hope for the future, the inheritors and shapers of the future.

Now there might not *be* a future for any of them.

As much as Menethis tried to remain optimistic about the coming fight, he found it difficult in the face of such a ferocious enemy that came in such numbers. To either side of his warriors were long lines of archers, resplendent in long cream robes over shirts of mail. Each archer in the front rank had emptied their quiver, placing their arrows in the ground before them, indicating that they would not run in the face of the enemy.

Their lines were thin, and would not stand long against a determined enemy charge.

Numerous spear hosts formed the centre of Lord Swiftwing's army, though the finest troops were positioned just behind the front lines. Stormweaver's Silver Helms looked magnificent in their polished ithilmar armour and gleaming helms, but there were only two hundred of them. Every warrior's helm was decorated with ribbons, gemstones or golden edging, indicating that these were the bravest of Lord Swiftwing's knights. Galadrien Stormweaver rode at their centre, his helm additionally embellished by swept-back eagle feathers of gold and white.

The enemy army was marching towards the river, and Menethis fixed his gaze on the disciplined ranks of druchii warriors directly across from him. They wore heavy hauberks of blackened iron and purple robes embroidered with fierce runic emblems of death. Bronze helms concealed their faces, and the fearsome swords resting on their shoulders marked them out as Executioners.

The weapons they carried were known as *draich*, killing blades forged in the blackest temples and blessed by priests of Khaine. Menethis had seen their skill with such executioners' swords on the walls of the Eagle Gate, and shivered at the bleak memory.

Behind these veteran warriors came something huge and crafted from bronze and jade, a towering effigy of murder and blades. A red-lit mist billowed around it, and hideous shrieks were carried on the wind alongside the bitter taste of iron. The red mist seeped out to envelop the Executioners, and their chants grew louder as they breathed in the sanguineous fog. Some drew their palms along the blades of their swords, while others reached up to touch their loathsome battle standard, a hateful icon with a grotesque mannequin chained to the upright and crossbars.

Its limbs jerked and twisted in a horrid parody of life, and Menethis turned away from the vile creation, but a broken voice called out to him from across the river. Suspecting some druchii trickery, Menethis paid the sound no mind, but it came again, and though it was the last gasp from a ruined throat there was a familiarity to the sound that was unmistakable.

He looked back at the Executioner's banner in horror as he realised it was no mannequin, but a living being nailed to timbers, one who had been horrifically disfigured through unimaginable torments only the insane could devise. His eyes had been put out, his limbs broken and every portion of his anatomy burned and flensed with skinning knives, yet this was a living being Menethis recognised.

It was Alathenar.

'Isha's mercy…' hissed Menethis.

The warriors to either side of him glanced over at his reaction, and Menethis knew he should reprimand them for such a lapse in focus, but he could not tear his eyes away from the horrors wrought upon the archer's body. How could he even know Menethis was here? Had he somehow sensed his former comrade's presence, or had he simply been repeating a familiar name ever since his capture?

The archer's lipless, toothless mouth worked up and down, crying out for Menethis, and he felt his heart moved to pity despite Alathenar's treachery. No one deserved such a fate, and Menethis pulled an arrow from his quiver and nocked it to his bow. He pulled back on the string, sighting down the length of the arrow, letting his breathing slow and imagining the path it would take. His focus shifted from the arrowhead to the mewling wreckage of the archer's body.

Menethis loosed between breaths, watching as his arrow arced out over the river. The point glittered in the weak sunlight as it slashed downwards. Alathenar turned what was left of his ravaged features to the sky, as though sensing his torment was about to end.

The arrow buried itself in Alathenar's throat, and the archer's head slumped over his chest as he died. A bawdy cheer went up from the Executioners, and Menethis hated that he had provided them any sort of pleasure.

'I give you peace, Alathenar,' Menethis said, 'but I do not forgive you.'

Chapter Thirteen

Blood of Ulthuan

THE BLACK ARK filled the horizon, a shard of Ulthuan now filled with evil and twisted to serve the druchii. The castle fortresses worked into the cliffs had been abandoned as the black ark ground its way deeper into the straits, crushing them to rubble against the sea walls. Every warrior of Lothern now stood on the glittering ramparts of the Sapphire Gate, ready to face an army of druchii that drew closer with every breath.

Every day had seen the black ark draw nearer to the sea gate, but today would see it close enough for the killing to begin. Black clouds swirled in a vortex above it, spreading out over the mountains to either side like oil in water. Every now and then, Tyrion would catch fleeting glimpses of a monstrous winged form in the darkness, a figure in purple-limned armour astride its serpentine neck.

The Witch King himself had come to see Lothern

humbled, and Tyrion longed for the chance to cross blades with the ancient foe of Ulthuan. The sea battered the cliffs of the black ark and crashed against its lower reaches, but what could the waves do to so towering an edifice as a mountain in so short a time? Tyrion felt the sea's anger as it sought to eject this thorn from the flesh of Ulthuan, and shared its frustration that it was powerless against it.

Powerless? No, that was not right.

He *could* have the power, but he chose not to wield it.

Tyrion gripped the hilt of Sunfang tightly, feeling the conflicting pulls on his heart as deep aches in his soul. His beloved Everqueen was beyond his sight in Avelorn, wounded and in need of his comfort, while Lothern would surely suffer greatly without his presence. Yet the greatest pull on his heart was that which turned his eyes to the north whenever his attention wandered or his focus slipped.

In those moments, he would see the storm-lashed isle in the cold, grey northern seas and feel the pull of that blood-bladed sword. Countless thousands had died over that hostile scrap of rock, their bones littering its desolate shale, their blood soaking its gritty black sand. All for possession of a weapon that could destroy the world. How ridiculous such a notion was. Why would anyone kill to possess a weapon that was doom incarnate?

Yet he *would* draw it and drive the druchii from Ulthuan if only he could be sure that he would set it back into the dripping altar as Aenarion had done. Tyrion knew he was strong, but was he strong enough to resist the lure of such a powerful weapon once it had been unsheathed? He didn't know, but the world would be a grimmer place were he to find out.

He heard someone call his name and shook off thoughts of the Blighted Isle.

'What?' he said.

'The island again?' asked Belannaer.

Tyrion nodded. 'Am I so transparent?'

'The Sword of Khaine is a mighty and terrible artefact,' said the Loremaster. 'And you are the greatest warrior of the asur. A hero of the line of Aenarion. Who else would it call to?'

Tyrion nodded towards the black ark as it ground its way along the straits of Lothern towards the Sapphire Gate.

'I fear what will happen if I do not answer its call,' said Tyrion. 'Yet my greater fear is of what will happen if I *do* answer it.'

'Then I am reassured,' said Belannaer. 'Only the foolish dream of such dangerous power; the wise know when not to meddle.'

'I am not wise, Sire Belannaer,' said Tyrion.

'You are wiser than you know, my friend.'

Tyrion shrugged, uncomfortable with such compliments, and said, 'Thank you, but I do not wish to speak of it further. Let us change the subject.'

'As you wish,' said Belannaer.

'Did my brother ask you to counsel me?'

Belannaer smiled. 'I am here to offer counsel to any who will heed it.'

'That's not an answer.'

'It is, just not the one you were looking for.'

'You mages and your secrets…'

'I keep no secrets, Tyrion,' said Belannaer. 'I am here as a representative of the White Tower. No more, no less.'

Tyrion said, 'Very well, I will press no further. But I

would value any counsel you would give. Like how we will stop the druchii from sweeping over us when that rock is upon us.'

'You will stop them with heart and courage,' said Belannaer. 'Every warrior on this wall is looking to you to show them how a prince of the asur fights. Finubar may be king, but *you* are the one they would wish to be. Remember that as you fight.'

Tyrion shook his head. 'No one should wish to be me.'

'In this instance, the truth of *being* Tyrion does not matter, it is the *idea* of Tyrion that is paramount. Every warrior here knows of your exploits; the rescue of the Everqueen, the duel with Urian Poisonblade, and the battle against N'Kari. You are a hero, whether you see it or not, and you *must* live up to that ideal.'

'So the legend of Tyrion becomes more important than who I really am?'

'In this case, yes.'

Tyrion said nothing for a moment, then gave a mirthless chuckle. 'You do not offer comforting counsel, Loremaster.'

'I offer the truth,' said Belannaer, 'and that is sometimes unwelcome.'

Further discussion was prevented by the arrival of the Phoenix King and his retinue of White Lions. Korhil was easy to spot, his lion-pelted shoulders and braided hair bobbing above those of his fellow warriors. Finubar's scarlet armour shone like polished ruby, and he carried his helm in the crook of his elbow so that all might see his mane of silver-blond hair streaming in the wind coming in off the straits.

'My king,' said Tyrion with a curt bow.

'Tyrion,' said Finubar. 'And Sire Belannaer, I trust you

and your mages stand ready to defend my city?'

'We do, my lord,' answered the mage, resting his hand on the pommel stone of the sword of Bel-Korhadris. 'With spell and with sword if need be.'

'Good, good,' said Finubar. 'If only all my subjects were so loyal.'

'Sire?' said Tyrion.

Finubar stood at the edge of the battlements, looking out at the dark clouds gathering above the black ark. Shards of lightning split the gathering gloom and the spread wings of a mighty dragon could clearly be seen silhouetted against the actinic light.

'We face Ulthuan's greatest foe, and yet there are those among my people who do not answer the call to fight. Prince Imrik seals himself in the volcanic caverns of the mountains and refuses to ride his dragon into battle. And messages to Eltharion are answered only by empty silence. I fear the Warden of Tor Yvresse has fallen too far into despair to lead his warriors in battle ever again.'

'I know Eltharion,' said Tyrion. 'He is a cautious warrior, it's true, but I cannot believe he will allow Ulthuan to fall without fighting in its defence.'

'Then perhaps you should go to Tor Yvresse and convince him to come,' snapped Finubar.

Tyrion shared a glance with Korhil at the Phoenix King's outburst, and the mighty White Lion gestured to the city behind the gate with his eyes. Far below, gathered in neat ranks on Lothern's quayside, a thousand grim-eyed warriors in pale white armour and cloaks of vivid scarlet edged with golden flames stood beneath a banner of a fiery phoenix.

Tyrion now understood the cause of Finubar's discomfort, for these were the Phoenix Guard, the silent guardians of the Shrine of Asuryan. It was said that within the temple was a forbidden vault known as the Chamber of Days, whereupon was inscribed the fates of every Phoenix King that had ever lived and ever would. The Phoenix Guard were privy to the secrets of time, and would arrive without warning to escort a newly-chosen Phoenix King to the fires of Asuryan.

Or carry a dead Phoenix King to his final rest.

THE ICE SPREAD over the water like sickness from a wound. Issyk Kul's savage warriors charged onto the solid surface of the river, brandishing heavy axes and swords and screaming filthy chants to the Dark Gods. Their horned helms gave them the appearance of daemons, and Caelir knew that was very nearly the case. Every one of the mortals who lived in the frozen north was touched by the warping power of Chaos.

The warrior hosts of Tor Elyr fought the twisted beasts, rank upon rank of spearmen thrusting their sharpened points into the heaving mass of furred flesh over and over again. It was an unequal struggle, for their foes were many times stronger. But where the beasts fought as raging individuals, the asur host gave battle as a cohesive whole. In perfect unison, elven spears were withdrawn and then rammed forward, each time bathed in the unclean blood of the monsters.

The arrival of the tribesmen would tip the balance of this flanking battle, but Caelir would not let that happen. The ice had reached the near shore, and Caelir saw Anurion the Green and his mages fighting to hold back its spread down the length of the river. Anurion's magic caused fresh blooms of grass and flowers to rear from the water's edge as he brought forth the life-giving magic of

Ulthuan, only for it to be withered by the cold and corruption of the dark magic from the tribal shamans.

This was an aspect of the battle Caelir could do nothing to affect, and he led his charging warriors onto the frozen surface of the river as powerful enchantments were woven, cast, countered and deflected. Any steeds other than Ellyrians would have slipped and fallen on the smooth ice, but there were no more sure-footed mounts in the world.

The tribal warriors saw his riders coming and loosed a wild cheer, as eager for the fight as the charging Reavers. Caelir tucked his spear into the crook of his arm and picked out the tribesman he would kill first. A barbarian wearing a bearskin cloak and a spiked helm lined with fur. His armour was crudely fashioned from lacquered leather and burned with a curving rune that brought bile to Caelir's throat.

The Reaver Knights smashed into the horde with a deafening clatter of blades. Caelir's spear punched into the tribesman's chest, tearing down through his heart and lungs before erupting from the small of his back. Caelir's spear snapped and he hurled away the broken haft. He drew his sword as Irenya smashed a path into the heaving mass of warriors. Blades flashed and blood sprayed the ice as the Reaver Knights wreaked fearsome havoc on the mortals. Armoured warriors slipped and went under the hooves of the Ellyrians, crushed against the diamond hard surface of the ice.

Irenya spun and kicked out as Caelir fought the northern tribesmen with the ferocity of a berserker. He heard elven voices calling his name, but he ignored them, driving his horse ever deeper into the sweating, stinking horde of savage mortals. Ahead, he could see Issyk Kul, his powerful form dwarfing those around him.

The warlord saw him coming and grinned with what looked like genuine pleasure, opening his arms as though welcoming home a prodigal son. Caelir screamed his hate and drove Irenya straight at the champion. Kul laughed and goaded his red-skinned beast towards Caelir. Both riders pushed their mounts hard, and as they passed, Caelir struck out with his sword, the blade slicing across the flesh of Issyk Kul. The warlord's skin was like iron, and Caelir's blade slid clear.

In return Kul's monstrous blade swept out and beheaded Irenya with a brutal overhead cut.

Caelir was hurled from the corpse of his mount as she crashed to the ice. He twisted as he fell, landing on his feet atop a fallen tribesman. Blood flooded from his headless steed, and he stared in horror at the twitching remains. Warriors surged forward, but Kul reined in his horse and waved them away. The raw-fleshed steed radiated heat, and the ice steamed with every step it took.

'You have returned to join us?' asked Kul, his voice wetly seductive, and Caelir wanted to laugh at the ridiculous question. Tears streamed from his eyes at Irenya's death, and he hurled himself at the warlord, oblivious to the swirling combats going on around him. Warriors were dying on the ice, *his* warriors, but all he could see was the gloating form of Kul as he loomed over Caelir's steed.

'You killed her!' screamed Caelir, charging at Kul.

The mounted warlord batted aside Caelir's clumsy attack, and slammed an armoured boot into his face. Caelir reeled from the power of the blow as Kul dropped from his horse, the beast snarling and stamping the ground in its eagerness to trample him underfoot. Kul thrust his sword into the ice, a black malevolence radiating from the blade and into the ice.

'Why are you fighting me?' asked Kul, 'I made you what you are, little elf. Have you not realised that yet?'

Caelir spun on his heel, slashing for Kul's throat, but the blow struck the champion's armoured forearm as it came up to block. Kul's fist hammered Caelir's chest and something cracked inside. He dropped to one knee, struggling to catch a breath. Issyk Kul shook his head and reached up to remove his helm, hanging it from his saddle horn. The warlord retrieved his sword from the ice and swung it around his body, as though loosening up for a mildly diverting sparring session.

'You were nothing until we remade you,' hissed Kul, his repulsively handsome face more disappointed than angry. 'A pathetic life wasted on petty cruelties and dabblings on the fringes of true excesses. You called yourself free, but you were just as much a prisoner of the grey chains of life as the rest of your dull kind. I did you a favour, and you welcomed it.'

'No!' screamed Caelir, surging upright and stabbing his blade at Kul's groin.

Kul stepped aside and thundered his knee into Caelir's side. A right-cross slammed Caelir to the ice, and his sword skittered away from him. He scrabbled across the ice to retrieve it. Kul followed him with long strides and grabbed him by the scruff of the neck.

Caelir twisted in his grip, but Kul was too strong for him.

'Pathetic,' sneered the warlord, and Caelir spat in his face.

Kul laughed and dropped him to the ice. 'That's more like it. Show me your hate and passions! Accept the ecstasies of the dark prince and you will know true freedom!'

Caelir's sword lay within his reach, and he swept it up, scissoring himself to his feet in a blur of motion. He stepped in and drove his blade into Kul's belly, but the blade snapped as though he had stabbed it into the side of a mountain.

'The dark prince protects his favoured sons,' sneered Kul at Caelir's attack. 'And if you choose to deny his seductions, then it is time to be rid of you.'

Kul's sword sang for Caelir's neck, its many blades glittering like icy shards of blood.

THE CHILL WINDS blowing from the far bank carried the foul odour of the cold ones: rotting meat, stagnant water and oily, scaled bodies that shunned the light. It caught at the back of Eldain's throat, and he retched at the rank, dead taste.

'Isha's mercy, how can they stand it?' he spat.

Eldain rode towards the crystal horses at the end of Korhandir's Leap in time to see the black knights thunder onto the bridge with terrifying speed as they dug razor-tipped spurs into the reptiles' flanks. The crystal bridge shook with the force of their charge, and the knights raised a crimson banner as they lowered their lances.

Arrows bounced uselessly from the scaled hides of the cold ones, spinning off into the dark waters of the river below. A shimmering skin of freezing fog crept across the water and Eldain saw that some of the arrows skittered across the surface of the river instead of sinking.

'The riders!' shouted Eldain. 'Kill the riders!'

His Reavers wheeled their mounts and stood tall in their saddles, bringing their bows to bear on these armoured knights. Flurries of arrows sped towards the black knights and a handful fell as particularly skilful or lucky archers found a gap between breastplate and helm, but it was not enough to stop the charge.

Eldain loosed a shaft at the exposed neck of a lancer. The arrow sliced deep into his flesh and the warrior toppled from the saddle. His mount snapped at the dangling corpse, biting it in two with one swipe of its jaws. Eldain sent another shaft into the knights, but this arrow ricocheted from a curved shield.

Perhaps a dozen knights were pitched from their saddles, but it was nowhere near enough to stop the charge from hitting home. The druchii heavy cavalry smashed into the bulwark of spears before them and the carnage was terrible. The sheer force of the impact obliterated the front two ranks of the asur battle line, their bodies crushed beneath the clawed feet of the reptilian monsters. Dark lances plunged home, punching screaming elves from their feet as the cold ones bit and tore at those who avoided the stabbing blades.

Eldain reined in his horse at the end of the bridge as blood-maddened cold ones rampaged amongst the dead. Despite the barbed spurs and goads of the black knights, the reptiles paused to gorge themselves on the warm meat laid before them like a feast. The bridge's defenders fell back from the slaughter, and only the shouted commands of the Sentinel prevented the retreat from becoming a rout.

Though every fibre of his being wanted to ride onto the bridge, Eldain knew his lightly armed Reavers could not hope to stop the black knights. The broken ranks of infantry would need time to rally before marching back into the fray. Eldain's warriors could not give them that time, but help was coming from a different quarter.

Mitherion Silverfawn stood amid the flow of warriors from the bridge, his silver robes billowing in the cold winds coming off the river. A small band of mages and Sword Masters attended him, and even from here, Eldain saw Rhianna's father was gaunt and drawn, though the battle had only just begun. Eldain recognised one of Master Silverfawn's Sword Masters, and he nodded to Yvraine Hawkblade as she unsheathed her mighty greatsword.

Mitherion Silverfawn threw his arms out to the side before bringing his hands together in a mighty thunderclap. The booming echo of the sound was like the hammer of Vaul upon the anvil of the gods, and Eldain's heart was instantly transported to the days of heroes, when Aenarion and Caledor Dragontamer bestrode the fields of Ulthuan like gods. He hauled back on the reins as a surge of vitality and confidence pounded through his body like the war drums of ancient armies that might conquer the world. He felt as though he could slay every one of the black knights and their monstrous mounts single-handed, riding through them to Morathi herself and cleaving her fell heart in two.

Eldain reluctantly shook off the effects of Mitherion Silverfawn's magic, knowing it was too dangerous for his warriors to get drawn into such a fight. Fleetness of hoof was their greatest weapon, not charging headlong into heavily armed warriors riding killer beasts.

All around him, elven warriors who had, moments ago, been in full retreat now turned back to the twin piers of crystal horses at the end of the bridge. Light seemed to dance within them, like sunlight in ice, and every warrior felt their wise eyes upon him. They braced their spears and marched back onto the bridge, a cold and merciless fire burning in their eyes.

More warriors manoeuvred towards the bridge, as though drawn by the raw courage of the bridge's defenders. While the cold ones feasted on the flesh of the dead, the asur marched back onto the bridge with aching laments of Aenarion wrung from every throat.

The dark knights cursed and struck their mounts, but such tender morsels were a rare luxury to these monsters and no amount of threats could rouse them from their feast.

With a rousing war cry, the elven warriors charged into the dark knights, spears thrusting home with strength enough to penetrate mail shirts and iron plates. A score of knights died to the vengeful spears of the asur, and their reptilian mounts screeched with agony as long blades stabbed them repeatedly. The surviving knights saw the murderous determination in the eyes of their foes, and fell back before their grim resolve.

Yet even this would not be enough.

Druchii warriors, fresh to the fight, marched onto the bridge beneath a banner dripping in blood and emblazoned with the rune of Khaine. Their armour and cloaks were plum-coloured and their barbed spears were as black as their hearts. They charged past the slaughtered cold ones and fallen knights to hammer into the scattered spearmen in a clash of blades.

Centuries of bitterness gave the druchii strength, and their spears were red and bloody in moments. The enchantment of Mitherion Silverfawn was losing its power, and the magic that had steeled the hearts of the asur faded like the last rays of sunlight in winter. The fighting was desperate and bloody, shouts of anger and pain echoing from the sides of the bridge as the sundered kin of Ulthuan fought without thought of quarter or clemency.

Warriors from both sides fell to the freezing river below, and blood seeped through the bridge's rainholes as though Korhandir's Leap wept for the slaughter being performed upon its divinely crafted arches. The banner of the druchii pulsed with life, as though with a heart-beat of its own.

Eldain twisted in the saddle and sought out Mitheri-on Silverfawn amid the fog and marching warriors. At last he spied the mage's silver robes at the edge of the river, and he urged Lotharin through the press of bod-ies towards him. Silverfawn looked up as he approached and smiled weakly.

'Eldain,' he said. 'I am glad to see you alive.'

'Master Silverfawn,' said Eldain. 'Any aid you can give us would be most welcome. The bridge will not hold long, and there are druchii across the river to the south.'

'I feared as much,' said Silverfawn cryptically, but Eldain had no time to dwell on the mage's eccentricities.

'Can you help or not?'

The Sword Masters attending Silverfawn stepped for-ward, angered by his tone, but Yvraine held them back as the mage nodded.

'I can, Eldain,' said Silverfawn. 'But the bridge will fall, I have seen it in every reading of the stars.'

'You have seen the future?' asked Eldain.

'Parts of it, yes,' admitted Silverfawn. 'Enough to know that the bridge will fall, and that we must hold this line as long as possible. You understand, time and the future are not linear, but curved, yes? What will be has to be *made* in the present by our own deeds. We work to create the future, and thus nothing is certain.'

'I do not understand you, Master Silverfawn,' said Eldain. 'All I understand is that our people are dying here, and more will die if you do not help.'

'Not help? Of course I will help,' snapped Silverfawn, striding towards the end of the bridge with Yvraine's Sword Masters at his heels. 'As though I would not, the very idea!'

Eldain made to follow, but before he could urge Lotharin onwards, Laurena Starchaser rode next to him. Her hair was matted with dried blood and she had lost her spear somewhere along the way.

'The druchii are crossing the river in ever greater numbers,' she said. 'Heavy horse as well as the fast riders.'

Eldain swore. 'Our flank is turned.'

'The spear hosts at the southern edge of Tor Elyr are aligning to meet this new threat,' said Starchaser. 'But if the druchii take the bridge, we will have no choice but to fall back to the city itself.'

Eldain glanced at the bridge, remembering Mitherion Silverfawn's words. The bridge would fall, the mage had said, but if there was one thing Eldain had managed to take from his rambling words it was that nothing was set, nothing was ever inevitable.

'Gather thirty of your best riders and follow me, Laurena,' said Eldain.

'Where are we going?' asked Starchaser, even as she wheeled her mount.

'Onto the bridge!' cried Eldain, riding after Mitherion Silverfawn.

THE EXECUTIONERS CROSSED the river with heavy strides, though how such a thing could happen was a mystery to Menethis. In a land of endless summer, how could a river suddenly freeze? Red mist clawed up from the water's edge, and the heavily armoured warriors came up the slopes of the hills with their *draich* swinging in glittering arcs.

With the Executioners on this side of the river, Menethis finally saw the terrible effigy of bronze and jade on the opposite bank. A towering automaton of blades, it was a mechanical representation of the murder god himself, shaped by madmen and hellions with bare hands on molten metal. Blood streamed down the carven limbs and flowed in endless rivers from the serrated blades held in the statue's outstretched hands. That blood was collected in a vast bronze reservoir below, a bloodstained cauldron that hissed and spat with poisonous fumes, reeking of spoiled meat.

Chanting, slender-limbed elves with pale skin and near-naked bodies danced around the construction, and the blood of uncounted sacrifices made Menethis want to retch. The malign influence of the thing was potent, and stank of the blackest murder and sorcery.

Menethis tore his gaze from the hideous effigy as arrows slashed down upon the Executioners. Hundreds of shafts were loosed from archers positioned behind and on the flanks of the spear hosts. The red mist clung to the grim warriors, and many of the arrows were burned to ash before they struck home. Hideous beasts came behind the Executioners: draconic creatures with numerous reptilian heads atop serpentine necks, and disfigured abominations goaded by hunchbacked mortals.

Then the charge hit. A forest of stabbing spears punched through the armour of the Executioners' front rank, drawing blood and then ramming home again.

'Thrust!' cried Menethis, and the warriors behind him

shouted as they drove their spears into the enemy ranks.

'Twist! Withdraw!'

Over and over Menethis shouted the mantra of thrust, twist and withdraw, but these cold-eyed killers had no fear of death. Fresh warriors stepped over the bodies of the slain, chopping spear heads from hafts or gripping the weapon that killed them with blood-slick hands and keeping it wedged in their bodies.

Grunts of pain came from the druchii, but no screams. These were tough, grim warriors who understood that pain was a warrior's lot, and accepted it. Their blades hacked into the spear host, lopping heads and limbs with every stroke. The precision of their blows was extraordinary, honed over a lifetime of beheadings and executions in the name of Khaine.

Though his warriors fought magnificently, the Executioners were now living up to their name, hacking down rank after rank of Ellyrion's finest. Menethis understood the ebb and flow of a battle well enough to know when the courage of warriors was at its most brittle.

This was that moment, and there was nothing he could do to prevent it breaking.

The terror of the Executioners' blades became too much for his spear host, and they fled from their murderous strokes, breaking ranks and sprinting for the lines of archers behind them. They fled in ones and twos, all cohesion forgotten in the desperate flight for life. The Executioners cut down those not quick enough to flee, methodical to the last.

'Hold! Stand fast!' shouted Menethis, though it was far too late for mere words to keep the line from disintegrating. As his warriors fled, Menethis stood his ground before the black line of Executioners, his anger at what they had done here like a forest fire in his heart.

'You took Cerion, you took Glorien and now you come for me,' he said, calmer than he would have believed possible. His heartbeat was like thunder over the Annulii as he lifted his sword to his shoulder and charged towards the Executioners with the name of Asuryan upon his lips.

His sword slashed across an Executioner's chest, the blade sliding up under the cheek plate of the warrior's helmet to slice his face open. A flap of skin flopped down over his jaw, but still he did not scream. A sweeping two-handed blade arced towards Menethis's neck, but he leaned into the blow and rammed his sword through the eye slits of the Executioner's helm.

The warrior dropped with a strangled grunt, but another stepped over his corpse without pause and crashed the pommel of her sword into his forehead. Menethis reeled back, blood streaming down his face as the Executioner closed in for the kill.

He looked up through the visor of her helm. She had the most beautifully violet eyes.

Menethis tried to raise his sword, but the *draich* was too fast.

The thunder of his heartbeat swelled, but before the Executioner's blade parted his head from his shoulders, a silver lance punched her from her feet and lifted her high into the air. Thundering shapes of white and silver streamed past him, heavy horse armoured in ithilmar mail and caparisoned in ivory and gold.

Warriors clad in gleaming plate and high silver helms that shone like moonlight on still water rode these mighty steeds, and their lances and swords cut like lightning from the hand of Asuryan himself.

CHAPTER FOURTEEN

BREAKING POINT

CAELIR HAD HEARD that at the moment of death, a person's life would flash before their eyes, but as Issyk Kul's sword swept towards him, he knew that was a lie. It was not the deeds of the life about to end that paraded through a mind, but the life unlived and the roads not taken.

He saw himself as lord of Ellyr-Charoi with Rhianna at his side, and children playing in the meadows beyond. Horses filled the stables and summer's calm lay upon the hillsides. In the space of a single heartbeat, Caelir saw the joys, the tears and the absurdities of existence that make up the rich pageant of lives intertwined. Eldain was there too, his brother sat astride Lotharin as he rode the endless plains of Ellyrion with a song in his heart.

It was fiction, a dream of a future that never was and never could be; but it gave him a moment's comfort in this last breath of life left to him. Caelir closed his eyes, but instead of death, he heard an earthy sound like a Chracian's axe biting fresh wood.

Standing before him was a glistening tree trunk, and embedded in the wood was Issyk Kul's monstrous sword. Ice and water ran from its branches, and the sweet smell of new sap filled Caelir's nostrils as it poured like amber blood from where Kul's blade had hacked into it. The ground creaked beneath Caelir, and he saw the splintered hole in the ice where the tree had burst through the ice covering the river's surface.

Kul wrenched his sword from the soft wood, and Caelir sprang away as the ice bucked and heaved beneath him. Jagged black cracks split the ice, racing away in zigzag courses from the new roots and branches pushing their way up from below. An entire forest was rising from the depths of the river, growing with incredible ferocity.

'Life magic!' hissed Kul, as though the presence of such things were anathema to him.

Caelir was astounded, and scrambled away from this burgeoning forest as the ice heaved and split apart. This was no passive greenery, but aggressive growth like the ancient forest trees said to dwell within the forgotten heart of Athel Loren. Jagged roots speared up into the tribesmen, piercing their flesh and growing up through their bodies.

He lost sight of Issyk Kul as spreading branches ensnared terrified warriors and looped around limbs to tear them off with wrenching heaves of growth. Scores of armoured tribesmen were lifted from the ground and impaled upon sharp, new-grown wood or ripped in two by spreading branches. Within moments, a thick forest of dripping trees had arisen from the river, and hundreds of torn bodies hung from their branches like corpses in gibbets.

Nor was the threat of the forest the only danger.

As roots burst the ice, a measure of the sorcery holding the water in its frozen state was unravelled, and screaming warriors dropped through into the river. In the midst of this rampant fecundity strode a mage in emerald robes that swirled in the billowing streams of magic that spiralled around him like a caged whirlwind.

'Anurion!' cried Caelir.

The mage ignored him and strode into the howling mass of tribesmen. His arms wove complex patterns, and where he gestured new life erupted from the ground to entangle, to stab and to tear. The river became a thick forest, dense with dark trees and overhanging boughs of thorny wood. So complete was Anurion's mastery of life-giving magic that it mattered not that thick sheet ice lay between him and the touch of earth.

Baying and blooded tribesmen who had escaped the slaughter of the rampaging forest threaded a path through the trees towards the mage. A throwing axe was turned aside by the swaying branches of a willow, and a hurled spear changed in flight to become a twisting sapling that spun harmlessly away. A raven-fletched arrow sliced into Anurion's thigh, and blood stained his robes with vivid scarlet.

A tribesman in a wolf-faced mask hurled himself at Anurion. The mage pointed a finger at him, and the branch of a tree lashed out to take his head off with the precision of a rapier. More closed in, and the forest defended its creator, grasping roots dragging men beneath the river and long saplings slashing like razor-edged whips to open throats and remove limbs.

Yet it had cost Anurion dear to raise a forest from the depths of the river, and already its rapid growth was slowing. Caelir took up a fallen spear from the body of a slain Reaver Knight and half ran, half slipped towards Anurion.

The mage saw him and shook his head.

A wall of thorns and thick, grasping briars arose, completely blocking Caelir's path towards Anurion.

'No!' shouted Caelir. 'Anurion! Come back!'

Caelir's voice was lost in the bellows of the mortal warriors, and tears stung his eyes at the thought of the line of Anurion the Green being ended forever. No sooner had the thought arisen, than a spectral voice sounded in his mind.

So long as one blade of grass or flower blooms in Ulthuan, I will live on.

Caelir tore at the jagged coils of briars. The thorns, recognising one of their own, turned their barbs from his skin.

'Anurion, no!' he yelled. 'Please! Come back to us!'

Make them pay, Caelir. That is all I ask, make them pay…

Caelir nodded and turned from the sheets of briars, weeping and stumbling over the disintegrating ice towards the riverbank. Reaver Knights rode back to solid ground as yet more of the ice cracked and came away from the riverbank. He leapt as the ice beneath him retuned to water, breathless and grief-struck at the loss of Anurion.

He took a heaving breath and reasserted a measure of control. Anurion was gone, and that was a grievous loss, but the battle had yet to be won. Caelir turned and ran to where his Reaver Knights awaited him. Around sixty still lived, and he vaulted onto the back of a bay mare with a silver mane and midnight black tail.

'I am Caelir Éadaoin of Ellyr-Charoi, and I grieve with

you for the loss of your rider,' said Caelir, 'but if you will have me, I will be your brother in this fight. What say you?'

The mare tossed her mane and stamped the ground in assent, and Caelir rubbed a hand over her neck as a name appeared in his thoughts.

Liannar.

'I will be a loyal companion, Liannar,' he promised as his knights formed up around him.

The northern flank of Lord Swiftwing's army was still holding. Remorseless spear hosts drove the bestial monsters that had first crossed the river back to the water's edge. A combination of unending arrows dropping from above and elven stoicism had prevailed, and the beasts were being slaughtered in ever greater numbers.

The mist was clearing, and Caelir saw the summit of the rounded hill and its marble crown of waystones. As the conjured mist dissipated still further, the bolt throwers unleashed a hail of arrows into the druchii forces massing on the far bank of the river. Caelir wheeled Liannar southwards, shielding his eyes from the low sun to gauge how the rest of the army fared.

The ground to the north of Tor Elyr sloped gently down towards the bay, levelling out to a wide plain to the south, and Caelir's jaw clenched as he saw the druchii had crossed the river south of the city. The army's centre was bending back like a bowyer testing the strength of a bow stave, but Galadrien Stormweaver's Silver Helms were fighting hard to give the infantry time to rally and reform the battle line.

The Reavers around him saw what he saw, and he sensed their dismay at the ring of blades closing in on Tor Elyr like a hangman's noose. If the centre broke, then this battle was as good as over. He saw that same realisation on every face around him, and knew that the courage of his warriors hung by a thread.

Caelir rode out before the Reavers around him, and turned his horse to face them. More scattered horsemen rallied around his warriors, until hundreds were ready to listen.

'This battle is *not* lost,' he shouted. 'The druchii have crossed the river, but the centre still holds and Stormweaver's Silver Helms are fighting to keep it so. We hold the north, and Anurion the Green gave his life that we might continue to do so! The enemy will attempt another crossing, and it is up to us to stop them. Either we stop them or Tor Elyr is lost. We fight here, or we die elsewhere. It is that simple.'

He lifted his spear and Liannar reared up on her hind legs.

'We are Ellyrians, and this is our land!' yelled Caelir. 'Are you ready to fight for it?'

Hundreds of spears stabbed the air, and a wordless Ellyrian war cry echoed across the water and corpse-thronged forest to their enemies. Caelir turned Liannar back to the riverbank as the icy mist once again crept across the water to freeze its surface.

A war horn sounded from the opposite side of the river.

Far to the north a glittering curtain of light shimmered on the horizon, and a sparkling rain fell beneath a rainbow's arch like diamond tears.

'Isha be with us,' said Caelir.

TYRION DIVED BENEATH a slashing line of iron barbs loosed from a bolt thrower situated on a craggy bluff of the black ark and rolled to his feet with Sunfang held out before him. The entire length of the Sapphire Gate was swathed in the shadow of the vast, seaborne fortress, its monstrous bulk finally wedged deep in the rocks of the straits some thirty yards from the sea portal. Heavy iron corvus ramps slammed down on the ornamented battlements, and druchii swordsmen poured from inside the hellish mountain.

Asur warriors stood frozen in death alongside him, their bodies turned to glassy ice by the bleak sorceries of the druchii magickers. One body lay shattered into crystalline fragments beneath the spiked end of a boarding ramp, like a marble statue struck by a sledgehammer. Tyrion leapt onto the iron ramp bridging the gap between the black ark and the Sapphire Gate as warriors in scaled cloaks like dragonhide charged at him with curved sabres and cutlass daggers unsheathed. Tyrion ran to meet them, his golden-bladed sword cleaving through the first three attackers in as many strokes. Crossbowmen took shots at him from rocky bluffs high above the ramp, but Tyrion was always in motion, ducking, spinning, leaping and lunging.

Many of their bolts hit their fellow druchii, sending them falling thousands of feet to the churning waters below. The ramp swayed and bounced with the weight of bodies upon it, and Tyrion used its motion to help him dodge the clumsy blows of his enemies. Yet he was only a single warrior, while the druchii were many, and time and time again, he found himself having to take a backwards step to avoid being flanked.

'Asur!' he yelled, vaulting back onto the battlements of the Sapphire Gate.

'Ho!' came the shouted reply, and a score of

goose-feathered shafts sliced home into the attacking druchii. He watched as warriors were pitched from the ramp, falling like flower seeds blown from a gardener's hand. Elven warriors took up position at the end of the ramp, hacking at the stonework with heavy hammers and axes to dislodge the penetrating spikes.

Belarien was at his side a heartbeat later, a bent bow in his hand as he pulled the string taut. He loosed and another druchii was punched from the ramp.

'Must you always run off on your own?' hissed Belarien. 'It makes it much harder to keep you safe.'

Tyrion gave a wry smile. 'You must be getting old, my friend. You never had any trouble keeping up with me at Finuval.'

'I was young and foolish back then,' said Belarien. 'Now I am just foolish.'

'We are all foolish, else we would not be warriors, but poets and dreamers.'

'If only life gave us the chance, eh?'

'If only,' agreed Tyrion, as the ramp was broken loose from the ramparts. It dropped from the walls, but heavy chains looped around iron rings stopped it from falling too far. A grinding windlass mechanism within the ark started turning, and the ramp began to rise, ready for more druchii to pour across it in yet another attack. A dozen ramps disgorged hundreds of druchii onto the Sapphire Gate, and the fighting on its glittering structure was fierce indeed. Flights of arrows and swarms of bolts cut the air back and forth, and streams of magical fire lit up the unnatural darkness as Belannaer's mages burned the rock of the black ark to glass.

In return, freezing winds swept the Sapphire Gate as the Witch King's sorceries sucked the life from the elven defenders, and writhing tendrils of darkness snaked up over the walls to drag screaming warriors to their doom. The vast brazier atop the black ark bathed the battle in a hellish orange glow, and each battle was fought in its leaping shadows.

Like a single colossal siege tower, the black ark unleashed thousands of druchii onto the Sapphire Gate in an onrushing tide. Finubar's warriors had fought off every attack thus far, but all it would take was one boarding ramp to capture its part of the ramparts for the defenders to lose control of the gate.

Tyrion scanned the fighting, looking for any weaknesses the druchii could exploit.

At the meeting point of the two halves of the sea gate, he saw Finubar's crimson armour amid a brutal swirl of daggers, axes and barbed shields. Korhil fought beside the Phoenix King, his enormous axe cleaving druchii in two with every blow. Those he could not strike with his axe, he picked up and hurled from the battlements.

A pair of ramps hammered down on the ramparts to either side of the Phoenix King, and Tyrion immediately saw the danger.

'Belarien, with me!' he yelled and ran towards the centre.

Tyrion sprinted through the morass of struggling warriors, ignoring all but the most pressing dangers. He cut and slashed as he ran, killing the enemy even as his attention was focussed on the Phoenix King. Druchii warriors poured down these new ramps, cutting the king off from his warriors.

Tyrion felt his sword grow hot in his hands and swept it around in a wide arc, holding it two-handed and unleashing a brilliant ray of fiery sunlight from its blade.

It cut through the druchii, setting light to their dragonscale cloaks and melting the flesh from their bones.
Burning warriors screamed in agony and hurled themselves from the sea gate to the waters below, while others
sagged on heat-softened bones to fall in pools of molten
skin and liquefied organs.

The screaming was terrible, and the stench even worse,
but Tyrion felt nothing for the warriors he killed. They
were his enemies. They had attacked his homeland and
his people, and deserved no more. Tyrion ran through the
flame, and blackened lumps of crackling meat, Sunfang
now cold in his grip. The heat of his sword's fire hazed the
air, and a druchii warrior appeared before him, his skin
blackened and his armour fused to his skin in glossy black
runnels. Tyrion took his head off without missing a step
and ran to where he heard the bellows of the White Lions.

A sharp metallic flavour bit the air, and Tyrion tasted
the taint of sorcery. Heat gave way to cold in an instant,
and Tyrion pulled up short at the shock of it. It billowed
out like debris from a falling star, and Tyrion dropped to
one knee as it blew over him. Freezing fog enveloped the
centre of the sea gate, and flash-formed icicles hung like
ice dragon teeth from the overhanging machicolations.

The sounds of battle faded to silence, and Tyrion
forced himself to run into the icy mist. The marble flagstones were slippery with ice, and as Tyrion came upon
the fighting, it was akin to entering the winter gardens
of Lothern at festival time. The mages of Saphery would
amaze visitors to their gardens with startlingly lifelike
creations fashioned from ice that could move and inter-
act with the patrons.

Except the figures that populated the ramparts were
not simple creations of water, they were living beings.

Or they *had* been…

The White Lions stood frozen in place, layers of frost coating their thick pelts like icing on a feast cake. Their skin was translucent and ghostly, their veins vivid red and blue against the white. Frozen arcs of crimson curved from the edges of weapons and wounds spilled blood in a frozen tableau.

In the centre of the frozen scene was Finubar, the brilliant red of the Phoenix King's armour ice-dusted white and blue. Before the king, frozen in mid-leap, was Korhil, his powerful frame draped in icicles and crackling webs of frost like spider webs.

'Isha's mercy!' cried Tyrion, weaving a path through the frozen figures towards the king.

Beyond the icy figures, Tyrion saw druchii hacking a path towards the king with heavy-bladed felling axes. The targets of their axes shattered and fell to the ramparts with glassy cracks, and Tyrion felt his smouldering anger turn to incandescent rage.

A druchii axeman smashed a frozen White Lion aside, but died a heartbeat later as Tyrion buried his sword in his chest. Tyrion kicked the axeman from his blade and leapt to intercept the others. He could hear shouted voices behind him, but dared not take his eyes from the druchii warriors facing him. Cold-eyed and thin-lipped, they wielded their heavy executioner's blades as easily as a child would swing a wooden sword.

An axe swung past him, missing his ear by a hair's breadth, and he jumped back, almost losing his footing on the ice. He turned that slip into a spin, bringing Sunfang up into his attacker's midriff. The warrior grunted and dropped to his knees, his glistening entrails steaming in the cold air.

Arrows whickered through the frozen statues of the White Lions, carefully aimed and lethally accurate. Tyrion knew Belarien's warriors would no sooner hit him than they would the Phoenix King, and fought the druchii as arrows passed fingerbreadths from his body.

'Come on and die!' he yelled, when the axemen hesitated.

Tyrion saw their cruel smiles and, in that moment, knew their attack had been but a diversion. He turned and ran back towards the Phoenix King in time to see a black-cloaked figure land on the ramparts with finesse that spoke of only one possible profession.

'Assassin!' yelled Tyrion.

The hooded figure drew a black dagger from an iron sheath and ran towards the Phoenix King. Arrows sliced by him as he moved like liquid; twisting, swaying and leaping over every incoming shaft. Tyrion sprinted towards the assassin, though he was too far away to save the Phoenix King. The black dagger came up and Tyrion screamed Finubar's name.

As the weapon plunged down, another warrior leapt in front of the Phoenix King. Mail links parted before the blade, and blood squirted as it twisted in the wound. Tyrion screamed as he saw Belarien fall at the Phoenix King's feet, his heart pierced by the assassin's dagger. The black hood fell away from the killer's face, a wholly unremarkable face that would pass unnoticed in a crowd and leave no impression upon anyone who saw him.

The assassin wrenched the dagger free of Belarien's chest and turned back to the Phoenix King. Tyrion drew back his arm, ready to hurl Sunfang in a last ditch attempt to prevent the assassin from carrying out his mission.

Before he could throw, a cracking sound like a gallery of windows breaking echoed over the gate, and a mighty, frost-hardened fist swung around to slam into the assassin's shoulder. Korhil of the White Lions shrugged off the last of the ice encasing him in an expanding mist of ice shards, his fury like that of the beast whose pelt he wore upon his shoulders. The black-cloaked killer twisted at the last moment to rob the blow of its power, and spun around Korhil. The black dagger stabbed out again, and Korhil grunted as it was withdrawn bloody.

The White Lion staggered against the parapet as the assassin moved in to finish him. Before the dagger could stab home again, Korhil surged forward and wrapped his arms around the assassin, dragging him into a crushing bear hug. The killer fought to free his arms, but the champion of the White Lions kept them pinned at his sides and exerted every ounce of his legendary strength.

Tyrion heard something give way with a sickening crack, and the assassin went limp in Korhil's arms. The White Lion released the assassin, who fell to the ground like a limp marionette. Korhil picked him up by the scruff of the neck and swung the corpse around to dangle it over the edge of the sea gate.

'You nearly made me fail,' he growled. 'And I *never* fail.'

With those words, Korhil hurled the assassin out to sea, watching as the body bounced and flopped down the craggy sides of the black ark to the hungry waters below.

Tyrion ran past Korhil, and skidded to a halt beside Belarien's limp form.

His friend was dead, of that there could be no doubt. Whatever venom had coated the assassin's blade had been deadly enough to slay him a dozen times over. Belarien's face was slack, his limbs already cold, and Tyrion felt a lifetime's rage coalesce in his heart.

A crushing hand gripped his shoulder and pulled Tyrion to his feet.

He lashed out, but a wide palm caught his fist.

'Grieve later, young prince,' said Korhil, releasing Tyrion's hand and shaking the last of the icy sorcery from his limbs. 'We have greater enemies to face now.'

Tyrion looked at the White Lion through a mask of tears. Korhil's face was ashen from the after-effects of sorcery and the assassin's venom, and how he had not succumbed to their effects was beyond Tyrion's ability to understand.

'He saved Finubar's life,' said Tyrion.

'Aye, that he did,' agreed Korhil. 'And he will be remembered for his sacrifice. But this fight isn't over yet, not by a long way. Look!'

Tyrion followed Korhil's outstretched axe, and saw the midnight black form of a mighty dragon swooping overhead. Its scaled body glistened like obsidian, and the warrior astride its neck was encased in armour of curved black plates, spines and barbed horns. Flares of dark magic slicked the air around the Witch King, and he threw searing purple lighting from his hands as he flew over the sea gate. Explosions of actinic light swept the sea gate, and elven warriors were hurled to their deaths or burned to cinders where they stood.

'Malekith,' hissed Tyrion, but Korhil gripped his arm before he could charge off to face the Witch King.

'Unhand me, Korhil,' demanded Tyrion.

'We'll get to the traitor king in good time, young prince,' said Korhil, turning him around as an adult might turn a child. 'We have other druchii to gut first.'

The druchii axemen were surging forward in the wake of the assassin's failure, hacking a path through the frozen figures of Korhil's White Lions. The sorcery that had frozen them in place was wearing off, and these warriors screamed as the axe blades cleaved them. Tyrion forced his grief at Belarien's passing aside, and distilled the fury raging within him down to a diamond hard core of utter clarity of purpose.

He swept Sunfang up to his shoulder, and nodded to Korhil.

Before they could charge to meet the axemen, a flurry of arrows arced down from the rocks on the eastern side of the gate. Each one found its mark with uncanny accuracy, dropping an axeman with a single arrow to the throat. A single volley of arrows had felled two score armoured warriors.

'Blood of Aenarion!' swore Korhil. 'Where did those arrows come from?'

Tyrion squinted through the gloom to see who had loosed these incredible arrows, but could see nothing. It was as though the cliff itself had let fly.

Then he glimpsed movement, but it was movement he saw only because the warrior making it *wanted* him to see it. Almost invisible against the rocks of the straits, Tyrion saw an archer clad in slate grey and gorse green, with a dun cloak pulled tightly around his body. He wore a conical, face-concealing helm of burnished bronze and silver, and Tyrion knew of only one group of warriors who went to war so attired.

'The rangers of Tor Yvresse!'

'But how can they be here?' said Korhil. 'Unless…'

From the darkened sky came a screeching roar, and a

powerful beast with the hindquarters of a jungle cat and the upper body of a ferocious beast of prey stooped from the storm clouds wreathing the upper reaches of the black ark. Its wide wings were feathered gold and brown, and its powerful beak was the colour of ebony and mahogany. Sat in a heavy leather saddle on the griffon's back was an elven warrior clad in golden, gem-encrusted armour and a winged helm of white and blue feathers. He unsheathed a rune-encrusted longsword that broke the darkness like a fang of silver light, and even over so great a distance Tyrion could see the grim set to the warrior's features.

'Eltharion has come!' shouted Tyrion.

KORHANDIR'S LEAP WAS slick with blood. Druchii spearmen shouted with every thrust of their spears, pushing the bridge's defenders back with every step. Barbed spears bit flesh and tore armour, and even a touch of their blades was agony, for they snagged skin and ripped wounds wider.

A thin line of elven warriors was all that stood before the druchii, and Eldain could sense their despair as they took yet another step backwards. The rippling blood banner writhed upon its cross pole, as though feeding on the carnage being wrought in its shadow. Ghostly laughter drifted at the edge of hearing, and Eldain tasted bile in the back of his throat as he rode through the terrible sprawl of ruptured bodies.

The bodies of slain elves lay together in death; but for their armour it would have been impossible to tell asur from druchii. That thought alone made Eldain want to weep, for what had divided them all those thousands of years ago but one individual's arrogance and lust for power? Could such a sin be worth thousands of years of war and death? That his race, so proud and aloof and superior had allowed themselves to be caught up in such a terrible cycle of hatred astounded Eldain.

We make lofty claims to be an elder race, greater than any other, yet we hold to ancient wrongs like spoiled children...

Ahead, Mitherion Silverfawn strode to the centre of the bridge, streamers of raw magic feathering the air with translucent fire. The mage walked with purposeful steps, and the cloaks of the dead flapped and billowed in his wake. Eldain felt the build up of powerful magic, and urged Lotharin to greater speed.

The line of elven spearmen finally broke, and they turned to flee before the triumphant druchii. The hideous banner cackled gleefully as black-bladed spears stabbed and spilled yet more blood. A host of druchii warriors broke from the ranks and ran towards Mitherion Silverfawn, eager to claim so valuable a trophy. Yvraine's four Sword Masters stepped to meet them with their great, silver blades looping around them in shimmering arcs. Trained and schooled by the Loremasters of the White Tower, the Sword Masters fought with a grace and precision the likes of which even legendary heroes like Laerial Sureblade or Nagan of Chrace would have struggled to match.

Yvraine and her fellow warriors wove a silver path of destruction through the druchii, slaying any who came near Mitherion Silverfawn with graceful strokes of their blades. They wielded their mighty swords with an ease that only decades of training could provide, ducking, swaying and leaping over the weapons of their enemies like acrobats. In less than a minute two score druchii lay dead, cut to pieces with contemptuous ease.

Seeing that the Sword Masters would not be taken by such futile heroics, the druchii line advanced en masse with their barbed spears lowered. But the Sword Masters had no intention of fighting an entire battle line of spears. Without any command being spoken, Yvraine moved her warriors behind Mitherion Silverfawn as he unleashed the full power of his magic.

A coruscating stream of blue fire poured from his outstretched hands to engulf the druchii. Iron weapons melted, flesh boiled from bones and the screams of the enemy warriors were mercifully brief. Shrieking bodies tumbled from the bridge, blazing fireballs that not even the waters of the river could extinguish. The banner of writhing blood went up like an oil-soaked rag, an incandescent plume of fire that screamed like a child as it died.

The druchii line collapsed as the dozens of warriors disintegrated like ashen statues, and the cries of terror that came from those who saw their comrades immolated was music to Eldain's ears. The druchii reeled as the cackling blue flames danced over the crystalline structure of the bridge, and Eldain spun his spear up to point at the druchii.

'Now, Starchaser!' he yelled. 'With me! For Ulthuan and the Everqueen!'

Lotharin leapt forwards, and Eldain clung tight to the reins as his faithful mount carried him over the smouldering, blackened ruin of the druchii. Starchaser's Reavers followed him, a thundering wedge of vengeful horsemen with lowered spears. The druchii saw them coming, but their line was scattered and broken, easy meat for cavalry.

The Reavers punched into the reeling druchii, spears thrusting and swords slashing. Eldain stabbed his spear through the neck of a warrior whose armour and cloak smouldered with blue flame. Even before the druchii fell, Eldain was moving on, plunging the leaf-shaped blade into the panicked mass of enemy warriors. A sword sliced up at him, but Lotharin sidestepped and lashed out with his hooves, hurling the druchii champion from the bridge.

The druchii fled from the blades of the Reavers, but there was no mercy to be had, and no way to escape the speed of an Ellyrian steed. None survived to reach the end of the bridge. Eldain circled his horse as Mitherion Silverfawn waved to him. The mage's skin was pallid and his features drawn by the expenditure of such powerful magic. Unleashing the fiery conflagration had cost him dear.

'Eldain, you should not be here!' said Mitherion.

'And yet I am,' countered Eldain. 'You still think the bridge will fall?'

'I *know* it will,' said Mitherion in exasperation. 'Do you think something as obvious as a charge of the Reaver Knights would prevent it? Look, the druchii are already gathering crossbows and swordsmen.'

Eldain swore as he saw the truth of Mitherion's words. Hundreds of druchii were moving towards Korhandir's Leap, bearing spears, crossbows, and swords. Too many for their small Reaver band to fight.

'Our charge was glorious,' said Laurena Starchaser, riding alongside and voicing Eldain's fear, 'but we will not hold against so many without more warriors.'

Eldain turned to Mitherion Silverfawn. 'Is your magic spent?'

'Not yet, but what power I have left will not keep the druchii from crossing.'

'More warriors will come,' said Eldain. 'We will hold the druchii here until they do.'

Mitherion shook his head. 'If you stay on this bridge you will die. You must ride!'

'Retreat?' said Eldain. 'After we fought to drive the druchii away?'

'I did not say retreat,' said Mitherion. 'I said ride. Ride on, Eldain, it is the only way!'

'Ride on? Into the druchii army? Have you lost your mind?'

Mitherion gripped Eldain's hand, and he felt the coruscating heat of the magic fire within the mage. Eldain saw the desperation in Mitherion's eyes, the aching need to be believed.

'Trust me, Eldain, you must cross the river and destroy the red giant,' said Mitherion. 'It is the only way you live.'

'Red giant? What are you talking about?' said Eldain, snatching his hand back and turning Lotharin towards the druchii. At least five hundred warriors were marching towards the bridge, a force many times beyond what he would ever think of riding straight towards. He saw no red giant among them, and wondered what foolishness had taken hold of the mage.

He caught Starchaser's eye, and she gave an almost imperceptible nod of acceptance. Whatever he ordered, she and her riders would obey.

'Death surrounds us,' she said. 'One way to face it is as good as another.'

'Better to face it head on then,' said Eldain.

ITHILMAR-TIPPED LANCES SPLIT the Executioners apart. Caparisoned in blue and white and gold, the Silver Helms of Galadrien Stormweaver smashed through the close packed ranks of the heavily-armoured druchii. Bravest of all the riders in Ulthuan, the Silver Helms were called headstrong by some, reckless by others, but all agreed that they were the most magnificent warriors of the land. Only the Dragon Princes of Caledor could lay claim to superiority, but such was the arrogance of those riders that their boast was largely discounted, save by those who had seen them in battle.

Stormweaver leaned hard into the stirrups and drove his lance through the breastplate of a druchii warrior. The blade tore free of his victim and he lined up another target. The druchii swept his unwieldy sword around in an effort to smash the head from Stormweaver's lance, but it was a move of desperation. He looped the lance tip around the *draich* and its tip plunged into the warrior's belly. Stormweaver lifted the screaming warrior off the ground, letting his own weight tear him from the blade, and enjoying the sound of his scream.

The Silver Helms bludgeoned their way through rank after rank of druchii, and Stormweaver saw a banner go down, trampled into the mud beneath his clarion's horse. The white mounts of the Silver Helms were bred to be stronger than almost any other horse in Ulthuan, and fought with as much pride and power as their riders.

The Executioners fought back, and Stormweaver had to grudgingly admit that they were not without skill. He saw Irindia plucked from his horse by a well-aimed strike to the belly, and Yeledra thrown to the ground as her horse was beheaded in a single stroke. These were just the last gasps of hate, not real courage, and they were far too late to alter the outcome of this charge. Scores of druchii were ground to smashed bone and ground meat beneath the hooves of the Silver Helms' mounts, and those few that remained were aghast at such swift slaughter.

Onwards the Silver Helms plunged into the druchii, killing with every yard gained from the lofty heights of their saddles. Gods of the battlefield, the Silver Helms slew and crushed all before them, revelling in their pre-eminent power and skill. The noise was incredible, like a drunken mortal hammering every plate of metal in a smith's forge with clumsy missteps.

An Executioner leapt to meet him, sword swinging low for his horse's legs. His steed leapt over the blow, lashing out with its hind legs to shatter the druchii's skull with a sharp blow from its hooves. Another cloaked druchii stabbed his murderous blade towards Stormweaver's chest, but a jink of the reins stepped him away from the blow. Too close for a lance strike, Stormweaver released the reins and drew his sword in one, fluid motion. Stormweaver wheeled his horse in around the Executioner and slashed his blade down onto his neck, hacking down past the druchii's collarbone and into his lungs.

The Executioners could take no more and turned to flee from the silver horsemen in their midst. Some threw down their weapons to aid their escape; others clung to them in the mistaken belief that they would live to fight with them again.

What had, moments before, been a desperate struggle of blades now became a slaughter as the Executioners fled from the storm of blades and lances. But their flight only brought more doom down upon their heads. Dozens were hacked down in the first moments of their panic, others run down beneath the heavy horses of the Silver Helms, yet more skewered on the tips of still-sharp lances.

As much as he loved the moment of the charge, this was the moment Stormweaver relished the most; riding down a defeated foe. Every horseman dreamed of the enemy broken and fleeing before him, easy prey to the glorious rider with fire in his heart. The Silver Helms ran amok, slaying and laughing and singing as they unleashed furious wrath upon their dark kin.

Stormweaver pictured his warriors pursuing the druchii all the way back to Eagle Gate and beyond. Riding over them until only a handful remained alive to reach their black ships on the coast.

'No mercy!' shouted Stormweaver. 'Drive them into the river!'

The Silver Helms followed his lead and broke apart into hunting groups as they slew the druchii with wild abandon. Stormweaver led the massacre, riding for the river and plunging his lance into unprotected backs. This was joy! This was vengeance!

He heard heavy cracks of splintering ice and splashes from up ahead, and imagined the Executioners' desperate struggles as the weight of their armour dragged them under the water. As his lance sliced clear of another dead druchii, he looked up to see how few remained.

His elation turned to horror as he saw the titanic scaled beasts climbing from the river.

'Hydra,' he said, as the nearest monster spread wide its jaws and unleashed a burning stream of volcanic ichor.

It was the last thing he ever said.

Chapter Fifteen

Despair

LIKE A GOLDEN arrow loosed from Asuryan's silver bow, Eltharion cut through the air on Stormwing's back with his glittering runesword held before him like a lance. The Witch King had not seen him, and only when the griffon slowed its descent with a thunderous boom of spreading wings did the master of the druchii look up. Malekith hauled the chains looped around his dragon's maw and its vast form banked quicker than anything of such size should be able to move.

Yet still it was not fast enough.

Stormwing's forepaws took hold of the membranous frill where the dragon's wing met its body, and his rear claws raked the underside of its belly, drawing a wash of brackish blood. Eltharion's sword looped out and bit into the pauldrons of the Witch King's armour. The runes worked into the blade shone with trapped moonlight as the sword came free, and Eltharion twisted in his saddle to avoid a strike from Malekith's ensorcelled black blade.

The dragon bellowed and its long neck twisted around to tear at Stormwing. Ichor-dripping teeth like dagger blades snapped on empty air as the griffon pushed off the dragon's body and the aerial combatants broke apart.

Wild cheering greeted the arrival of Eltharion, but he cared nothing for their jubilation. With the element of surprise now gone, this fight had just become far more dangerous.

'Up, Stormwing!' he cried. 'Height is everything.'

The griffon beat its wings furiously, and Eltharion looked over his shoulder to see the Witch King's dragon surging towards him. Thousands of feet below, the Sapphire Gate was a thin line of white marble, blue gemstones and golden ornamentation set in the midst of pale rock. The dragon's jaws spread wide and Eltharion knew what was coming next.

He leaned left and exerted pressure with his knee, and Stormwing obeyed instantly. A seething geyser of noxious black gases vomited up from the dragon's belly. It went wide, but the caustic reek of it caught in the back of his throat. Stormwing tucked one wing into his body, twisting and stooping down onto the rising Witch King.

Eltharion looked into the shimmering emerald glow of Malekith's eyes, remembering the last time he had seen that dread iron mask. Looking upon him from a cold tower of bleak obsidian, the Witch King had prophesised an agonising death for Eltharion. Moments later, the poisoned blade of a druchii witch cut him, and he had hovered at the edge of life for days.

By rights he should have died, but the ghost of his father had called him back to fight for Ulthuan against the rampaging horde of the Goblin King. If that had been the worst the Witch King could do to him, then Eltharion welcomed this fight.

Malekith's armour was black as midnight and Eltharion's keen eyes could make out the runic script worked into the plates of star iron. The Witch King thrust a clawed gauntlet towards Eltharion and a booming voice echoed from within his horned helm. It was a single word, yet a word that should never be uttered or heard by any mortal.

Shrieking pain blitzed around Eltharion's body, and he screamed as every nerve in his body was bathed in fire. His vision greyed and he felt his heart spasm fit to burst. Blinding lights exploded before his eyes, and it was all he could do to retain a grip on his sword. Sensing his rider was incapacitated, Stormwing screeched and banked to the side as the dragon roared in to the attack. Its jaws snapped. Hind legs swung up to claw, and its enormous wings beat the air to pummel the griffon into a spin.

Stormwing twisted out of the way of the dragon's teeth, and dipped his wings to avoid a lethal clawing. Buffeting turbulence spun him around, but he pulled his wings in tight and aimed himself towards the earth. The dragon followed him round, slower and less agile than the griffon, yet murderously powerful.

Eltharion gritted his teeth and fought through the pain, letting it bleed from his body as he and Stormwing plummeted back to earth. The Witch King was right behind him, and the dragon's onyx eyes glittered with terrible appetite. Its jaws drooled acidic saliva and Eltharion could see it was building another gullet of toxic breath to exhale. He jinked Stormwing left and

right as the Witch King hurled crackling arcs of purple
fire from his iron gauntlets. The Sapphire Gate rushed
up to meet him and Eltharion pulled Stormwing left and
dug his heels into his feathered flanks.

The griffon spread his wings and the force of decelera-
tion almost tore Eltharion from the saddle. He risked a
glance over his shoulder in time to see the crimson jaws
of the dragon upon him. Stormwing rolled and looped
around underneath the dragon as the two creatures
passed within a few feet of one another. The dragon's tail
slammed into the griffon, and Eltharion felt his mount's
pain as he fought to right himself.

He pulled Stormwing around in a tight turn, swooping
back to the fight as a black sword sang for his neck. He
brought his runesword up and a blazing rain of sparks
flew from the two weapons as they struck. Stormwing
fought to keep out of reach of the dragon's claws as he
and Malekith traded blows. With every clash of iron,
Eltharion felt the destructive power of the dark sorcery
worked into the Witch King's blade.

But his sword had been fashioned by the first Warden
of Tor Yvresse and its enchantments were too strong to
be overcome by the pretender's magic of unmaking.
Time and time again their swords clashed as Stormwing
and the dragon twisted and spun and climbed and dived
as though engaged in some bizarre mating dance.

Their battle was fought with blade and spell, and every
blow was followed by a blast of white fire or crimson
lightning. Stormwing's feathers were burned from his
shoulder and portions of the dragon's neck were fused
to glass by the lethal magic. Eltharion knew his magic
was nowhere near as powerful as that of Malekith, and
he was nearing the limit of his endurance. The Witch

King's blade hammered down again, and Eltharion felt its cackling glee as it devoured a portion of the magic empowering his runesword.

Stormwing spun away from the dragon, and Eltharion fought to stay upright as his faithful griffon used every ounce of its speed and agility to outmanoeuvre the Witch King's mount. He pulled Stormwing into a tight turn, one wing stooped, the other spread wide. Malekith passed beneath him, and Eltharion slashed down with his sword. The blade bit into the Witch King's armour, but slid clear before tasting flesh. In return, Malekith's sword stabbed up into Stormwing's belly, opening a long gouge that drew a shriek of pain from the noble creature.

The two creatures spun around one another, clawing and tearing. Stormwing was the more agile of the two, twisting aside from the dragon's powerful jaws and slashing talons. Yet what the dragon lacked in speed, it made up for in sheer power. Stormwing looped over the dragon's neck, and a slicing talon tore out the mighty creature's right eye. The dragon roared and thrashed its heavily muscled limbs in agony. A slicing blow from its hind legs cut deep into Stormwing's flank, gouging down to the bone. Stormwing screeched and Eltharion held on tight as the griffon bucked in pain.

In such a close quarters fight, there could be only one winner, and it would be the dragon.

'We have done all we can for now, old friend,' said Eltharion.

Stormwing folded his wings and dropped away from the dragon, diving hundreds of feet before levelling out over the walls of the sea gate. Flights of arrows flew from the defenders' bows towards the dragon. Most bounced from its thick scales, but a lucky few pieced its body where the battle with Eltharion had torn them loose. The enraged dragon turned about and was flying after him, its wings pounding the air and scattering the fighters on the wall below with the force of the downdraught. A flurry of iron bolts zipped past Eltharion and he swung his mount lower, passing within ten feet of the ramparts.

The cliff wall was fast approaching. He was running out of space.

A sibilant voice sounded in his head, and it was a voice he knew to trust implicitly.

Fly to me, Eltharion! By the western cliff!

Eltharion obeyed instantly, turning in a sharp bank and roll manoeuvre as he flew back the way he had come. The dragon matched Stormwing's turn, but Eltharion could hear his mount was blowing hard now, a sure sign of imminent exhaustion.

'Fly just a little more, brother,' said Eltharion.

The griffon extended its wings and flew westwards as the Witch King's dragon roared in anticipation of the kill. They sped over the wall, through a mist of arrows and bolts, weaving through the air and jostling for position. Eltharion scanned the walls for any sign of his friend, and spotted the star-cloaked mage exactly where he had said he would be.

Loremaster Belannaer stood swathed in a cerulean cloak of moon-writ runes and read aloud from a heavy golden book, its kidskin covers embossed with the motif of a rising phoenix. His voice was ancient beyond reckoning and the words he spoke were of Asuryan and the creation of the world.

Eltharion drew Stormwing in, and the griffon spun as the Witch King and his dragon closed. The dragon's wings boomed wide as it slowed its flight, and no sooner had Malekith reared up to strike down at Eltharion than Belannaer unleashed a coruscating vortex of pure white fire from the tip of his crescent-topped staff. The flames enveloped the Witch King and his dragon, but instead of bellows of agony, there came only gloating laughter.

The flames vanished in a heartbeat, and Eltharion saw the Witch King's shield glowing with a blistering light where it had swallowed the full force of the magical fire.

Stormwing landed on the ramparts of the sea gate, and Eltharion saw Belannaer stagger away from the wall as though struck. The Loremaster held himself upright with the aid of his golden staff and though he was greatly weakened, he kept reading from his magical tome.

'In Vaul's name, I unweave the winds of magic, their colours to be unmade, their enchantments to be undone!'

The air between Belannaer and Malekith buckled with unleashed force and the Witch King's shield shattered into a thousand fragments. The dark plates of his armour cracked, and searing lines of magical fire clawed his light-starved flesh. The Witch King roared in pain, and pulled his draconic mount away from Belannaer's magic. As the dragon pulled up and away, its long neck rippled with peristaltic motion.

Eltharion shouted a warning and Stormwing leapt into the air as a black torrent of lethal fumes and searing bile erupted from the dragon's jaws to envelop the Loremaster. Eltharion could only watch in horror as Belannaer's body erupted in incandescent flames that burned hotter than the forge of the Smith God himself until nothing remained.

* * *

THE MIST ROLLING in from the river thinned as it reached the riverbank, and Caelir saw vast blocks of marching warriors emerge from its edges. They were big men, thick of limb and wide of shoulder; each armed with a great felling axe that dripped with amber sap. The flesh of their bodies was sliced open from head to toe, and barbed thorns were snagged on their armour or embedded in the meat of their arms and thighs.

They came on in a screaming host, beneath a forest of crude banners and braying war horns. A thousand warriors, and then a thousand more emerged from the mist, a multitude of warbands, sword-packs and axe-brothers. Caelir felt his courage sink to his boots at the sight of so many warriors.

Riding tall in the centre of the host was Issyk Kul, his shoulder guards draped with a fresh cloak of torn emerald robes and pale flesh. Stretched over the warlord's spiked pauldrons, Anurion the Green's face gave voice to a silent scream, while the emptied skin of his body flapped as a grotesque rag of bloody flesh.

'Gods above!' hissed Caelir. 'Anurion…'

He fought down his rising panic as he tried to think of some way they could hold the northern flank. The Reaver bands numbered fewer than five hundred riders, and the spear hosts barely a thousand. The fighting around Korhandir's Leap had drawn in too many warriors, and the north was now dangerously exposed.

And that weakness had been exploited.

The spear hosts angled themselves to meet the oncoming horde of tribesmen as the clear notes of elven battle horns trumpeted. The sound gave Caelir hope, and he smiled wryly as he thought of the tales Narentir had told of Aenarion in the performance circles of Avelorn. The poet always sang of hope in the darkest hours, of how heroes never gave in to despair and always clung to the hope of victory. He would spin spellbinding tales of all the great heroes of Ulthuan: Aenarion, Caledor Dragon-tamer, the sword-mages, Firuval and Estellian, and of course Tyrion and Teclis.

One night Caelir had asked Narentir why he never told the tale of Eltharion, for it was an epic tale that surely best exemplified his belief in holding on to hope in the darkest hour.

Narentir had shaken his head and said, 'Dear boy, you are young and beautiful. Some stories should not be told too often, for the soul is heavier for hearing them.

Caelir had sensed evasion and said, 'Save your fancy words for the circles, poet. Tell me. Why do you not speak of Eltharion?'

'Because I choose not to,' said Narentir. 'He is a warrior of great sadness and anger. Not someone about whom one should speak without his leave. Dear Caelir, you met Eltharion in Tor Yvresse, and even you must have realised that about him without someone like me having to explain it to you.'

'I met him, yes,' agreed Caelir. 'He seemed sad more than angry.'

'And with good reason.'

'Have you met him?'

'Once,' said Narentir. 'And before you ask the question I sense is rushing towards those exquisite lips of yours, it is not an experience I care to relive, so do not ask.'

Caelir had cajoled him all night, but Narentir would not be drawn on the matter. Events had overtaken them, and Caelir guessed he would never get the chance to learn the reasons for the poet's reluctance to speak of Eltharion.

'You were a fool, Narentir,' whispered Caelir. 'A wonderful, brilliant fool. I wish you were here to tell me there was still hope.'

On the ride to Tor Elyr, Caelir had chided Eldain for not believing there was still hope.

How naïve he must have sounded. How childish.

The enemy had crossed the river, and there was no hope of holding them back.

ELDAIN AND LOTHARIN rode onto the western bank of the river, and Starchaser's Reavers followed close behind. It was glorious madness to be on this side of the river, with enemies all around them, but where else should an Ellyrian Reaver Knight be but deep within enemy territory with the threat of death all around?

He had a handful of warriors against an army, which were the odds an Ellyrian liked.

But where to lead them?

'The red giant,' said Eldain. 'Gods, Mitherion, what in Isha's name did you mean?'

To the south, hundreds of druchii hurried to the ford, which became more passable with every moment as fell magicks were brought to bear to hold back the waters of the river. The spear hosts were already embroiled in battle, and though the line was holding, the druchii could simply hurl warriors at it until it broke. Hundreds of warrior bands of druchii were marching towards the bridge, eager to flank the elven spears, and as much as Eldain dearly wished to oppose them, he knew it was a fight his riders could not win.

Eldain could not see what was happening in the north, for a thick fogbank obscured all but the distant hill of waystones and the Eagle's Claws upon its slopes.

To left and right, druchii crossbows and bolt throwers unleashed withering hails of arrows. Small bands of crossbowmen were, even now, making their way from the riverbank to take aim. Iron-tipped bolts whickered from the undergrowth, and two of Eldain's riders were pitched from their saddles. A bolt embedded itself in the thick leather of his saddle horn, and Lotharin reared up as the tip pricked his flesh beneath.

Eldain angrily tore the bolt free and hurled it aside.

'Ride north along the riverbank!' he shouted, guiding Lotharin around with pressure on his right knee. His black steed turned on the spot and galloped away from the bridge with Starchaser's Reavers behind him. Less than a hundred yards to his left, thousands of druchii warriors marched towards the river, so close he could pick out individual faces and shield designs. It was madness to be riding so close to the front of the enemy host, but where else was there to go?

Eldain felt the snap of druchii crossbow bolts flashing past them, and heard the screams of Reavers as they were cut down. He shouted in anger and took up his bow, loosing shaft after shaft in return. He saw enemy warriors fall, but took scant comfort in their deaths. No matter if each of his riders killed a druchii with every arrow in their quivers, there would still be ten times too many for them to fight.

'Damn you, Mitherion!' shouted Eldain as he heard another of his Reavers die.

The ground became harder under Lotharin's hooves, and Eldain felt the air grow icy, like the depths of winter in Cothique. Ellyrion never knew winter's touch, and it chilled his soul like nothing else to know that his land could be so touched by the fell influence of the druchii.

Cold mist oozed from the river, and Eldain heard the slap of water on ice… the tramp of booted feet on ice.

Eldain could see nothing save the grey curtain of mist before him. To ride blind was madness, but to ride slow would see them skewered on the bolts of the druchii crossbowmen.

'Ride sure, old friend,' he shouted to Lotharin.

The horse tossed its mane and plunged into the mist, the cold wetness of it soaking Eldain through in moments. He could see nothing save vague shapes, dark outlines and hazy silhouettes as Lotharin rode deeper and deeper into the mist. The sounds of hideous chanting came from all around him, mired in the muffled sound of clashing blades, screams of pain, beating war drums and wildly blowing horns.

Mired in the mist, the battle might already be won or lost for all Eldain knew.

Something vast, golden and jade loomed in the mist, the towering outline of a warrior. Taller than any elf could ever be, it was swathed in red mist that tasted of burned metal and set his nerves afire with its hateful resonances of pain, murder and fear. Vast blades descended from outstretched arms, and Eldain saw writhing forms leaping and dancing around a steaming cauldron that sopped and sloshed with blood. The taste of the air set his teeth on edge, and brought tears to his eyes.

'The red giant,' said Eldain, amazed that they had come upon it in the mist.

The red mist parted, and Eldain saw the lithe forms of near-naked druchii warrior women spinning around the mighty effigy of their bloody-handed god. Each was a dark beauty of sinister allure, and each carried dripping black-bladed daggers in both hands. Khaine himself leered down at the Reavers, and the ruby eyes of the statue pulsed in anticipation of bloodshed. Eldain let fly with his last arrow at one of the women, who leapt over the speeding shaft and bounded towards him like an acrobat.

Eldain was reminded of the elf-maid Lilani he had met in Avelorn, but where her grace was natural and sinuous, these druchii women had the predatory agility of stalking cats. One of the women vaulted into the air and leapt at him feet first. Lotharin reared up and flailed the air with his hooves, smashing her ribcage and hurling her back. Eldain used the respite to take up his spear as the Reavers rode into the women.

Two were killed almost instantly, crushed beneath the sheer mass of horses, and another pair were pinned to the ground by a flurry of arrows loosed by archers more skilled than Eldain. The Reavers outnumbered the dancers of Khaine, but they cared nothing for their own deaths and slew for the cruel enjoyment of the deed. Eldain felt something tear along his shoulder, and ducked over Lotharin's neck as a pair of iron razor-stars slashed by his head.

A naked elf with dark tattoos garlanding her body balanced on the edge of the slopping cauldron of blood like a witch-hag from the terror stories used to frighten children. Her hair billowed around her thorn-crowned head, and barbed torqs of thornvines wound their way along her legs and arms. Though her body was that of the fairest elf-maid, her face was a loathsome melange of youth and ancient malice.

Eldain turned Lotharin toward the witch, feeling his hatred intensify the closer he rode to the looming statue and its dripping blades. The eyes of the effigy burned with the light of a furnace, hot, raging and always in motion. Eldain's lip curled in anger as he stared at the witch-hag, letting his hate build as she sprang from the edge of the cauldron with a hateful scream that tore at his nerves. It was a name he had never heard uttered from a living being, it was the name carried in the death rattle of those with a knife in their back or a murderer's hands wrapped around their throat. It was the wordless exultation of murder.

At that moment, Eldain knew the terror of prey.

Lotharin reared in panic, and Eldain dropped his spear as the witch queen's word of power took him back to the days of darkness, when even the elves huddled close to the fire for fear of what might lurk beyond its light. He wanted to reach for his sword, but his muscles were terror-locked in paralysis. Even as she came at him with twin daggers that hissed with venom, he could not move, could do nothing save imagine the pain as she cut out his heart.

The witch sailed through the air as though in defiance of gravity and Eldain saw her face split apart with the feral grin of a savage killer. Her blades never connected, for a leaf-bladed speartip erupted from her ribcage and plucked her from the air.

Laurena Starchaser rode past like the Huntress of Kurnous herself, her auburn hair wild and unbound and trailing behind her like a fiery comet. The witch queen slid from her spear, punctured clean through and wailing impotent curses from bleeding lips.

'Have you forgotten how to fight?' asked Starchaser, circling her horse and whipping the blood from her spear.

Eldain shook off the terror of the witch-hag's spell and said, 'No.'

'She bewitched you?'

'Maybe,' said Eldain, unwilling to dwell on the naked fear he had felt.

'This is the red giant Mitherion Silverfawn spoke of?' she asked.

'I believe so.'

'Then let's hurry up and destroy it, there are more druchii coming.'

'Any idea how?'

Starchaser slid from the saddle and waved the surviving Reaver Knights over. Eldain rode around the statue as Starchaser and another five Reavers put their shoulders to the brass cauldron and pushed. Eldain unhooked his lasso from his saddle and spun the loop once before hurling it up and over the statue's head. He wound the end of the lasso around Lotharin's saddle horn, as three other Reavers followed his example. One rope snapped on the drooping blades, and Eldain felt the statue's smouldering anger as the Ellyrians worked to bring it down.

'Now, Laurena!' shouted Eldain. 'Push!'

Lotharin strained against the heavy weight of the statue, and Eldain glanced over his shoulder to see the red glow of its baleful eyes spread throughout its metal body. He heard angry shouts of druchii warriors and leaned over Lotharin's neck.

'Come greatheart, you are the strongest horse I know,' he said. 'If any can pull this damned statue down it is you.'

Lotharin's shoulders bunched and he strained at the enormous weight at his back until at last the statue's base cracked, and it began to fall. Blood sloshed from the cauldron, hissing as it hit the good soil of Ellyrion and rendering it barren for years to come.

Then the statue tipped past its centre of gravity and fell without effort from the elves. Eldain's lasso unwound from the statue's neck, and he coiled it back onto his saddle as the cauldron fell from its mounting and flipped over. The bronze face of the murder god slammed into the ground as the cauldron rolled towards the mist-shrouded river.

Instead of a heavy splash, Eldain heard the booming clang of metal striking something solid. The sound continued as the cauldron vanished into the mist. Starchaser and her Reavers ran back to their horses as armoured warriors emerged from the mist around the fallen statue. Crossbow bolts flashed through the air as the Reavers took to their heels.

Eldain spun in the saddle, seeing druchii approaching from all sides.

All sides but one.

ELTHARION BROUGHT STORMWING in over the centre of the sea gate. The aerial duel with the Witch King had brought the fighting to a halt as all eyes turned to watch the awesome clash of might and magic. His armour torn open and his dragon wounded, the Witch King had flown high into the boiling clouds. The sight of Eltharion's triumphant entry to the fighting galvanised the defenders to push the druchii from the walls for the time being.

Tyrion and Korhil stood to either side of Finubar as he went to greet the Warden of Tor Yvresse. The Phoenix King was still weak from the druchii sorcery that had slain his White Lions, but Tyrion knew it was more than luck that kept him alive. Finubar was the mortal vessel of Asuryan's fire, and the Creator God did not suffer weaklings to guide his chosen people.

The griffon's claws gripped the edge of the wall and he folded his wings back with regal poise. Tyrion saw the beast was lathered with sweat and its eyes filled with pain.

Tyrion and Eltharion had once been close, but ever since the Goblin King's assault on Yvresse, they had barely spoken. Tyrion had learned the particulars of the battle from those who had fought the goblins, but Eltharion had always refused to speak of it. Whatever had happened in the Warden's Tower at the height of the fighting had changed Eltharion in terrible ways. His grim demeanour was understandable; his lands had been ravaged and his family slain, but the haunted lifelessness of his eyes was hard to bear.

Tyrion's old friend now shunned company, avoided his boon companions and brooded alone in his sullen city of ghosts. As timely and welcome as his arrival had been, Tyrion found it hard to be glad that the Warden of Tor Yvresse now fought with them.

'Eltharion,' said Finubar, as the grim-eyed warden dismounted and dropped to the ramparts. 'You are a sight for sore eyes, my friend.'

Eltharion nodded curtly. 'My king was in danger. I had to come,' he said, and Tyrion heard the hollowness of the sentiment immediately.

Finubar embraced Eltharion warmly, a gesture that looked forced and awkward to Tyrion, but which was greeted with a rousing cheer from the defenders of the Sapphire Gate. As the two warriors broke the embrace, Tyrion saw the simmering anger behind Finubar's façade of camaraderie. Yes, Eltharion had come, but he had taken his sweet time about it and brought precious few warriors with him. Aside from a handful of rangers, it was clear the armies of the eastern realms remained within the walls of Tor Yvresse.

'As king of Ulthuan, I am glad to have you,' said Finubar, ever the diplomat.

'Stormwing is injured,' said Eltharion. 'I would ask your healers see to his wounds.'

'Of course,' said Finubar, waving to a nearby archer. 'Immediately.'

Tyrion stepped forward. 'Sire Belannaer?' he asked. 'I saw the dragon...'

Eltharion shook his head. 'He is dead.'

'Are you sure?' pressed Finubar.

'I am sure,' said Eltharion. 'I saw the flames consume him. He is dead.'

Tyrion wanted to strike Eltharion for announcing the death of one of the White Tower's greatest Loremasters with so little emotion. Coming so soon after Belarien's death, Tyrion's anger surged to the surface. Before he did anything rash, Korhil took hold of his arm and gave an almost imperceptible shake of his head.

The sound of hunting horns echoed from the sides of the cliffs, and shouts of warning came from the watchtowers as the iron boarding ramps cranked down from the black ark.

'Druchii!' shouted Korhil, running to the edge of the ramparts. 'Stand to! Archers!'

Finubar nodded to Eltharion and Tyrion, then drew his sword and ran to muster the defenders. Warriors flocked to the Phoenix King as arrows and bolts flew between the black ark and the Sapphire Gate once more.

Eltharion turned to follow the king, but Tyrion grabbed his arm and said, 'Why did you really come?'

'Lothern is ready to fall, where else would I be?'

'Platitudes like that may appease Finubar, but I know you better,' said Tyrion. 'Tell me.'

Hostility and aching loneliness swam in Eltharion's eyes, but it was soon replaced by cold resentment. Tyrion saw a cruelty in his old friend that he liked not at all.

'You really want to know?' asked Eltharion.

'I do.'

'I remembered something a poet once said to me.'

'What did he say?'

'Nothing I will ever tell you,' said Eltharion, pulling his arm free and walking away.

CHAPTER SIXTEEN

BATTLE'S END

MENETHIS WATCHED IN disbelief as the monsters destroyed the Silver Helms. Three monsters with writhing masses of heads tore them apart with snapping bites and gouts of hellish red fire vomited up from their bellies. Alongside these scaled monstrosities, deformed abominations of flesh, bone, gristle and raw meat fought with lunatic fury. Snapped chains whipped from barbed collars, and mouths opened randomly in the elastic, warping flesh of the hell-spawned beasts.

The slaughter was so swift that Menethis could scarce believe it had happened at all. One moment, Stormweaver's Silver Helms were slaughtering the Executioners, the next, monsters had emerged from the mist and destroyed their salvation. Menethis watched a hydra snatch up a horse in its jaws and bite it in two. Half the beast went down the monster's gullet, the rest spat back into the killing. A Silver Helm, unhorsed and pouring blood from where his arm had once been, staggered back from the slaughter, but one of the spawn creatures swept him up in a gelatinous tentacle and swallowed him whole.

'Isha save us, sweet mother of mercy,' said a spearman behind him.

'Be silent,' ordered Menethis.

With the timely arrival of the Silver Helms, Menethis had rejoined his spear host on the gentle slopes before Tor Elyr. Once in sight of the spires of the city, the citizen soldiers had steeled their courage, and banded together around their banner. Menethis had discovered them marching back to join him, and not since he had stood on the walls of Eagle Gate had he felt such humbling pride.

'Raise spears,' he said, knowing it was futile. If such warriors as the Silver Helms could not fight such monsters, then they had little chance. That did not matter, for they had sworn to defend this land, and nothing could be gained by running save a few wretched moments of life. That they had no chance of prevailing was immaterial.

That they stood with courage unbroken before such beasts was all that mattered.

The mist at the river began clearing and Menethis saw the full might of the druchii army across the river. Despite the numbers their host had killed, the druchii still outnumbered them. No matter that they had fought with bravery and strength beyond what anyone could have expected; they were still doomed.

THE VORTEX OF storm clouds above the black ark seethed with elemental power, swirling and gathering strength with every passing moment. Torrential rain fell in soaking sheets, washing the ramparts clean of blood, and

Tyrion's robes were plastered to his skin. Sunfang hissed like an ingot fresh from the furnace in the downpour.

Deafening peals of thunder echoed from the cliffs and blinding forks of lightning burned crackling traceries across the sky. If this was to be the end of Ulthuan, then the heavens were providing a fitting accompaniment. Tyrion turned aside an overhand cut with his dagger and spun around the druchii swordsman, plunging Sunfang into his lower back. The warrior grunted in pain and fell to the blood-wet flagstones of the gate.

Two thousand elven warriors fought on the Sapphire Gate, faced with who knew how many druchii. Tens of thousands might lurk within the black ark for all Tyrion knew.

Let them come, he thought. Let them come and I will kill them all!

He almost smiled at the thought, welcoming the intrusion of the Sword of Khaine this time. Belarien was dead, as was Loremaster Belannaer. Who else was to die before this was over? Alarielle? Teclis? Finubar?

Tyrion?

Strangely, the thought of his own death did not trouble him, but the thought of losing those closest to him filled him with such dread that he had trouble breathing.

Two dozen druchii swarmed down the boarding ramps, howling their hatred. Arrows pierced a handful and sent them plummeting to their doom, but the rest came on without pause. They hurled themselves onto the gate, only to be met by cold steel and courage. Swords clashed and armour rang with the bitter songs of battle, and for the fifth time this day, the ancestral enemies of Ulthuan and Naggaroth fought to the death.

A broad-shouldered warrior in overlapping bands of

plate led these warriors, and arrows bounced from his armour. Armed with an axe-bladed polearm, he landed on the ramparts and spun his weapon around until it was aimed at Tyrion.

'The Tower of Grief will have your head!' promised the warrior, his voice muffled by the form-fitting helm of bronze he wore.

'Come and take it,' answered Tyrion in reply.

Tyrion's blade struck first, skidding from the druchii's breastplate. In reply, the polearm swept down. Tyrion raised Sunfang to block, before realising the blow was a feint. The haft of the polearm suddenly reversed and swept down to smash against the side of his knee. Tyrion leapt over the attack, ramming his dagger at the warrior's neck.

The druchii leaned into the blow, and Tyrion's blade snapped on the flared metal of his helmet. Tyrion landed lightly and ducked beneath a slashing blow of the axe head. He thrust, and it was deflected. He feinted, rolled and leapt, but each time his attacks were intercepted and turned aside by the halberd, its longer reach keeping him at bay.

More druchii were gaining the walls, pushing out from the space their champion had created. The elven line was bowing, and the druchii kept pouring on the pressure, sensing a chance for a breakthrough. Anger touched Tyrion. He was a prince of Ulthuan, its sworn protector, and some upstart druchii champion was fending him off?

The halberd swung at him again, but instead of parrying the blow, Tyrion stepped to meet it and hacked the blade from the haft with one blow. The druchii stared stupidly at the broken end of his weapon, and Tyrion gave him no chance to recover. He pushed the broken halberd aside and rammed his sword into the champion's gut, the enchanted blade sliding between the bands of contoured plate.

Tyrion pushed the dying warrior to the edge of the wall and lifted him onto the battlements, still skewered upon Sunfang's blade like a butterfly on a collector's pin. Behind the faceplate of his helm, the druchii's violet eyes were wide with agony as the sword's caged heat boiled his innards.

'Tell Kouran I will see his tower cast down within the year!' bellowed Tyrion.

He twisted his sword blade, and the champion fell from the walls, to howls of dismay from his fellow druchii. Thunder crashed across the heavens again, but something in the timbre of the sound made Tyrion look up. Nothing of the storm clouds raging above the black ark could be called natural, but this thunder was unnatural even for such a freakish phenomenon.

The Witch King dropped from the clouds of torrential rain on the back of his dragon as lightning split the sky with dazzling brightness. The dragon's left wing was torn and ragged from the battle with Eltharion and Stormwing, but Malekith's armour bore no traces of that desperate fight.

Those druchii still on the wall began falling back as though at some prearranged signal. Tyrion watched them go, but instead of elation he felt only an acute sense of danger. Instincts honed on a hundred battlefields were screaming at him that something terrible was about to happen.

Arcs of powerful lightning played across the Witch King's body, coiling around his dragon and flaring with a million hues of colour. Variegated light swirled within

Tyrion's sword and armour, and he tasted the bitterly metallic flavour of powerful magic in the air. He ran along the length of the gate, keeping one eye on the motionless form of the Witch King as he drew all the lightning in the sky to him.

In the centre of the wall, Finubar and Korhil watched the unfolding drama with wary eyes. Korhil's pelt was bloodied, yet Tyrion was heartened to see that not even an assassin's venom could lessen the Chracian's strength and power. Likewise, Finubar had thrown off the worst effects of the druchii sorcery, and his golden blade was wet with blood.

'I'll wager this bodes ill,' said Korhil as Tyrion approached.

'What do you think he is doing?' asked Finubar.

'Nothing good,' said Tyrion. 'The druchii pulled back inside the ark the moment he appeared.'

'I saw that,' said Finubar, as the coruscating sphere of rampant lightning built around the Witch King until he was almost completely obscured by the whipping cords of power.

A mage in robes of cream, blue and gold stood at the edge of the walls, staring up at Malekith with frightened eyes.

Tyrion hauled him to his feet and said, 'What is happening? What sorcery is this?'

'I... I am not sure,' gabbled the mage. 'It cannot be what I think it is...'

'You are not sure? Then what use are you? Did Teclis send us fools or mages?' growled Tyrion.

'It is magic, but... but of a kind I know only from legend. It has the feel of ancient power, creation magic from when the world was made. Only fragments of it are said to remain in forgotten places lost to the races of this world.'

'Creation?' spat Tyrion. 'The Witch King knows nothing of creation, only destruction.'

'They are two faces of the same aspect,' the mage gasped. 'Creation. Destruction. You cannot have one without the other. As one thing is created, another is destroyed. It is the most dangerous kind of magic, the magic of the Old Ones. It is said its misuse caused the fall of the world in the ancient days before the rise of the elder races.'

'You speak in riddles,' hissed Tyrion, before throwing the mage back against the wall. He watched as the lightning wreathing the Witch King grew even brighter, like a newborn sun hovering in the straits. Stark shadows were cast by its radiance, but the light was without life or warmth, only raw luminous power.

'We need to get everyone off this gate,' said Tyrion as he saw the truth of Malekith's sorcery. 'Now!'

'What?' demanded Korhil. 'Madness. The druchii will simply walk onto the gate.'

'Trust me,' said Tyrion. 'In a few moments I do not think there will *be* a gate…'

'What if you are wrong?' demanded the Phoenix King.

'I will stay on the gate.'

'Alone?' said Finubar. 'You cannot hold the druchii back alone.'

'If I am right, I will not need to.'

'If you are right, you had better be a damn good swimmer,' said Korhil.

Finubar nodded and gave the order to abandon the Sapphire Gate. That order was obeyed instantly, and elven warriors ran to the cliffs, where wide steps were cut into the sides of the straits. Sprays of power blazed from the Witch King as hundreds of elves hurried down the curving steps that led down to the quays of Lothern. Korhil and Finubar went with them, and Tyrion stood at the junction of the two halves of the gate.

He watched the defenders of Lothern fall back to the quays, each sentinel of spear and bow quickly reforming their warriors alongside the unmoving ranks of the Phoenix Guard already arrayed there. The storm winds bellied their banners wide and full, and as the warriors evacuating the wall took up position around them, Tyrion saw they were perfectly placed in this newly formed battle line.

'They knew,' he said. 'They *knew* this would happen…'

Then the Witch King unleashed his new and terrible power.

A streaming fountain of black light blazed from the sphere of lightning, striking the dead centre of the Sapphire Gate. Too bright to look upon, its power did not destroy that which it touched, rather, it *unmade* it. Tyrion watched through half-closed eyes as the very fabric of the gate was unwoven. Matter was unravelled, like a loose thread in a cloak that snags on a thornbush. Ithilmar, starwood and sapphires larger than a warrior's fist came apart like snow before the spring, broken down into their constituent fractions and consumed.

Tyrion staggered as the entire gate slumped and portions of its load-bearing structure were eaten away by this dreadful power. Vast swathes of the gate dissolved into nothingness as the ball of lightning surrounding the Witch King continued to pulse with ancient magic. He ran to the cliffs, now knowing there was no need to stay. The druchii were not going to be coming over the gate, they were going through where it *used to be*.

What remained of the gate cracked, and those portions of it that still stubbornly held on to existence now began to split apart. Flagstones cracked beneath Tyrion's feet as he ran for the cliff-side steps. He leapt to the battlements as the flagstones were consumed by the decay of its material form. Pieces of the gate were disappearing at random, and Tyrion leapt from solid ground to solid ground as the dissolution of the gate increased exponentially.

Fifty yards lay between him and safety, but it might as well have been five hundred.

Only fragments of the Sapphire Gate still existed, and what had taken thousands of artisans decades to construct was unmade in moments. Tyrion leapt for one of the last portions of the gate still maintaining its structural integrity, but no sooner did his feet touch the stone than its matter was unmade by the Witch King's stolen magic.

Tyrion's eyes told him there was stone there, but his feet passed through as though it were as insubstantial as the confounding mists wreathing the shifting islets to the east of Ulthuan. Panic gripped him as he tumbled downward, spinning and flailing his arms in a desperate attempt to control his descent.

Tyrion closed his eyes and let his body find its poise. He rolled and angled his descent towards the sea, but knew that falling into water from such a height was akin to landing on solid rock.

What a galling way for a prince of Ulthuan to die...

Not in battle, not at the claws of some ancient nemesis, but falling from a great height.

The ignominy of it angered Tyrion more than the thought of his own death.

'Extend your arms, Tyrion!' shouted Eltharion's voice above him.

Tyrion heard a screeching roar and felt a booming rush of air above him. He did as Eltharion commanded, and the griffon's ebon-hard claws seized his arms. His plummeting descent slowed and smoothed out as Stormwing took his weight and flew over the empty quays and the hastily assembling defenders of Lothern.

Eltharion brought Stormwing down into the port, coming in slow and allowing Tyrion to drop the last yard to the paved quay before setting the griffon down. Tyrion's heartbeat was racing at his brush with death, and he turned in gratitude to Eltharion.

'My thanks, brother,' said Tyrion.

Eltharion shrugged and said, 'It was nothing. I was there.'

Tyrion gripped Eltharion's hand. 'I owe you my life. That is not nothing. You understand?'

Eltharion shook his head, and Tyrion despaired of ever reaching his friend again. All understanding of the bonds of brotherhood engendered by decades of friendship had been scoured from his soul, and only an empty shell that wore the face of Eltharion remained.

'What happened in that tower?' whispered Tyrion. 'What price did you pay?'

'You of all people should know better than to ask such a thing,' snapped Eltharion.

'What do you mean?'

'You are of the line of Aenarion,' said Eltharion, 'accursed to the last generation by his blood and forever drawn to battle and death. Your soul is still yours for the moment, but mine is already forfeit.'

'I do not understand.'

'You will,' said Eltharion. 'And on that day you will know what it means to be cursed.'

Eltharion took to the air on Stormwing's back, but Tyrion did not watch him go.

Instead, he stared at the great gap where the Sapphire Gate had once stood and at the towering immensity of the black ark. Whatever power Malekith had used to unmake the great sea gate was spent, but its work was done, and the route into Lothern was open.

Iron portcullises at the base of the black ark clattered upwards and a crimson-sailed fleet of raven ships and troop galleys surged out towards the quays of Lothern.

Tyrion turned and ran to stand alongside his king.

LORD SWIFTWING WATCHED the battle for Tor Elyr from the spired ramparts of his castle and felt despair like the morning he had learned he would never ride again. He wore his ithilmar breastplate and carried his winged helm in the crook of his arm. His family blade was sheathed at his side in a scabbard specially modified to fit around his lopsided waist, and an azure cloak flapped in the wind that whistled around the high tower.

Casadesus stood beside him, and the mood was grim as they watched the mist lifting from the river and saw the scale of the enemy facing what remained of his army.

The southern flank was buckling under the weight of the enemy attack, and the horde of tribesmen was massing to charge the thin line of spears in the north. The noose was closing on Tor Elyr, and no amount of heroics would change the inevitable outcome of this battle.

In the centre of the army, amid a troupe of cavorting blade-maidens, was Morathi.

Seated astride her winged steed of darkness, the hag sorceress had taken no part in the fighting, which surprised Lord Swiftwing, for history told that she was a leader who relished the chance to get her hands bloody.

'Why do you not fight?' whispered Lord Swiftwing. 'What are you saving your powers for, she-witch?'

The wind blew cold, and Lord Swiftwing pulled his cloak tighter about himself.

'You should go from here, my lord,' said Casadesus. 'I have a ship waiting at the lower docks. It is fast, and the druchii will not catch it.'

'Go?' said Lord Swiftwing. 'Go where?'

'To Saphery perhaps,' said Casadesus. 'There are no reports of fighting there. You would be safe and could rally support to retake Tor Elyr.'

Lord Swiftwing shook his head. 'You would have me flee? You should know me better than that, Casadesus.'

'I would have been disappointed if you had said yes,' agreed Casadesus, 'but I had to ask.'

'I understand, old friend,' said Lord Swiftwing. 'How could I look myself in the mirror knowing I had fled my city and left my warriors to die? No, if this is to be the last day of Ellyrion, then I will die with my land. You should go, there is no reason for you to die too.'

'You tried to send me away once before, and I seem to remember telling you that I was where I needed to be, my lord.'

'Duty?'

'Duty,' said Casadesus.

'It will be the death of us all,' said Lord Swiftwing, watching as a small Reaver band rode across the frozen river with rank upon rank of druchii marching after them. Red mist trailed from their lathered horses, but how they came to be on the other side of the river was a mystery. Though if there was one thing that could always be said of Ellyrion Reaver Knights, it was that they would always cause havoc from the direction least expected.

'A river in Ellyrion turned to ice. Who would have believed such a thing was possible?' said Lord Swiftwing. 'The druchii do not fight with any notions of honour, though I should not be surprised at such a thing. It is hard to believe they were once like us.'

'They *were* us,' said Casadesus. 'But I agree, it is hard to credit.'

A shimmering light rippled the horizon to the north, and Lord Swiftwing saw the graceful arc of a glorious rainbow. A shimmering curtain of stars glittered beneath it, though he had no idea what could have caused such a wondrous display.

'What magic is this?' he wondered. 'Ours or theirs do you think?'

'Who can say?' replied Casadesus. 'Ellyrion is a land of mystery.'

'There is truth in that,' agreed Lord Swiftwing, turning away from the battle and placing a hand on the hilt of his sword. 'But that is one mystery that will need to remain so for today.'

'My lord?'

'Ready my chariot, Casadesus,' said Lord Swiftwing. 'I may not be a Reaver Knight this day, but I will take to the field of battle as my last act.'

'Will you permit me to be your spear-bearer, my lord?'

'I would be honoured,' said Lord Swiftwing.

THE CRYSTAL SPIRES of the city glittered like the icy stalactites in the Dragon Caves of the Frostback Mountains.

Issyk Kul had killed a mighty creature of ancient days in those caverns, dragging its monstrous skull down onto a spike of ice and earning the favour of the dark prince in the process.

His flesh burned with the need to defile, to violate and to debase. This battle had given him precious little chance to honour his god in the proper manner, and the few tortures he had managed to inflict on the green shaman had only served to inflame his passions further.

Blood coated his chin where he had drunk the blood of a dying elf-maid, and his hands were slick to the elbow where he had reached into the chest of an injured warrior to remove his still-beating heart. Petty debaucheries in which even the lowliest devotee of Shornaal would happily indulge, but trifling and dull to him. He needed to violate something innocent, to destroy something beautiful and to corrupt something pure.

His warriors bayed for blood, for battle and for the sheer noise of it. A deafening symphony of discord arose from the horde, a wailing, braying, honking, skirling wall of sound that was music to his ears. The blaring cacophony, the smell of sweat, blood, fear and exultation were a potent mix, and the striking colours of the landscape and sky and city all combined in a scintillating chorus of sensation.

His horse pawed the earth, its flesh hot and raw and heaving with the need to trample warm bodies beneath its clawed hooves. It had feasted on elven meat, and bloody saliva dripped from between its chisel-like fangs. The very air of this island was pain to its exposed flesh, but the beast welcomed it as a fellow creature of Shornaal.

The invasion of Ulthuan had been like no other

campaign, for the sheer potency of war waged on a land of magic was like nothing he had experienced before. He had led the northmen's wolfships over the Sea of Claws to the Empire, but its rain-lashed shores held little appeal for him. The men that called that land home were dull, mud-caked grubbers of the earth, who knew nothing of the wonders of the true gods.

He could feel the aching need of his warriors to be unleashed, but held them in check a moment longer. The wall of spears before them was thin and fear came off the silver-armoured warriors in delicious waves. Against his horde, they would break and run at the first charge. Horsemen rode at the flanks of the battle line, and Kul licked his lips as he saw the warrior he and Morathi had broken in the haunted dungeons of Naggarond.

The young elf had been a playful pet, and had taken a long time to break, but when he had, oh... the degradations he had enjoyed, the torments he had begged for. To have endured so complete a debasement and still retain even a scrap of sanity spoke of a measure of denial or fortitude that Kul could only admire.

Caelir, that was his name, and Kul imagined skinning him alive and taking his flesh for a scabbard in which he would sheath his many-bladed weapon. A lone warrior with a horned helm and a cloak of thick bearskin broke from the horde with an ululating scream of hatred, but a white-feathered arrow punched through the visor of his helm before he had covered more than ten yards.

The elven spears trembled, and Kul let their fear grow. His anticipation built until finally he could stand it no longer.

He raised his sword and loosed a battle howl of lustful

rage. It was answered by his horde, and they sprinted forwards in a mass of axes, swords, shields and clubs. Kul rode with them, keeping pace with his warriors to better savour the raging swell of emotions that surrounded them. This would be a charge like no other, a charge of blood, noise and joy. The air hazed with the sheer violence of the spectacle assaulting Kul's senses.

'Yes!' he yelled. 'Yes, Shornaal, yes!'

The sky behind the elven battle line shimmered like the lights that burned on the northern horizon when the Chaos moon waxed full. The rounded hill crowned with menhirs like the herdstones around which the forest beasts would gather was aflame with colour, and a dazzling rainbow soared from its centre. The stones raised atop the hill blazed with magic, and the runes cut upon them shone like the fires that burned in the hottest forges of the Kurgan metal-shamans.

Glittering rain fell like sparkling snow, and a rumble of thunder rolled across the plains of Ellyrion as a searing crack split the sky. It crackled and spat, like a blazing lightning bolt tapped in the moment of its birth. The charge of the horde faltered at such a sight, and Issyk Kul felt a rush of powerful magic. The crack spread wider, tearing open like a curtain at a window, and the overpowering scent of wild blossoms, new wood and fresh-grown grass gusted from beyond its light.

Shapes moved through the glow, large and small, capering and lumbering, and Issyk Kul spat a mouthful of blood as he tasted the raw power of unfettered life magic. Songs and music sounded from the hilltop, festival-wild and redolent with the promise of rebirth and the cycle of living things. It was a hatefully melodious counterpoint to the blessed din of his horde's noise, and Kul's anger grew.

The rainbow faded, and the light on the horizon vanished as suddenly as it had come.

In its place was an army of magic, a host of whiplimbed dryads, capering fauns with barbed tridents and glittering carpets of sprites that covered the hillside and the land to the north. Towering over the curved waystones came trees with vestigial faces and limbs of creaking, groaning timber. These wooden giants lumbered down the hillside, followed by a glittering host of wild creatures of all shapes and sizes.

Wild boars, silver-tailed wolves and huge bears with golden fur came alongside a garishly attired host of elves armed with bows, spears and swords. Flocks of birds erupted from a sky that had been empty moments before: ravens, doves, hawks, red-breasted falcons, starlings, white-tailed jays and a host of birds of myriad species and plumage.

Soaring over the flocks were three golden-winged eagles, wide of pinion and noble in bearing. They flew like the sky was their own private kingdom, and Kul dearly wished for a horn bow like those carried by the Hung horsemasters to bring them down. An eagle with a white-plumed head soared higher than his brothers, and Kul remembered this bird killing his warriors before the walls of the Eagle Gate. Kul instantly dismissed the birds as he laid eyes upon a vision of ancient, eternally enduring perfection at the centre of the magical army.

It was an elf-maid, but an elf-maid like no other.

The purest white light streamed from her supple limbs, like sunrise on northern ice or the shimmer of gold in a streambed. Hair the colour of ripened corn fell about her shoulders like a waterfall, and her face was a vision of perfect beauty.

Eyes of hazel flecked with gold. Full lips and a smile that forgave him all his violations.

Kul hated her with a passion.

By virtue of her race, she was innately more beautiful than Kul could ever be, and the fires of his jealousy burned hotter and fiercer than ten lifetimes worth of hatred.

There could be no doubt as to her identity.

This was the Everqueen of Avelorn.

Finally, something worth defiling.

CHAPTER SEVENTEEN

BREAKING THE NOOSE

NARENTIR FELT HIS stomach lurch as the magic faded, and his mouth dropped open at the sight of the enemy horde below. Thousands of savage warriors draped in animal skins, beaten pig-iron armour and horned helms advanced upon a perilously thin line of elven spearmen. Narentir had served his time in the citizen levy, and was no warrior, but even he could tell that the northern tribesmen would smash through the spear hosts with one charge.

He clutched the spear Lirazel had given him as though it was a dangerous serpent that might turn on him at any moment. A heavy shirt of mail weighed on his shoulders, and how anyone expected him to fight while carrying such an extraordinary weight was quite beyond him. Narentir had explained this to Lirazel, but no amount of protest had changed her mind.

'You are one of the asur,' she had said. 'You will fight for Ulthuan. There is no other option.'

That had been the end of the discussion, and though he knew he was quite useless as a warrior, he had marched with the Everqueen's army to a long line of waystones hidden in a mist-shrouded valley deep in the heart of Avelorn. Here, the Everqueen bid her army make camp, and there they had remained for Isha knew how many days, until, as the sunlight began to fade, the same wordless summons that had awakened the denizens of her forest to her presence now brought them to battle readiness.

'Remember to point the sharp end at the enemy,' said Lilani, startling him from his memory and putting a reassuring hand on his arm. 'Stay close to me, and you will live through this.'

Narentir took a deep breath and said, 'I believe you, my dear, though the gods alone know why.'

'Because you are in love with me,' she said.

'Obviously,' replied Narentir. 'But so is half of Ulthuan, and you can't be right about them all, now can you?'

'Maybe not, but you *will* live through this,' said Lilani. 'And you will tell tales of this day for hundreds of years.'

'Really?'

'Really,' she said, and Narentir took comfort from her certainty.

Cruciform shadows passed overhead as the three eagles banked low over the army of Avelorn. A chittering, cackling mass of sprites and faeries swarmed towards the tribesmen, as flocks of birds swooped down and obscured them in a mass of feathers. The elves of Avelorn followed them, all the dancers, poets and singers of the Everqueen's realm come together to fight for the land they celebrated in song and verse. Leading them was the Maiden Guard, a solid core of marble-limbed elf-maids with sculpted breastplates and long spears of bronze.

Narentir was carried along by the stream of bodies, one hand clutching his spear to his chest, the other holding on to Lilani's arm. Despite the dancer's assurance that he would live, fear took hold of him, and his mouth dried at the thought of facing one of these dreadful barbarian warriors in combat. The bloody heave of battle was for heroes and killers, and he was assuredly neither. He told tales of heroes, he was not a hero himself.

He might die on this hillside.

This could be his last day on Ulthuan.

Narentir turned to Lilani and looked deep into her eyes.

'You'll look after me, my dear, won't you?' he said, almost begging.

'Count on it, Narentir,' she replied.

ELDAIN LED STARCHASER and their Reavers around the rear of the elven army at the gallop. They had left the druchii army behind and now swung around the battered survivors of the attack over the river. The centre still held, and it was strong, but the flanks were buckling under the pressure.

The druchii stranglehold on Tor Elyr was closing ever tighter, and if this were to be the end, then he would face it by Caelir's side. He could not know for sure that his brother still lived, but the same intuitive belief that Caelir had not died on Naggaroth told him that he still fought on.

Tor Elyr rose up before him, beautiful and shimmering

like a dream. How long would it take the druchii and the tribesmen of the north to bring it down? How quickly would this unthinking enemy reduce a city that had endured for centuries to ash and broken glass?

Eldain pictured its marble castles aflame, its silver towers sagging in the awful, intolerable heat of tribal revel fires. He saw its beautiful inhabitants crucified from the highest spires, their blood staining the white cliffs, and the flocks of carrion as they flew in lazy circles, bloated by the feast of flesh below.

Great sorrow replaced the anger in Eldain's heart at the thought of such wanton destruction and needless murder. Against such bitter hate, what chance did any of the races of the world stand? When such forces of darkness were ranged against all that was bright and pure, how could anything of goodness endure?

Yet even as despair threatened to overwhelm him, he saw the gates of Tor Elyr opening and ten warriors ride through on black steeds, each as dark as Lotharin. They were few in number, yet it was the banner they rode beneath that restored Eldain's hope that there was always reason to fight on. Shining like the last sunset, the banner flapped from the armoured prow of a chariot constructed from lacquered black starwood edged in gold that thundered from the city in the midst of the horsemen.

Upon that banner was the rearing silver horse upon a crimson field of Lord Arandir Swiftwing.

'The lord of Tor Elyr rides with his warriors once more!' shouted Laurena Starchaser, and a chorus of skirling yells answered her. Eldain watched the crippled master of the city lift his sword high, a glittering blade of sapphire steel, and in that moment the images of Tor

Elyr in flames vanished, replaced with it shining at its most glorious.

The riders and the chariot charged down the statue-lined causeway from the bastion castle at the edge of the bay, and Eldain lifted his sword in salute as Lord Swiftwing's chariot plunged into the swirling combat in the centre of the battle. To fight alongside the master of Tor Elyr would be an honour, but the northern flank was in danger of collapse, and needed his warriors to keep it steady.

Bodies lay twisted on the frozen riverbank, sprawled next to monstrous beasts with the heads of wolves, bears and bulls. Everywhere Eldain looked, he saw death. The smell of blood, rotten meat and mangy fur was like a poison in the air. A raucous melange of horns, drums and beaten iron came from the mortal host of tribesmen, a sound to end worlds.

'But not this world,' swore Eldain, riding around groups of wounded elves. They cheered at the sight of Lord Swiftwing riding out, and turned their broken bodies back to the fighting ranks. Riderless horses milled around the edges of the battle, and with every passing moment, Eldain's Reaver band grew larger as these grieving mounts joined their wild ride.

He saw the horde of northern tribesmen, and his stomach turned at the sight of so terrible and numerous a foe. The savage warlord sat atop his red-raw steed at the centre of the enemy line, and Eldain angled the course of his Reavers towards the edge of a thin line of spears and archers.

The archers were strung in a line two deep and loosed the last of their shafts into the onrushing horde. It wouldn't be enough to stop the charge, and Eldain knew the spearmen did not have the mass of numbers to stop them either. With perfect synchrony, the Reaver hosts parted and flowed around the flanks of the elven host. Starchaser rode along the edge of the river, while Eldain curved around the eastern end of the line in the shadow of the waystone crowned hill. A bloodied Reaver band milled at the foot of the hill, and Eldain rejoiced to see his brother at its head. His brother had lost his helm and his armour bore all the hallmarks of hard fighting. Caelir saw him and raised his sword with a boyish flourish.

They shouted each other's name in unison, riding together as a burst of rainbow light blazed from the hillside above them and the warriors of Avelorn took the field. An army like nothing else on this world emerged from the shimmering curtain of light that parted the sky like a silken theatre curtain in a Lothern playhouse.

Creatures of myth and legend, even in a land such as Ulthuan, came at the behest of this army's leader, and both brothers felt the awesome light of her presence as she trod the grass of Ellyrion.

'She lives…' breathed Caelir. 'Thank all the gods!'

Eldain nodded, too dumbfounded to answer as he saw the beautiful elf at the Everqueen's side. Though outshone by the Queen of Avelorn's brilliance, she was in every way, more radiant and more precious to Eldain than any divine ruler could ever be.

'Rhianna,' he said.

ON THE WESTERN bank of the river, the spectacular arrival of the Everqueen's army caused a ripple of unease to pass through the ranks of the druchii warriors. Her powers were rightly feared by the denizens of Naggaroth, and their own legends were filled with terrible stories of the fey queen's ability to bewitch and unmake even the mightiest champion.

Only one amongst the druchii did not quail at her sudden appearance.

Morathi smiled as the glittering host stepped from the blazing portal opened through the waystones. It had only been a matter of time before the bitch of Avelorn intervened, and now that she had made her move, it was time for Morathi to make her own.

It had been hard to stay her hand from intervening in the battle, for her powers could easily have destroyed whole swathes of the asur, but in the battle to come she would need all her power to oppose the greatest mage the world had ever seen. No matter that he was completely insane, Caledor Dragontamer was still a force to be reckoned with. Centuries of study and disciplined training had enabled her to shield her thoughts from others, even ones as canny and watchful as Caledor.

He would not see her coming, and the threat he had made all those years ago was surely now as empty as when he had first bluffed her with it. Then she had been young and just discovering the full extent of her power; now she was the mistress of the dark arts, a sorceress unrivalled in ability and strength. No power in the world could match her, not even the shadowy guardians who faded with Caledor on the island.

Morathi's blood sang with the prospect of her final triumph. Let Malekith tear down the gates of Lothern, and let this host topple the castles of Tor Elyr. These were mere sideshows in the great battle that had begun over five thousand years ago when the fires of Asuryan had left her beloved son a burned and wretched husk.

She could feel the titanic energies swirling around the

island even from here. They were calling to her, and she would answer their siren song of salvation with one of destruction.

Morathi shrieked and jabbed her barbed spurs into Sulephet's flanks. The beast snarled in anger, spreading its wings and powering into the sky. Flocks of screeching, bat-winged harpies rose like flocks of startled carrion, their leathery wings flapping wildly as they struggled to keep up with her dark steed.

Morathi watched the world recede, the desperate life and death struggles playing out upon its surface now meaningless to her. Let whichever side carried the field have its moment of glory. By day's end it would be irrelevant.

The Everqueen had come to Ellyrion, but Morathi did not care.

She flew away from the battle, over the glittering spires of Tor Elyr towards the magical heart of Ulthuan.

THE TWO HOSTS came together in a clash of mortal bodies and magical flesh. Birds of many colours swooped and dived with razored beaks pecking out eyes and sharp talons raking the skin from exposed limbs. The eagles flew low over the enemy host, slashing with claws and beak as they plucked warriors from the ground and tore them apart in the air.

Elasir, the lord of the eagles, hunted the largest warriors, ripping them to pieces even as they shouted commands to their vassals and huscarls. His brothers did likewise, their ebon claws ripping armour as though it were no more substantial than silk.

Streams of liquid sprites coursed through the tribesmen, biting and tearing with glittering claws of sparkling energy. Towering figures formed from bark and centuries-aged timber and moss stomped through the swirling mêlée, arms of ash, oak and willow smashing men through the air or crushing them beneath root-formed feet. Fauns gored, wild animals snapped, arrows sliced home, and hurled spell-flames burned the northmen, but even under such fantastical assault they did not break.

These were warriors reared amid the harshest environments imaginable, where life was unimaginably brutal and only the strongest, most ruthless warriors survived. The tribes of the north lived on the very edge of the world, in the scrap of land where the division between the realms of men and daemons was at its thinnest. The touch of Chaos lay upon that land, and the things living in the northern wastes were far stranger and more dangerous than these capering sprites.

Northern axes clove the giants of wood and spears spitted the fauns and wild animals. Swords bludgeoned the birds from the air, and heavy wooden shields bore the brunt of the rain of arrows. In the centre of the northmen, Issyk Kul battered a path through the raging combats to face the oncoming Queen of Avelorn, roaring his eagerness for the fight like a bellowed challenge. His warriors followed him in a swirling mass of rabid blades and clubs, all cohesion lost in the rush to destroy the incandescent elf-queen.

Eldain and Caelir rode around the edges of the tribesmen towards the lower slopes of the hill, loosing arrows into the mass of grunting warriors as they went. They rode without heed for the rest of the battle. Right now, *this* was all that mattered. Both brothers knew that they owed their lives to the Everqueen, and they rode to fight at her side. They could never repay her mercy or undo the hurt they had done, but they could offer their souls as sons of Ellyrion.

Eldain saw Lirazel lead a charge of the Maiden Guard, their shrill war cries like the wails of a thousand banshees. Their bronze spears plunged into the closest warriors, and then they were in amongst them, leaping, stabbing, kicking, punching and slashing. Elves of both sexes who had no business being warriors fought men who had spent their whole lives in battle, and Eldain wondered at the kind of devotion that could inspire such courage.

Caelir let fly with his last arrow and threw aside his bow.

'Brother!' he shouted. 'It's time!'

Eldain knew exactly what he meant and nodded. 'Into them!'

He turned Lotharin towards the tribesmen and unsheathed his sword, riding hard towards the armoured warriors. Hundreds of Reaver Knights rode with him, and their charge was a thing of beauty, perfectly coordinated and smooth as glass. Four hundred horsemen smashed into the fur-clad army, trampling and spearing the mortal warriors in a stampede of shod hooves and blades.

Moving languidly, as though she ghosted down the hillside without touching the ground, the Everqueen came in a shimmering cloud of drifting flower petals and perfumed air. She brought the light with her, and where she so much as glanced, the land threw off the chill of winter and summer blooms rose from the ground. She cast no magic, content to draw the healing energies of the land within her and let it flow into the warriors around her.

At her side, Rhianna displayed no such restraint,

basking in the potent wash of magical energies to empower her own spells. Searing fires leapt from her hands, dancing among the tribesmen with screeching cries of predatory birds. Her face was carved from granite, harsh and merciless as she killed, but to Eldain's eyes she was still wondrous.

Surrounded from all sides, the tribesmen responded by pulling back and bringing their shields around in perfect concert. Arrows thudded into heavy timbers and the Reaver Knights were forced to turn away from the solid barrier of spiked shields and jutting blades. Issyk Kul rode to the edge of the shield wall and raised his sword in challenge to the Everqueen.

'Face me and I shall ruin you, woman!' he shouted.

The Everqueen said nothing, but stepped down to the earth as though to answer the warlord's challenge. Though the battle continued to rage around the shield wall, it seemed to Eldain that the world around these two combatants faded to shadowy echoes. Kul burst from the shield wall on the back of his mighty steed; a monstrous sword of many blades held over his head and poised to slice the Everqueen in two.

The grass around her surged with life, the green of every shoot and leaf becoming eye-wateringly brilliant and vivid. Until now, Eldain had thought Ellyrion a land of great life and vibrancy, yet the Everqueen's touch poured the power of primordial creation into its very soul. Sweetly perfumed air spread from her, and the sunlight followed her every step as she faced a warrior who was her opposite in every way.

What she could create, he would destroy.

Where she breathed life, he carried death.

Where his dark patron corrupted, she renewed.

The Everqueen lifted a slender arm and pointed at the red-fleshed steed. Kul's charge was undone as the horse reared in agony, but it was not the pain of some magical attack that caused it to scream. The warlord leapt from the saddle, as chestnut strands of colour wound their way around the thrashing beast's legs, like thread onto a weaver's bobbin. Exposed musculature was once again clothed in flesh and skin, the colour moving upwards until the warm, mahogany coloured coat was reknitting onto the horse's back. The raw stump of its tail grew again, and a lustrous mane of long black hair sprouted from its gleaming neck.

Within moments, the horse was transformed, the hideous changes wrought upon its form now undone. The horse climbed to its feet, eyes wide and ears pressed flat against its skull as it saw the world with eyes untouched by warping powers.

The northmen shouted oaths to their Dark Gods, horrified at the ease with which their power was broken. Eldain threw off his surprise at the Everqueen's magic to see that the gap opened in the shieldwall by Kul's charge was still open. While it remained solid, a shieldwall was virtually impregnable, but once it was broken...

Lotharin saw what Eldain saw and sprang toward the gap.

'Reavers, ho!' shouted Eldain. Some of the tribesmen recognised the danger and moved to close the gap, but Eldain was quicker. Lotharin barged through, using his weight and power to smash men from their feet. More warriors saw the danger and rushed towards the incoming Reaver Knights. Eldain wheeled Lotharin around, lancing his sword through the neck of a tribesman wearing a full-faced helm of iron.

More Reaver Knights joined Eldain and their charge split the shieldwall as a wooden wedge splits a log for the fire. Caelir kicked a warrior in the face and slashed his blade through another man's arm. Starchaser rode into the shieldwall and her Reavers tore into the northmen from within. What had once been a fortress was now a deathtrap. Hundreds of cavalry charged the disintegrating shieldwall, and the savage warriors of the north were forced to fight as individuals. Though they still outnumbered the elves, they were scattered and alone.

The northmen were doomed, and Eldain swung his horse around as Issyk Kul ran at the Everqueen with his sword swinging for her throat. Once again, she raised a hand, palm up. Kul's sword vanished into a haze of glittering sparks, as through remembering the fire from which it had been created. The warlord cast aside the hilt as it burst into flames, and screamed his hatred at the Queen of Avelorn.

'You do not hate me, Issyk Kul,' said the Everqueen. 'You love me, as I love you.'

'I... I... love no one,' hissed Kul, struggling to reach the Everqueen as though he walked through the thickest mud. 'I am to be feared, not loved.'

His every step was a battle, and sinews stood out like taut cables on his neck and chest as he fought to reach her. His hands closed around her neck, and Eldain wanted to scream at such an insult.

'That is a lie,' said the Everqueen. '*She* loved you, but you offered her to the prince of pleasure for power. You gave away the most precious thing in the world, and for what? Power? You think what you have is power? Mortal power is fleeting, a blink in the eye of the cosmos. Love is eternal, and lasts all the ages of the world.'

Kul screamed and his hands dropped to his sides as he fell to his knees. Eldain saw the healing light of her magic worming its way into his flesh. Kul's body was swollen with muscle, warped to gross proportions by the Dark Powers he served. The magic of Avelorn filled him, seeking to undo the horrific changes he had willingly accepted. The Everqueen wished to destroy him, but Alarielle would not, for it was anathema to end life when she could restore it.

Eldain saw the northern warlord *diminish*, as though his entire body was being drained of the corruption that had given him such impossible strength and hatred. The face that was both beautiful and monstrous reshaped itself, losing its magnificence and becoming pugnacious and, worst of all, ordinary. His hair darkened until it was the same sandy, flaxen colour as his warriors, his flesh dirty and bruised, hard and leathery.

But the changes worked on his flesh had been at the whims of the dark prince, and such a god was a jealous master who did not willingly abandon his playthings. Even as the Everqueen remade Kul's body in its original form, so the petulant god of pleasure incarnate poured his malice, his spite and his perverse glee back into Kul. Ancient powers warred within the champion's flesh, and the effect was as horrifying as it was sudden.

Renewal and the power of unfettered excess ripped Kul apart, his body expanding and tearing with new growth. Limbs swelled and bloated as the power of the dark prince ran riot within his blood and bone. Gristled extrusions of marrow erupted from the raw flesh of the mutating champion, along with spindly growths, rubbery bladders of meat and hairless body parts that had no business being on the outside of any creature.

Within seconds, nothing that resembled a man remained, simply a mewling mass of degenerate flesh that flopped and squealed and honked its insanity through a dozen flapping mouths. A hundred eyes oozed into existence all over its warp-spawned flesh, and each one of them burned with hatred and madness. A warrior who had once been the chosen of the gods had now been abandoned, cast aside by his master like a broken toy.

Yet this broken toy was still awesomely dangerous, its lashing limbs hooked and barbed with lethal claws, its many mouths filled with swollen, broken teeth and needle-like fangs. The Everqueen's light was eclipsed by the darkness boiling from the monster's myriad eyes and it came at her with all the fury of a thing that knows only that the source of its pain is standing before it.

Then Caelir was beside the Everqueen, his borrowed sword held before him.

A bladed limb slashed for the Everqueen, but Caelir's blade was there to intercept it. He cut it away as more spined, thorny limbs lashed out like a whipping forest of razor-edged blades. He fought with the speed and skill of a Sword Master, slashing grotesque appendages from the creature spawned from Issyk Kul's remains.

As swiftly as he sliced its unclean flesh, more growths erupted from its heaving bulk. The Maiden Guard surrounded the monstrosity, plunging their spears into its gelatinous body and putting themselves between its rampage and the Everqueen. Lirazel rammed her spear into the creature's body, gouging and twisting the blade to draw forth spurts of steaming black ichor. The monster screeched and attacked with even greater fury. A slicing barb took Caelir high on the shoulder as another tore his armour just above his hip. He staggered, and a host of blackened limbs struck him with gleeful frenzy.

Eldain leapt from his saddle and cut a path towards the creature through its whipping limbs, organic debris and thrashing, frond-like tentacles. Stinking fluids gushed from each wound, and Eldain retched at the miasma as a jelly-like limb of toothed suckers wrapped itself around Caelir and lifted him into the air. A pair of mouths rippled into existence on the monster's unquiet flesh, fangs like sword blades unsheathing from drooling gums of pus-yellow meat.

Before they could bite down, Eldain slashed his sword through the side of the creature's head. A flood of stinking black blood and fatty tissue frothed from the wound. The reek was incredible, rotten meat and decaying matter that smelled as though unearthed from a freshly opened grave.

The beast hurled Caelir aside, gurgling in lunatic amusement as it sensed a more succulent morsel nearby. Eldain ran to his brother's side as Rhianna stepped before Issyk Kul's new and repulsive form. The Everqueen's light filled her, white fire shining in her eyes and blazing along her body like the magic that thundered through the Annulii.

'Are you hurt?' said Eldain.

'I'm bleeding, but nothing serious,' answered Caelir. 'Come on, we have to help her.'

'No,' said Eldain, holding Caelir back. 'This is not a fight for the likes of us, brother.'

Rhianna stood before the monster, unfazed by its expanding horror, and magical vortices of fire spun around her body in pulsing waves.

Acidic drool and hissing spittle flew from the monster's

jaws as it hauled its lumpen mass towards her on twisted limbs of misshapen bone and roiling frills of undulant flesh. Faces blurred on its drum-taut skin as though a hundred bodies writhed within it, and claws, teeth and drooling orifices opened in the meat of its distended belly.

'I am a mage of Saphery,' said Rhianna, her voice resonating with wells of power no mortal ought to tap. 'And a daughter of Ulthuan. The blood of queens flows in my veins.'

Eldain and Caelir shielded their eyes as a torrent of blazing light erupted from Rhianna's body. A horizontal geyser of white fire shot from her hands and eyes.

It was killing magic. Dangerous magic. *Old* magic…

Alarielle would not destroy, but Rhianna was more than willing to do so.

The light played over Kul's transformed flesh, and where it touched, it burned like the fires of Asuryan himself. Like tallow before a flame, bloated flesh sizzled and ran like butter. Drooling ropes of it melted from grossly twisted and deformed bones that cracked in the heat with a sound of splitting wood. The creature's many mouths gave voice to one ululating shriek of pain and horror as its body was devoured by the cleansing flame of Avelorn.

Eldain tasted the ancient power of this magic. This was the energy that had brought the world into being, a fragment of the power that had shaped worlds and allowed its builders to cross from one side of the cosmos to the other in a single step. Against its awesome potency, the power of the dark prince was as a leaf in a hurricane.

Kul's body shrank before the firestorm, but whatever spark of life remained to animate his monstrous form remained alive until the last. The screaming went on until nothing remained of the creature save a molten pool of smouldering ash and liquid bone.

THE SPEAR HOSTS charged into the ragged horde of northmen, and drove them back with disciplined thrusts of their weapons. With graceful, methodical precision, the tribesmen were either slain or driven back to the river. Caught between the precise slaughter of the spears and the crazed whirl of magical beings, spells and creatures of legend, the warriors of Issyk Kul had already held beyond the limits of human endurance.

And, without him to lead them, they broke.

Here and there, small groups banded together, but the Reavers simply circled them and sent well-aimed shafts through helmets, exposed limbs and necks until they too collapsed. Fewer than a hundred warriors survived to reach the riverbank.

The spear hosts left the final slaughter to the creatures of Avelorn, obeying the shouted commands of their sentinels to reform and march to the aid of the centre. The Everqueen moved through the wounded, spreading her healing light to those who were still beyond the reach of Morai-Heg's banshees. She would take no part in the killing, and the magical beings she had brought to Ellyrion swarmed around the edges of the spear hosts, eager to take their killing to the centre.

Beneath the ragged, battle-torn banners of Tor Elyr's citizen levy, the victorious warriors of the northern flank turned south.

CHAPTER EIGHTEEN

THE LAST HOUR

THE RAVEN SHIPS hit the quayside first, sweeping the docks with iron bolts that killed any of the defenders not behind cover, and driving the rest back. Heedless of the damage to their ships, the slave-masters of the troop galleys cracked their whips and drove their hulls straight into the sloping quays. The ugly boats cracked and disgorged scores of druchii swordsmen onto stonework that had known the tread of many races, but had never seen Naggarothi in thousands of years.

Tyrion had joined the Phoenix King and Korhil in the centre of the battle line, amid a silent, armoured host of Phoenix Guard. Tall and unmoving, silent and grim of feature, these warriors were unlike any other of Ulthuan. It seemed a lambent light glowed beneath their skin, and their eyes were dark pools that had seen too much. Even standing next to them gave Tyrion a sense of ages passed and ages yet to come.

He felt the weight of grief borne by Ulthuan, the endless cycle of battle and bloodshed waged in the name of a power struggle begun thousands of years ago. He saw the bloody Sword of Khaine above it all, revelling in the long-burning hatreds that flared anew with every generation, as mothers and fathers told their children of ancient wrongs over and over.

Truly Aenarion had saved and cursed his people by drawing the sword.

'Would you have drawn it had you *truly* known the price we would pay?' Tyrion wondered aloud. 'If you had seen the millennia of woe it would bring, would you still have drawn the sword?'

He knew the answer to that, just as he knew what his own answer would have been.

The druchii were massing beneath a relentless hail of arrows, but still the Phoenix King did not give the order to advance.

Tyrion moved along the front of their line until he stood next to Finubar. The king gave him a weak smile, and Tyrion saw the fear in his eyes. He feared to give the order, and not without good reason. The Phoenix Guard's presence was a grim omen: praetorians and pallbearers all in one.

'Sire,' said Tyrion. 'We must advance. The druchii need to be driven from the quayside.'

'I know,' said Finubar.

'Then give the order.'

'I am afraid, Tyrion,' said Finubar. 'If I order the advance, I will die. I know it.'

'You will die anyway,' said Tyrion. 'We all die sooner or later. Better on our terms than theirs, my king.'

The warrior beside Finubar nodded, and Tyrion saw

the rune of Asuryan upon his brow. Clad in a shimmering hauberk of orange-tinted gold and ithilmar, he was swathed in a white cloak of mourning and carried a slender-hafted halberd with a shining silver blade. The warrior's face was full and roguish, like that of a libertine, yet his eyes were filled with the shadows of past regrets and future knowledge.

'Caradryan,' said Tyrion, recognising the famed Captain of the Phoenix Guard.

The warrior mimed drawing a sword and cocked his eyebrow.

Tyrion looked from Caradryan to Finubar and Korhil, seeing their incomprehension. It was the question only a warrior without words could ask, and Tyrion knew the answer even as the question was posed.

Yes, the Sword of Khaine would give him the power to end the druchii threat once and for all, but the price was higher than Tyrion was willing to pay. Aenarion might not have known the full truth of the damnation he laid upon his people by drawing the Widowmaker, but Tyrion knew it all too well. Power such as the sword would grant could never be given back by something so simple as driving it back into an altar. Once loosed, it was *always* loose; in the hearts of all who heard of it, and in their blood that sang of its slaughters.

Nothing could undo the damage Aenarion had done by wielding the Sword of Khaine, but Tyrion would not add to his people's woes by drawing it anew. He had the strength of his friends, and courage of his own to steel him in the face of the enemy. Yes, the sword offered a chance for victory, but Tyrion would not let its temptations draw him into its web. The faces of lost loved ones paraded before him, but Tyrion welcomed them, reliving the joy he had known in their lives instead of mourning their passing.

Tyrion held himself taller than he had in a great many years as the anger he had carried for so long vanished in a heartbeat.

Tyrion smiled, and Caradryan saw the revelation within him.

'You look *different*,' said Korhil.

'I am,' agreed Tyrion.

'What has changed?' asked Finubar.

'Me,' replied Tyrion. 'I have changed.'

Korhil shrugged, dismissing the matter as irrelevant, but Finubar continued to stare at him. The Phoenix King seemed to take a measure of comfort in Tyrion's calmness, and looked over to the druchii massing on the quayside. Crossbowmen were moving out with their black weapons tucked into their shoulders, and swordsmen marched behind them beneath freshly raised banners.

Above them all, the Witch King flew on the back of his dragon. The sky above Lothern was calm and peaceful, unsullied by so much as a single cloud, and Tyrion followed the Witch King as he swooped and dived over the city, unleashing bolts of purple fire from his gauntlets and noxious breaths of toxic fumes from the dragon's jaws. Flames leapt up from the stricken city, and the sight of his city burning galvanised the Phoenix King at last.

'Everyone dies,' he said at last. 'And if this is to be my time, then so be it.'

Finubar raised his sword, and the fiery banner of the Phoenix Guard caught its golden edge. All along the elven battle line, swords and spears were raised in answer.

'In Asuryan's name!' shouted Finubar.

The Phoenix King charged, and the host of Lothern went with him.

ELDAIN AND CAELIR rose to their feet as Rhianna approached. The light of borrowed power still shone in her eyes, and it seemed that she did not know them for a moment. Then the light of recognition arose and her face went through a complex series of expressions ranging from relief, to anger and regret. So many emotions churned within her that Eldain had no idea how she would react to seeing him again. The last time they had stood in one another's presence, Rhianna had tried to destroy him with her magic.

Caelir took matters into his own hands and swept Rhianna into a passionate embrace. Her arms hovered for a moment before returning the embrace, and Eldain let out a relieved breath as he saw tears of happiness spill down her cheeks.

'My love,' said Caelir. 'Gods above, but I have longed for this moment.'

'Caelir,' said Rhianna. 'I thought I would never see you again.'

'I have a habit of doing what others do not expect,' he said, kissing her on the mouth.

She returned the passion of his kiss, and Eldain felt his heart break anew. He had lost Rhianna to Caelir once before and it had hurt like no other pain ever could. That wound had festered, but this one was clean.

Caelir and Rhianna belonged together. Eldain knew that now, but still it hurt.

No one could ever lose a maiden like Rhianna without pain, but this was *good* pain, as though a barb he hadn't known was lodged in his heart had suddenly been removed by a healer's magic. Guilt had been a torment he had lived with for so long, he had forgotten what it was to live free of it.

He made to turn away, but a restraining hand took him by the arm.

'Eldain,' said Rhianna. 'I do not know what to say to you.'

'You do not have to say anything,' said Eldain. 'I do not expect your forgiveness, for I did you and Caelir great wrong. He and I have made a peace of sorts, but I expect nothing of the kind from you.'

Rhianna took a deep breath. 'I can forgive you, Eldain, but first you have to forgive yourself.'

Eldain shook his head. 'Look around you. All of this is my fault. I brought this death and destruction to Ulthuan, and I can never forgive myself for that. Do not waste your forgiveness on me, Rhianna. I do not deserve it.'

'The heart that does not want to heal cannot be remade.'

'Maybe some hearts should not be remade.'

'I said the very same thing once,' said Rhianna. 'I believed it then, but I do not believe it now. Broken hearts are empty, and empty hearts soon fill with all that is dark in this world. I would not see you live so.'

Eldain said, 'It is not your choice to make, Rhianna.'

'No, it is not,' said a sad voice of radiant wonder. 'And it never will be.'

They turned to see the Everqueen standing before them in a pool of golden light. None of them had heard her approach, and Eldain fought down a rising fear as he felt the presence of the ancient power of the Everqueen lurking behind the mask of Alarielle.

Which of the Queen of Avelorn's two faces would be in the ascendancy?

'Be at peace, Eldain of Ellyr-Charoi,' said Alarielle. 'You need not fear me. Nor should you, Caelir of Ellyr-Charoi. The Everqueen spared your lives, for reasons I could not fathom, but which I now understand. Ulthuan needs you like never before.'

'I am yours to command,' said Eldain, dropping to one knee.

'My life is yours,' vowed Caelir.

Warm approval greeted their pronouncements, as a black shape passed overhead, a stain on the purple sky as it passed over the face of the sinking sun. Eldain looked up and saw a black steed galloping through the air. Its sweeping midnight wings beat with powerful strokes, and there could be no doubting the identity of the ivory-skinned druchii sorceress sat astride its back.

'The Hag Sorceress,' hissed Caelir. 'She flees!'

'No,' said Rhianna, with a haunted look settling upon her features. 'She does not flee.'

'Then what is she doing?' asked Eldain.

'She seeks to unmake that which she cannot possess,' said the Everqueen.

Eldain said, 'Where is she going?'

'Rhianna knows,' said Alarielle. 'Don't you?'

'Isha, no...' said Rhianna, as though reliving a dark memory or despairing foresight. 'The vision of the oracle... the druchii princess... I saw her kill them.'

'Kill who?' asked Eldain.

'The mages!' cried Rhianna. 'Without them the ritual will be undone!'

'What does that mean?' asked Caelir.

'Aenarion's bride flies to the Isle of the Dead,' said Alarielle. 'To unmake the vortex of Caledor Dragontamer.'

* * *

THE SONG WAS killing him. He knew it, but kept singing it anyway.

His body was wasted, drained of energy to keep the melody alive, and his mind was lost in the darkness of ancient dreams. Prince Imrik, though the name now held little meaning for him, floated in the depths of the mountains. He had long since cast off the silver threads that bound him to his flesh in his desperation to reach the ancient minds of the slumbering dragons. Even were he to succeed, his mind would be lost forever in the spaces between thought and physicality. Unable to return to his body, his mind would wander in darkness for all eternity, or at least until his empty frame eventually succumbed to the ravages of time.

Yet it would be worth it if he could only reach the minds of the sleeping dragons.

He raged and pleaded for them to awake, but still they ignored him. He offered them riches, magic and servitude if only they would rouse themselves from their dreams. They took no heed of his blandishments, and dreamed on.

He felt them moving around him in the darkness; vast, mountainous consciousnesses that rolled and turned like vast leviathans of the deep. They took no notice of him, lost in their own dreams of glory and open skies. What lure did the world above have for such minds?

The magic of the world was in decline, drawn away by an ancient ritual, and without that magic, the world of mortals was a cold and tasteless realm. Better to live in dreams, where magic was all powerful and never faded.

Who would ever choose to leave such a place?

Why would *he*?

Imrik finally accepted the truth of the naysayers in Lothern.

The dragons were sleeping away the ages of the world, and would never reawaken.

He had avoided that conclusion for so long, but now it was inescapable. With its acceptance, Imrik felt his will to awaken the dragons erode until there was nothing left, just a broken mind bereft of a body to which he could return.

Imrik surrendered to despair, adrift on currents of ancient thought.

Lost forever in the shared dreamspace of dragonkind.

THE AIR ABOVE the Inner Sea was cold and flecked with clouds like rumpled snow. Eldain held tight to the feathers of the eagle's neck, though he knew it would never let him fall. Primal fear of heights kept Eldain's grip firm, and though the view beneath him was spectacular, he tried to keep his eyes fixed on the creature beneath him.

Its plumage was gold, not the gold poets spoke of when describing a beautiful elf-maid's hair, but the gold that would drive a dwarf to madness with its lustre. Only the eagle's head was different, pure white and unblemished by so much as a single feather of another colour.

The bird's name was Elasir, and he was the lord of the eagles. Such a self-proclaimed title among mortals would have invited ridicule, but for Elasir it was completely appropriate, and, indeed, seemed entirely too prosaic for so magnificent a creature. Its two brothers were no less spectacular, and when they had landed behind the Everqueen, Eldain felt the need to bow to them as he had bowed to her.

'Follow Morathi,' said the Everqueen. 'Stop her.'

Simple commands, yet Eldain had not the faintest idea as to how they would obey them.

The first part had been easy. Two of the eagles stooped their wings, and Caelir and Rhianna had eagerly leapt upon their backs. Eldain had only reluctantly climbed aboard Elasir's back, for he was a rider who preferred his mounts to remain earthbound. No sooner had he settled himself on the back of the eagle than it lifted with a deafening cry, spreading its wings and powering high into the sky.

I am Elasir, Lord of the Eagles. Be calm and grip the feathers of my neck.

The voice was powerful and layered with wisdom gathered from across the world. Eldain obeyed instantly, and felt the noble bird's amusement at his nervousness.

Your companions have no fear of flying on Aeris and Irian, came the gently chiding voice of the eagle, *nor should you. I will not let you fall.*

'Rhianna is a mage of Saphery, she is used to such strangeness. And Caelir, well, he relishes this kind of thing.'

Few earthwalkers earn a chance such as this.

'Believe me, I know that, and I am grateful, but I will be glad when I am back down.'

I doubt that, said the eagle, and Eldain wondered what he meant.

The ongoing battle at Tor Elyr had faded behind them in the mist, and Eldain felt a pang of guilt at leaving before the outcome was decided. Even with the magical forces of the Everqueen, the army of Lord Swiftwing was still in dire straits. Neither force would emerge from the battle without grievous losses, but it was clear that the outcome of the battle held little meaning for Morathi.

The Inner Sea was a churning blue shimmer of breaking waves and foaming crests. Eldain remembered crossing that sea on the *Dragonkin*, and it had been like a mirror, smooth and untroubled by much in the way of waves. Captain Bellaeir had complained that the seas were troubled, and Eldain wondered what he would make of them now.

Scraps of islands passed beneath them, tiny dots in the expanse of sea that looked like shapes on a map instead of actual landscape. To the north, Eldain saw a smudge of smoke on the horizon from the ever-smouldering volcano on the Gaen Vale. Only reluctantly did he allow his eyes to be drawn to the shimmer in the air before them that masked their destination.

The Isle of the Dead.

No one with any sense sought to travel to that doomed rock, for it was a place of mist and shadow, grief and loss. Eldain forced himself to look at the seas around the island. Where the rest of the ocean was unsettled and threatening, the waters around the Isle of the Dead were calm and smooth, as though painted on the surface of the world by an ancient artist. A grey and craggy smear of land was just visible through the mists that hugged the shoreline, and Eldain was reminded of Narentir's tales of the Ulthane and the lost island they guarded.

Did anything similar protect the Isle of the Dead?

No, the island has protection of its own, came the voice of Elasir.

Eldain nodded and said, 'Yet it still needs us to fly to save it?'

I did not say those defences were on the island.

Eldain could not argue with that logic, and watched as

the island grew larger on the horizon. They flew into the mist, and Eldain felt the clammy touch of it. His breathing grew shallow, for the air here was cold and without life, like a mansion left empty by the death of its owner. It tasted of abandonment, a place where nothing has stirred the air for centuries, and nothing ever would.

Even their presence left no mark.

The beating of the eagles' wings did not stir the clouds, and their cries back and forth to one another did not echo. Caelir shouted over to Eldain, but his words were swallowed in the dead space between them. Here and there, he saw glittering lights and distant glows in the mist and cloud, but no sooner were they noticed than they faded away.

'What are they?' he asked, knowing Elasir would understand.

Souls who approached too close and were trapped by Caledor's great magic. Do not look upon them too long or your heart will break with sadness.

Eldain took that advice and averted his gaze whenever he saw the flickering corpse-candles. Instead, he concentrated on the lost island that faded in and out of perception as the eagles flew ever deeper into the deathly mist. It had been thousands of years since this land had last known the tread of elves, caught forever in a timeless, deathless embrace of powerful magic.

Just thinking of the Isle of the Dead was enough to settle a lump of cold dread in his stomach, for it was a place of incredible heroism and awesome tragedy. The fate of the asur had been sealed and saved on this island, as had the lives of the mages who made the ultimate sacrifice in joining Caledor.

Elasir began to drop through the air, his wings folding

back and dipping as he lost altitude and began his approach to the island. Eldain swallowed as the clouds enveloped them once more. He could see nothing but the cloying mist and the dim lanterns of the souls trapped by the island's magic. Would he be such a light for some future traveller to see? The idea terrified him, and his mouth went dry at the thought of being trapped here for all eternity.

Then they were clear of the clouds, and the Isle of the Dead spread out before him.

A bleak shoreline of tumbled boulders rose from the sea, leading to shingled beaches of polished stones and thence to forests of leafless trees. Though the sea around the island was like a polished mirror, it pounded the rocks of the island itself. Booming waves hammered the island, and Eldain felt the sea's fury at being kept from these shores for so long.

Elasir brought him in low, coming in fast over the shoreline. Broken swords with black blades and skull-topped pommels drifted in the surf, and the bones of long-dead monsters lay half-buried in the sand. The eagle landed high up the beach, and Eldain dropped to the black sand with a relieved sigh.

Aeris and Irian landed a moment later, and Caelir vaulted from the back of his mount, his face flushed with excitement.

'That was incredible, Aeris,' he said, running his hands along the eagle's flank as he would an Ellyrian steed. 'I don't think I've known anything like it.'

The eagle ruffled its feathers, and Eldain felt its pride. Rhianna slid demurely from the back of Irian, adjusting her mage's robes as she turned to face them. She bowed to her eagle, and whatever words passed between them were for her and Irian alone.

We will take to the air now, said Elasir.

'You will not come with us?' asked Eldain.

We cannot. Mortals cursed this place, and only mortals may walk its paths.

'So how do we get back?' asked Caelir.

We will be here, replied Elasir, and Eldain caught the note of hesitation in his words.

Caelir looked around the dismal beach. Grey fingers of mist eased from the forests higher up on the scrubby bluffs overlooking the beach, and the surf spread yet more weapons and bones over the sand. Caelir picked one up, its hilt still sticky with blood and the blade razor-sharp. A skull-rune was stamped on the pommel stone, and Caelir threw it away in disgust.

'I thought this place was supposed to be timeless,' he said.

'It is,' said Rhianna.

'Then why does the sea still surge and recede? Why does the mist writhe in the trees?'

'The island is cut off from the rest of the world,' said Rhianna. 'If anyone could see us, we would appear to be standing still. Time flows around us here, not with us.'

A faint tremor shook the beach, and stones rattled as they were carried down to the water.

'What was that?' asked Caelir.

'Morathi,' answered Rhianna.

'We'd best get a move on,' said Eldain, setting off for the bluffs overlooking the shore.

BEYOND THE BEACH, the island was just as bleak and desolate. It had all the hallmarks of a battlefield, for the dunes were formed from piles of skulls and heaps of rotted armour. The noise of the sea receded, and the island became utterly quiet. The forest was unnaturally silent. No birds nested in the leafless trees, no burrowing animals made their lairs amid their roots, and not a breath of wind stirred the skeletal branches.

'What was this place?' asked Caelir as they followed a path that wound a serpentine route through the trees. 'I mean, I know the stories of what happened here, but what was it before then?'

'I do not know,' said Eldain, glancing nervously between the narrow trunks at the scraps of mist that seemed to be following them. 'I have only ever known it as the Isle of the Dead.'

'It was where the asur were born,' said Rhianna. 'This is where Asuryan made the first of us. It was once a place of creation, the cradle in which our race was first given form.'

'How do you know that?'

Rhianna hesitated. 'I am not sure. I feel it as though I have always known it, though the thought never occurred to me until now. It feels like… like memory.'

'We should hurry,' said Eldain, glancing over his shoulder. 'I believe we are being followed.'

Caelir drew his sword. 'By who? Morathi?'

'No,' said Eldain. 'I don't know what it is, but I can feel it drawing near.'

Eldain scanned the trees, his eyes darting from shadow to shadow as he saw the sinuous form of a slender figure ghosting between the trees. Dark of eyes, and with black fingernails and black hollows for eyes, he knew he should know this figure, but could not place its identity. He knew him, he *did* recognise him, but from where?

Eldain searched the recesses of his memory, but could

not think of this figure's name. There was something dreadfully familiar to the cruel cast of his smile, the empty blackness of his gaze and the spidersilk weave of his dark robes.

'Stand forth and make yourself known!' he yelled, but the mist and the trees swallowed his words. He heard mocking laughter and spun around as it seemed to come from all around him. Only then did he notice that he was alone.

Caelir and Rhianna were nowhere to be seen.

'Who are you?' he demanded.

Eldain stood alone in the dark forest, and the mist gathered around him. The lights he had seen in the clouds were all around him, sparkling and dancing as though amused at his ire.

'They are pleased to see you,' said a voice from the trees.

A tall elf, slender and thin-limbed, walked from the trees, his robe rustling softly around him as he walked. He wore a pale ivory mask, and Eldain saw he had mistaken the features painted onto its surface as the elf's true expression. Long white hair gathered at his shoulders, and a jade amulet in the form of a black-bladed sword hung at his neck. The name of Khaine was stitched into his robes with silver thread, and Eldain saw variations on that theme in the hems and cuffs of the figure's attire.

'Why are they pleased to see me?' asked Eldain, trying not to show fear as he recognised the elf. 'They don't know me.'

'Oh, but they do,' said Death. 'They have nothing to do but watch the comings and goings of the world. You have amused them greatly, for they have seen your path lead you inexorably to this place. And they do so love to welcome new souls to their ranks.'

'New souls?' asked Eldain. 'Am I dead?'

Death cocked his head as though considering the question. 'Not in the way you would consider it, but for the purposes of our conversation you might as well be dead.'

'I think I am still alive,' he said.

'In that your heart still beats and you have breath, then I suppose you are,' conceded Death with a noncommittal shrug. 'In that you are part of the world and its grand pageant, you most certainly are not.'

'Is this even real?' asked Eldain.

Death sighed. 'Another one who wants to argue about the nature of reality... what is this obsession you mortals have with reality?'

'Well? Is it real?'

'Real is such an ambiguous term, Eldain,' said Death. 'This is as *real* to you as it needs to be, but others would doubt it were you to tell them of it. Is that good enough for you?'

'Real or not, I have nothing to say to the likes of you,' said Eldain, turning away.

Death was at his side in an instant, walking beside him as though they were old friends out for a convivial stroll in the forest.

'The likes of me?' said Death, sounding almost hurt. 'That was uncalled for, especially as we have so much to talk about.'

'What could we possibly have to talk about?'

'What do you imagine Death and a mortal would talk about?' said Death, lacing his hands behind his back. Eldain saw they were beautiful hands, craftsman's hands. The nails were black, but not painted black. They were the black of the void, nails that could mould the warp and weft of reality in ways unknown to those who did not have the power of a god.

'Am I going to die?' asked Eldain.

'Of course,' answered Death. 'All living things must die.'

'Even Morathi?'

'Even Morathi,' laughed Death. 'She can avoid me for only so long. She thinks she "cheats" me every time she emerges from that tinker's cauldron, dripping with the blood of babes and innocents, but she is not immortal. Not yet. She only postpones the inevitable. Even this is just another parlour trick to delay my touch upon her flesh.'

'She is going to destroy the world,' said Eldain, feeling more at ease talking with Death, though the nature of the experience was still confusingly surreal. 'That hardly seems like a parlour trick, as you call it.'

'Exist as long as I have existed and even the mightiest deeds will seem trifling to you too.'

'Even the end of the world?'

'Even the end of *worlds*.'

Though Eldain knew this was a realm of magic and deceit, he was quick to spot the lie.

'If that were true, why are you here now? Shouldn't this bore you?'

Death shrugged and said, 'I have an affection for this world, and I have grown fond of the grand players in its performances. Some are mad, some are deluded and others are so very nearly gods that it amuses me to watch them weave their plans as though they will last forever. As to why I am here, some mortals need their endings to be witnessed. Otherwise their lives will pass unremarked, and that would be a terrible tragedy.'

'Are you speaking of me?' asked Eldain.

Death laughed. 'No, Eldain. At best, you are a minor player in this world's drama.'

The masked figure put a hand on Eldain's shoulder and said, 'Yet even the minor players may make the greatest of differences.'

'How?'

'By accepting the inevitable,' said Death. 'By knowing when to give in.'

'That sounds like grim counsel,' said Eldain.

'You *are* talking to Death, you know.'

The path they were following led out through the trees, and Eldain saw they had come to a wide plain of black sand that had turned to obsidian in the fires of some ancient cataclysm. Lightning-shot mist gathered on the plain, swirling around its perimeter in a ceaseless vortex. Crackling lines of power raged in the depths of the howling mist, and pillars of light stabbed into the sky from its centre. Eldain had the sense of unimaginable power being drawn to this place, lines of convergence that had taken a lifetime to map and devise. The air was rich with magic, and he felt his blood sing with its proximity. His flesh tingled with the desire to drink that power and reshape itself into new and ever more wondrous forms.

Only with an effort of concentration was he able to force that desire down.

Thousands of carved waystones were strewn around the exterior of the vortex, some toppled, some still standing, but all rendered glassy by whatever infernal heat had vitrified the plain.

'What is this place?' he asked.

'You know what it is,' said Death. 'Every part of your body can feel where you are.'

'This is where Caledor Dragontamer enacted his great ritual,' said Eldain. 'This is where Caledor died.'

Death laughed again, and there was real amusement in the sound.

'You are half right,' agreed Death. 'This is indeed where Caledor drained the magic from the world. But *died*? Perhaps. It is hard to tell sometimes, I have not been kind to the old elf and his mind is not what it once was. In any case, it is a moot point, for this is where I will leave you, Eldain Éadaoin. Just remember what I told you and you may yet leave this place alive.'

Eldain wanted to ask more, but the world blurred around him and Death had vanished.

In his place were Caelir and Rhianna, both with the same expression of surprise he was sure was plastered across his features. They looked into the vortex of magical energy, elated and horrified in equal measure that they had reached their destination.

'Eldain! Rhianna!' cried Caelir, sweeping them both into a powerful embrace. 'I lost you both. I was lost and alone in the forest, but then I felt someone else beside me.'

'Who was it?' asked Eldain.

'Our father,' replied Caelir, as a tear ran down his cheek. 'We rode through the woods of Ellyrion, and he told me that he loved me and was proud of me. We spoke for hours, and I said all the things I wished I had said to him while he still lived.'

'I saw an old man,' said Rhianna. 'I did not know him at first, but then I recognised him from a colour plate in one of the books my father keeps in the Tower of Hoeth.'

'Who was he?' asked Caelir.

'His name was Rhianos Silverfawn, and he lived a very long time ago.'

'He was an ancestor of yours?' said Eldain. 'How long ago did he live?'

'In the time of Caledor Dragontamer,' said Rhianna. 'He was filled with sadness to see me, but before he could say any more, he vanished and I found myself at the edge of this obsidian plain.'

'Who did you see, brother?' asked Caelir.

Before Eldain could answer, the very air rumbled and a crack split the ground. The world shuddered as a powerful earthquake shook it. The trunks of the trees split open and they toppled, disintegrating into billowing clouds of dust as they struck the ground. Flickering magical fire seethed from the cracks in the earth, like the fire at the heart of the world oozing up through wounds in its surface. Forks of lightning arced from the vortex and struck deep in the forest. Fire bloomed as tinder-dry trees caught light.

One of the towering columns of light in the centre of the plain was snuffed out, and the heaves of the ground intensified. Like the gods themselves bestrode the earth with titanic footsteps, the ground bucked with thunderous heaves.

The spiralling mist split apart as whipping tendrils of mist and light began spinning off, like debris from an apprentice potter's wheel that spun too fast. Monumental power sheared from the vortex and bled ferociously back into the world.

'What's happening?' asked Caelir.

'We are too late,' said Rhianna. 'Morathi has unmade the vortex, and everything is unravelling.'

CHAPTER NINETEEN
THE VORTEX UNDONE

No sensation in the world came close to the thrill of battle, and that thought saddened Lord Swiftwing, even as he drove his spear through the heart of another druchii warrior. Casadesus steered with great skill, wheeling and twisting the heavy chariot in exquisite arcs that carried it close enough to the enemy to strike, but fast enough that they could not board it.

Iron bolts hammered the chariot's armoured flanks, but the enchantments woven into its timbers kept it from harm. Lord Swiftwing could not draw a bow, but Casadesus passed him long javelins that he hurled with deadly accuracy. They rode away from the druchii line as the spear hosts marched forward with their blades lowered to engage the enemy.

Lord Swiftwing saw Menethis of Lothern in the front rank, his tunic bloodied and his face set with resolve. The young elf had earned great glory this day, and Lord

Swiftwing only hoped he would be able to reward him properly at battle's end. Command of a squadron of Silver Helms would be good for him.

'Coming about, my lord,' said Casadesus, as he brought the horses around in a tight turn.

'Once more, dear friend,' said Lord Swiftwing, as two Reaver Knight hosts formed up on his flanks. Laurena Starchaser commanded one group, while an elf-maid with hair of crimson and gold, held in place by a butterfly pin worked in silver, led the other.

'Take us in, Casadesus!' shouted Lord Swiftwing.

Archers loosed arrows into the druchii, as Mitherion Silverfawn sought to counter the druchii's sorcery with spells of his own. His Sword Masters were led by a fierce-looking elf-maid with auburn hair. A little too square-featured for Lord Swiftwing's tastes, but her prowess with the heavy broadsword she carried set his blood afire.

Cavalry skirmishes broke out on the left flank as the dark-cloaked riders who had crossed the river fought with a scattered band of Reavers. Both groups of horsemen swirled around one another, stabbing, loosing and riding in, only to break apart in dusty spirals. Each clash left elves and horses on the ground, bloodied and dead, but neither side showed any sign of breaking.

A glittering host of light and magic filled the horizon to the north, and Lord Swiftwing anxiously awaited news of what it heralded. Frantic word had come that it was the army of Avelorn, but he had received no clear confirmation as to what was happening on his right flank. Even atop his chariot, he could see little that made sense. Phantoms of light and colour shimmered on the fields he knew, and from that rainbow miasma he could hear the sounds of battle. But who was doing the majority of the dying was a mystery to him.

Salvation or doom awaited on that flank, and only when it arrived would he know which.

Lord Swiftwing led the charge in the centre, and though it was anathema to throw a chariot straight at the enemy, there was little room left for subtlety in this fight. The Reaver Knights alongside him kicked their horses to the gallop, and Lord Swiftwing loosed an ancient war cry in the old tongue of Ellyrion.

The two hosts of warriors came together with a resounding clash of blades and flesh. Casadesus threw the chariot into a long skid. The spinning wheels swung around and smashed into the druchii, scattering them like children's skittles. Axle blades scythed them down in droves, and blood splashed Lord Swiftwing's armour.

The Reavers slammed into the druchii and their spears stabbed and broke as they rammed them home like lances. They switched to swords, hacking at the druchii as they turned to flee from the thundering hooves and slashing blades of the Reavers. The wedge of the charge had punched deep into the druchii, but still they held on.

The chariot bucked as enemy warriors went under the wheels, ground to red paste as Casadesus tugged the reins and pushed deeper into the mass of druchii. Lord Swiftwing threw his last javelin and drew his sword, leaning out over the edge of his chariot and stabbing down. His blade parted mail links and cut through plate with pleasing ease, and his buckler deflected the worst of the return strikes.

'I overestimated our enemies' prowess!' he yelled as the chariot rumbled onwards.

His spear hosts shouted as they drove their weapons forward, the archers raised their bows and let fly in arcing lines over the fighting ranks. He laughed as he struck left and right, letting Casadesus pick their route through the killing. A crossbow bolt struck his left shoulder and ricocheted away. Another hit him square in the chest and wedged there, the tip an inch from penetrating his heart.

The chariot circled around and carried him out of reach of the druchii, and he broke the shaft of the bolt with the hilt of his sword; angry more than shocked at so close a brush with death. Druchii milled in confusion, bodies lay broken and bloodied all around, like stalks of corn in a trampled field. Swords, bows and spears lay discarded like unwanted playthings, and the soil of Ellyrion was stained red with the blood of slaughter.

'Come, Casadesus!' he shouted. 'Into them once more!'

'As you say, my lord,' replied Casadesus, turning the chariot back to the fighting.

Once again the chariot carved a gory path through the druchii, the ithilmar axle blades cutting through greaves, meat and bone to leave only screaming cripples in their wake. Swords and axes slammed the wood and metal of his chariot, some biting deep and splintering armoured plates, others sliding clear. Lord Swiftwing lopped limbs and heads with each blow of his sword as Casadesus swung the chariot like a madman, weaving a bloody course through the druchii.

'Again, Casadesus! Again!' yelled Lord Swiftwing. 'Turn and ride them down again!'

The chariot swung around, but all thoughts of another charge were forgotten as the druchii swarmed them. A spear punched through the timber sidings of the chariot and punctured Lord Swiftwing's leg armour. He grunted and hacked the haft in two. Blood streamed down his leg, but he could barely feel it. Crossbow bolts zipped past him, and he ducked.

An ear-splitting roar echoed over the field, and Lord Swiftwing saw a rearing hydra creature with a huge body and a multitude of serpentine necks. It reeked of decaying meat and soured sweat, its many mouths screaming one discordant wail of fury.

Casadesus didn't even wait for Lord Swiftwing's order, turning the chariot towards the creature. Druchii and asur alike fled from the beast's rampage as its grossly swollen tail of chitinous barbs swept warriors from their feet and fed them into gaping maws filled with grinding teeth.

Its pendulous heads turned towards Lord Swiftwing's chariot with a roar of monstrous appetite. It vomited up a host of half-digested remains, and bellowed in hunger.

The chariot slashed along its flanks, the scythe blades opening up a yard long gash that sprayed foaming ichor and black blood. A rippling frond of torn muscle tangled itself around the wheel of the chariot. Such was the speed of the attack that the muscular tissue was ripped out of the hydra's body, but not before its drag slewed the chariot around and threatened to tip it over.

Lord Swiftwing gripped the edge of the chariot with his free hand and fought for balance. Casadesus braced himself against the fairings, but the horses pulling the chariot had no such luxury, and the first had its jaw broken by the sudden jerk of the bit in its mouth. The second had its back legs shattered as the yoke snapped and the entire bulk of the chariot rolled over them. The horses screamed horribly and thrashed in agony.

Casadesus leapt from the ruined chariot and lanced his sword through the throats of each stricken beast. Both were beyond help, and no horse of Ellyrion should suffer such pain. Lord Swiftwing twisted around in the specially modified seat in the chariot as the hydra hauled its body around to face him.

Asur warriors ran to his side, spears stabbing its bulk, but the beast had clearly set its sights on him. A long neck curled towards him, and he hacked it away. Another swung at him, and it too was despatched. Then Casadesus was at his side, keeping the beast at bay with jabs and swings of his spear.

'Still glad you stayed at my side?' said Lord Swiftwing.

'I am beginning to have second thoughts,' replied Casadesus.

The beast spat a hawking wad of burning phlegm at them, and Lord Swiftwing ducked behind the cracked fairings of the chariot. Instantly, the chariot's sides began melting, the molten heat of the venomous mucus eating through ithilmar plates with horrifying ease. Droplets had spattered his armour, and burned rivulets streaked the unblemished lustre of his breastplate.

'Damn you!' he cried. 'This was hand-crafted by the Old Man of Vaul himself!'

He reared up, though a shooting lance of white hot pain burned its way up through his twisted pelvis. His sword swung out and cut deep into the meat of the hydra's head, splitting one of its eyes open in a popping spray of white fluid. The beast shrieked, and Lord Swiftwing stepped down from the chariot, taking painful step after painful step towards it.

Its flesh melted before the enchantments woven into his blade, and each strike was hideously painful to it.

Lord Swiftwing lost all sense of the battle around him, the screams of asur and druchii mingling into one constant death note. Shimmering light, like droplets of rainbows, fell around him and he heard the most wondrous music from the very air itself. It made him want to dance, and that angered Lord Swiftwing, for he never danced now.

His sword rose and fell, each time cutting deep into the muscular flesh of the hydra. Its cries were feeble now, hideous, gurgling, honking sounds of something dying. At last he halted his mechanistic swings. The monster was dead, its flesh collapsing in on itself like a deflated bladder, and its limbs snapping and twitching as the last spark of life fled its carcass.

'Asuryan and Isha preserve us,' he gasped as the world snapped back into focus around him. His armour and cloak were matted with blood and ichor and other, less identifiable, fluids. Cheering warriors surrounded him, waving bloodied spears in the air as they rejoiced at having fought alongside the master of Tor Elyr.

The surge of adrenaline that had kept him on his feet drained from him in an instant, and Lord Swiftwing gasped as the pain of his crippled leg and pelvis shot through him once again. He sagged, and a spearman caught him. Another two helped, and they carried him away from the awful stench of the hydra's body, which was already beginning to decay like a week-old cadaver.

'Casadesus? Casadesus, where are you?'

He looked into the faces around him, and knew none of them.

'Where is Casadesus?' he asked, almost blind with pain. The spearman looking at him was nonplussed. He shared a look with one of his spear-host brethren.

'I do not know who that is,' he said.

'My spear bearer,' said Lord Swiftwing. 'My chariot…'

'He's gone, my lord,' said the spearman. 'I am sorry.'

'What? No! Impossible!'

Lord Swiftwing threw off their supporting arms and searched for his chariot. There it was, listing badly where the hydra's fire had devoured the timber and supports. One wheel was little more than spokes and a slowly dissolving hub. The scythe blade drooped like a melting candle.

'Casadesus?' he said, upon seeing the slumped form of his bondsman. 'No!'

He lowered himself to the ground and placed a hand on Casadesus's chest. His face and upper body was all bloody meat and scorched bone, eaten away by the corrosive flame of the creature's breath.

'Damn you and your duty,' he snarled. 'You wouldn't listen and now look where it's got you. You glorious fool, you stupid, glorious fool…'

Lord Swiftwing wept for his lost friend, and almost didn't notice the gentle hands lifting him from the ground. He felt the hard edges of the grips and looked up into faces formed from bark and moss and broken edges of timber. They were creatures of the forest, knots of wood and splinters for eyes, slender trunks for bodies and twisting root legs to bear them.

'No!' he cried. 'I will not leave him for the druchii!'

The tree creatures did not answer him, but the bark around where their mouths would have been creaked and rasped with clicking, cracking sounds. If it was language, it was no language Lord Swiftwing understood. A nimbus of radiant light shone in the heart of their bodies, and he saw they had not come alone.

Wild wolves snapped at the druchii and capering fauns

with emerald skin fought them with shimmering axes of light. Gambolling sprites swirled like water around the druchii, nipping and biting and clawing. Something tall and in flames battled another many-headed hydra, its heavy limbs of bark and timber breaking necks and rupturing spines with every blow of its heavy branch limbs. Another two such creatures joined their oaken brother, a whip-limbed willow and a clawed pine.

'What is happening?' he yelled, and one of the creatures of wood turned its bole towards him. Its bark cracked into a semblance of a face and a soft voice issued from its mouth, utterly at odds with the harsh lines and earthy nature of the creature.

'I am Alarielle, and my army is here to fight alongside you.'

'The Everqueen? You are the Everqueen?'

'I am all things in Avelorn,' said the Everqueen in the guise of the wooded creature. 'I am speaking to you through this dryad, but I am close at hand.'

'Then we are victorious?' said Lord Swiftwing, hardly daring to believe it.

'No,' said the Everqueen sadly, as the dryads stood him up. They had carried him far and fast, and Lord Swiftwing found himself on the slopes of the causeway that led up to the great bastion castle of Tor Elyr, looking over the battlefield.

The centre had broken, and the warriors that had fought so valiantly alongside him were being driven back by heavily armoured blocks of druchii infantry. Mitherion Silverfawn and his Sword Masters coordinated the retreat, and their courage alone kept the retreat from becoming a rout.

The south was folding rapidly, the spear hosts and

Reaver Knights falling back to the city in good order. It was clear that the Everqueen's army had indeed come from the north, and though its magnificence was wonderful and beautiful to behold, its troubadour warriors, poet archers and acrobat swordsmen were no match for Morathi's determined and ferociously disciplined army.

The noose had finally closed on Tor Elyr, and his city was doomed.

'We are defeated,' said Lord Swiftwing.

'Not yet,' said the dryad with the voice of beguiling sweetness. 'Wait...'

The world exploded with light and magic.

ALL ACROSS ULTHUAN, the magical lines of force devised by Caledor Dragontamer surged with power. Conduits of magic blazed through the landscape, like lines of mercury fire poured onto the land. Power that once drained from the world now found no outlet, and unimaginable energies spilled into its magical winds.

The Annulii screamed as the titanic power chained within their peaks surged like a molten river of light at floodtide. Streamers of fire poured down the mountainsides in glittering waterfalls, sparkling with unleashed power and uncontained magic. Where it touched would never be the same, the solid substance of matter reshaped and born anew in chaotic jumbles of random form.

The wild creatures of the mountains – the chimera, the cockatrice, the jabberwocky and other magical beasts of incredible form and myriad variety – came down from the highest peaks. Lonely hunters' cabins high in the mountains were ripped apart by voracious beasts driven to madness by the surging power boiling their brains, or destroyed in the tsunami of raging magical energy.

Nor was the devastation confined to the mountains. Earthquakes of terrifying power ripped across Ulthuan, shearing kingdoms from one another and cracking the earth like a second Sundering. The walls of Tor Yvresse broke open and whole swathes of the city were buried beneath a monstrous avalanche. Three hundred souls were lost, from a city that could ill-afford to lose any of its sad inhabitants.

In Lothern, the fighting on the quayside halted as the city threatened to tear itself apart. Grand villas of marble slid down the hillside of the lagoon as the land rumbled and heaved and shook. The towering statues of the Everqueen and Phoenix King that stood sentinel over the city cracked and swayed and the outstretched hands of the pair finally met as the Phoenix King toppled forwards and smashed into the marble face of the Everqueen.

Floodwater spilled over the docks and through the streets of the city as Ulthuan tipped and the seas roared over its coastal regions. Once again, Tiranoc knew the terror of being lost beneath the waves as seawater gushed through it fjords and spilled onto its fields. Towns and villages along the coasts of Naggarythe and Caledor sank beneath the waves, their people obliterated in a heartbeat as the pulse of magical energies threatened to break the island apart.

Throughout Ulthuan, the waystones blazed like spears of fire, desperately venting magical energies as they tried to dissipate the colossal power building within them. Some exploded as that power became too much for them to contain, others melted to liquid rock in the searing heat.

On the Gaen Vale, the smouldering volcano at the heart of the island exploded, filling the air with ash and smoke. Vast rivers of lava poured down the flanks of the volcano, boiling the waters around the island to steam.

Wherever the currents of magic met the surface of the world, they buckled and twisted like colts in heat, breaking the earth and burning the air with its power. Hundreds of the asur died in the opening moments of the cataclysm, and hundreds more were soon to follow them as the waves of destruction and unfettered magical energy spread out from the Isle of the Dead.

Piece by piece, Ulthuan was tearing itself apart.

'How does it feel, old ghost, to know that I have undone your great work?' yelled Morathi.

She shrieked to the misty air, for she stood alone on the glassy plain of basalt. Howling winds surrounded her, yet the space within the vortex was silent, an eye of a hurricane of magical energy that was unravelling before her eyes.

Crackling shapes moved in the mist, mighty figures that shimmered and faded as they endlessly described complex patterns with their hands. The motions required of the great ritual were complex and exacting, and these mages had been weaving them for thousands of years, never changing and never stopping.

Except one *had* stopped.

Morathi laughed and brandished a golden-bladed dagger of strange design above her head. Coagulating blood dripped from its edge onto the body at Morathi's feet. It decayed at a furious rate, skin and hair flaking from bone that powdered in an instant. In moments, even that was scattered by the wind until all that was left was an empty robe of silver weave.

'It took me hundreds of years to learn how to shield

my thoughts from you,' she said. 'Hundreds of years, thousands of lives and an age of searching for the right weapon to slay your all-powerful mages.'

Morathi stalked the plain, shouting to the empty air, gloating, though there was no one over whom to gloat. Her body was slathered in old blood, and her black steed pawed the hard ground as though here under sufferance. It was eager to be away, and its wings ruffled at its flanks.

'You scared me once, I'll admit that,' said Morathi. 'When last we spoke, I was afraid of you. I believed you when you said you would destroy this place rather than allow me to take it. What a fool I was! You had no power then, and you have none now.'

'Is that what you think...?'

Morathi spun, and there he was, just as she remembered him.

Caledor Dragontamer, if this revenant could still be called such, was ghostly pale, his skin near translucent. The meat of his muscles wriggled on his skull, and his eyes were black coal, devoid of life and sanity.

'It is what I know,' said Morathi, gesturing to the empty robes. 'One of your precious cabal is dead by my hand and your ritual is broken.'

'Always so literal, Morathi,' said Caledor. 'It is one of your greatest failings.'

Morathi scowled, knowing the old ghost was simply trying to make her angry.

'You look terrible, Caledor,' said Morathi. 'You were once a fine specimen of an elf, tall, broad-shouldered and handsome, but all that is left of you is a skeletal wreck.'

'I am reminded daily of how deathly I look,' said Caledor. 'I think it amuses him.'

'What are you talking about?' asked Morathi. 'To whom do you talk on this dead island?'

'Why, Death, naturally,' said Caledor, as though she had asked a particularly obtuse question. She smiled and threw back her head to laugh.

'I believed you mad before. Now I know it.'

'Mad? A distinct possibility,' agreed Caledor. 'Mad, but not stupid. I created the vortex, and I told you once that I would not allow you to have it.'

'I do not *want* it, I am here to destroy it.'

'Why?'

'Why not?'

Caledor laughed. 'That is your answer for destroying a world? *Why not?*'

'That you desire it saved is enough for me to want it destroyed.'

'How petty you have become, Morathi,' said Caledor, sounding more disappointed than angry. 'Death may not suit me, but immortality suits you even less. You may hide behind a fair face, but your heart is rotten to the core. I warned Aenarion about you, but he would not listen. Too wrapped in grief to see the corruption behind your mask of beauty. What would he think were he to see you now?'

'Aenarion is dead, Caledor,' snapped Morathi. 'As you should be. We are not so different you and I, for we have both cheated death.'

'Not so,' said Caledor. 'As you say, I am an old ghost, nothing more.'

'Then I am done with you,' said Morathi. 'Your vortex is coming apart and Ulthuan is doomed. My vengeance is complete knowing that you will die with it.'

Caledor shook his head. 'All those thousands of years, and you *still* do not understand…'

'Understand what?' shrieked Morathi.

'That I will never let that happen,' said Caledor.

'There is nothing you can do to stop it,' answered Morathi. 'It has already happened.'

Caledor smiled. 'One age ends, another begins. You do not realise what you have done, what you have begun.'

'And what is that?'

'A new age,' said the old ghost.

RECLINED UPON HIS padded litter atop the Tower of Hoeth, Teclis closed his eyes and ran his hands across the obsidian moonsphere. For six hours he had attempted to send his spirit eyes within its impenetrable surface. It was said the secrets of the future were locked within its impossibly dense structure, the course of every possible event encoded in the complex lattice of its formation. Most likely that was not true, but Teclis had never been one to allow the impossibility of a task deter him from trying.

Not even Bel-Korhadris had been able to unlock the secrets of the moonsphere, and generations of Loremasters had similarly failed to discover what lay within. It had been gathering dust in the archive chambers of the Tower of Hoeth for hundreds of years, forgotten by all save the most dedicated of scholars.

Teclis did not know what had compelled him to send one of the Sword Masters to fetch it, but he had little else with which to occupy his time. The potions that had kept him strong as a youth now did little to sustain him, and only sufficed to take the edge away from the constant pain that wracked his limbs. Though the healers remained optimistic, Teclis knew he was dying, his weakened frame finally succumbing to Morathi's sorcery.

He had observed the battles raging at Lothern and before the walls of Tor Elyr, lamenting every death, and rejoicing in each turn in the asur's favour. He wept as the fire consumed Belannaer, then laughed as he saw the book from which the old Loremaster read. His spirit soared as he felt Tyrion's rejection of the Sword of Khaine's influence, even though he knew it was but a temporary reprieve. Such a dread shard of the murder god's power would not easily surrender its most treasured son.

That was a struggle for another time, and Teclis savoured this small victory.

His eyes snapped open a moment before the surge of magical energy roared up through the tower. Like magma boiling up from the heart of a volcano, raw power filled every stone in the White Tower and blazed from the golden finial where the Sword of Bel-Korhadris would sit in times of peace.

Teclis surged to his feet as the unbridled power of magic poured into him, reknitting torn flesh, mending ruptured blood vessels and making whole necrotic tissue in his heart and lungs. In an instant, his flesh was reborn, healed more fully than any potion could hope to cure. His body was still the frail shell of flesh it had always been, but the hurt done to him in the fires that burned the tower was undone as surely as though it had never happened.

The moonstone fell from his hands and fell to the patterned marble floor of the tower.

It cracked open in the storm of magical energy that blazed through the tower, and Teclis looked upon its internal structure with eyes that shone with titanic power. Greater than any wielder of magic in this or any other age, Teclis saw the insane geometries within the moonsphere and laughed as he saw the fate of a million futures mapped out.

Teclis spoke a word of power and his plain robe was instantly transformed into one of cobalt blue, ivory white and shimmering gold. A shining sword and moon-topped staff appeared in his hands, and upon his head, a crown of gold and sapphire glittered with lambent light.

Fire billowed around Teclis, but did not touch him.

He roared with the sheer joy and terror of commanding all the magic in the world.

Then he vanished.

IMRIK WAS NO more, and yet he could hear song.

Who could be singing in this place of dreams, where ancient minds slept away the cares of the world? He had sung songs of glory once, but no one had heard them and he had stopped when he had run out of will to give them voice. His life was a flickering ember, a dying spark lost in the darkness.

No, not darkness…

Fire, blazing fire, surrounded him. What had been a fading glow now leapt to life as a great song enfolded him. It was the greatest song in the world, yet he knew he would never be able to do it justice were he to live long enough to recount this event. It had no words, no melody and no tune, just an exultant evocation of wondrous times of glory when Ulthuan was young and still cooling from the molten fires of creation that had shaped it.

Light pulsed from the heart of the world, billowing up in great waves that filled the air with hot thermals of the purest magic. On these winds flew the first dragons, the chosen children of the gods and the inheritors of all that magic could achieve. These were the glory days, when anything was possible, and impossible was a concept that simply did not exist.

Imrik saw all this and more.

Days of glory where cycles of the universe were but the blink of an eye. Voyages between the stars, where a dragon's wings could carry it to distant suns with a single beat. Imrik saw fierce battles fought between rival dragons that snuffed out worlds and birthed them anew in the fires of their great wars. It was an age undreamed and unknown, a secret history known only to dragonkind, and told to him now by the mightiest of dragons.

Imrik found himself face to face with a vast eye. It was the size of a star, and he a mote in its eye, yet still it saw him. All that had been lost in his endless wanderings was remade by the music of the oldest dragons. They sang songs unknown to the elves and younger dragons, and bore Imrik up through the white heat of their dreamings, where no mortal was ever meant to venture.

Imrik cried out as he opened his eyes and found himself once more in the vast cave beneath the mountains. His wasted flesh was whole once more, the effort of singing the songs of awakening undone by the magic of this last song. What the power of the elves could not achieve was child's play to the dragons.

Steam and ashen smoke filled the air and the ground shook with violent tremors.

Imrik rose to his feet as mighty shapes moved and shifted in the steam.

Dragons. Hundreds of awakened dragons.

A huge beast with a body that glittered as though constellations were captured in its scales loomed over him. Its vast head dipped, and its eyes shone with ancient fire.

We are the dragons of Ulthuan, and we come to fight!

CHAPTER TWENTY

SACRIFICES

THE VORTEX WAS unravelling, and it was madness to run into its collapsing heart, but that was what they were doing. Eldain and Caelir ran side by side, with Rhianna matching them stride for stride. Howling winds tried to push them back and random flares of raw magic burst with painful brightness all around them. Their skin glistened with magic, and even their breath sparkled with the nearness of such boundless creative energy.

Eldain's blood shone like painted rubies, and though it had long since dried on his armour, it ran as though fresh from the vein, eager to *become* something. The life-giving properties of the vortex tugged at their flesh, urging it to change, to reshape itself and take advantage of this magical boon.

What else could you be? What might you become?

The lure was strong, and colours swirled around him in washes of brightness: reds, golds, white, orange and lilac. Colours that had no names, and which the mages and wizards of the world had forgotten, bled into existence, their power magnified in this place of confluence.

Rhianna staggered under the effect of so much magic, like a reveller after too many goblets of dreamwine. The power here was intoxicating and overwhelming. It overloaded the senses until nothing else mattered. Caelir was lifted from his feet by the force of the magic, laughing like a maniac as febrile energies coursed through his body. Their headlong run into the vortex was halted in an instant, and all three came to a dazed halt as their senses swam in the myriad complexities of the vortex's power.

Magical energy surrounded them, passing around and through them, drawn to their mortal desires and flesh by the beat of their hearts. It bathed them and filled their bodies with limitless potential. Against such power, what could three mortal elves achieve?

Eldain held out his hands.

'Hold on to me!' he yelled, the words taking shape as colour and light as soon as they left his mouth. His hair whipped around his head and he saw a thousand spinning concepts at play in the air above him. Dreams, nightmares and the amorphous things in-between. The vortex was a towering loom of potential, a thundering engine of creation that could make the impossible commonplace, the unreal solid.

He felt Caelir take his hand, his brother staggering as though bowed under a heavy load. Rhianna took his other hand, and they followed his lead as he pushed on into the vortex. There was no way to tell if he was heading in the right direction, for nothing in this swirling morass gave any clue to forwards or backwards, left or right. Such mortal constraints held no sway here and for all Eldain knew he might be walking in circles.

Caelir cried out, waving his free hand at some terror only he could see. Rhianna wept tears that flew off like tiny winged jewels, and screamed meaningless words to the howling winds. No sooner had one emotion seized them than another would replace it. They laughed, danced with joy and tried to pull away from him to chase invisible heart's desires.

Eldain dragged them after him, like a master with two recalcitrant hounds.

They screamed and raged and cried into the vortex, assailed by visions of things only they could know. Eldain wondered why he was unaffected by the power of the vortex. Were his dreams so banal and mundane that they were beneath its notice?

Perhaps it was because he had no dreams left, and wasn't that all magic was?

Wasn't that what made magic wondrous? That it could make any dream reality?

The magic of the vortex could reach deep into the furthest recesses of a heart and make real anything it desired. It was the power at the heart of creation, and there was nothing beyond its ability to conjure into being. Yet all Eldain saw was the raging heart of the disintegrating vortex, its lightning spalls, its fiery unmaking and the destruction being wrought on the landscape by its death throes.

Though every step was a battle, like walking in a dream where everything is arrayed in opposition, Eldain struggled onwards, dragging Caelir and Rhianna behind him. He bowed his head against the fierce magical winds and concentrated on simply putting one foot in front of the other. The ground beneath his feet was no longer the glassy plain, but a swirling sea of luminescent colours that was solid only because he believed it to be so. No sooner had the thought taken shape than the ground became soft and spongy.

Eldain gritted his teeth and willed the ground to solidity, and grinned as it instantly transformed into marble flagstones that ran with silver light. Understanding the potential of the magical gale buffeting him, Eldain lifted his head into the wind.

'Be still and grant me passage!'

The wind dropped immediately and the swirling colours parted before him, as though he walked through an invisible tunnel of force that bored through the maelstrom of raging magic. He knew better than to believe he was the master of this power, and hurried onwards to where he saw a pale stillness ahead. Caelir and Rhianna came with him, blinking and panting as the delusions beguiling them vanished.

'How...?' gasped Caelir.

'What did you do?' said Rhianna.

'I'm not sure,' said Eldain. 'But the way is clear.'

They moved onwards, the passage through the howling vortex sealing behind Eldain as he walked towards the eye of the hurricane. He did not ask what they had seen in the magic, for there was a haunted look on both their faces that spoke of some dreams that ought never to be dragged into the light.

At last they emerged from the swirling vortex and found themselves standing at the edge of a glassy plateau of shimmering rock. The funnel of the vortex towered above them, its top lost to sight in thundering storms of magical discharge as the power it was intended to contain flooded back into a world unready for it.

In the centre of the plain stood Morathi and another elf who looked more like a cadaver than a living being. Her back was to them, and Eldain saw the same dread weapon that had so terrified him before the battle at Tor Elyr had begun strapped to her back.

'Morathi…' hissed Caelir, drawing his sword.

She turned at the mention of her name, and smiled as though greeting a long lost friend. The gaunt elf beside her looked up into the storm raging above him, and Eldain saw his eyes were black and lifeless, his face like a skeleton with a thin layer of flesh pasted over it. He wondered who this was and what terrible fate had seen him trapped in such a place. The old elf seemed pleased to see them, and began moving his hands in esoteric patterns that left glittering trails in the air.

Rhianna gasped as she drew the unchained magic into her body, her hands crackling with power as she whispered the first syllables of a spell. Caelir went left, and Eldain went right. Morathi faced Rhianna with a withering look of contempt. She spared a glance for the old elf of no less contempt.

'This is it, Caledor? *This* is the best you can summon to your defence?'

Eldain pulled up in shock at Morathi's casual use of the name.

His eyes flicked to the old elf, now seeing him for who he truly was.

He was Caledor Dragontamer, and he was dead.

The legends spoke of a towering mage of awesome power. A giant of magic. A wielder of power like no other in the world. The greatest mage in Ulthuan's long history, he was Aenarion's boon companion, a mighty warrior-mystic who fought the daemonic horde with spell and sword. He was a hero of the ages, all powerful and all knowing.

Perhaps once, but no more.

This was Caledor…?

Yet if Eldain's passage through the vortex had taught him anything, it was that nothing was as it seemed. In life, there had been no mage as powerful and subtle as Caledor. Who knew how powerful he had become in death…?

Morathi's gaze bored into Caelir, and she threw back her head and laughed.

'My little slave,' she said, drawing her barbed weapon from over her shoulder. 'You have come back to me.'

'I am no one's slave,' said Caelir. 'I am here to kill you for what you did to me and what you have done to Ulthuan.'

'Kill me, little slave? Oh no, you won't be doing that.'

Rhianna unleashed a stream of crackling fire from her hands, but Morathi casually batted it aside. The vortex greedily sucked it in to its swirling mass, and Morathi loosed a crackling orb of purple fire from her barbed weapon. Rhianna caught it in a shimmering prism of light and crushed it between her palms.

'The she-elf has some power,' said Morathi. 'Not nearly enough though.'

Cold wind gusted from the Hag Sorceress, like a swirling tornado laid upon its side. Rhianna was swept up by the wind, and crackling webs of frost spread over her mage's robes. Caelir ran at Morathi, and Eldain followed him.

His brother's sword stabbed for Morathi's belly. She spun into the air, twisting over Caelir's head and driving her heel into the back of his neck. Caelir fell flat on his face as Eldain brought his sword around in a disembowelling sweep. Morathi blocked the blow without looking and spun around him, hammering her elbow into his cheek. Eldain staggered and brought his sword up to parry a return stroke of her rending lance. Sparks flew from the impact, blinding him, and he threw himself away from Morathi.

He heard laughter and rolled to his feet as Caelir picked himself up.

They circled Morathi, wary of her speed as she bounced on the balls of her feet with a feral gleam of malicious enjoyment. Caledor seemed content to watch the unequal contest of arms without intervening, if he even could. Eldain met Caelir's eyes and they nodded, circling in opposite directions to come at Morathi from two sides.

They attacked together. Morathi leapt towards Eldain, swaying aside from an elegantly delivered thrust and launching herself at him, feet first. Her legs scissored around his waist, and she spun around him. A slender dagger nicked the skin of his neck as she vaulted clear.

Caelir's sword stabbed past Eldain, but Morathi was long gone.

She danced from foot to foot, spinning her longhafted weapon before her.

Eldain's vision blurred, and terrible weakness slipped along his limbs.

'Are you all right, brother?' shouted Caelir.

'No,' said Eldain, as Rhianna dropped from the storm above to land between him and Morathi. Words of mystic significance spilled from her lips and a cage of white fire sprang into being around Morathi. It burned with searing brightness, and Eldain shielded his eyes.

Morathi snapped her fingers and the cage vanished, its bars of light transformed into writhing black snakes that she hurled towards Rhianna. With a gesture, they became streamers of golden mist. Silver fire erupted from the ground beneath Morathi, but the druchii sorceress leapt into the air, somersaulting over Caelir and landing in a cat's crouch on the glassy rock.

Eldain forced himself to his feet. His limbs felt like water, and a throbbing pain flared in his lower back. He took a step forward, but dropped to one knee as his legs lost their strength. He knew he had been poisoned, and the realisation that he could do nothing against it galled him. He lost his grip on his sword and it fell to the ground with a glassy clatter.

Rhianna and Morathi traded spells back and forth, each one drawing on the thundering power of the vortex to augment their attacks. Blazing tongues of white fire leapt from Rhianna's fingertips, and forking traceries of amethyst lightning arced back in answer from Morathi. Magic powerful enough to level cities and destroy armies was unleashed, all to no effect. Spell and counterspell. Killing magic and destructive power flared between them, flaring, building and bleeding off as the vortex sucked at their violence. Caelir tried to help Rhianna, but the backwash of deadly magic kept him from getting too close.

Eldain felt the world go grey around the edges of his vision, and fought to stay conscious.

This was end of the world fighting, and he had to see how it ended.

Dimly, he felt a touch, and looked down. Fingers like reeds and skin like poorly made parchment rested on his shoulder. Yet for all their frailty, Eldain felt incredible power in that hand. He gasped as that power flowed through him, burning Morathi's poison from his blood.

'I may be dead,' said Caledor, 'but I am not without a few tricks of my own.'

Eldain surged to his feet. 'Then help her,' he demanded. 'Morathi is too powerful.'

'She is powerful,' agreed Caledor, the black pits of his eyes and the deathly countenance of his face twisted in what might have been a faint smile. 'But I was shaping world-changing magic before she could even master the simplest enchantment.'

Caledor lifted his hands and the vortex above bent inwards, its awesome power his to command. Morathi and Rhianna paused in their magical battle as Caledor drew the swelling power building in the world to him. The eye of the hurricane had been calm, but the power of the vortex was destabilising, drawn within itself as Caledor spoke incantations that were unknown beyond the time of Aenarion.

Eldain stepped away from the old elf as he *swelled*, his gaunt frame filling out with powerful muscle and youthful flesh. His face bloomed with vitality until he was an elf in the prime of his life. Eyes that were once black and dead were now sparkling and green, flecked with gold and silver. His lips were full and lush, his hair regrown to its youthful lustre.

This was Caledor Dragontamer, the mage who had shackled the riotous magic of the world and bound it to his will. His robes billowed in the raging winds and the storm of magic descended with booming peals and blasts of lightning.

'I warned you, Morathi,' he said with a voice that

commanded respect from elf, man and dragon alike. 'I told you what would happen if you pressed me. You loosed the power of the vortex, but only I know how to harness it!'

Caledor's growth had gone beyond any simple restoration of his previous form. His body swelled to titanic proportions, twice, then three times the size of even the largest elf of Ulthuan. He towered over them, and his powers were growing by the second. Morathi quailed before him, and Eldain saw Caelir circling behind her with his sword poised to strike.

Eldain shouted a warning, but his voice was lost in the tempest of Caledor's mighty growth. Caelir hurled himself at Morathi, his sword held two-handed to plunge between her shoulder blades.

Eldain ran toward Caelir.

Time slowed, Eldain screamed.

Rhianna held out her hands.

Too late.

Morathi swayed aside from the blow. Her own rending blade came up and rammed into Caelir's chest. She wrenched the blade and a squirting arc of crimson misted the air. Caelir staggered, a look of disbelief twisting his boyish features. He collapsed into Rhianna's embrace, and her arms were instantly soaked with blood.

Eldain screamed Caledor's name, but the enormous mage had concerns greater than the lives of mortals who had foolishly ventured into this place of his making. Morathi ran to her black pegasus and vaulted into the saddle. Her bladed lance dripped with Caelir's blood, and Eldain ran towards her.

Caledor said, 'You were always too arrogant to *listen*, Morathi. I told you that the destruction of the vortex would liberate an enormous amount of magical energy. And I told you I would use it for one purpose, to slay you. I gave you my word.'

'I remember, Caledor,' said Morathi, her dark mount taking to the air. Hurricane winds buffeted it, but Morathi held it steady in the storm. 'But it makes no difference now. Your great work is undone and the world is doomed.'

'Once again you underestimate me,' said Caledor. 'Now begone.'

Caledor waved a contemptuous hand, and Morathi and her mount were hurled from the vortex. They vanished into the roiling clouds of magical energy as though swatted by an enormous fist. Caledor dropped his hands to his side and the enormous growth that had propelled him to giant proportions began to reverse.

Eldain dropped his sword and ran to Caelir's side.

One look at the blood soaking his ruined chest told Eldain that the wound was mortal.

Rhianna looked up at him with tear-filled eyes.

'Eldain...' she said. 'He's dying.'

ONCE AGAIN THE hill of waystones above Tor Elyr erupted with magical light, but instead of an entire army stepping from the glow, a lone figure emerged from the gateway. He was clad in the shimmering finery of a Loremaster of the White Tower, and all who saw him knew him in an instant.

Teclis!

A blinding corona of titanic energies surrounded him, cracking the sky with its brightness and pulsing from him in uncontrollable waves. Teclis floated over the battlefield, his body awash with magical energy like never before. His eyes burned with the fire at the heart of the world, and the druchii looked upon him and saw their doom.

The armies of Avelorn and Ellyrion gathered before the walls of Tor Elyr, but there would be no heroic last stand, no futile bravery to stem the advance of the druchii.

It would not be needed.

Crossbow bolts and powerful sorcery flew up at Teclis, and though the unmaking of the vortex had enhanced the spells of Morathi's pet magickers also, they were like children before the might of Teclis. Iron bolts were transformed into seeds that fell upon Ellyrion's soil, and spells were turned aside by the shimmering arcs of power that played about Teclis.

The Everqueen's magic flowed into the land. The icy mists smothering the summerlands of Ellyrion dissipated, and the river was returned to flowing water. The black corruption of the bloody cauldron's demise was reversed, and no trace of the spoor left by the hydras and spawn creatures was allowed to remain.

Such was the Everqueen's duty, yet Teclis was here not to heal, but to destroy.

He was the greatest practitioner of the arcane arts since Caledor Dragontamer himself, and the power he now commanded had last been wielded when the builders of this world first shaped its continents into shapes pleasing to them.

Yet with all the power of a god at his fingertips, Teclis yielded to the first inclination of mortals, and used it to kill. He swept his hands out before him, and a wall of white fire engulfed the druchii army.

Warriors and heroes, monsters and steeds all burned in the fire. It left no mark upon the ground, but no creature of darkness could be touched by the fire of Teclis and live. The screams of the druchii were terrible to behold, but no tears were shed for their death agonies.

Teclis hovered in the air above Tor Elyr and burned an army to death.

LOTHERN. THE END.

The druchii swarmed the docks, and the battle was fought in knee-deep water. Tyrion slashed his sword through the neck of a druchii axeman, and ducked beneath an avenging blow from another cold-eyed killer. Behind him, Lothern burned in the fires of the Witch King's malice, and the citizens of the city fled to the high villas overlooking the cityport.

Perhaps some would escape, but not many.

The Witch King contented himself with watching his enemies die from above, drifting on the lazy thermals from the burning city. His dragon roared and the Witch King's hateful laughter drifted over the doomed warriors below.

'Come down here and fight, and I will choke you with that laughter,' promised Tyrion.

The Phoenix Guard fought with silent menace, their halberds cutting down any druchii who dared to come near with brutally efficient strikes. The flanks of the asur line bent back and crumbled, but the centre held strong. Korhil swept his mighty axe left and right, while Finubar fought like a berserker, all thoughts of restraint lost in the fury of battle. Caradryan of the Phoenix Guard swept his halberd in killing arcs, his blade reaping a fearsome tally in druchii dead.

Eltharion flew above Lothern, diving on Stormwing's fury to attack the druchii from the air. Brave fighters all, killing many enemy warriors, but just spots of light against the darkness. Not enough to counter the encroaching night.

Tyrion had killed two score druchii already, and the battle was still young. He had lost track of time, but the autumnal cast to the sky spoke of sunset. Appropriate, he thought, that we should face our ending as light vanishes from the world. He fought with all the skill he possessed, but could already see that it would not be enough. The druchii had limitless numbers to call on. Thousands more warriors were crossing from the black ark in yet more troop galleys. The sea was awash with black-tarred vessels bearing druchii killers.

He fought through a mass of druchii swordsmen towards the Phoenix King as the sky lit up with a dazzling eruption of light. Another earthquake ripped across the city, and a high tower of blue marble and crystal sculpture toppled into the lagoon. Pieces of the Everqueen's statue broke off and fell into the water, smashing a slender bridge of golden crystal and a handful of raven ships. A fresh wave swept into the collapsing city.

The sky to the west burned with orange light where the volcanoes of the Dragonspine had erupted. Blistering, red-lit clouds smeared the tops of the cliffs, and the sharp tang of sulphur tainted the air. Ash fell in a black rain, and Tyrion felt that the world was weeping.

The fighting paused with each fresh disaster, and Tyrion splashed through the floodwater as he saw a host of warriors in black armour and scaled cloaks advance on the Phoenix King. Finubar had plunged deep into the mass of druchii and was cut off, but before the Corsairs could attack, a host of sailors bearing the blue cloaks of Lord Aislin charged into the fray. They were without armour, but took on the druchii with a fury that could only have its roots in vengeance.

Tyrion ran to join them, and cut down the last of the druchii as Finubar came to his senses and fell back to the battle line with a grateful look on his face. The sailors went with him, and Tyrion stopped one with the look of command about him.

'You are a ship's captain?' asked Tyrion.

'Aye, my lord. Captain Finlain of *Finubar's Pride*,' said the sailor.

Tyrion laughed and let him go, pleased with the aptness of the captain's ship.

He jogged back to the fighting line as the druchii regrouped and hundreds of fresh warriors disembarked from their ugly galleys onto the cracked and sunken quayside.

Korhil gave him a nod, and Finubar shot him a weak smile. Caradryan thumped the butt of his halberd against the wet cobbles in a gesture of respect between warriors.

'Ready for one last fight?' asked the Phoenix King.

'Always, my lord,' answered Tyrion.

'This will be it, Tyrion,' said Finubar. 'They will break us with the next charge. This will be my last battle. I know it.'

'Never say that,' said Tyrion. 'If there is one thing Teclis has taught me, it is that there is always hope.'

Finubar shook his head and indicated the glowering forms of Caradryan's warriors. 'The Phoenix Guard are here, and they would only have come unasked to take me to my final rest.'

Beside him, Caradryan shook his head and pointed to the two enormous statues that dominated the sky-line of Lothern. The Everqueen's statue was battered and portions of it had fallen into the sea, but the Phoenix King's statue had taken the brunt of the damage. Its colossal plinth had split, and the statue listed drunkenly at an angle, the helmeted head resting on the shoulder of the Everqueen across the bay.

Finubar and Tyrion looked at the Captain of the Phoenix Guard in confusion, and it was left to Korhil to fathom the meaning of the gesture.

'They made a mistake,' he roared.

'What are you talking about?' demanded Finubar.

'I don't know exactly what they saw in that Chamber of Days, but I am willing to bet it was something about a Phoenix King *falling*. True enough, but they got the wrong one!'

The light of understanding dawned, but the answer brought another question.

'How is it possible that any of us survive this battle?' asked Finubar as the druchii hefted their spears and axes. War horns sounded the advance.

The answer came a second later as a series of deafening roars echoed from the cliffs.

All heads turned to the sky as the red-lit clouds of the west broke apart and a host of dragon riders swooped overhead.

They came in many colours, golden, crimson, silver and white. Copper and bronze, glittering with sunlight and starlight. Ten came, then ten more, then too many to count. They swept over the mountains in their hundreds and fell upon the druchii in a tide of fang and claw that could not be resisted.

The sky was filled with dragons, and Tyrion would see no finer sight in all his days. To see one dragon upon the field of battle was an honour, but to lay eyes upon such a host was something no elf had witnessed for thousands of years.

The dragons stooped on the close-packed galleys and raven ships in the harbour, breathing great blasts of fire from their jaws. A score of ships immediately caught light, a dozen more a second later as the beating of the dragons' wings spread the fire. Astride the neck of many of the dragons were mages clad in robes edged with red-gold. They hurled streaking bolts of blue light from outstretched hands and staffs, and the druchii burned in the flames of their magic.

Leading the winged host was the Lord of Dragons himself, Prince Imrik of Caledor.

Sat astride the neck of Minaithnir, Imrik flew towards the Witch King, his lance glittering like captured starfire and his dragonhorn sounding a high note of challenge. The Witch King answered his challenge and angled his dark mount towards Imrik.

Tyrion watched the two dragons climb as they flew at each other, but it was Malekith's beast that climbed higher. His dragon drew in its wings and its long neck extended as frills of scales opened at its throat. Before the monstrous dragon could unleash its noxious breath, Imrik's horn sounded again and the Witch King's mount convulsed as though struck. Its wing beats faltered and in that moment of pain, Imrik leaned low over his saddle to drive the shimmering point of his lance deep into its belly.

The dragon roared in agony as the starmetal of the lance pierced its scaled hide and tore into its body. Its claws raked Minaithnir's flanks, but it was an attack of flailing spite. Malekith hauled his dragon away, as Imrik drew back his lance for another strike. Once again the lance stabbed home, gouging a long scar down the dragon's rump.

Malekith struck with his sword and only Imrik's superlative reflexes saved his life. The dragons broke apart, but as Imrik circled Minaithnir for another tilt at the Witch King, his opponent was already flying towards the Straits of Lothern.

Tyrion cheered as Malekith fled, willing Imrik to turn and ride him down. Younger dragons chased the Witch King, mage riders hurling shimmering fireballs of incredible power. Though wounded and defeated, their quarry was still incredibly dangerous. Just as the fire mages' magic was enhanced, so too was his. Malekith froze dragons and their riders to sculptures of ice with a glance and sheared the wings from others with chopping gestures of his bladed gauntlets.

The pursuit of the Witch King was abandoned, and Malekith's dragon limped away to the south through the straits, its wings dipped and a drizzle of hot blood falling from its torn belly to the black ark below.

The harbour was alight from one side of the bay to the other with blazing ships, and the druchii trapped on the quayside watched with growing terror as the dragons turned towards them. Fire scoured them from the quaysides, and the water boiled to steam around their legs. Some of the druchii attempted to swim to the black ark, but it was an impossible goal, and their armour dragged them to the bottom of the ocean. The defenders of Lothern cheered and embraced one another as the dragons did in moments what they could not have done in a hundred lifetimes.

'We are saved!' cried Finubar as the dragons burned the druchii from Lothern.

'We are indeed, my king,' said Tyrion, putting up his sword as Imrik flew over the burning waters of the bay with his silver lance raised in salute.

RHIANNA CRADLED CAELIR, wiping blood from his face and letting her tears fall onto his face. Eldain knelt at Caelir's side and took his hand. The wound gouged in his chest was deep, and blood flowed from between his splintered ribs. Caelir's Ellyrian armour had offered no protection against Morathi's dread lance, and his heart had been all but plucked from his chest.

His brother was dying in front of him, and there was nothing he could do.

Only one person could save Caelir now, and she was far away in Ellyrion.

'Alarielle of Avelorn!' he yelled, hoping against hope that she might somehow hear his desperate plea over the miles that lay between them. 'I beg of you, help my brother!'

Caelir groaned and his eyes fluttered open.

'Eldain?'

'I'm here, Caelir,' he said. 'Do not move. I will save you, I promise.'

'You should not make promises you can't keep, brother,' said Caelir. 'I thought you'd have known that by now.'

'I will keep this one, and you will not die. You won't dare. Not now.'

'Remember,' hissed Caelir, painfully. 'I have a habit of disappointing you.'

Eldain shook his head. 'You never disappointed me, little brother. I was so very proud of you. Always.'

Rhianna wiped Caelir's brow and wept tears like

shimmering diamonds. Eldain looked into her eyes and he felt the last shreds of animosity melt away in the face of Caelir's ending. The power of her battle with Morathi still clung to her, a haze of white light that danced just beneath her skin with a luminous glow.

'Can you save him?' asked Eldain.

'I have not the power,' she said.

'Here, in this place, you do not have the power?'

'I am not the Everqueen,' said Rhianna.

A figure appeared behind them, and Eldain saw Caledor Dragontamer standing over them.

He looked down at Caelir and grimaced.

'She always did have a penchant for needless cruelty,' he said.

'You!' said Eldain, surging to his feet. 'You have the power to save my brother. Please, you have to help him.'

Caledor shook his head. 'He is beyond saving, Eldain. His hurt runs deeper than you know. His soul is torn and bleeding. Even the Everqueen could not save him.'

'I cannot accept that,' said Eldain.

'It is not up to you,' said Caledor, extending a hand towards Rhianna. 'Come, my dear. It is time for you to fulfil your destiny. The world does not have time for grief.'

'What are you doing?' said Eldain.

'What needs to be done,' said Caledor. 'I am powerful and have held the vortex from collapsing, but I cannot hold it on my own, and I do not have long before *he* returns to vex me.'

'You are not on your own,' stated Eldain, suspecting the truth of Caledor's purpose. 'You have your cabal.'

'One of them is dead. A mage named Rhianos Silverfawn. Morathi cut his throat with a dagger forged from the golden metal once used to construct the great gateway above the northern polar regions. My ritual is complex and precise. It needs all the mages to keep it in balance. One had died, and one must take his place. Who better than his descendant?'

Eldain knelt with Caelir as Rhianna stood before Caledor.

'The Everqueen spoke of this moment,' said Rhianna.

'I warned her not to,' said Caledor. 'She has a loose tongue.'

'What would you have me do?'

'Rhianna, no!' cried Eldain. 'Whatever he wants you to do, don't do it!'

'I have to, Eldain,' said Rhianna. 'You know what will happen if I do not. Ulthuan will be destroyed, and the rest of the world will soon follow. I think I have known that this moment was coming for a long time.'

'You can't do this!' shouted Eldain. 'Caledor Dragon-tamer would never demand such a sacrifice! He was a hero!'

Caledor's face hardened to granite. 'A hero? No, Eldain, he was a mage who sought to stop the dae-mons, that is all. And I *did* demand such sacrifices, Eldain. That is exactly what I did all those years ago. I told my cabal that they would never leave the Isle of the Dead, that they would be forever bound to my rit-ual. It was a sacrifice they all made willingly. And now Rhianna Silverfawn, daughter of Mitherion Silverfawn and descendant of Rhianos Silverfawn makes that same sacrifice.'

'No, please! You cannot take her!'

'He is not taking me, Eldain,' said Rhianna. 'I go of my own free will.'

Tears spilled down Eldain's cheeks, and he reached out to Rhianna with a bloodied hand.

'Don't leave,' he begged. 'Don't leave me alone!'

'We are all alone, Eldain,' said Caledor. 'It is the one truth I have come to realise in this place. We may gather many friends and loved ones to us throughout the long years, but we all walk alone in the end.'

'Rhianna will not walk alone,' said Caelir, grunting in pain as he pushed himself to his feet. 'I will walk with her. Until the end of time, the way it was always meant to be. The way I would have pledged to you had we been wed.'

'Caelir, what are you talking about?' cried Eldain.

Caelir coughed a wad of blood and held himself upright only with Eldain's help.

'If I return to the world beyond the vortex I will die,' he said. 'Here I will live forever.'

'You would stay here?'

'With Rhianna, brother,' said Caelir, gripping his shoulder tight. 'We will not be dead, we will be everlasting. You know it is the only way.'

Eldain bowed his head and nodded, remembering the words Death had spoken to him on their journey through the empty forest.

'By accepting the inevitable,' he said. 'By knowing when to give in.'

'This is not giving in,' hissed Caelir with the last of his strength. '*This is our victory.*'

'Come,' said Caledor. 'It happens now or it does not happen at all.'

Eldain released Caelir, and Rhianna and Caledor carried him to where a loose robe of silver weave lay discarded on the reflective ground. Eldain watched them go, Caledor's shoulders becoming more stooped the further away he went.

Rhianna and Caelir embraced, two souls entwined at last, and Eldain cried tears of sorrow and tears of joy as the light of the vortex swallowed them up. They were gone, but not dead. Trapped forever in the vortex, they would live in a perfect moment of union for all time, and Eldain envied them that eternal bliss.

Almost immediately, the raging anger of the vortex began to subside as Rhianna took up the role she had been born to play. Ancient plans and temporal designs laid down long ago finally came to fruition as the cascade of magical energy once again began to drain from the currents of the world.

Caledor turned back to Eldain, and the great hero of the asur had once again assumed his mantle of frailty. Eldain wanted to hate him, to spit curses at him for what he had lost, but the words would not come.

'You should go, Eldain,' said Caledor. 'The vortex is sealing and Lord Elasir waits to carry you back to Ulthuan. If you remain much longer, you will be trapped like me, cursed to live forever as a deathly revenant neither alive nor dead. A wraith of ancient days.'

'What is there left for me on Ulthuan?' said Eldain.

'More than you know,' said Caledor.

'Everything I love is gone.'

Caledor smiled. 'Not everything.'

EPILOGUE

GRIEF HUNG OVER Ulthuan for a long time after the victories of Tor Elyr and Lothern. The fire of the dragons consumed the druchii fleet in less than an hour, and as the black ark attempted to extricate itself from the Straits of Lothern, the dragons attacked it with all their fury. It could not last long against so mighty an assault, and its ramparts and crooked castles were cast down by creatures older than Ulthuan itself.

Tyrion led a host of Silver Helms into the mountains, driving the few druchii survivors back over the rocky peaks to the shoulder fortresses at the Emerald Gate. The warriors of the asur offered no mercy to their foes, and beneath a banner of the Everqueen, Tyrion charged across the pontoon bridge linking Ulthuan to the Glittering Lighthouse.

At battle's end, Eltharion took his leave of the Phoenix King and returned to Tor Yvresse to count the cost of the invasion among his own people. He said farewell to no one, and as Tyrion watched him fly away, he felt nothing but sorrow for his old friend.

In Ellyrion, the dead were gathered and mourned, every rider and citizen carried to their final rest as aching laments were given voice by the singers of Avelorn. A poet who had fought in the battle composed an epic verse as the sun rose on a new day, dedicating it to a young elf of his former acquaintance. Of the druchii who had fought at Tor Elyr, there were no traces. The fire of Teclis had been thorough, and only grief remained to speak of their invasion.

Thus were the druchii driven from Ulthuan.

The magic of the vortex pulsed through the veins of the world for many weeks, but as geomancers and mages spread through the land, toppled waystones were lifted and new ones established in freshly-mapped areas of mystical confluence. Slowly, and with great pain, the damage done to Ulthuan was healed.

The island would never be quite the same, for it was not in the power of those who lived in the world to undo every hurt done to it. Only those who had built the world were capable of such feats, and they were long gone. As with all damaged things, what could be done to keep life going was done, and the scars would simply have to be borne.

Nor were those scars confined only to the land of Ulthuan.

Too many lives had been lost for the asur to ever forget this war.

Good lives and bad had been spent in the defence of their island, miracles worked and dark wonders played out. The Eagle Gate was rebuilt and Menethis of Lothern appointed its castellan. Lord Swiftwing had offered him command of a company of Silver Helms, but Menethis had, instead, asked for Eagle Gate.

Lord Swiftwing stepped down from his role as master of Tor Elyr, and word was sent to the Old World for his sons to return home. The Great Herd returned to the wilds of Ellyrion, though many bonds of companionship had been forged in the battle, and many were the people of that land who would go on to become fine Reavers in time.

The Everqueen returned to Avelorn, and her army of fauns, dryads and treemen went with her. Her entourage of poets, dreamers and dancers went with her, and from amongst them was picked a young dancer named Lilani, who became a warrior of the Maiden Guard and one of Lirazel's most trusted captains. The revellers of Avelorn travelled north in a grand carnival of light and magic, and wherever they passed, the land bloomed in gold and green. Ellyrion was already a land of eternal summer, but the coming of the Everqueen made the sun shine a little brighter, the warm winds more welcome and the rivers just a little fresher.

Seasons passed, the world turned, and the decline of the asur continued.

Nowhere was this more evident than in Ellyr-Charoi.

THE LEAVES BLEW on…

Ellyrion basked in the warm, honey-gold light of a drowsy summer, but within the walls of Ellyr-Charoi, only autumn held sway. Eldain sat in the Hippocrene Tower and looked out over the endless plains as the dust gathered on his bookshelves and tables of his domain.

Golden leaves filled the summer courtyard, and the trough on the eastern wall was blocked once again.

Drifts of fallen leaves were heaped at the open gates of the villa, and filled the air with playful swirls as cold winds blew down from the mountains. Leaves rested on the roof of the Equerry's Hall, and tumbled from the eaves of the stables.

Dust rolled through Eldain's study, but he had neither the interest nor inclination to clear it away. Days passed without him moving from his chair, content to watch the passing of the sun and moons across the thin windows of his tower.

He ate and drank when necessary, but the actions were mechanical.

He took no joy in wine or fresh meat. The pleasures of the flesh were forgotten, and it seemed as though his heart had turned to stone.

The leaves blew on.

HE ENTERTAINED FEW visitors, for he was not viewed through the same heroic lens as others who had fought in the battles against the druchii. While other heroes were heaped with plaudits, Eldain quietly retired to Ellyr-Charoi to nurse his broken heart.

Lord Elasir had carried him back to Ulthuan. Aeris and Irian flew with their golden wings dipped in honour of those they left behind, and the mighty eagle left Eldain to his silence. Mitherion Silverfawn and Yvraine Hawk-blade had journeyed to Ellyr-Charoi, seeking news of Rhianna, and Eldain told them all that had happened on the Isle of the Dead. Mitherion wept for his daughter, but was consoled by the words Caelir had spoken as he and Rhianna followed Caledor into the vortex.

Eldain did not invite them to stay, and they did not seek his hospitality.

They were gone within the day, leaving Eldain to walk the empty halls of his villa.

The leaves blew on.

TIME BECAME MALLEABLE. Eldain tried to stave off the worst of his isolation by taking long rides through Ellyrion on the back of Lotharin. The black steed shared his melancholy, galloping with less and less joy at each ride. At last, Eldain led him to the gates of Ellyr-Charoi and removed his saddle.

'Ride, my friend,' he said. 'Be free. Join the Great Herd and live your life in joy.'

Lotharin nuzzled him, and all that their friendship had meant passed between them in a single, beautiful moment of connection. The horse tossed its mane and cantered down the overgrown path to the bridge. As Lotharin crossed the gurgling stream, he reared up in salute to Eldain before trotting off into the evening's light to rejoin the wild herds of the plains.

Eldain watched him go, knowing the last shred of what held him to this land was gone.

He shut the gates of Ellyr-Charoi.

SEASONS PASSED, THOUGH Eldain had no idea of how many.

On the rare occasions he could rouse himself from his study, he would walk the cold halls of the villa like a sleepwalker, moving from room to room as though in a trance. Though he had spent nearly all his life within its walls, the villa was lost to him now. Its rooms were unknown, and places that had once been familiar and homely were now bereft of feeling. He *knew* its halls and corridors, but he was disconnected to them, as though the villa now belonged to someone else.

He paused by an empty window as a cold wind gusted through a cracked pane of glass.

Snowflakes drifted through, dancing in the air for a moment before settling on the floor and melting to tiny spots of water. Eldain opened the window, and saw the leaves that carpeted the courtyard below were now white and frosted. Snow fell in drifting clouds, lying thick and still upon the edges of the high wall surrounding the villa.

Eldain walked outside, barely feeling the cold, and wondering how snow could fall in a realm of eternal summer. He trudged through the courtyard, not knowing where his steps were carrying him, but knowing that there was somewhere he needed to be.

He entered the Equerry's Hall, shivering with cold, and looking upon the dusty emptiness within. The firelit revelries that had once filled this hall were now ghostly memories, and Eldain could barely recall them. He circled the dusty table, and stood before the frosted portrait that hung on one of the long walls.

Eldain had not looked at this portrait since he and Caelir had last stood here.

Until now, he had not been able to even *think* of his brother's name.

The portrait was a good one, and he remembered the shame he had felt as Uthien Sablehand had first revealed the result of his labours. Now it was a reminder of happier times, and Eldain felt a moment of wistful pleasure at the sight of his younger brother. Yet even the thought of happiness was too much for him, and he turned away from the picture, unwilling to allow even a single ember of joy to lodge in his heart.

Winter closed a fist around Ellyr-Charoi, and the ice in Eldain's heart was no less bitter.

* * *

NOW, AS ALWAYS, Eldain wrapped himself in furs and a heavy cloak before venturing outside. The freezing temperatures were like nothing he had known, and there was no end in sight to the winter. Snow fell every day, wreathing the villa in a chill blanket, but through the windows of his tower, Eldain could see nothing but the golden light of summer.

It seemed this winter was for him and him alone.

It was no less than he deserved.

Until, one day, a visitor came to Ellyr-Charoi.

HE WAS A warrior, but a warrior like none Eldain had ever seen.

He arrived one morning as the snow was falling within the walls of the villa, and presented Eldain with a token of his authority: a golden phoenix set in an amulet of jade. Clad in a shimmering hauberk of orange-gold and silver, he was a head taller than Eldain, and carried a long-bladed halberd. His robes were of cream and azure, and tailored with exquisite care.

He came alone, and his forehead bore the glittering rune of Asuryan, but it was in his eyes that Eldain saw the truth of his identity. The warrior's eyes were dark pools of hurt and unasked for wisdom. They were eyes that had seen too much, but which had not shied away from that knowledge.

Eldain saw a terrible weight of sorrow in those eyes, and understood all too well what that could do to a soul. He saw the same expression every day in the mirror.

Though the warrior spoke no words, Eldain knew exactly what was required.

He dressed in simple travelling clothes and followed the warrior from Ellyr-Charoi.

He left the gates open, and together they walked east over the sunlit hills and grassy meadows of Ellyrion. Eldain turned for one last look at the villa that had been his home for so many years, and felt a sudden pang of regret as he saw the first signs of spring breaking around the snow-locked walls.

A black horse led a wildly galloping herd in the distance.

Eldain knew this was the last time he would ever see the land of his birth.

THEY CROSSED THE sea in a ship named *Dragonkin*, commanded by a venerable captain named Bellaeir who welcomed Eldain with great warmth.

'I dreamed I would see you again,' said Captain Bellaeir, but Eldain did not reply.

The ship sailed east across the waters of the Inner Sea, and Eldain did not venture above deck during the journey. He felt the presence of the Isle of the Dead, but could not bring himself to look out over that mist-shrouded rock for fear of what he might see.

At last, the ship docked in an island harbour of tall pillars and masked statues.

In the centre of the island stood a vast pyramid, and the fire burning at its peak lit the waters for miles around.

THE SILENT WARRIOR led him into the pyramid, along high, fire-lit corridors of red marble and golden carvings of the many aspects of the Creator God. They had not spoken during the entirety of their journey from Ellyr-Charoi, and Eldain found nothing unusual in that. The temple was home to many other silent warriors, and Eldain felt a kinship with them he had not felt with any other soul in a long time.

At last his silent guide brought him to a huge chamber at the peak of the pyramid, its walls golden and lit by a thousand torches. It had the feel of a temple, and Eldain knew he was standing in one of the most sacred sites of Ulthuan. A masked statue of Asuryan sat on a glassy throne at the far end of a long processional, and a wide portal was carved into the statue's legs, tall enough for a giant to walk through.

A host of armoured warriors lined a marble-floored path towards the portal, and the warrior that had brought him from Ellyrion led him between them. Golden doors led beyond, though what lay on the other side was a mystery. Curling runes lined the coffered panels, and Eldain saw many contradictory ideas represented there. He saw *Urithair* next to *Harathoi*, *Elthrai* abutting *Quyl-Isha*, but foremost among the runic concepts was *Saroir*, the symbol representing eternity and infinity, the flame of love that burns all it touches. He blinked as the runes seemed to pulse with their own heartbeat. Eldain had the prescient notion that the runes he was seeing were different to the runes another supplicant might see.

Supplicant…?

Yes, he supposed that was exactly what he was, though he had not thought so until now.

The golden doors swung wide and warm light shone from within the chamber beyond. It grew brighter than the sun, spilling out into the temple, and Eldain looked to his guide.

The warrior nodded and gestured towards the doors.

Until this moment, Eldain had not been afraid, but as the warm light beckoned him in, he dreaded taking even a single step into the chamber at the heart of the pyramid. The warrior gestured again, and this time Eldain obeyed.

Golden light enfolded him, and he felt the warmth of a nearby flame. He entered the chamber as the great doors closed behind him with a soft brush of metal. The light dimmed to a level where he could see, and he looked around at the vast space he found himself within. It was enormous beyond imagining, surely too vast to be contained within the top of the pyramid. A vast circle of black marble filled the centre of the chamber, and a towering flame of the purest white burned at its heart.

The walls of the chamber tapered inwards and were covered from top to bottom with runic script. A thousand lifetimes worth of words were written on the walls, maybe more, and Eldain marvelled at the wealth of information inscribed here.

This was the Chamber of Days, a living record of all the Phoenix Kings who had ever lived and ever would. The walls told the story of Ulthuan as it was known, and the story of Ulthuan that was yet to be written.

Even as he understood what was chronicled here, he felt the flame at the heart of the chamber burn hotter and brighter. A chorus of song issued from the fire, and Eldain closed his eyes as the dead and unborn spoke to him with one voice, the echoes of all the Phoenix Kings of the past and the voices of those yet to be crowned.

This was history and legend combined, a tale of days that had no beginning and no ending.

The kings spoke to him of their reigns, and Eldain lived their lives in a heartbeat.

He learned of their loves, their joys, their sorrows and their great deeds. He lived the history of an entire land and its people in one bright and shining moment. Eldain felt Caelir and Rhianna within the grand sweep of the tale, and wept as he relived their final sacrifice on the

Isle of the Dead. His remembrance of them had grown cold and lifeless, but in this chamber of eternal life, they burned as bright as stars.

The heart that does not want to heal cannot be remade...

Eldain finally understood those words, and with that understanding, he was made whole.

He had seen all that had ever been and all the future held; the wonders yet to come to pass, the resurgent glory of the asur and the last great battle for the fate of the world.

Eldain would be part of that, though he would never speak of it.

The temple doors opened and the Phoenix Guard awaited the return of their chosen warrior.

ABOUT THE AUTHOR

Hailing from Scotland, **Graham McNeill** worked for over six years as a Games Developer in Games Workshop's Design Studio before taking the plunge to become a full-time writer. Graham's written a host of SF and Fantasy novels and comics, as well as a number of side projects that keep him busy and (mostly) out of trouble. His Horus Heresy novel, *A Thousand Sons*, was a New York Times bestseller and his Time of Legends novel, *Empire*, won the 2010 David Gemmell Legend Award. Graham lives and works in Nottingham and you can keep up to date with where he'll be and what he's working on by visiting his website.

Join the ranks of the 4th Company at
www.graham-mcneill.com